Buffy the Vampire Slayer™

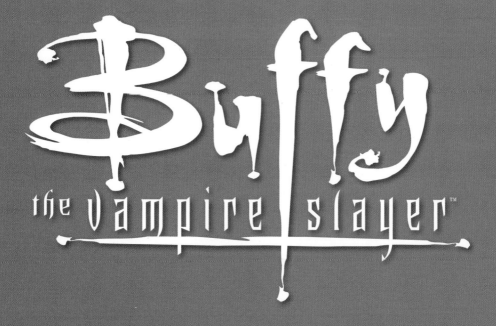

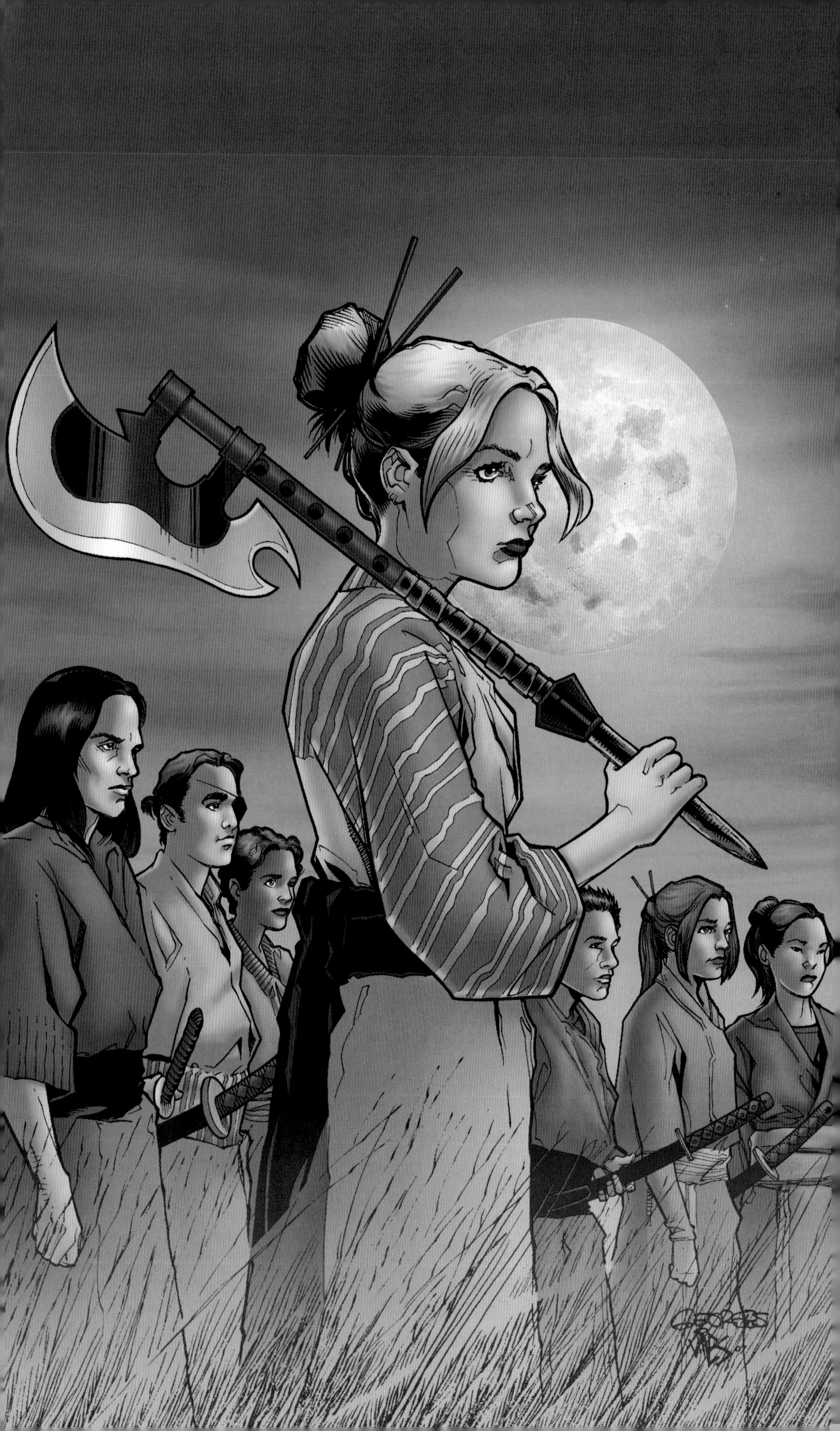

Buffy the Vampire Slayer™

SEASON EIGHT VOLUME 3

WOLVES AT THE GATE

Script DREW GODDARD

Pencils GEORGES JEANTY

Inks ANDY OWENS

Colors MICHELLE MADSEN

Letters RICHARD STARKINGS
& COMICRAFT'S JIMMY & ALBERT

Series Cover Art JON FOSTER

Collection Cover Art JO CHEN

"A Beautiful Sunset"
Script JOSS WHEDON

Executive Producer JOSS WHEDON

Dark Horse Books®

Publisher MIKE RICHARDSON

Editor SCOTT ALLIE

Associate Editor SIERRA HAHN

Collection Designer HEIDI WHITCOMB

This story takes place after the end of the
television series *Buffy the Vampire Slayer*
created by Joss Whedon.

Special thanks to Debbie Olshan at Twentieth Century Fox, Julia Dalzell, and Natalie Farrell.

This volume reprints the comic-book series *Buffy the
Vampire Slayer* Season Eight #11–15 from Dark Horse Comics.

Published by
Dark Horse Books
A division of
Dark Horse Comics, Inc.
10956 SE Main Street
Milwaukie, OR 97222

darkhorse.com

To find a comics shop in your area,
call the Comic Shop Locator Service toll-free at (888) 266-4226.

First edition: November 2008
ISBN 978-1-59582-165-2

1 3 5 7 9 10 8 6 4 2

Printed in China

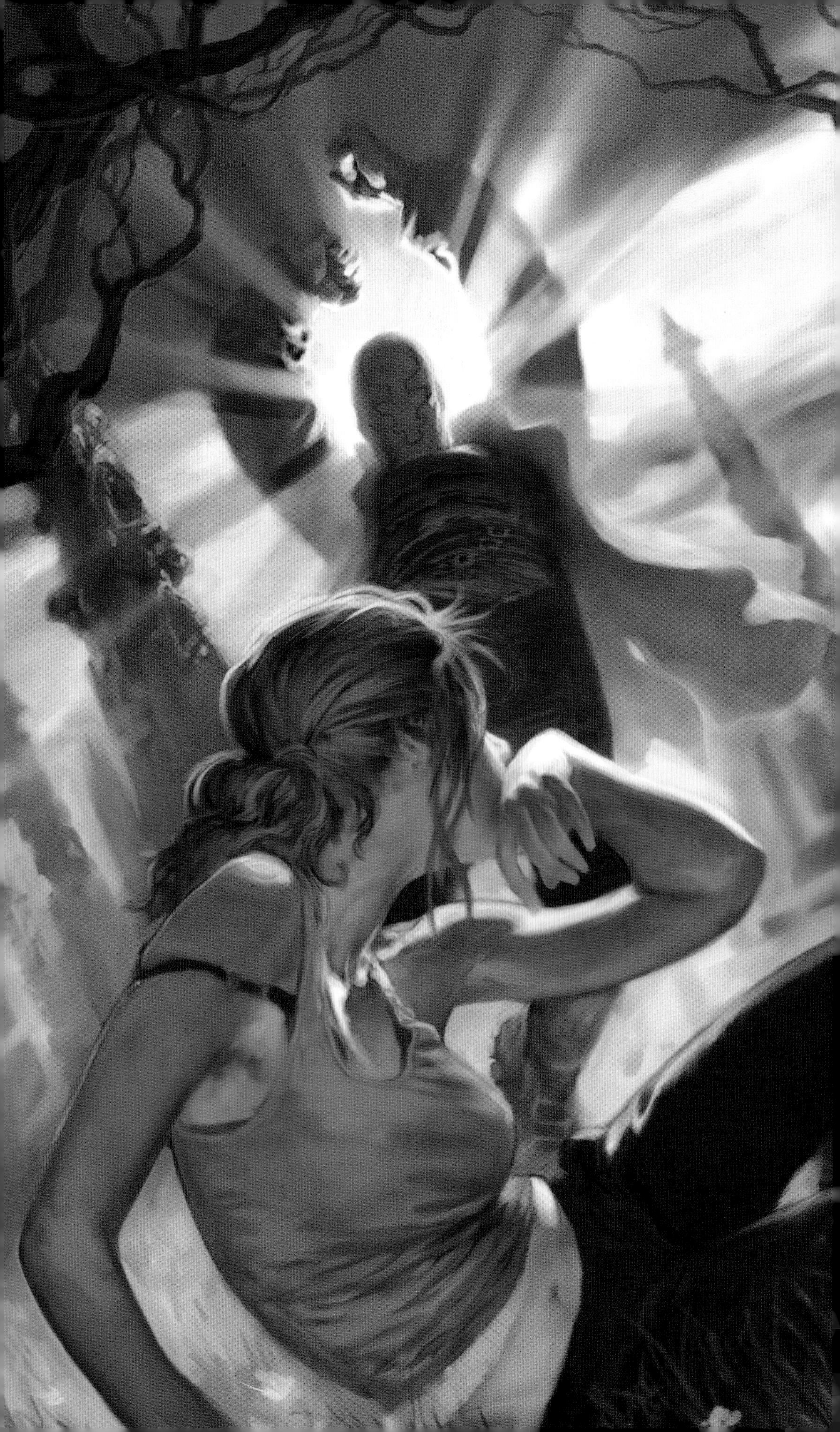

A BEAUTIFUL SUNSET

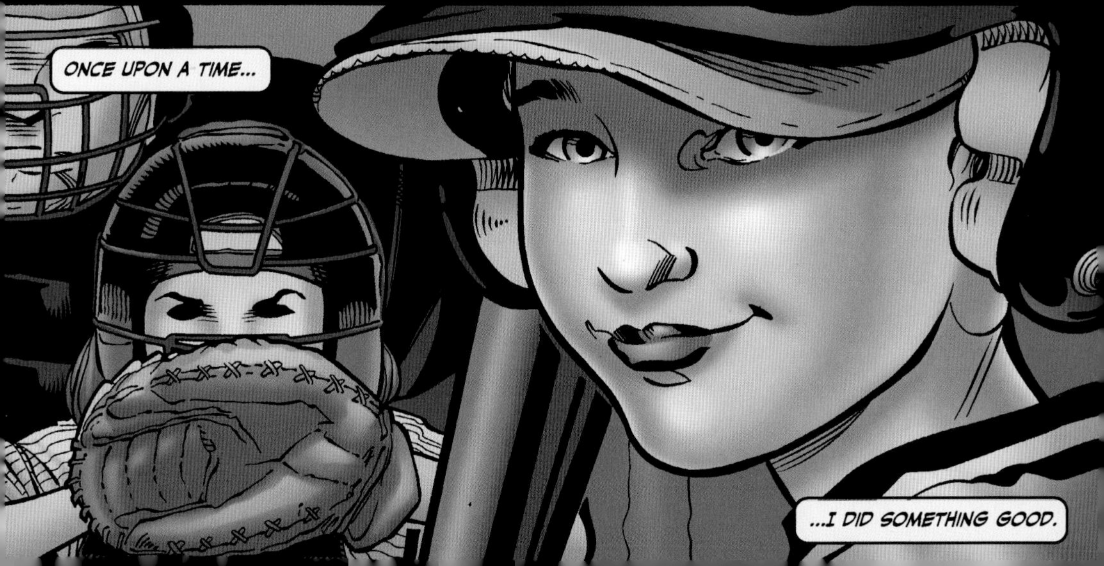
ONCE UPON A TIME...
...I DID SOMETHING GOOD.

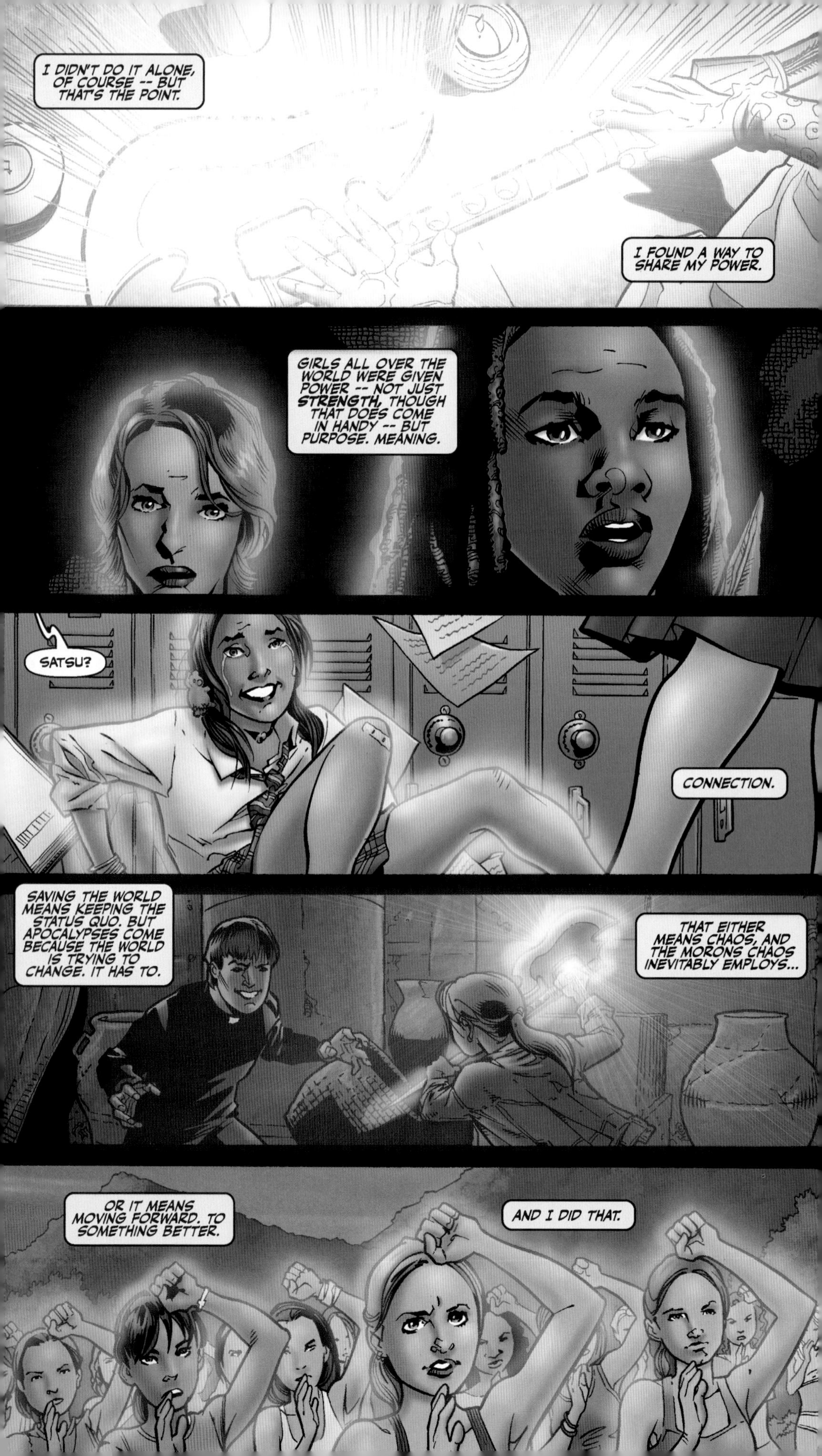
I DIDN'T DO IT ALONE, OF COURSE -- BUT THAT'S THE POINT.
I FOUND A WAY TO SHARE MY POWER.
GIRLS ALL OVER THE WORLD WERE GIVEN POWER -- NOT JUST STRENGTH, THOUGH THAT DOES COME IN HANDY -- BUT PURPOSE. MEANING.
SATSU?
CONNECTION.
SAVING THE WORLD MEANS KEEPING THE STATUS QUO. BUT APOCALYPSES COME BECAUSE THE WORLD IS TRYING TO CHANGE. IT HAS TO.
THAT EITHER MEANS CHAOS, AND THE MORONS CHAOS INEVITABLY EMPLOYS...
OR IT MEANS MOVING FORWARD. TO SOMETHING BETTER.
AND I DID THAT.

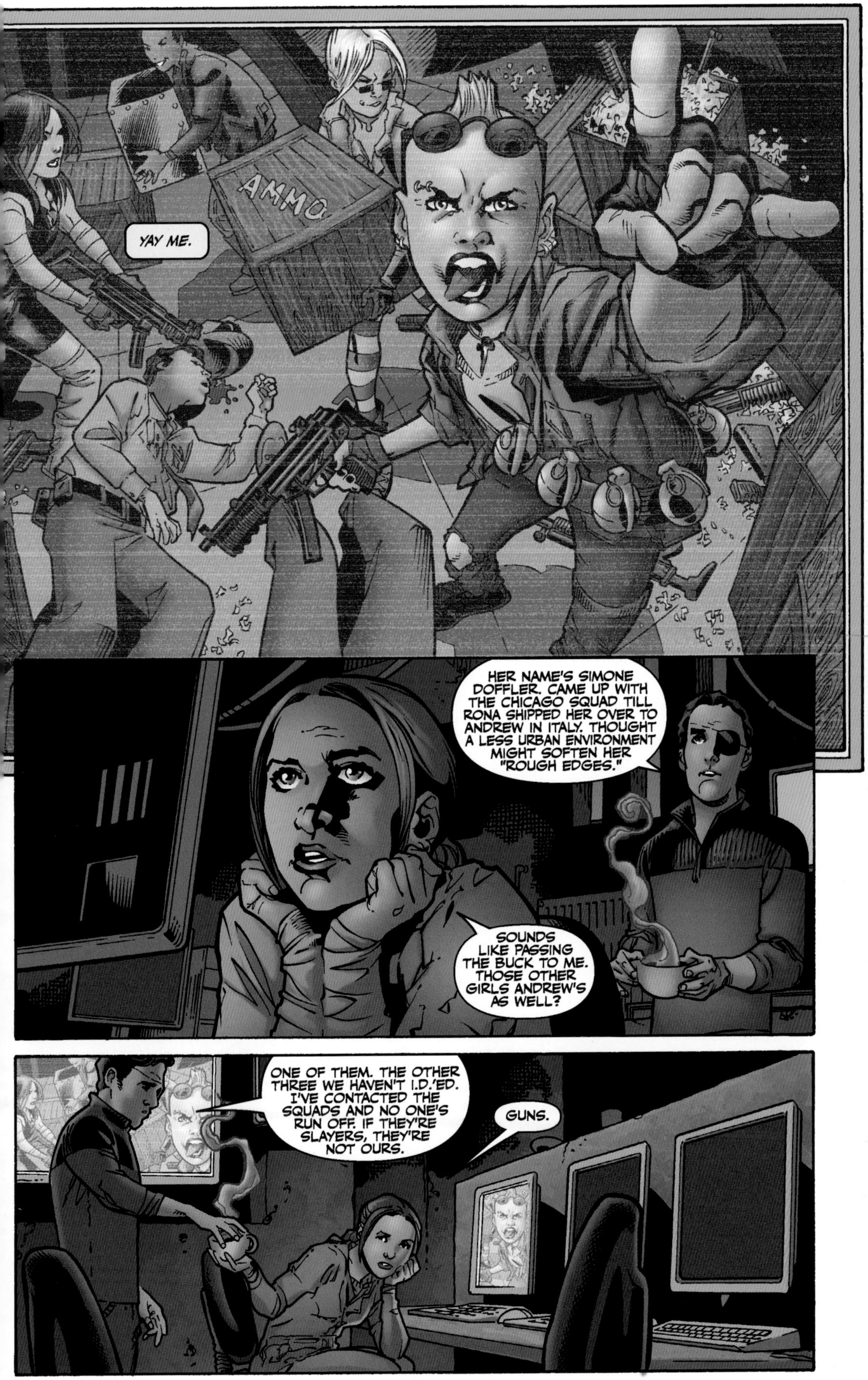

YAY ME.
HER NAME'S SIMONE DOFFLER. CAME UP WITH THE CHICAGO SQUAD TILL RONA SHIPPED HER OVER TO ANDREW IN ITALY. THOUGHT A LESS URBAN ENVIRONMENT MIGHT SOFTEN HER "ROUGH EDGES."
SOUNDS LIKE PASSING THE BUCK TO ME. THOSE OTHER GIRLS ANDREW'S AS WELL?
ONE OF THEM. THE OTHER THREE WE HAVEN'T I.D.'ED. I'VE CONTACTED THE SQUADS AND NO ONE'S RUN OFF. IF THEY'RE SLAYERS, THEY'RE NOT OURS.
GUNS.

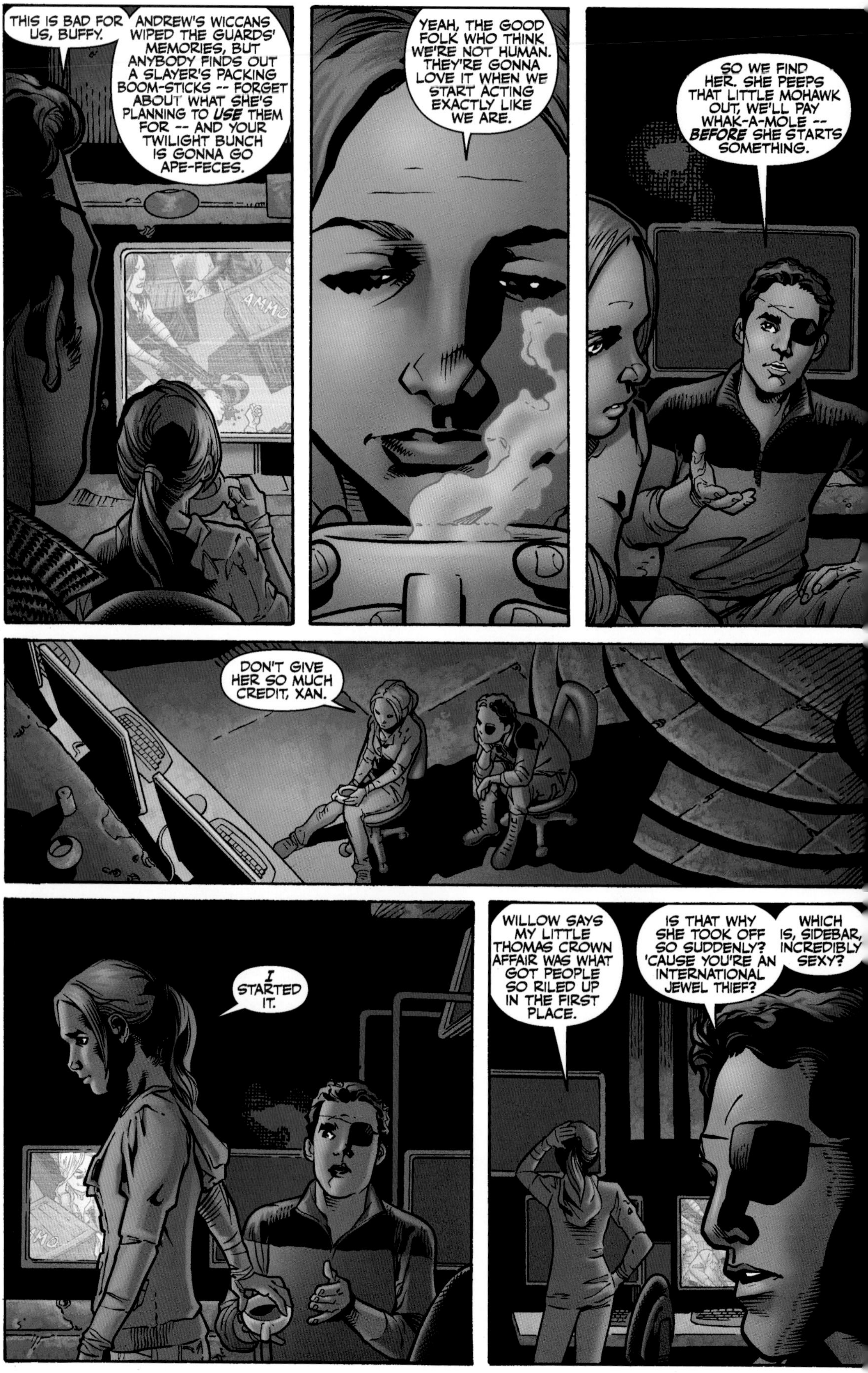
THIS IS BAD FOR US, BUFFY.
ANDREW'S WICCANS WIPED THE GUARDS' MEMORIES, BUT ANYBODY FINDS OUT A SLAYER'S PACKING BOOM-STICKS -- FORGET ABOUT WHAT SHE'S PLANNING TO USE THEM FOR -- AND YOUR TWILIGHT BUNCH IS GONNA GO APE-FECES.
AMMO
YEAH, THE GOOD FOLK WHO THINK WE'RE NOT HUMAN. THEY'RE GONNA LOVE IT WHEN WE START ACTING EXACTLY LIKE WE ARE.
SO WE FIND HER. SHE PEEPS THAT LITTLE MOHAWK OUT, WE'LL PAY WHAK-A-MOLE -- BEFORE SHE STARTS SOMETHING.
DON'T GIVE HER SO MUCH CREDIT, XAN.
I STARTED IT.
WILLOW SAYS MY LITTLE THOMAS CROWN AFFAIR WAS WHAT GOT PEOPLE SO RILED UP IN THE FIRST PLACE.
IS THAT WHY SHE TOOK OFF SO SUDDENLY? 'CAUSE YOU'RE AN INTERNATIONAL JEWEL THIEF?
WHICH IS, SIDEBAR, INCREDIBLY SEXY?

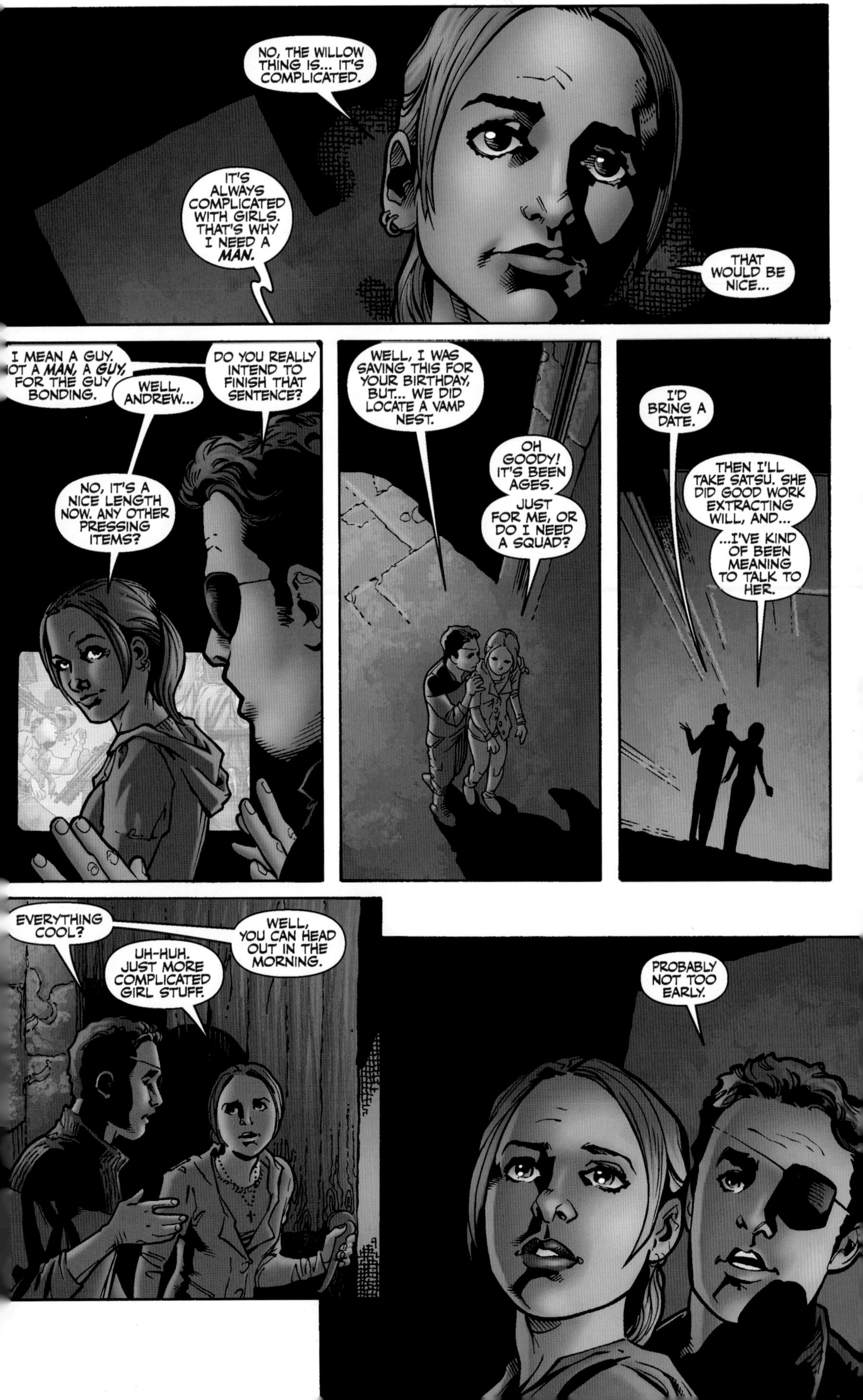
NO, THE WILLOW THING IS... IT'S COMPLICATED.
IT'S ALWAYS COMPLICATED WITH GIRLS. THAT'S WHY I NEED A *MAN.*
THAT WOULD BE NICE...
I MEAN A GUY. NOT A *MAN,* A *GUY,* FOR THE GUY BONDING.
DO YOU REALLY INTEND TO FINISH THAT SENTENCE?
WELL, ANDREW...
NO, IT'S A NICE LENGTH NOW. ANY OTHER PRESSING ITEMS?
WELL, I WAS SAVING THIS FOR YOUR BIRTHDAY, BUT... WE DID LOCATE A VAMP NEST.
OH GOODY! IT'S BEEN AGES.
JUST FOR ME, OR DO I NEED A SQUAD?
I'D BRING A DATE.
THEN I'LL TAKE SATSU. SHE DID GOOD WORK EXTRACTING WILL, AND...
...I'VE KIND OF BEEN MEANING TO TALK TO HER.
EVERYTHING COOL?
UH-HUH. JUST MORE COMPLICATED GIRL STUFF.
WELL, YOU CAN HEAD OUT IN THE MORNING.
PROBABLY NOT TOO EARLY.

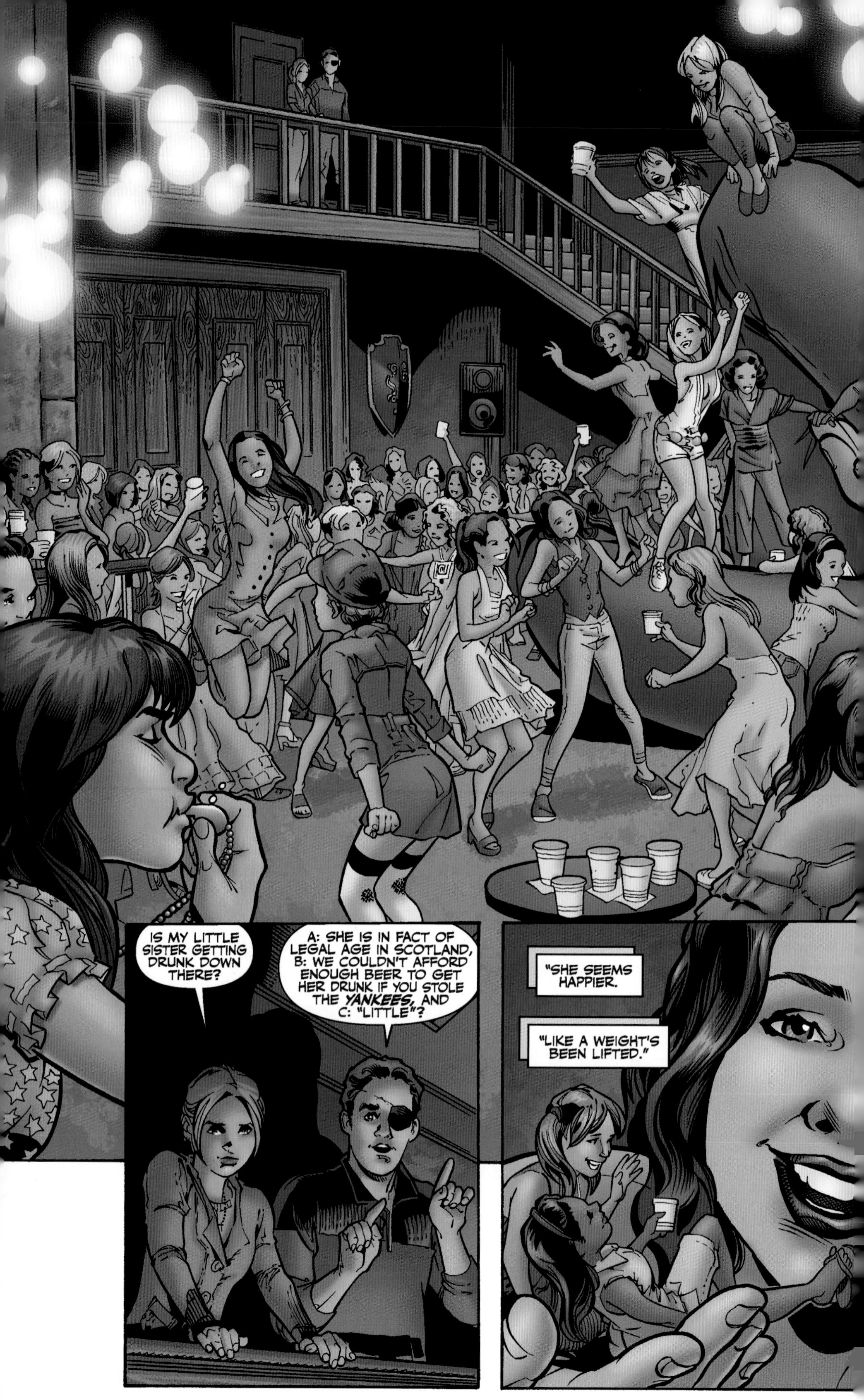

IS MY LITTLE SISTER GETTING DRUNK DOWN THERE?
A: SHE IS IN FACT OF LEGAL AGE IN SCOTLAND, B: WE COULDN'T AFFORD ENOUGH BEER TO GET HER DRUNK IF YOU STOLE THE *YANKEES,* AND C: "LITTLE"?
"SHE SEEMS HAPPIER.
"LIKE A WEIGHT'S BEEN LIFTED."

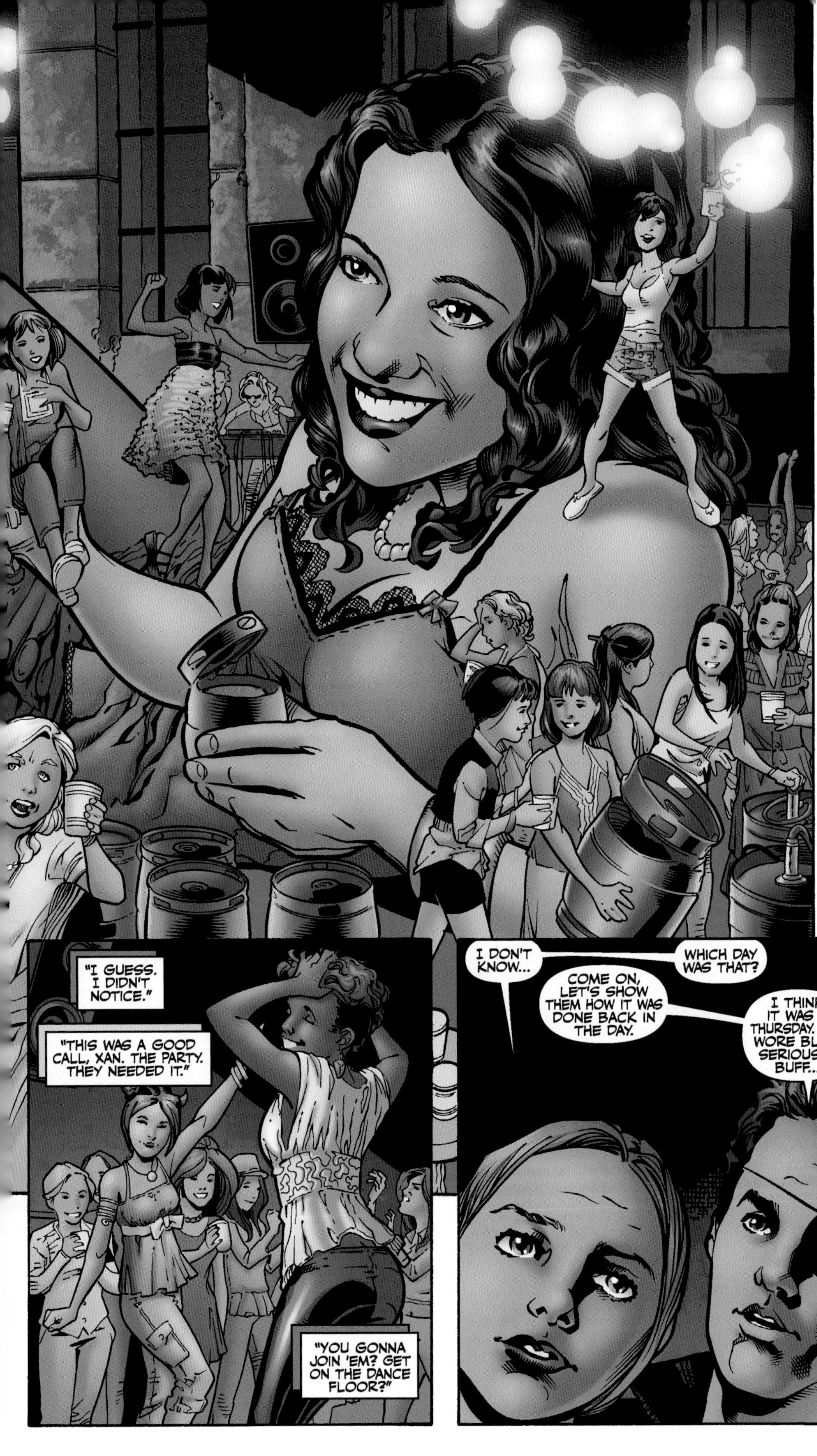
"I GUESS. I DIDN'T NOTICE."
"THIS WAS A GOOD CALL, XAN. THE PARTY. THEY NEEDED IT."
"YOU GONNA JOIN 'EM? GET ON THE DANCE FLOOR?"
I DON'T KNOW...
WHICH DAY WAS THAT?
COME ON, LET'S SHOW THEM HOW IT WAS DONE BACK IN THE DAY.
I THINK IT WAS A THURSDAY. YOU WORE BLUE. SERIOUSLY, BUFF...

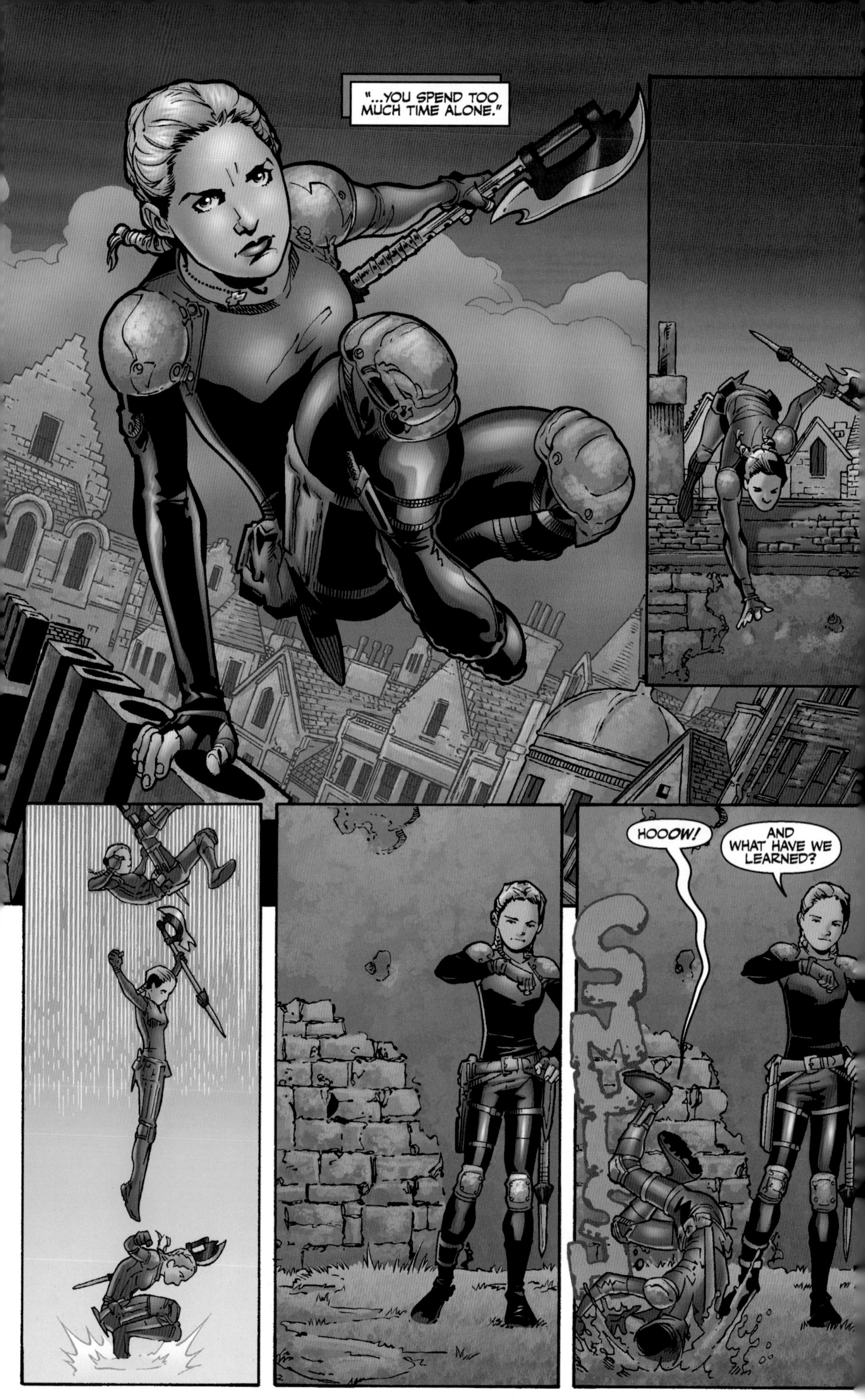
"...YOU SPEND TOO MUCH TIME ALONE."
HOOOW!
AND WHAT HAVE WE LEARNED?

SCOTLAND IS SLIPPERY?

DO I LOOK AMUSED?

I REALLY CAN'T SAY.

WOW, YOU LOOK... ACTUALLY YOU LOOK LIKE ME IN A DREAM I HAD ONE TIME.

I'M NOT AS FAST AS YOU.

YOU WILL BE.

YOU'RE MY BEST FIGHTER, SATSU. YOU COULD LEAD THIS CREW SOME DAY.

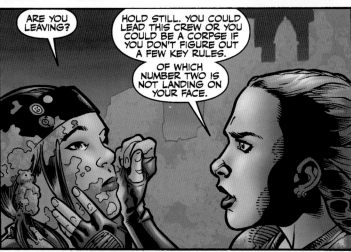

ARE YOU LEAVING?

HOLD STILL. YOU COULD LEAD THIS CREW OR YOU COULD BE A CORPSE IF YOU DON'T FIGURE OUT A FEW KEY RULES.

OF WHICH NUMBER TWO IS NOT LANDING ON YOUR FACE.

DID WE... SKIP NUMBER ONE?

NUMBER ONE IS YOU ARE ALWAYS IN DANGER.

RIGHT NOW, YOU'RE IN TERRIBLE DANGER.

...WHY...?

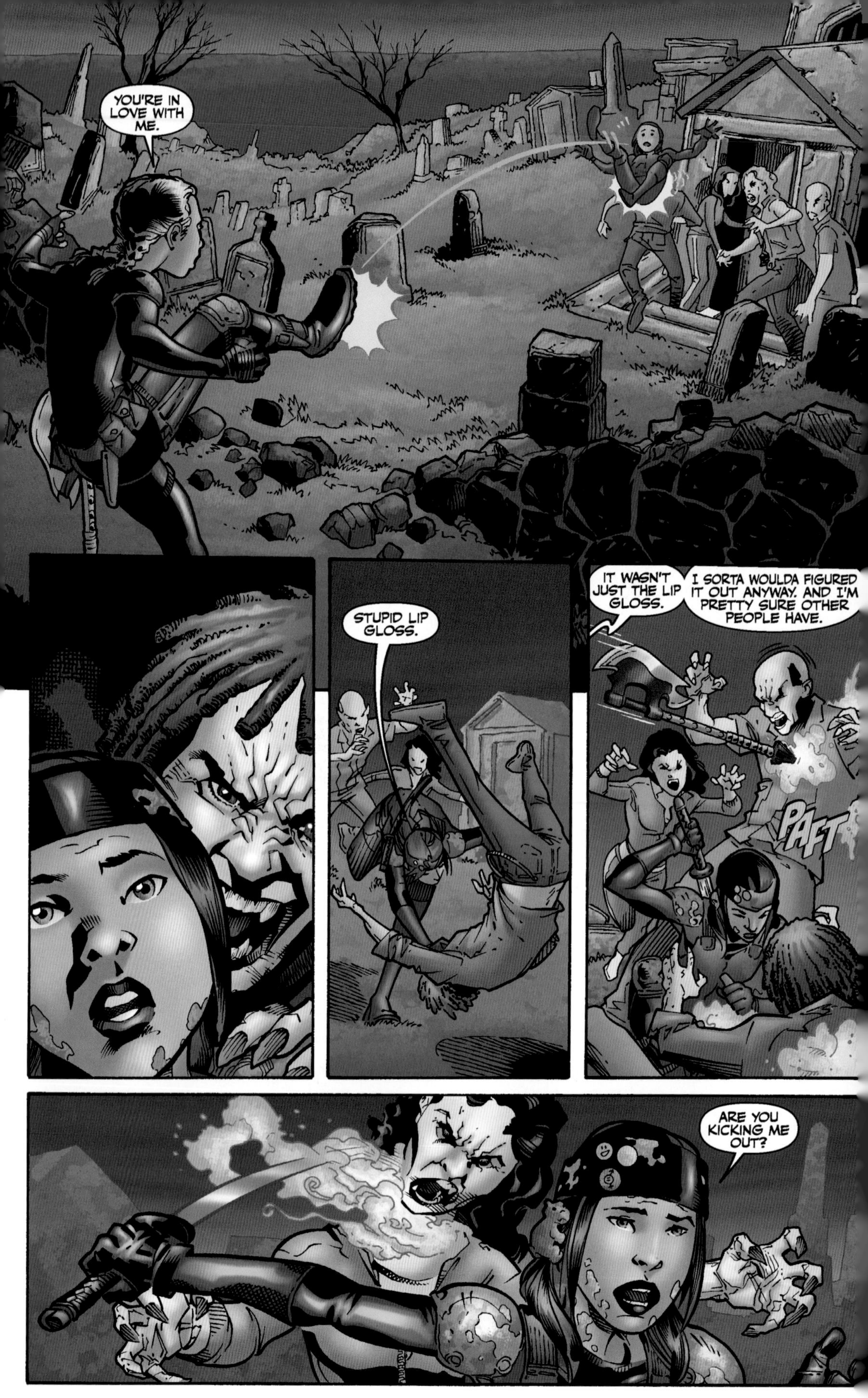
YOU'RE IN LOVE WITH ME.
STUPID LIP GLOSS.
IT WASN'T JUST THE LIP GLOSS.
I SORTA WOULDA FIGURED IT OUT ANYWAY. AND I'M PRETTY SURE OTHER PEOPLE HAVE.
PAFT
ARE YOU KICKING ME OUT?

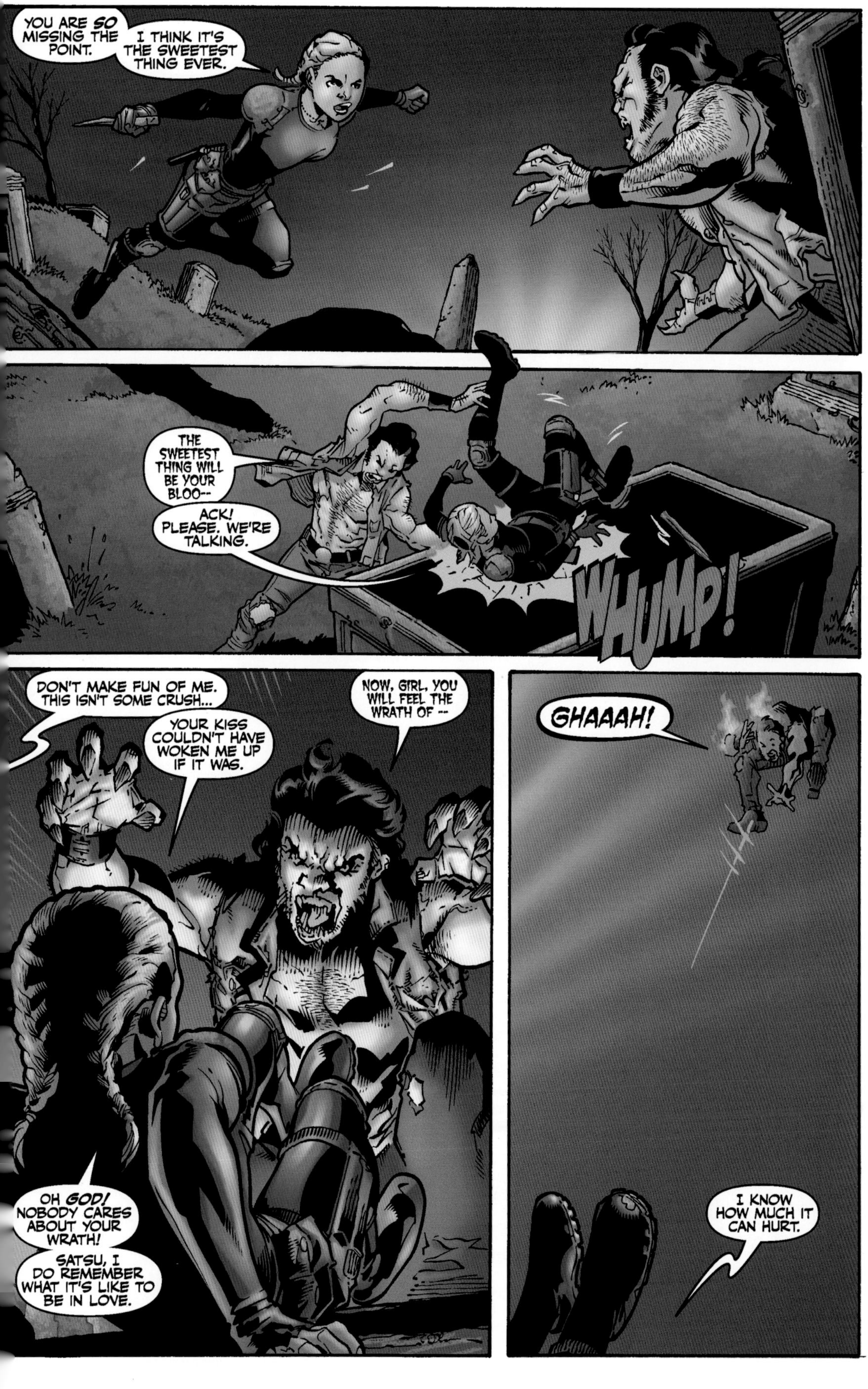
YOU ARE SO MISSING THE POINT.
I THINK IT'S THE SWEETEST THING EVER.
THE SWEETEST THING WILL BE YOUR BLOO--
ACK! PLEASE. WE'RE TALKING.
WHUMP!
DON'T MAKE FUN OF ME. THIS ISN'T SOME CRUSH...
YOUR KISS COULDN'T HAVE WOKEN ME UP IF IT WAS.
NOW, GIRL, YOU WILL FEEL THE WRATH OF --
OH GOD! NOBODY CARES ABOUT YOUR WRATH!
SATSU, I DO REMEMBER WHAT IT'S LIKE TO BE IN LOVE.
GHAAAH!
I KNOW HOW MUCH IT CAN HURT.

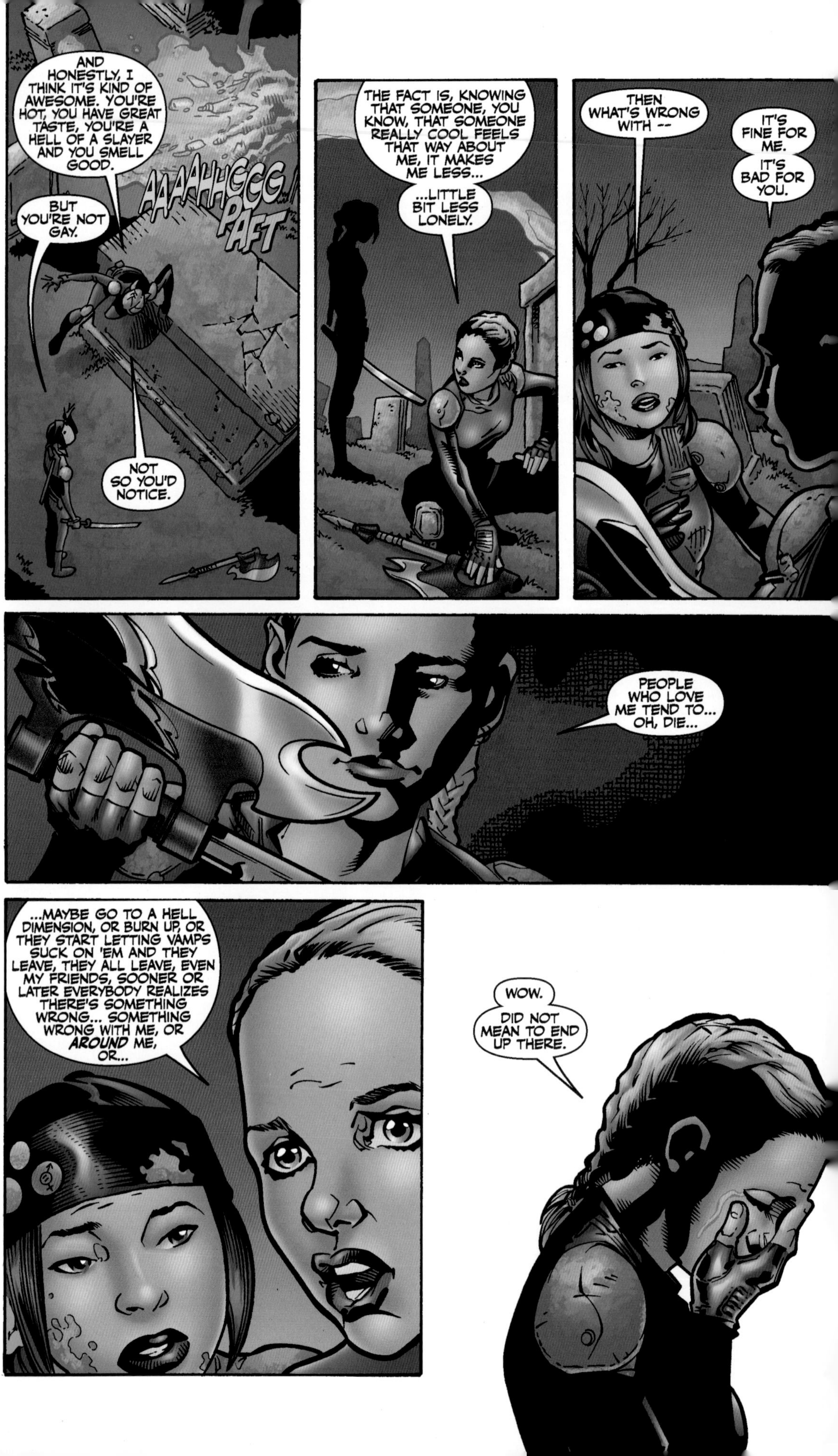
AND HONESTLY, I THINK IT'S KIND OF AWESOME. YOU'RE HOT, YOU HAVE GREAT TASTE, YOU'RE A HELL OF A SLAYER AND YOU SMELL GOOD.
AAAAHHGGG
PAFT
BUT YOU'RE NOT GAY.
NOT SO YOU'D NOTICE.
THE FACT IS, KNOWING THAT SOMEONE, YOU KNOW, THAT SOMEONE REALLY COOL FEELS THAT WAY ABOUT ME, IT MAKES ME LESS...
...LITTLE BIT LESS LONELY.
THEN WHAT'S WRONG WITH --
IT'S FINE FOR ME.
IT'S BAD FOR YOU.
PEOPLE WHO LOVE ME TEND TO... OH, DIE...
...MAYBE GO TO A HELL DIMENSION, OR BURN UP, OR THEY START LETTING VAMPS SUCK ON 'EM AND THEY LEAVE, THEY ALL LEAVE, EVEN MY FRIENDS, SOONER OR LATER EVERYBODY REALIZES THERE'S SOMETHING WRONG... SOMETHING WRONG WITH ME, OR *AROUND* ME, OR...
WOW.
DID NOT MEAN TO END UP THERE.

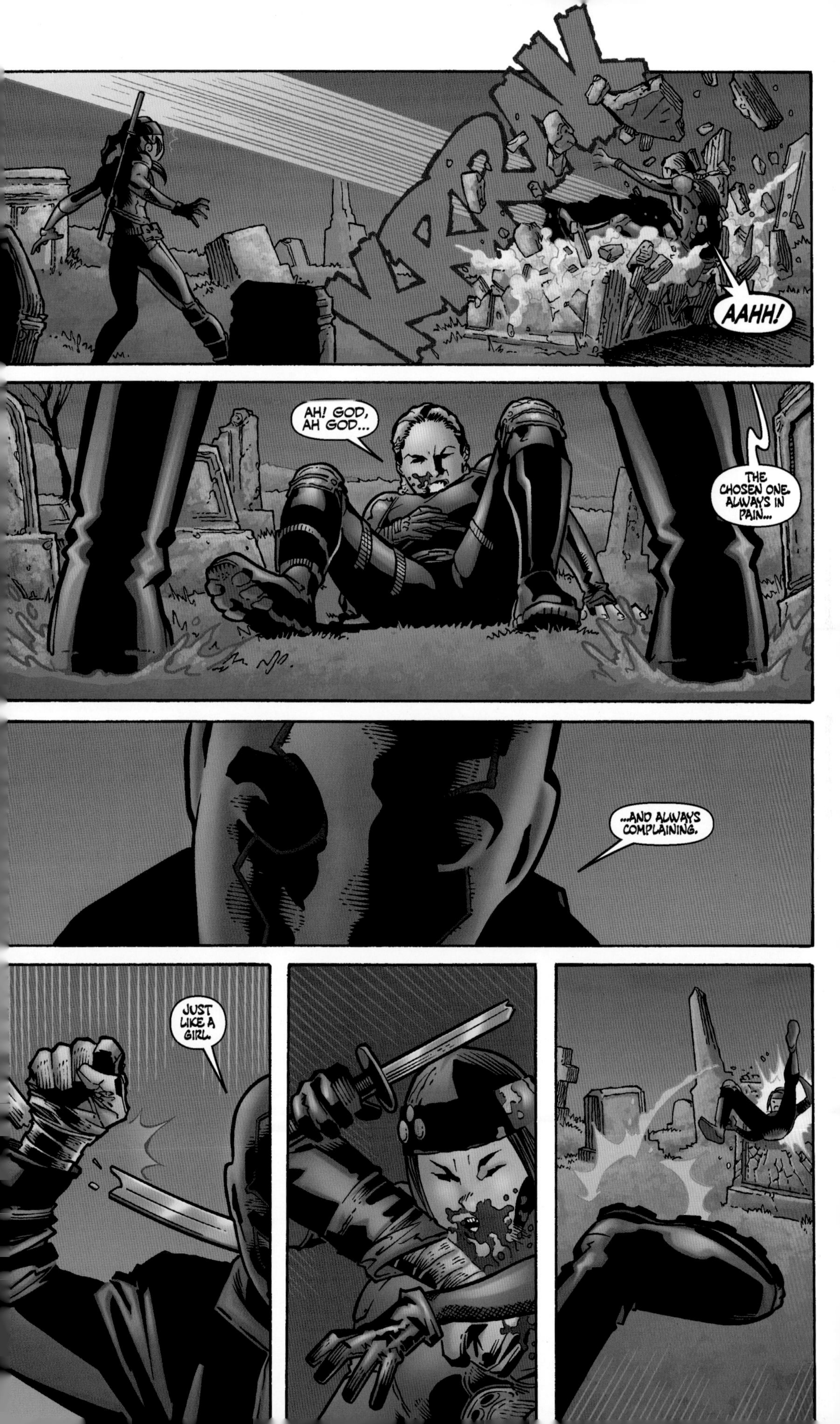
KRAK
AAHH!
AH! GOD, AH GOD...
THE CHOSEN ONE. ALWAYS IN PAIN...
...AND ALWAYS COMPLAINING.
JUST LIKE A GIRL.

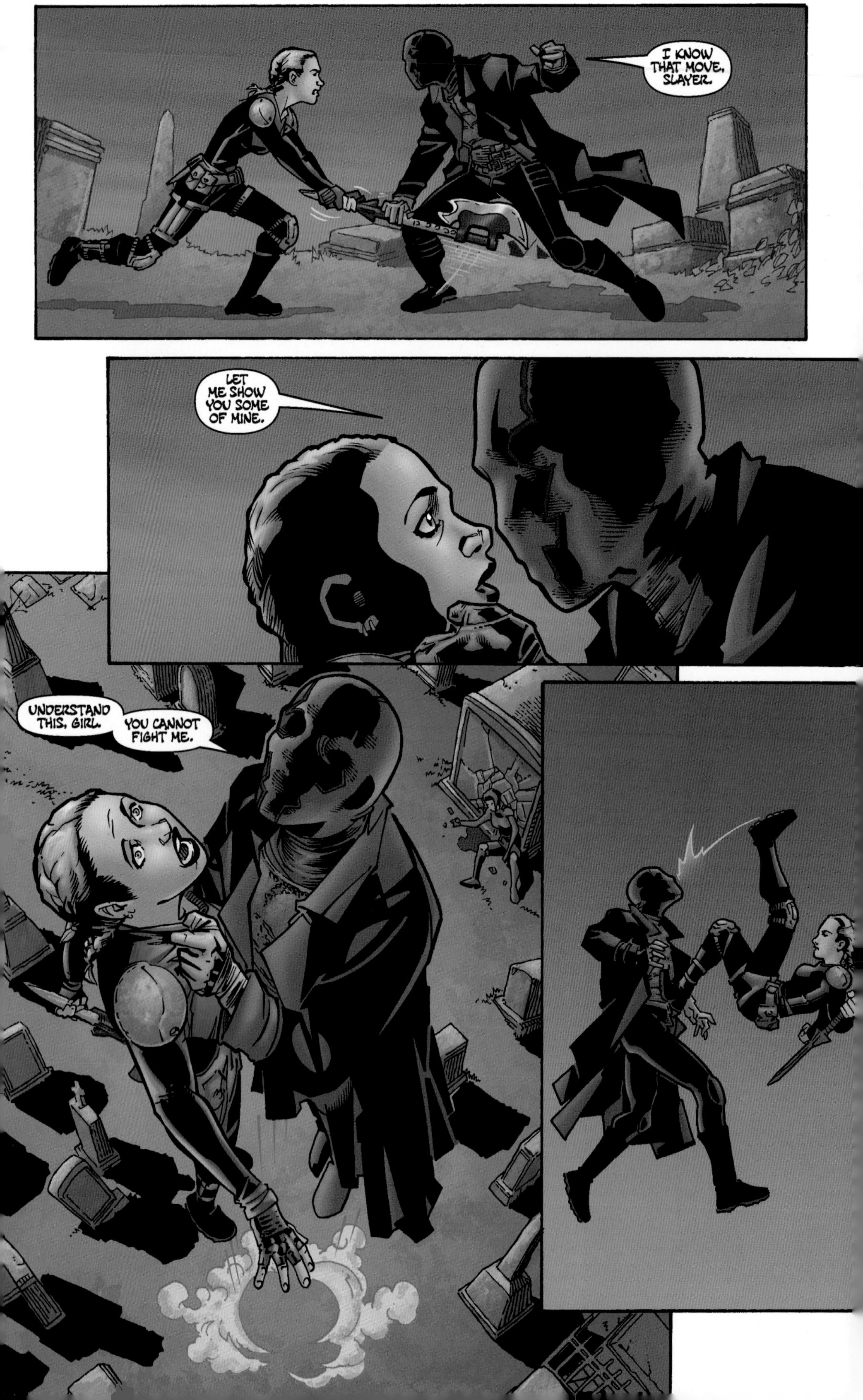
I KNOW THAT MOVE, SLAYER.
LET ME SHOW YOU SOME OF MINE.
UNDERSTAND THIS, GIRL.
YOU CANNOT FIGHT ME.

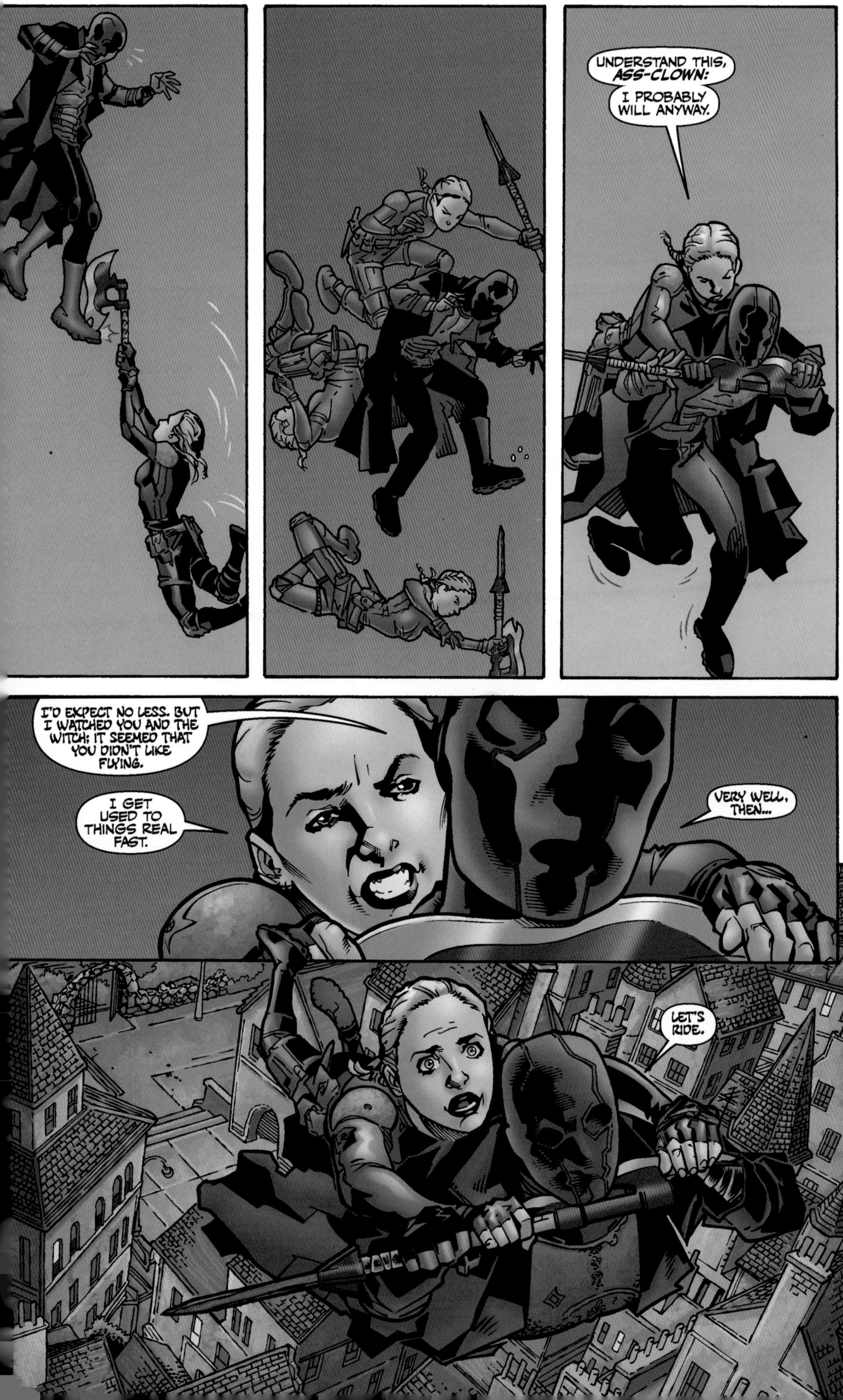
UNDERSTAND THIS, ASS-CLOWN:
I PROBABLY WILL ANYWAY.
I'D EXPECT NO LESS. BUT I WATCHED YOU AND THE WITCH; IT SEEMED THAT YOU DIDN'T LIKE FLYING.
I GET USED TO THINGS REAL FAST.
VERY WELL, THEN...
LET'S RIDE.

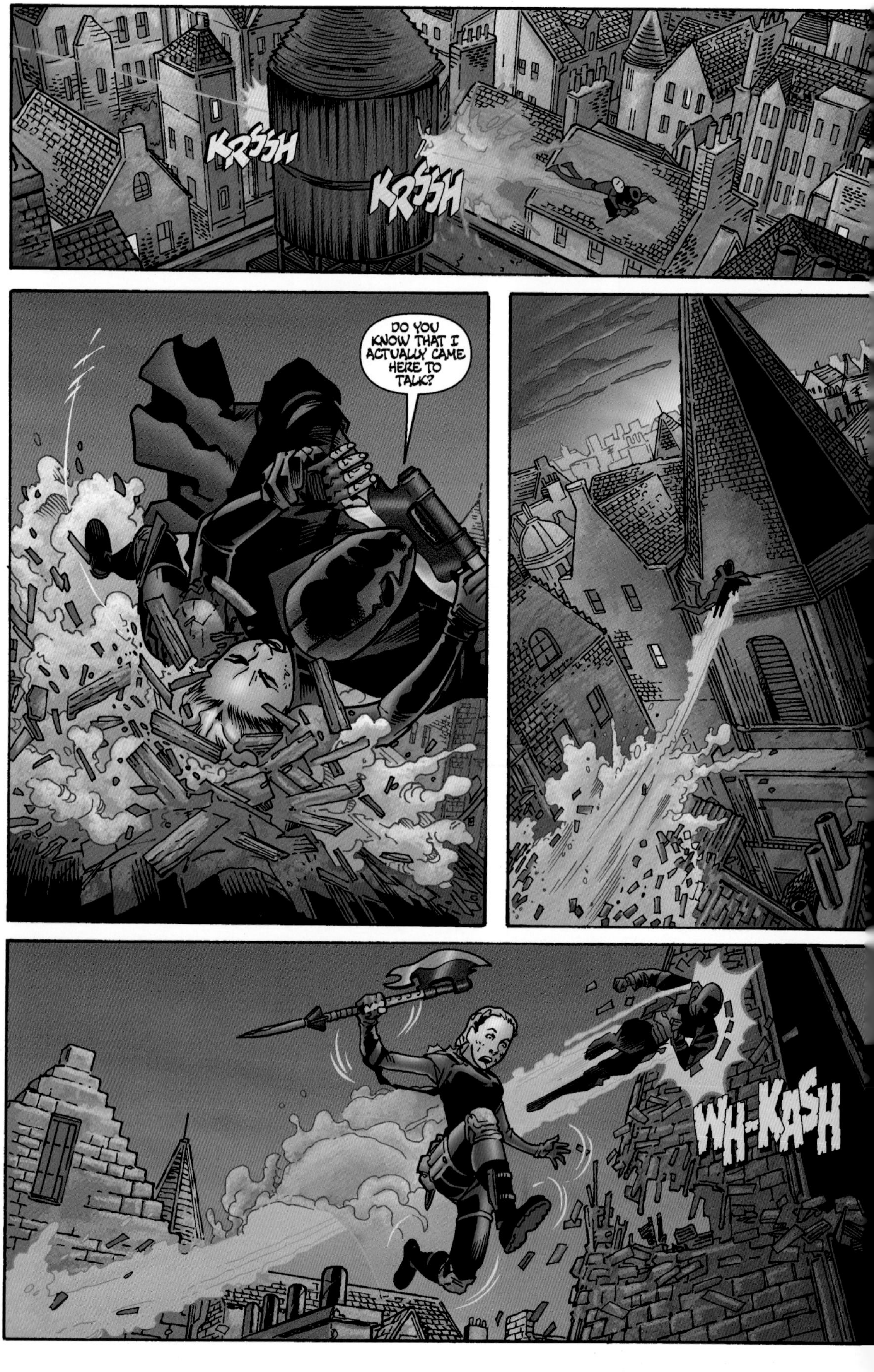
KRSSH
KRSSH
DO YOU KNOW THAT I ACTUALLY CAME HERE TO TALK?
WH-KASH

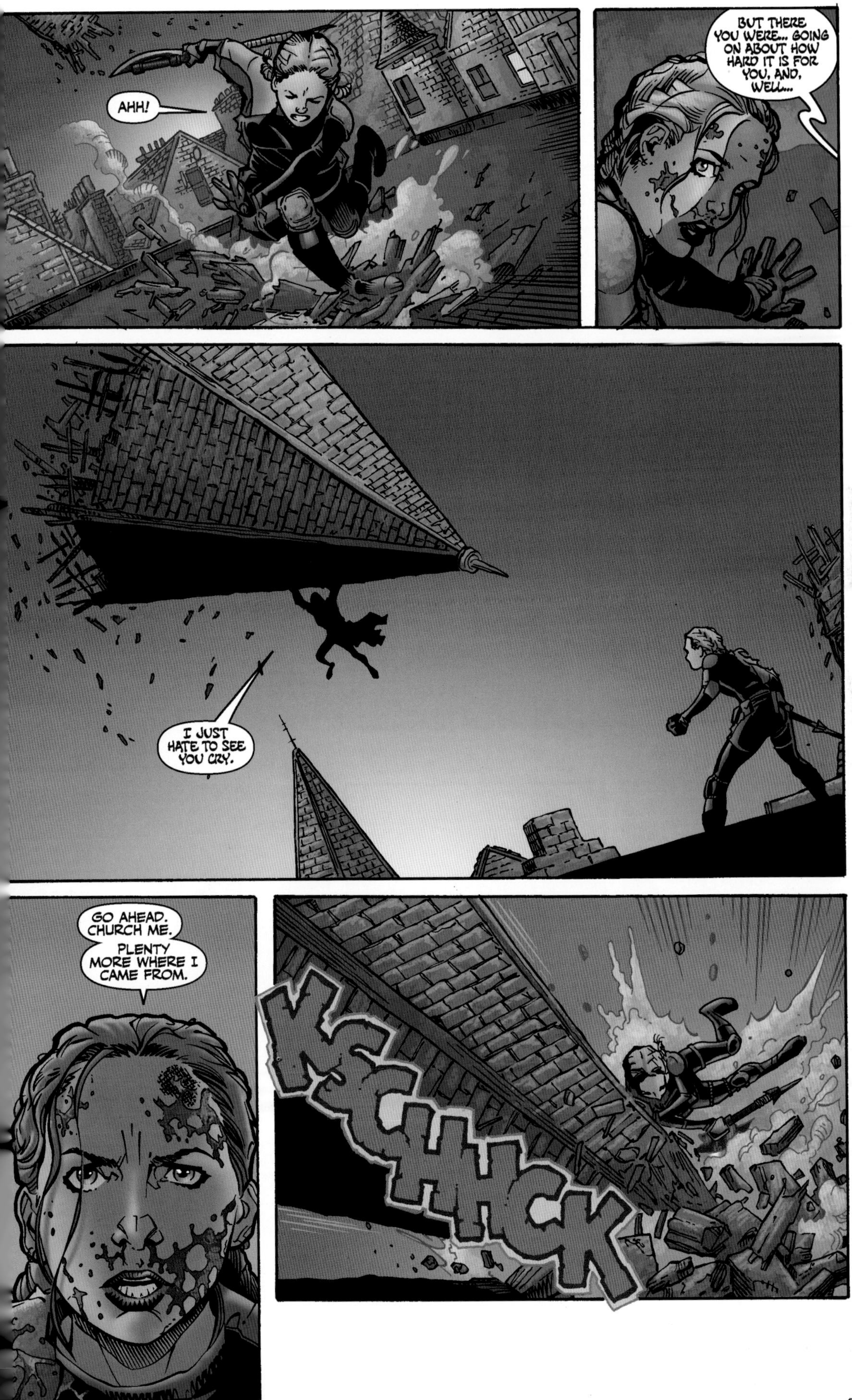
AHH!
BUT THERE YOU WERE... GOING ON ABOUT HOW HARD IT IS FOR YOU, AND, WELL...
I JUST HATE TO SEE YOU CRY.
GO AHEAD. CHURCH ME.
PLENTY MORE WHERE I CAME FROM.
KSSHHCK

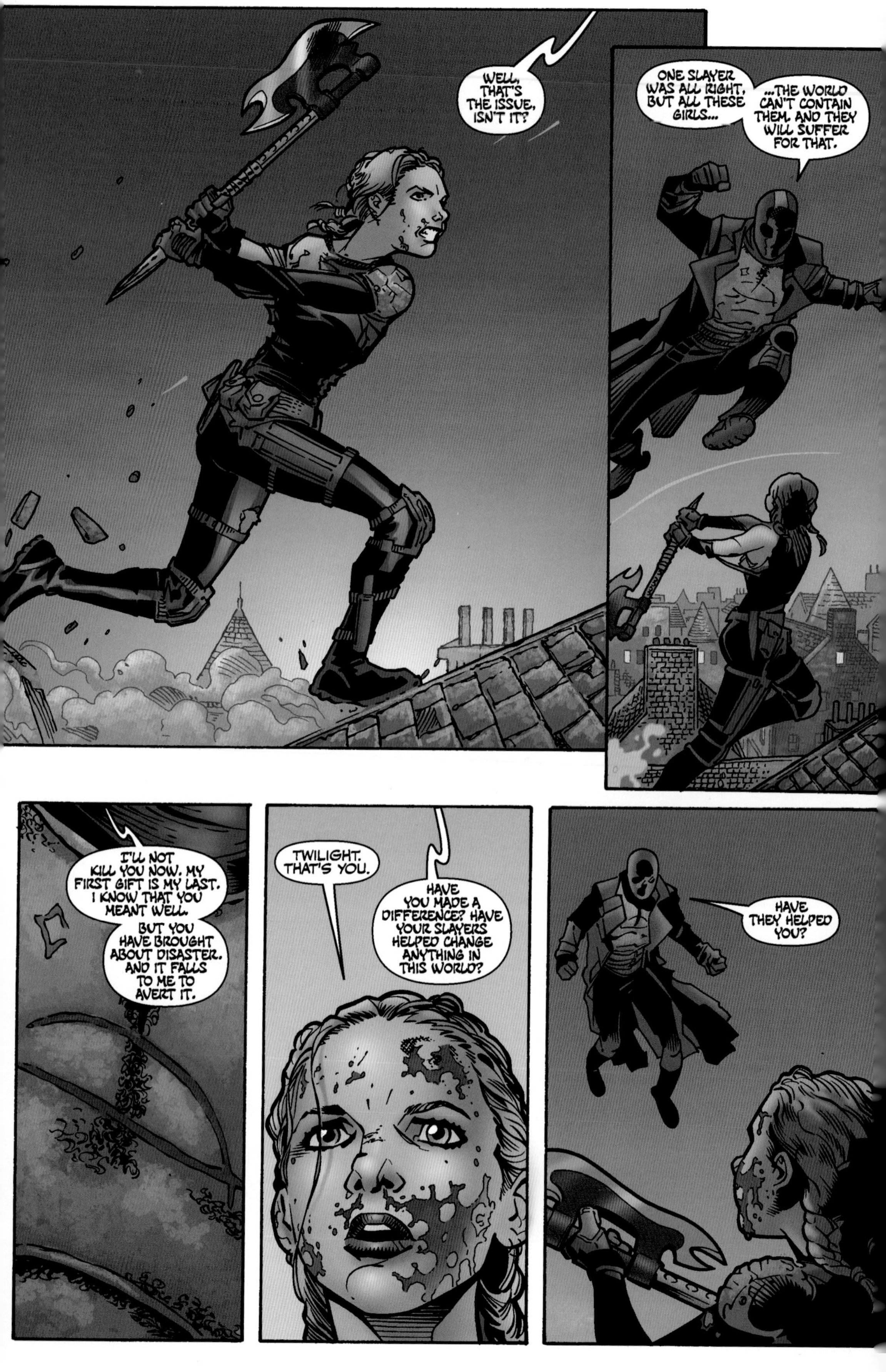
WELL, THAT'S THE ISSUE, ISN'T IT?
ONE SLAYER WAS ALL RIGHT, BUT ALL THESE GIRLS...
...THE WORLD CAN'T CONTAIN THEM, AND THEY WILL SUFFER FOR THAT.
I'LL NOT KILL YOU NOW. MY FIRST GIFT IS MY LAST. I KNOW THAT YOU MEANT WELL.
BUT YOU HAVE BROUGHT ABOUT DISASTER. AND IT FALLS TO ME TO AVERT IT.
TWILIGHT. THAT'S YOU.
HAVE YOU MADE A DIFFERENCE? HAVE YOUR SLAYERS HELPED CHANGE ANYTHING IN THIS WORLD?
HAVE THEY HELPED YOU?

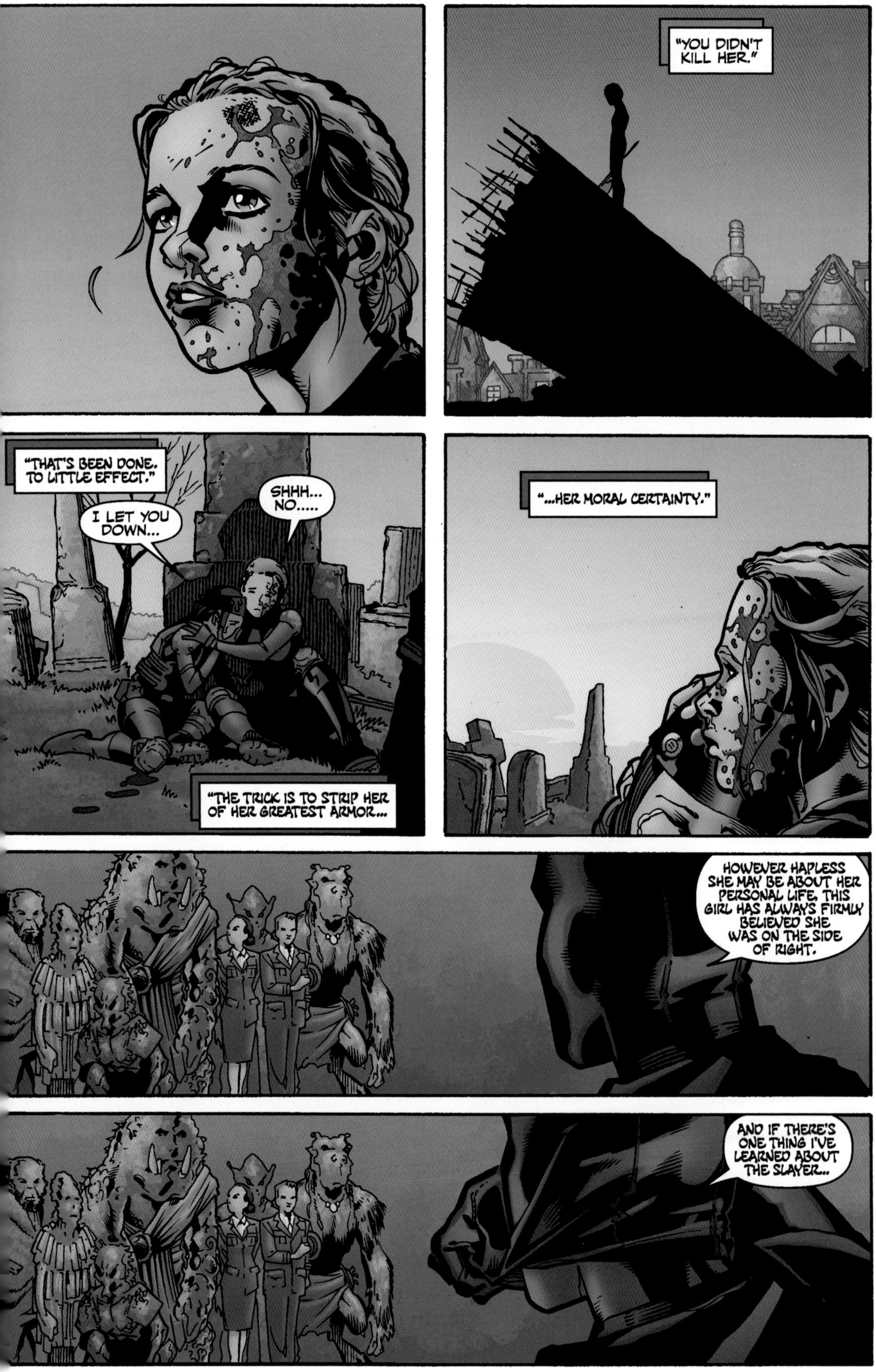
"YOU DIDN'T KILL HER."
"THAT'S BEEN DONE. TO LITTLE EFFECT."
I LET YOU DOWN...
SHHH... NO.....
"THE TRICK IS TO STRIP HER OF HER GREATEST ARMOR...
"...HER MORAL CERTAINTY."
HOWEVER HAPLESS SHE MAY BE ABOUT HER PERSONAL LIFE, THIS GIRL HAS ALWAYS FIRMLY BELIEVED SHE WAS ON THE SIDE OF RIGHT.
AND IF THERE'S ONE THING I'VE LEARNED ABOUT THE SLAYER...

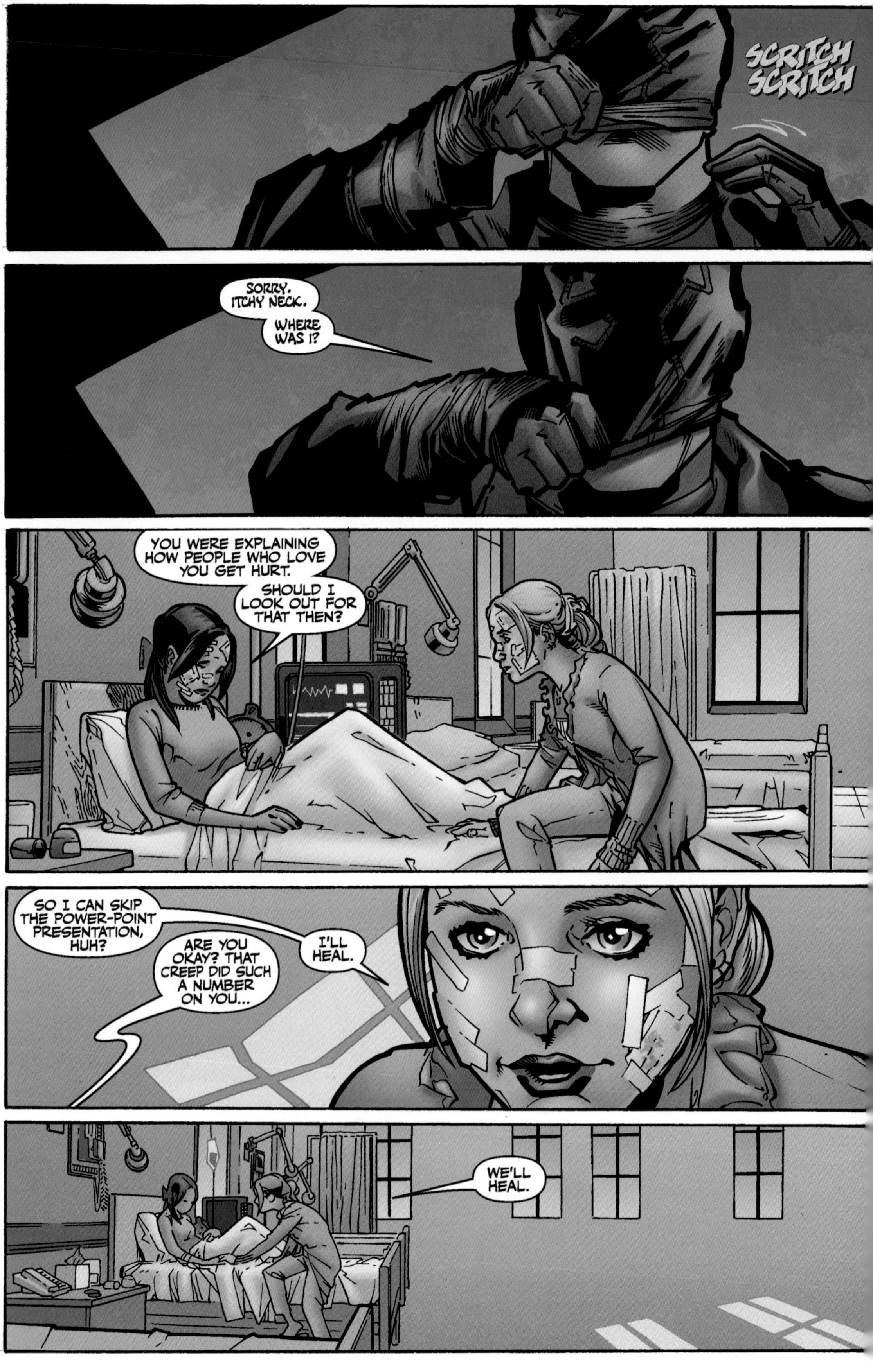
SCRITCH SCRITCH
SORRY. ITCHY NECK.
WHERE WAS I?
YOU WERE EXPLAINING HOW PEOPLE WHO LOVE YOU GET HURT.
SHOULD I LOOK OUT FOR THAT THEN?
SO I CAN SKIP THE POWER-POINT PRESENTATION, HUH?
I'LL HEAL.
ARE YOU OKAY? THAT CREEP DID SUCH A NUMBER ON YOU...
WE'LL HEAL.

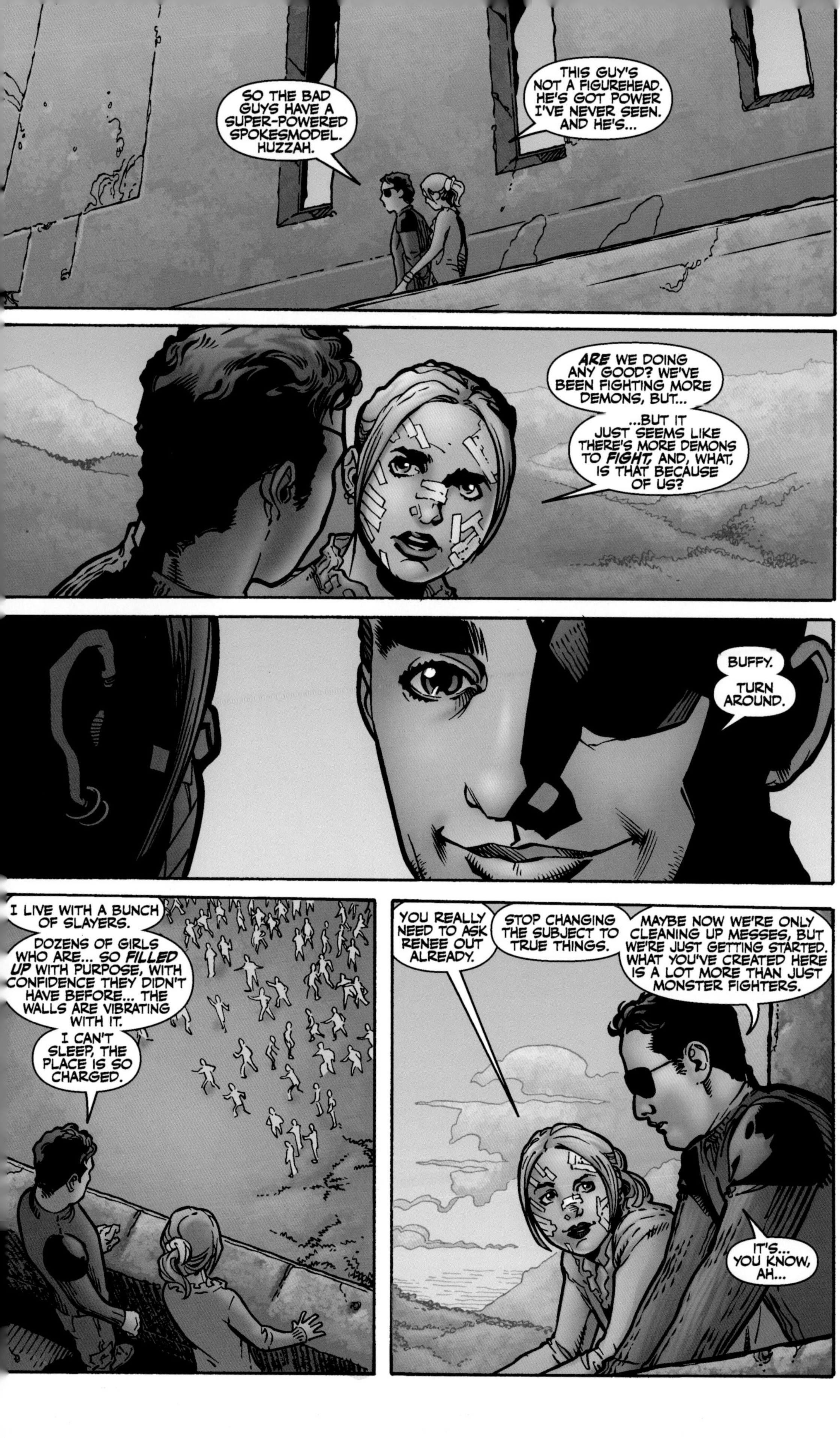
SO THE BAD GUYS HAVE A SUPER-POWERED SPOKESMODEL. HUZZAH.
THIS GUY'S NOT A FIGUREHEAD. HE'S GOT POWER I'VE NEVER SEEN. AND HE'S...
ARE WE DOING ANY GOOD? WE'VE BEEN FIGHTING MORE DEMONS, BUT...
...BUT IT JUST SEEMS LIKE THERE'S MORE DEMONS TO FIGHT, AND, WHAT, IS THAT BECAUSE OF US?
BUFFY.
TURN AROUND.
I LIVE WITH A BUNCH OF SLAYERS.
DOZENS OF GIRLS WHO ARE... SO FILLED UP WITH PURPOSE, WITH CONFIDENCE THEY DIDN'T HAVE BEFORE... THE WALLS ARE VIBRATING WITH IT.
I CAN'T SLEEP, THE PLACE IS SO CHARGED.
MAYBE NOW WE'RE ONLY CLEANING UP MESSES, BUT WE'RE JUST GETTING STARTED. WHAT YOU'VE CREATED HERE IS A LOT MORE THAN JUST MONSTER FIGHTERS.
IT'S... YOU KNOW, AH...
STOP CHANGING THE SUBJECT TO TRUE THINGS.
YOU REALLY NEED TO ASK RENEE OUT ALREADY.

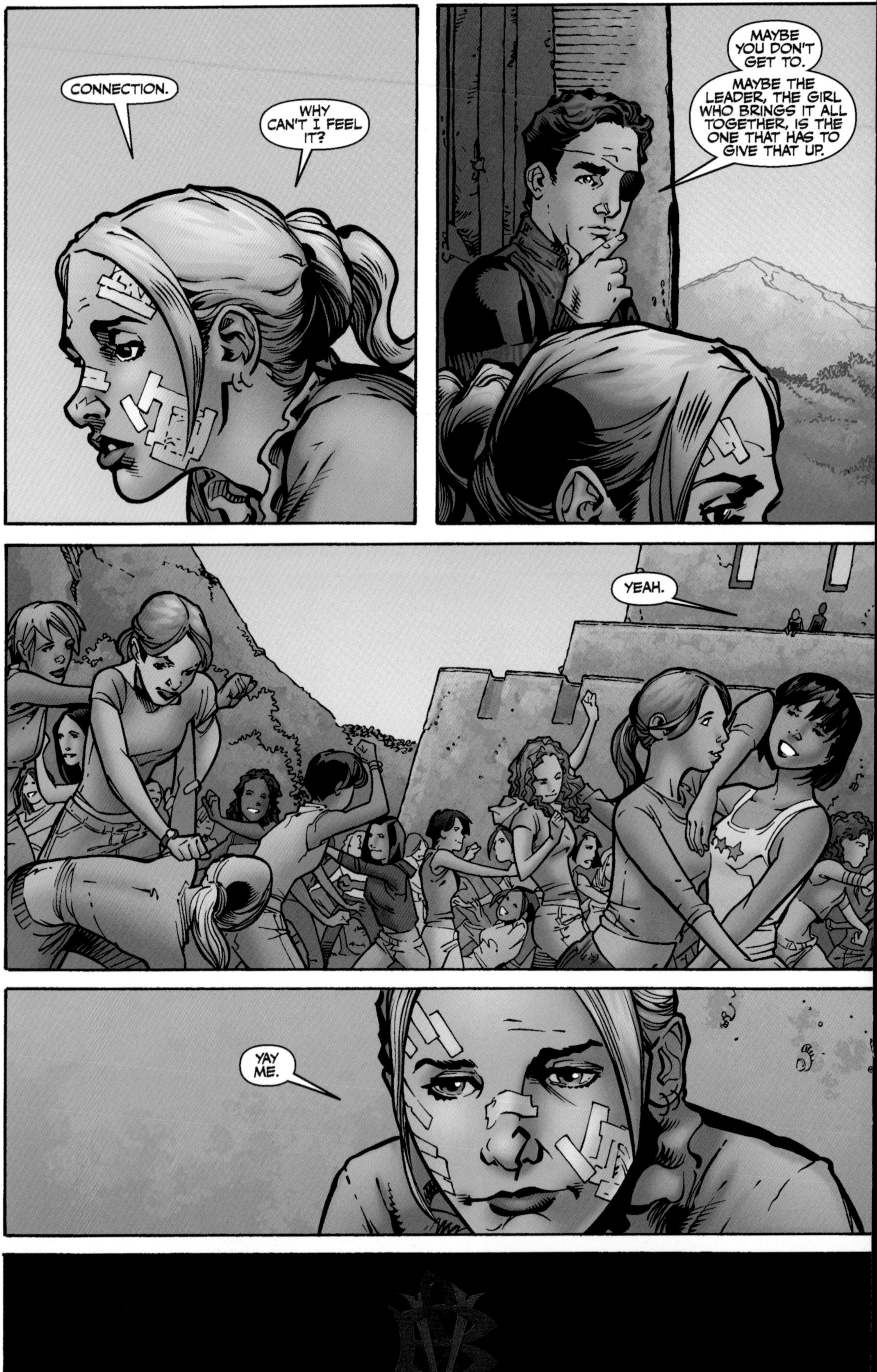
CONNECTION.
WHY CAN'T I FEEL IT?
MAYBE YOU DON'T GET TO.
MAYBE THE LEADER, THE GIRL WHO BRINGS IT ALL TOGETHER, IS THE ONE THAT HAS TO GIVE THAT UP.
YEAH.
YAY ME.

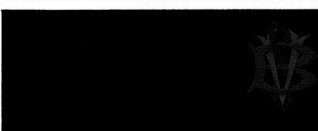

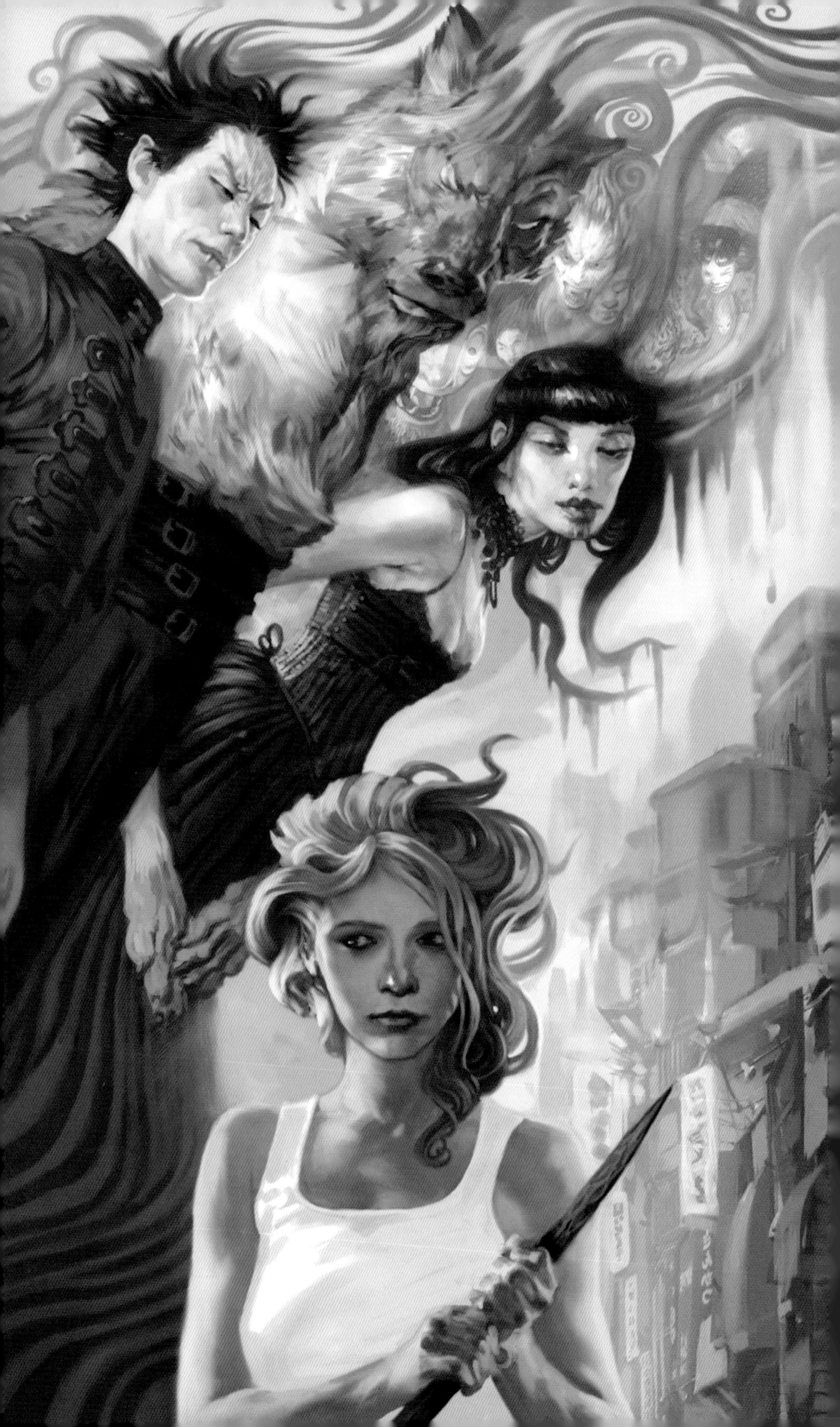

WOLVES AT THE GATE

PART ONE

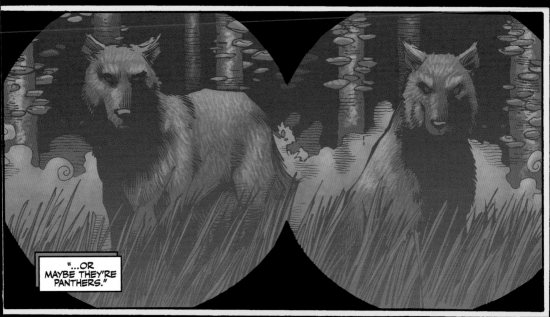

"...OR MAYBE THEY'RE PANTHERS."

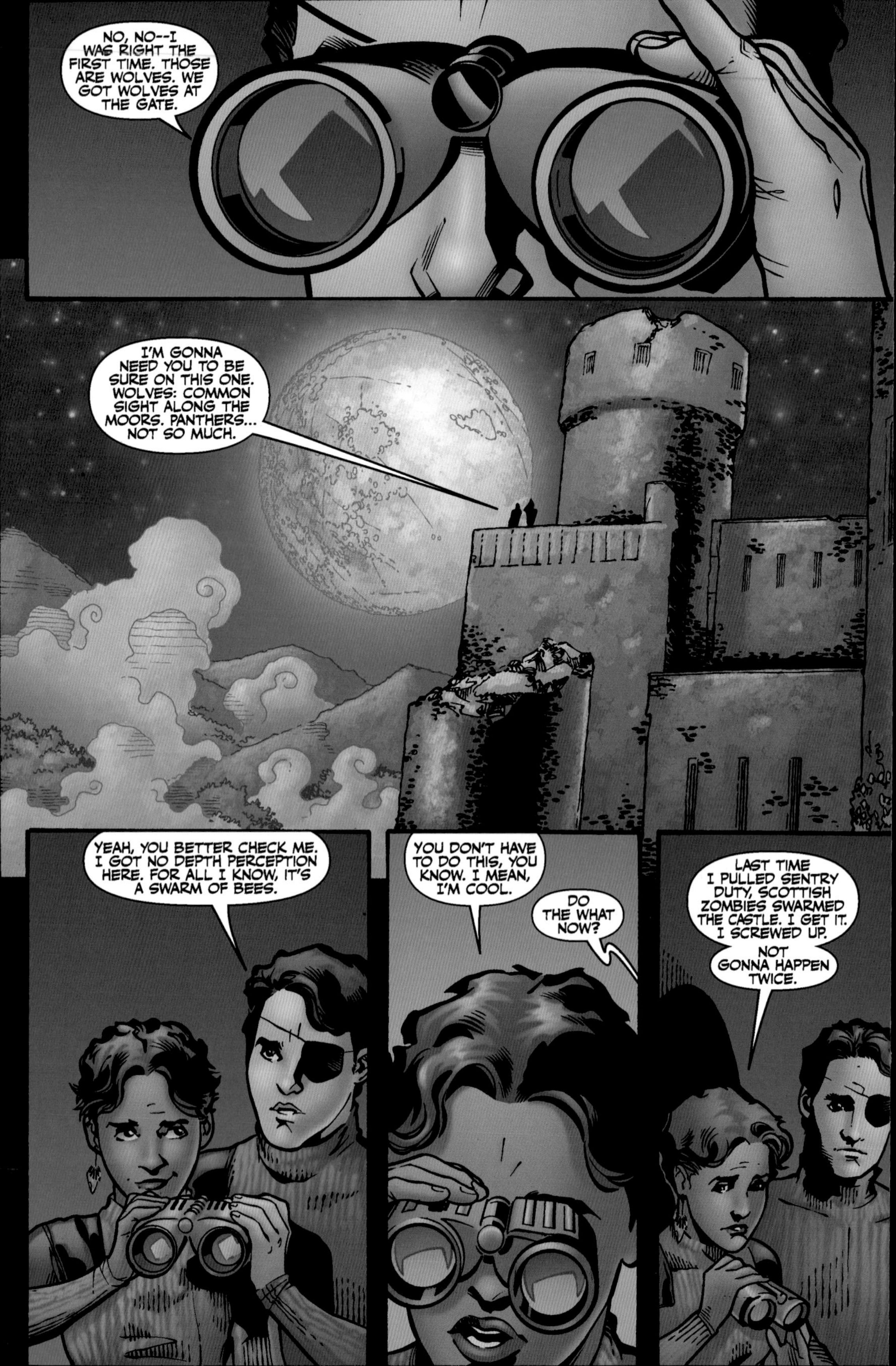
NO, NO--I WAS RIGHT THE FIRST TIME. THOSE ARE WOLVES. WE GOT WOLVES AT THE GATE.
I'M GONNA NEED YOU TO BE SURE ON THIS ONE. WOLVES: COMMON SIGHT ALONG THE MOORS. PANTHERS... NOT SO MUCH.
YEAH, YOU BETTER CHECK ME. I GOT NO DEPTH PERCEPTION HERE. FOR ALL I KNOW, IT'S A SWARM OF BEES.
YOU DON'T HAVE TO DO THIS, YOU KNOW. I MEAN, I'M COOL.
DO THE WHAT NOW?
LAST TIME I PULLED SENTRY DUTY, SCOTTISH ZOMBIES SWARMED THE CASTLE. I GET IT. I SCREWED UP.
NOT GONNA HAPPEN TWICE.

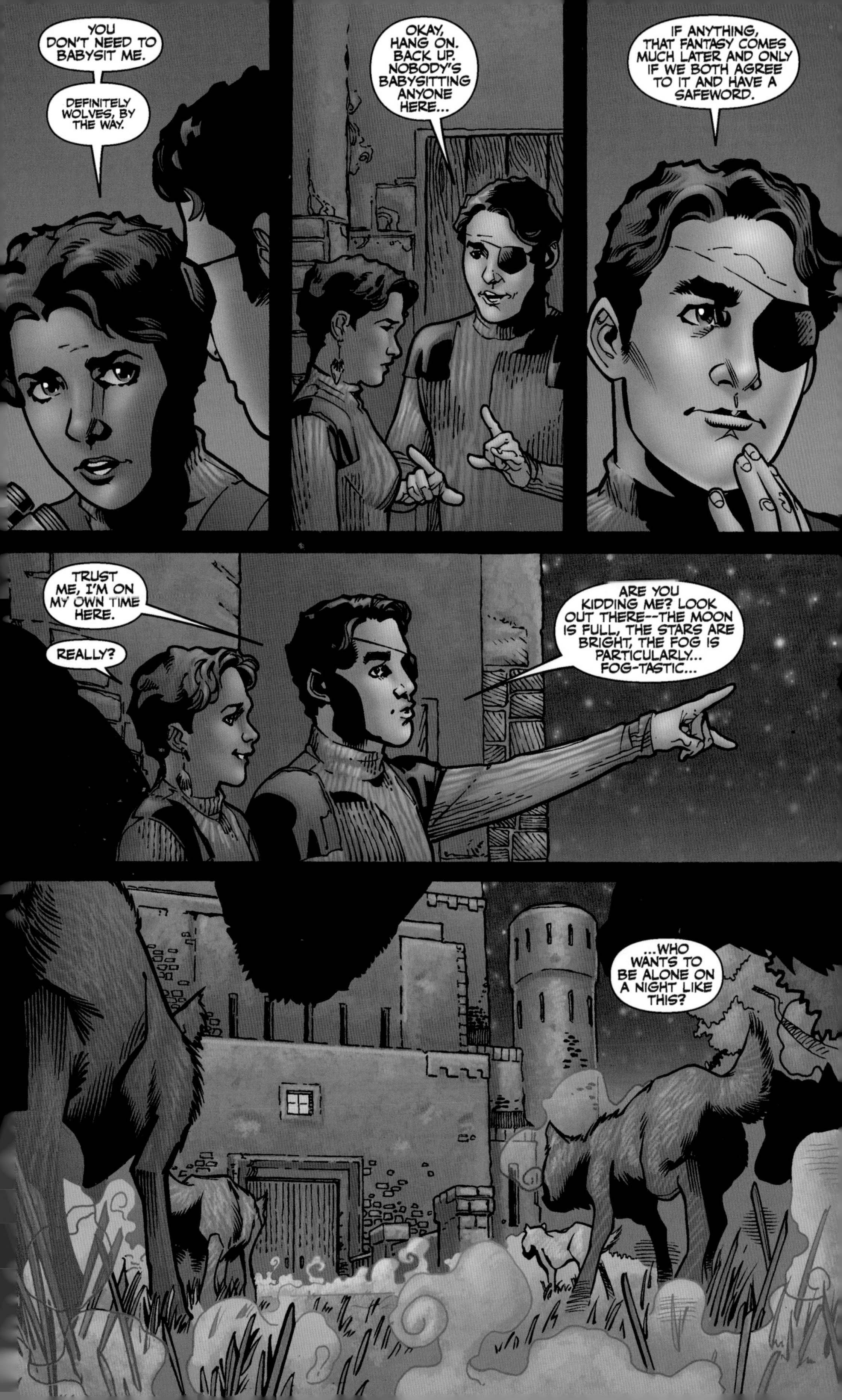

YOU DON'T NEED TO BABYSIT ME.
DEFINITELY WOLVES, BY THE WAY.
OKAY, HANG ON. BACK UP. NOBODY'S BABYSITTING ANYONE HERE...
IF ANYTHING, THAT FANTASY COMES MUCH LATER AND ONLY IF WE BOTH AGREE TO IT AND HAVE A SAFEWORD.
TRUST ME, I'M ON MY OWN TIME HERE.
REALLY?
ARE YOU KIDDING ME? LOOK OUT THERE--THE MOON IS FULL, THE STARS ARE BRIGHT, THE FOG IS PARTICULARLY... FOG-TASTIC...
...WHO WANTS TO BE ALONE ON A NIGHT LIKE THIS?

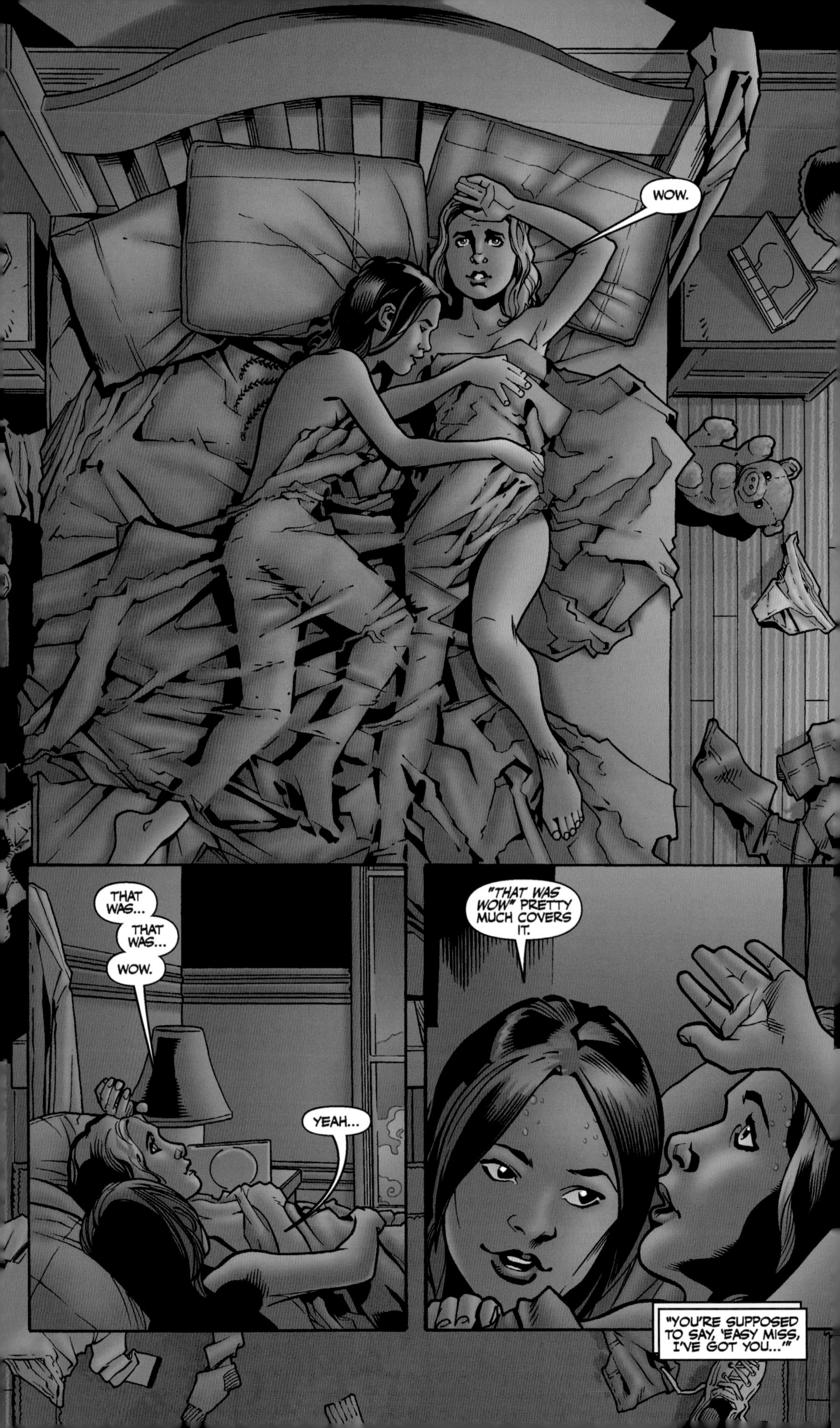
WOW.
THAT WAS...
THAT WAS...
WOW.
YEAH...
"THAT WAS WOW" PRETTY MUCH COVERS IT.
"YOU'RE SUPPOSED TO SAY, 'EASY MISS, I'VE GOT YOU...'"

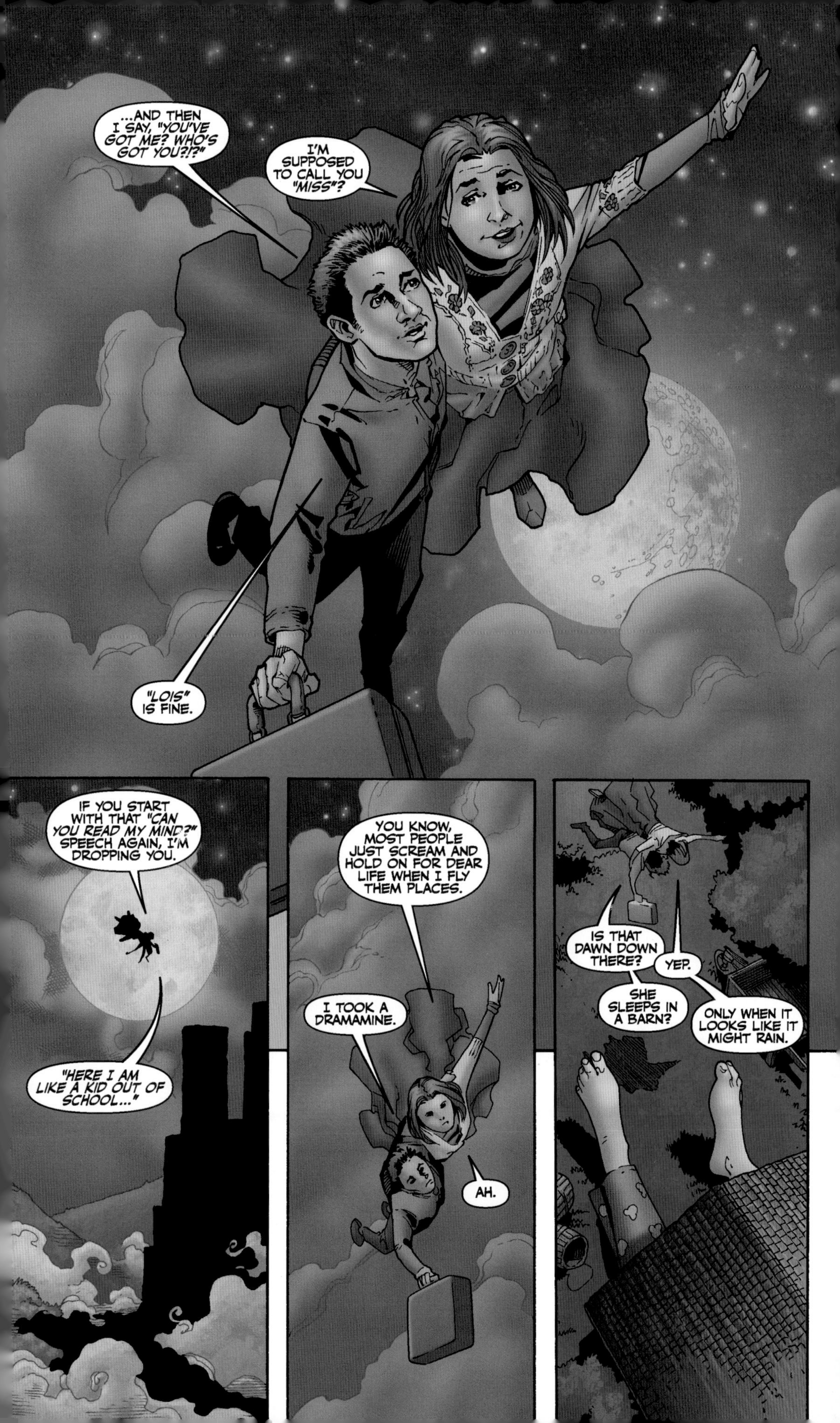
...AND THEN I SAY, "YOU'VE GOT ME? WHO'S GOT YOU?!?"
I'M SUPPOSED TO CALL YOU "MISS"?
"LOIS" IS FINE.
IF YOU START WITH THAT "CAN YOU READ MY MIND?" SPEECH AGAIN, I'M DROPPING YOU.
"HERE I AM LIKE A KID OUT OF SCHOOL..."
YOU KNOW, MOST PEOPLE JUST SCREAM AND HOLD ON FOR DEAR LIFE WHEN I FLY THEM PLACES.
I TOOK A DRAMAMINE.
AH.
IS THAT DAWN DOWN THERE?
YEP.
SHE SLEEPS IN A BARN?
ONLY WHEN IT LOOKS LIKE IT MIGHT RAIN.

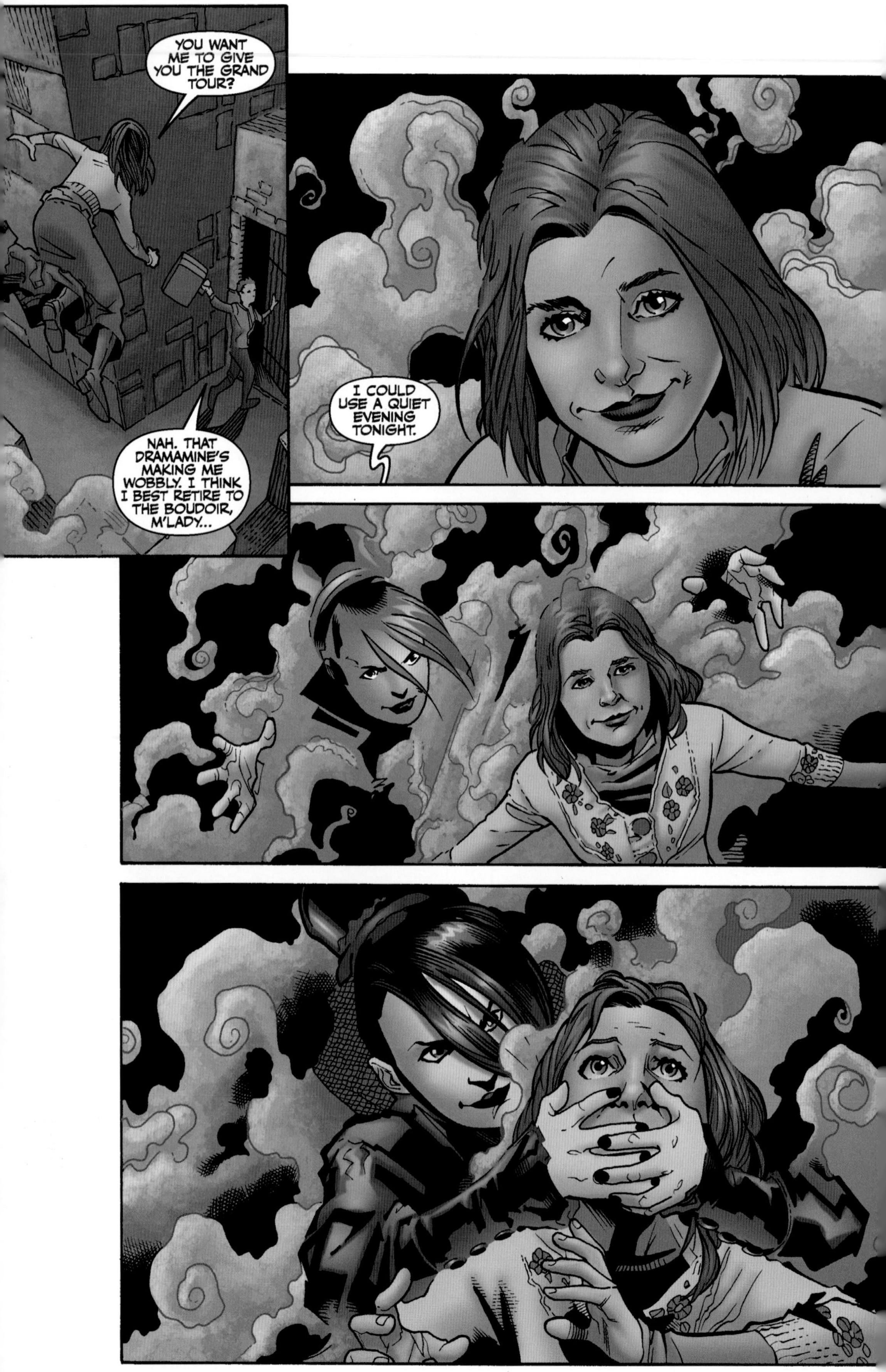
YOU WANT ME TO GIVE YOU THE GRAND TOUR?
NAH. THAT DRAMAMINE'S MAKING ME WOBBLY. I THINK I BEST RETIRE TO THE BOUDOIR, M'LADY...
I COULD USE A QUIET EVENING TONIGHT.

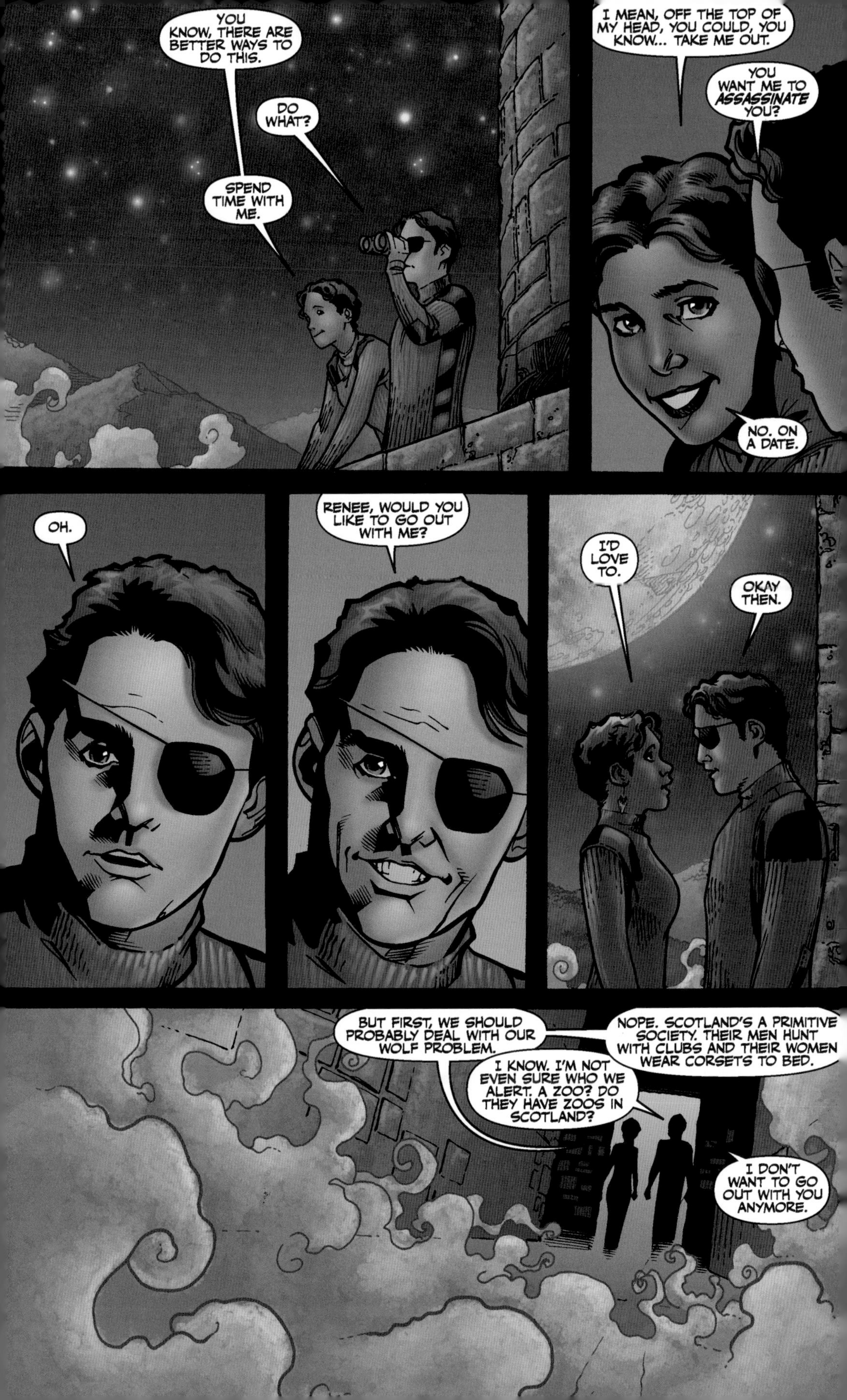
YOU KNOW, THERE ARE BETTER WAYS TO DO THIS.
DO WHAT?
SPEND TIME WITH ME.
I MEAN, OFF THE TOP OF MY HEAD, YOU COULD, YOU KNOW... TAKE ME OUT.
YOU WANT ME TO *ASSASSINATE* YOU?
NO. ON A DATE.
OH.
RENEE, WOULD YOU LIKE TO GO OUT WITH ME?
I'D LOVE TO.
OKAY THEN.
BUT FIRST, WE SHOULD PROBABLY DEAL WITH OUR WOLF PROBLEM.
I KNOW. I'M NOT EVEN SURE WHO WE ALERT. A ZOO? DO THEY HAVE ZOOS IN SCOTLAND?
NOPE. SCOTLAND'S A PRIMITIVE SOCIETY. THEIR MEN HUNT WITH CLUBS AND THEIR WOMEN WEAR CORSETS TO BED.
I DON'T WANT TO GO OUT WITH YOU ANYMORE.

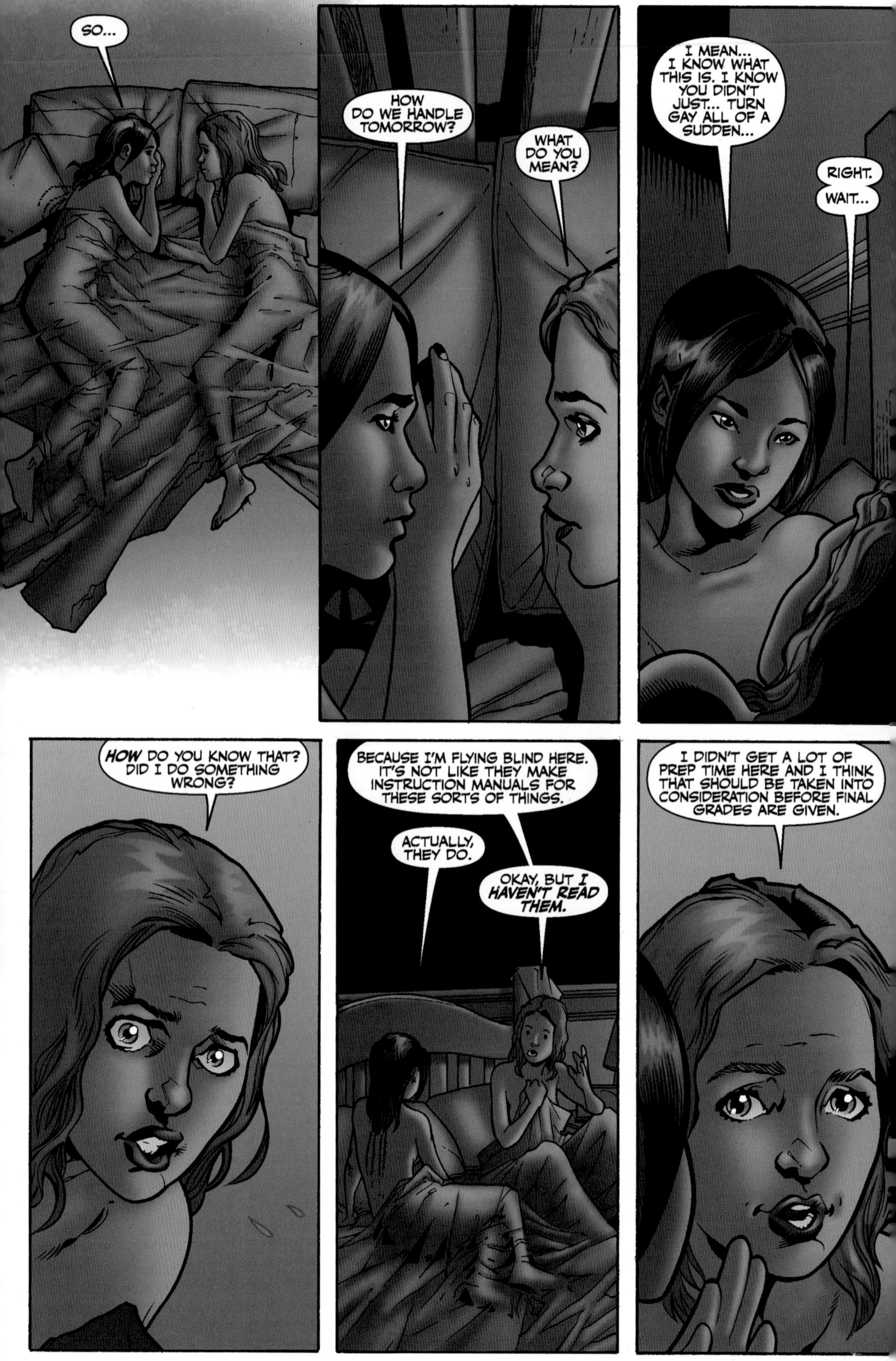
SO...
HOW DO WE HANDLE TOMORROW?
WHAT DO YOU MEAN?
I MEAN... I KNOW WHAT THIS IS. I KNOW YOU DIDN'T JUST... TURN GAY ALL OF A SUDDEN...
RIGHT.
WAIT...
HOW DO YOU KNOW THAT? DID I DO SOMETHING WRONG?
BECAUSE I'M FLYING BLIND HERE. IT'S NOT LIKE THEY MAKE INSTRUCTION MANUALS FOR THESE SORTS OF THINGS.
ACTUALLY, THEY DO.
OKAY, BUT I HAVEN'T READ THEM.
I DIDN'T GET A LOT OF PREP TIME HERE AND I THINK THAT SHOULD BE TAKEN INTO CONSIDERATION BEFORE FINAL GRADES ARE GIVEN.

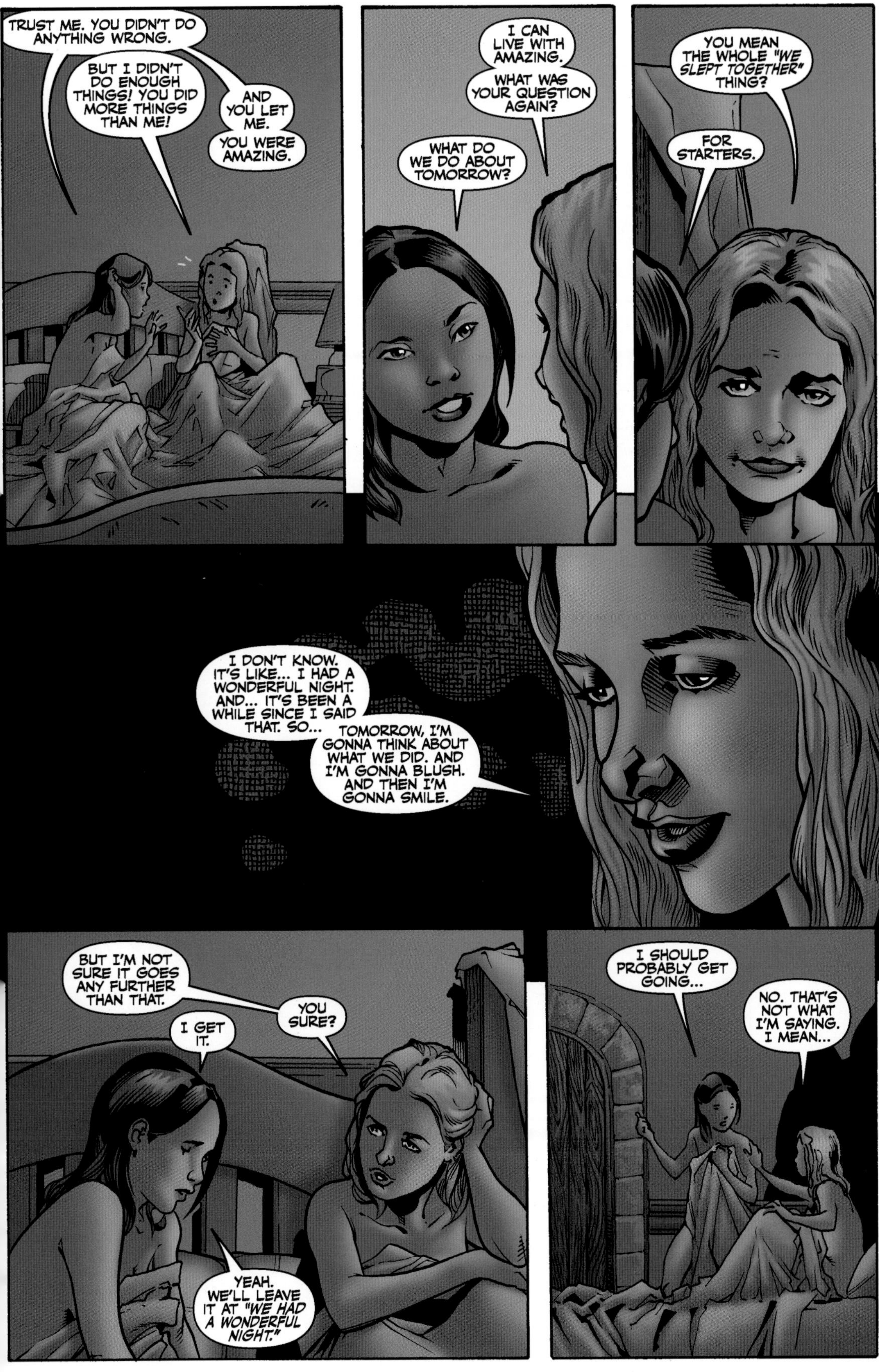
TRUST ME. YOU DIDN'T DO ANYTHING WRONG.
BUT I DIDN'T DO ENOUGH THINGS! YOU DID MORE THINGS THAN ME!
AND YOU LET ME.
YOU WERE AMAZING.
I CAN LIVE WITH AMAZING.
WHAT WAS YOUR QUESTION AGAIN?
WHAT DO WE DO ABOUT TOMORROW?
YOU MEAN THE WHOLE "WE SLEPT TOGETHER" THING?
FOR STARTERS.
I DON'T KNOW. IT'S LIKE... I HAD A WONDERFUL NIGHT. AND... IT'S BEEN A WHILE SINCE I SAID THAT. SO...
TOMORROW, I'M GONNA THINK ABOUT WHAT WE DID. AND I'M GONNA BLUSH. AND THEN I'M GONNA SMILE.
BUT I'M NOT SURE IT GOES ANY FURTHER THAN THAT.
YOU SURE?
I GET IT.
YEAH. WE'LL LEAVE IT AT "WE HAD A WONDERFUL NIGHT."
I SHOULD PROBABLY GET GOING...
NO. THAT'S NOT WHAT I'M SAYING. I MEAN...

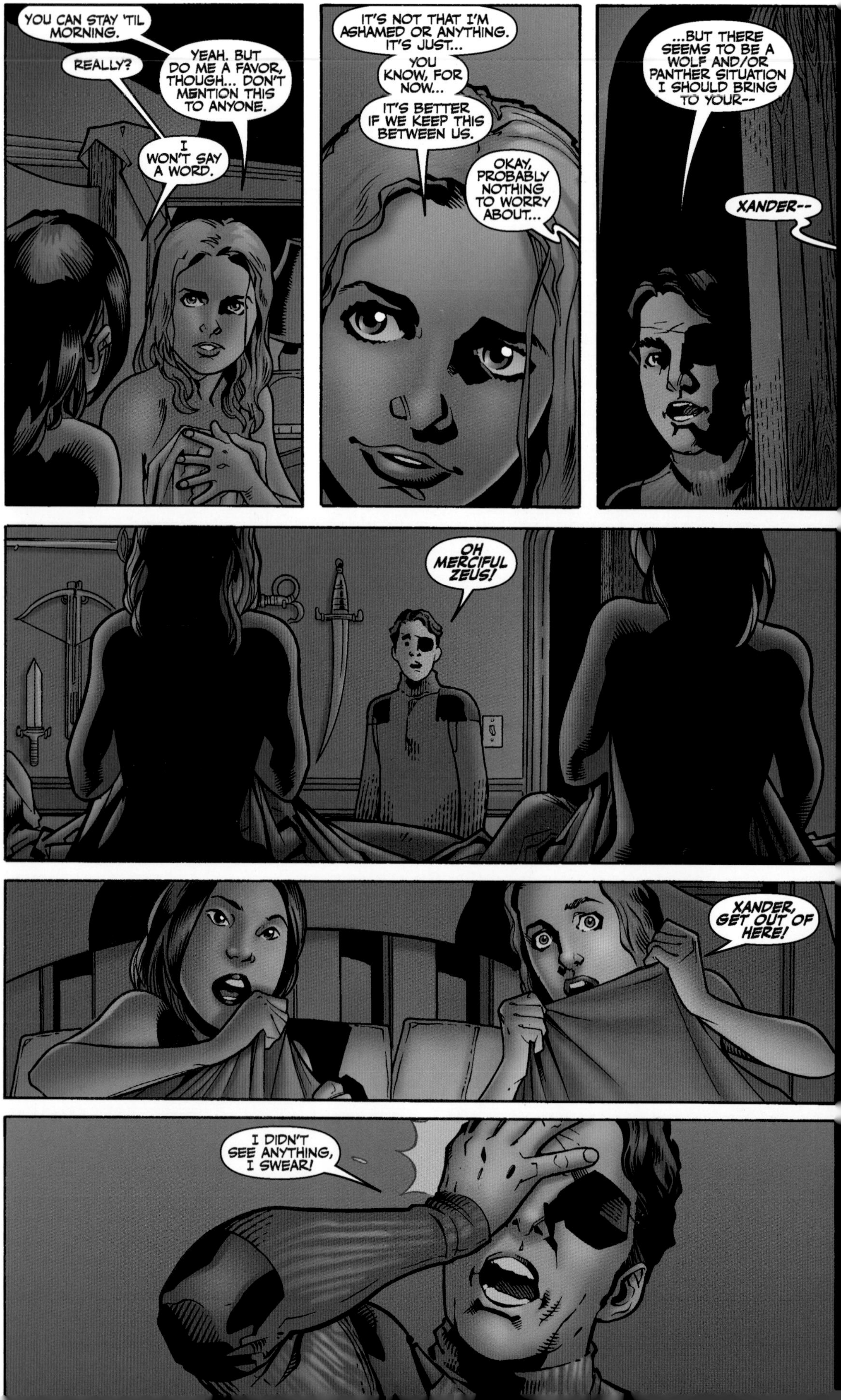
YOU CAN STAY 'TIL MORNING.
REALLY?
YEAH. BUT DO ME A FAVOR, THOUGH... DON'T MENTION THIS TO ANYONE.
I WON'T SAY A WORD.
IT'S NOT THAT I'M ASHAMED OR ANYTHING. IT'S JUST...
YOU KNOW, FOR NOW...
IT'S BETTER IF WE KEEP THIS BETWEEN US.
OKAY, PROBABLY NOTHING TO WORRY ABOUT...
...BUT THERE SEEMS TO BE A WOLF AND/OR PANTHER SITUATION I SHOULD BRING TO YOUR--
XANDER--
OH MERCIFUL ZEUS!
XANDER, GET OUT OF HERE!
I DIDN'T SEE ANYTHING, I SWEAR!

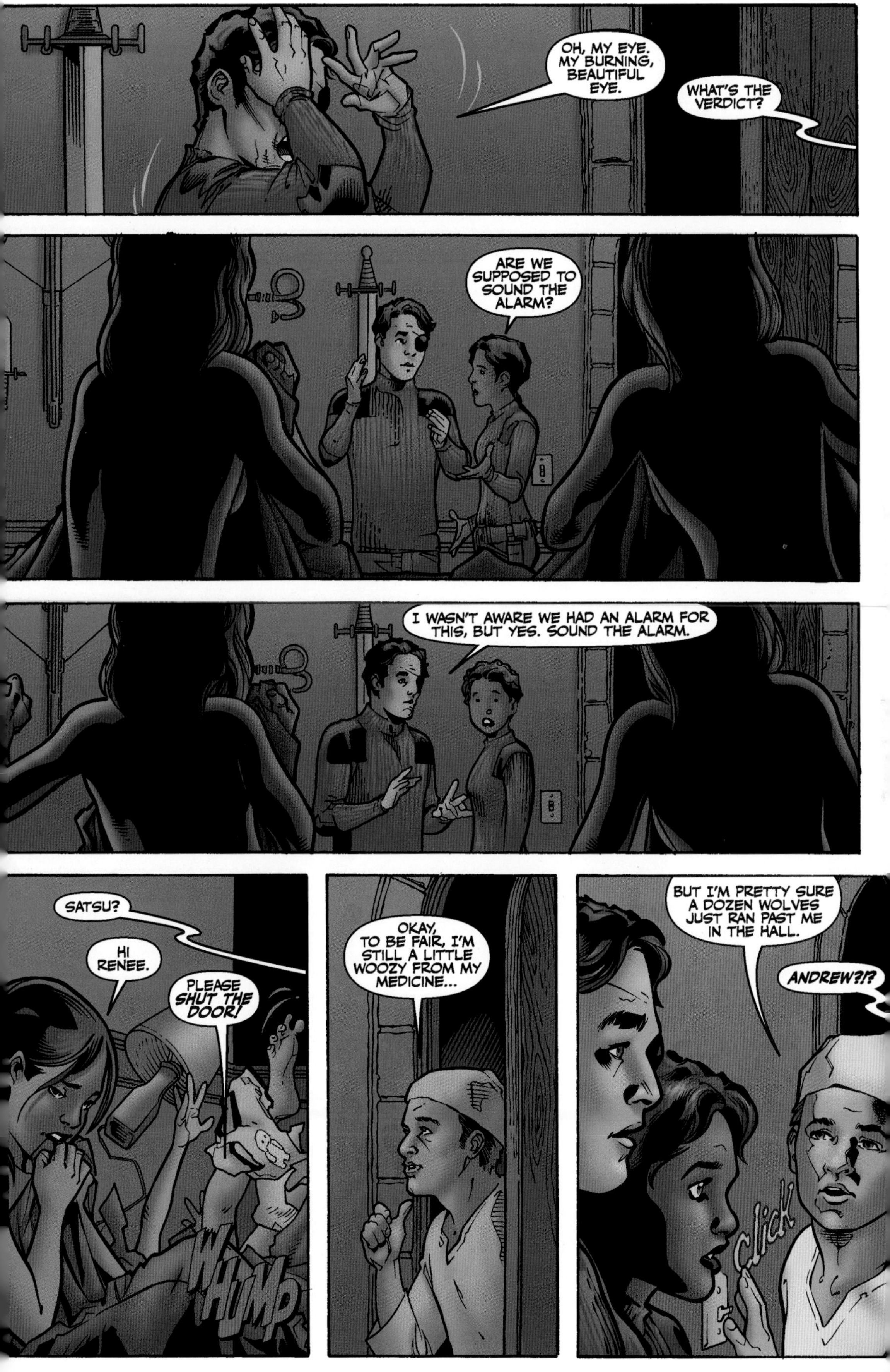
OH, MY EYE. MY BURNING, BEAUTIFUL EYE.
WHAT'S THE VERDICT?
ARE WE SUPPOSED TO SOUND THE ALARM?
I WASN'T AWARE WE HAD AN ALARM FOR THIS, BUT YES. SOUND THE ALARM.
SATSU?
HI RENEE.
PLEASE *SHUT THE DOOR!*
WHUMP
OKAY, TO BE FAIR, I'M STILL A LITTLE WOOZY FROM MY MEDICINE...
BUT I'M PRETTY SURE A DOZEN WOLVES JUST RAN PAST ME IN THE HALL.
ANDREW?!?
CLICK

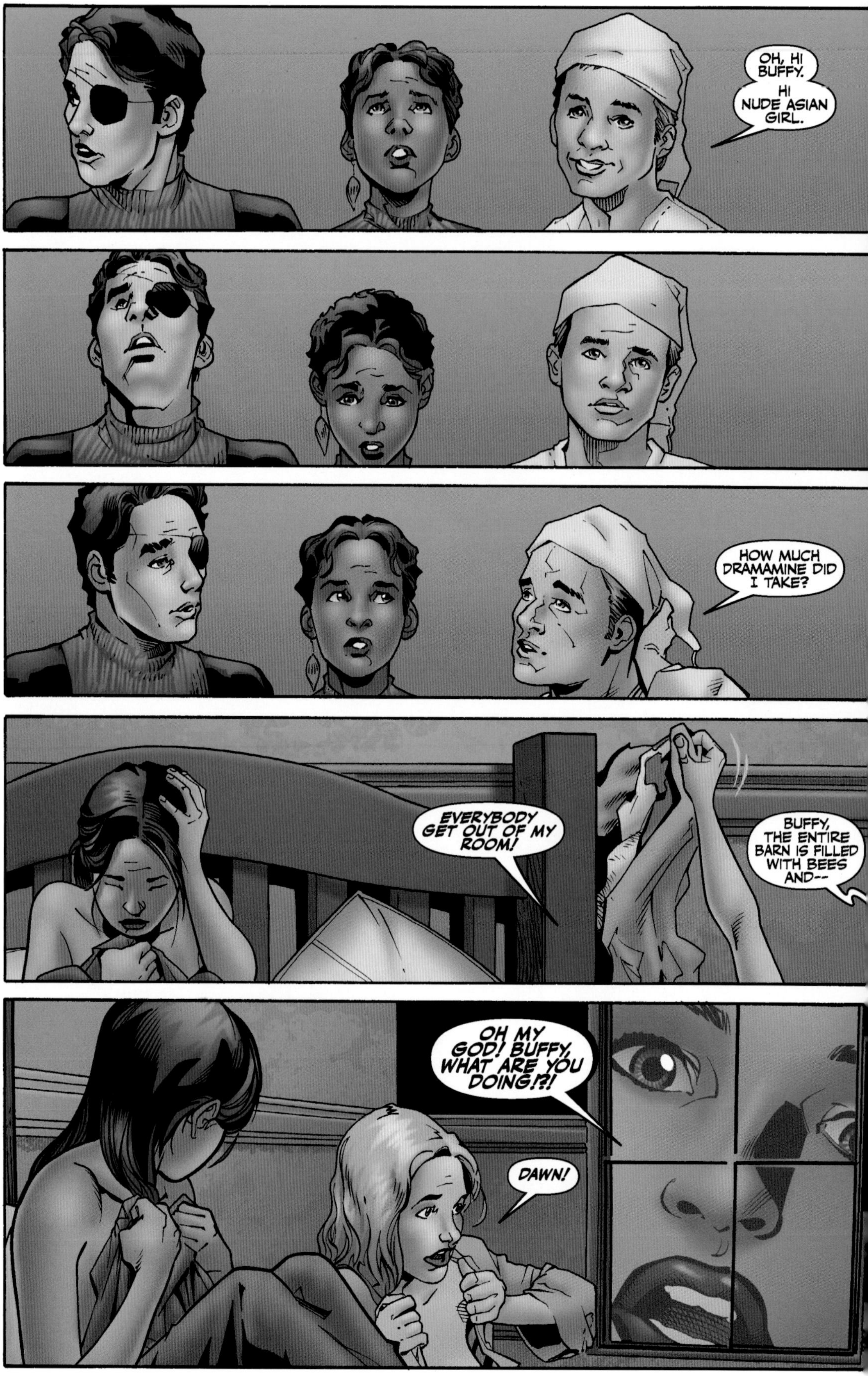
OH, HI BUFFY. HI NUDE ASIAN GIRL.
HOW MUCH DRAMAMINE DID I TAKE?
EVERYBODY GET OUT OF MY ROOM!
BUFFY, THE ENTIRE BARN IS FILLED WITH BEES AND--
OH MY GOD! BUFFY, WHAT ARE YOU DOING!?!
DAWN!

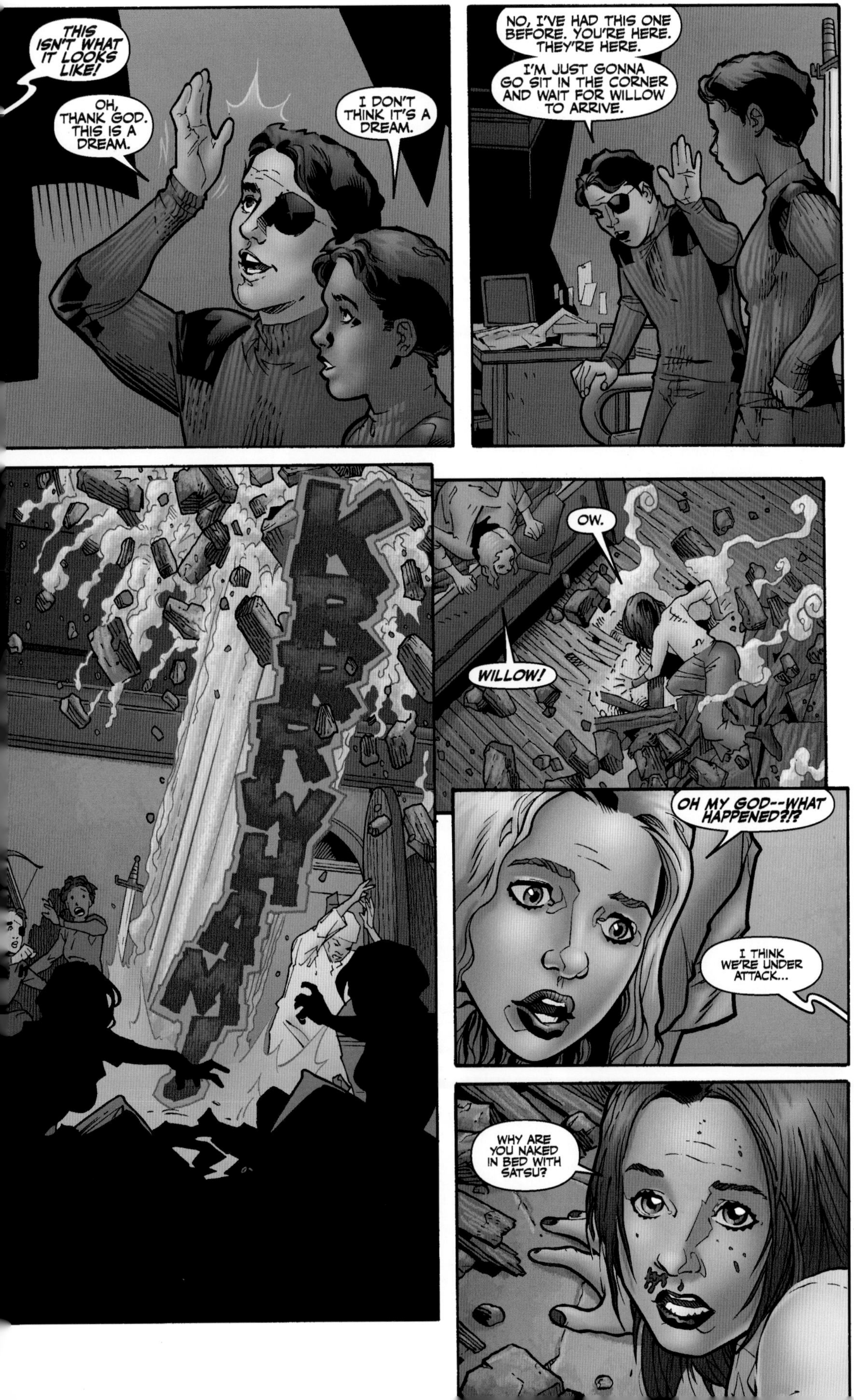
THIS ISN'T WHAT IT LOOKS LIKE!
OH, THANK GOD. THIS IS A DREAM.
I DON'T THINK IT'S A DREAM.
NO, I'VE HAD THIS ONE BEFORE. YOU'RE HERE. THEY'RE HERE.
I'M JUST GONNA GO SIT IN THE CORNER AND WAIT FOR WILLOW TO ARRIVE.
OW.
WILLOW!
OH MY GOD--WHAT HAPPENED?!?
I THINK WE'RE UNDER ATTACK...
WHY ARE YOU NAKED IN BED WITH SATSU?

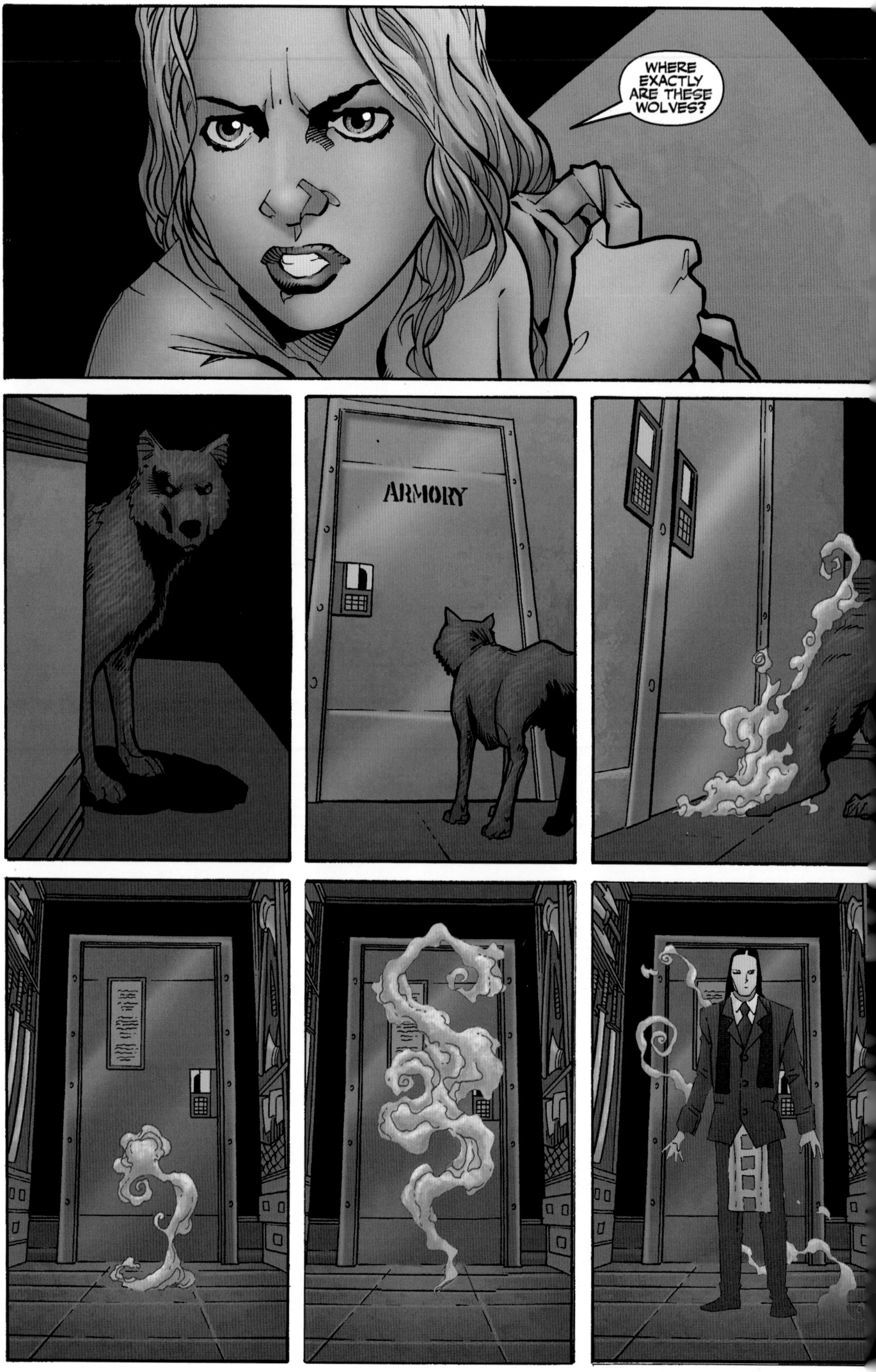
WHERE EXACTLY ARE THESE WOLVES?
ARMORY

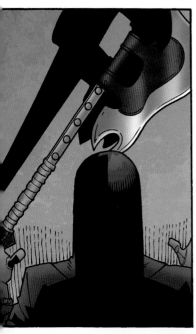

KUMIKO BROUGHT DOWN THE WITCH. WE'VE ENGAGED THE SLAYER FORCES AT THE PERIMETER.

ANY CONFIRMED FATALITIES?

NONE SO FAR. THEY'RE STRONGER THAN WE EXPECTED.

OH, DON'T SOUND SO DOUR, RAIDON...

THE FUTURE IS BRIGHT.

OKAY, I TRY TO BE MISS SHARE-AND-SHARE-ALIKE...

BUT I REALLY DON'T LIKE IT WHEN PEOPLE TOUCH MY STUFF.

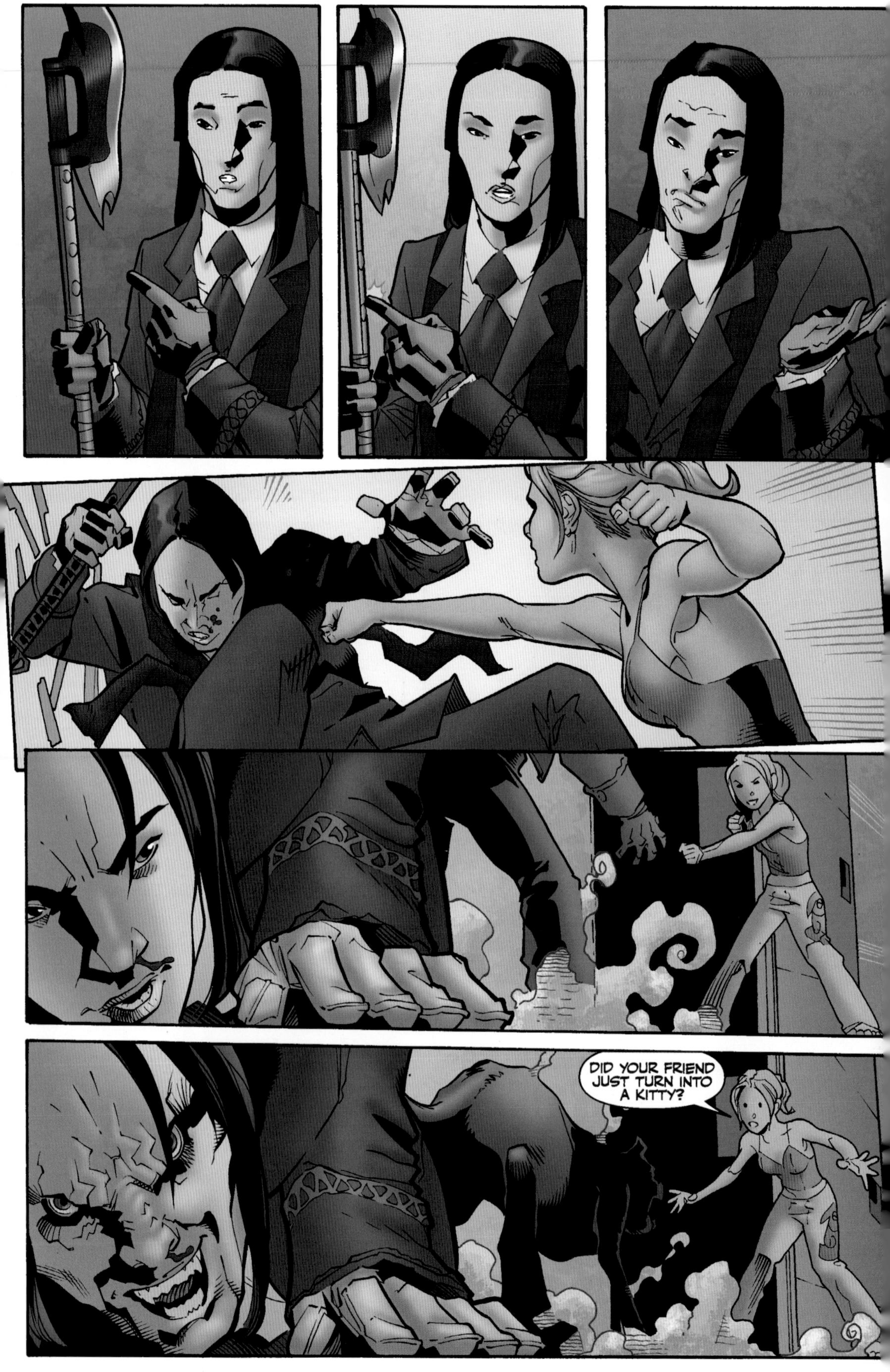
DID YOUR FRIEND JUST TURN INTO A KITTY?

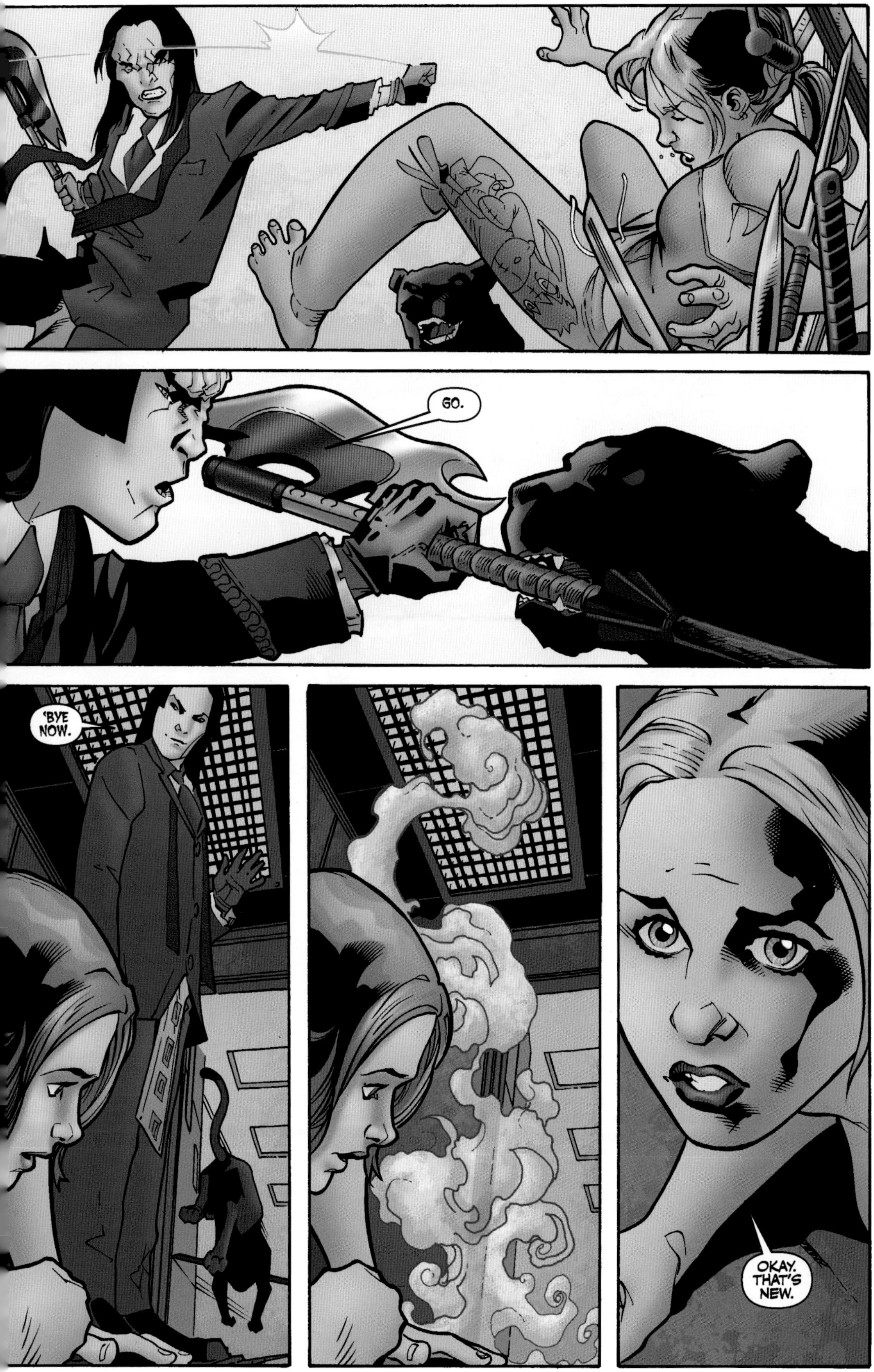
GO.
'BYE NOW.
OKAY. THAT'S NEW.

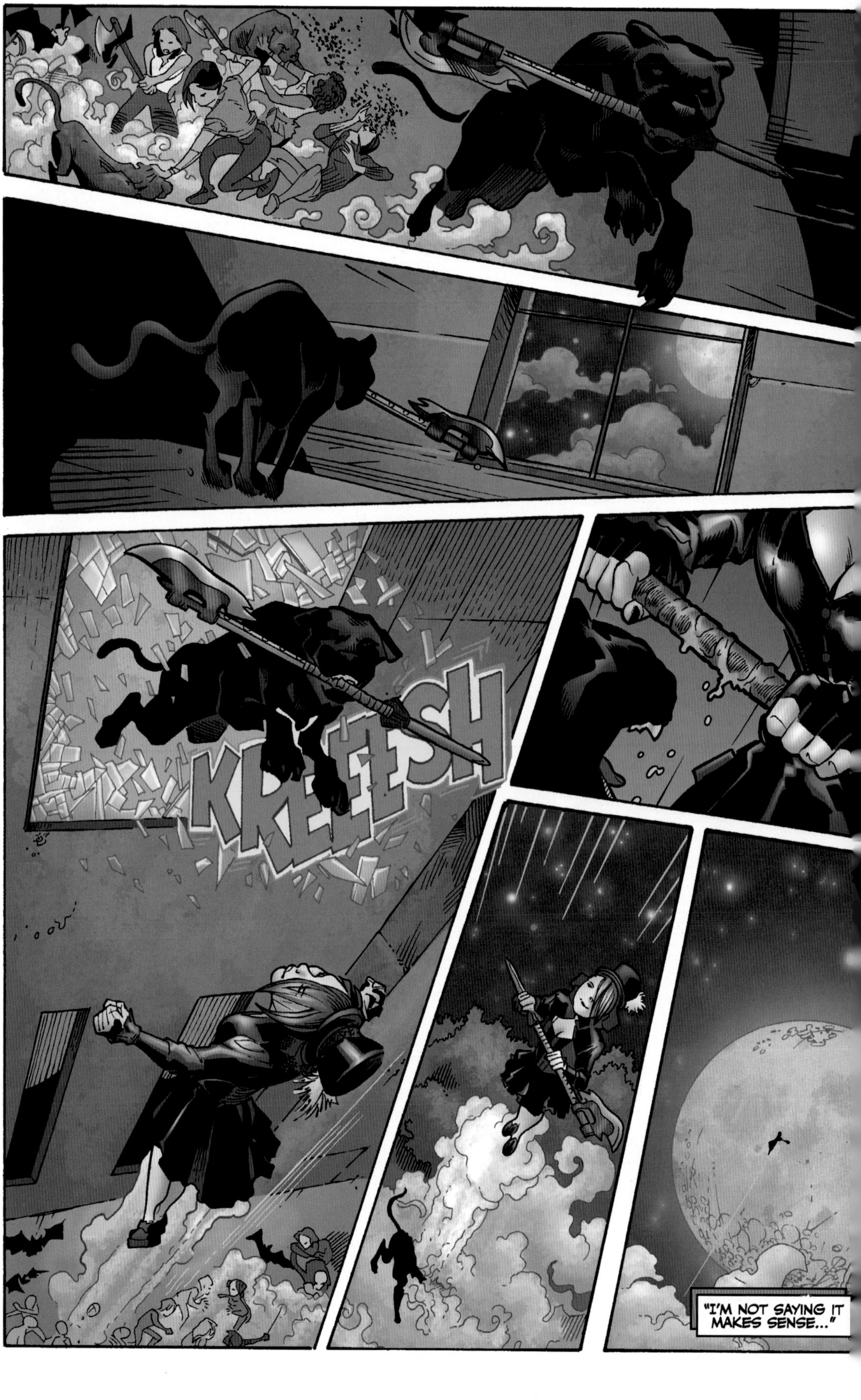
KREEESH
"I'M NOT SAYING IT MAKES SENSE..."

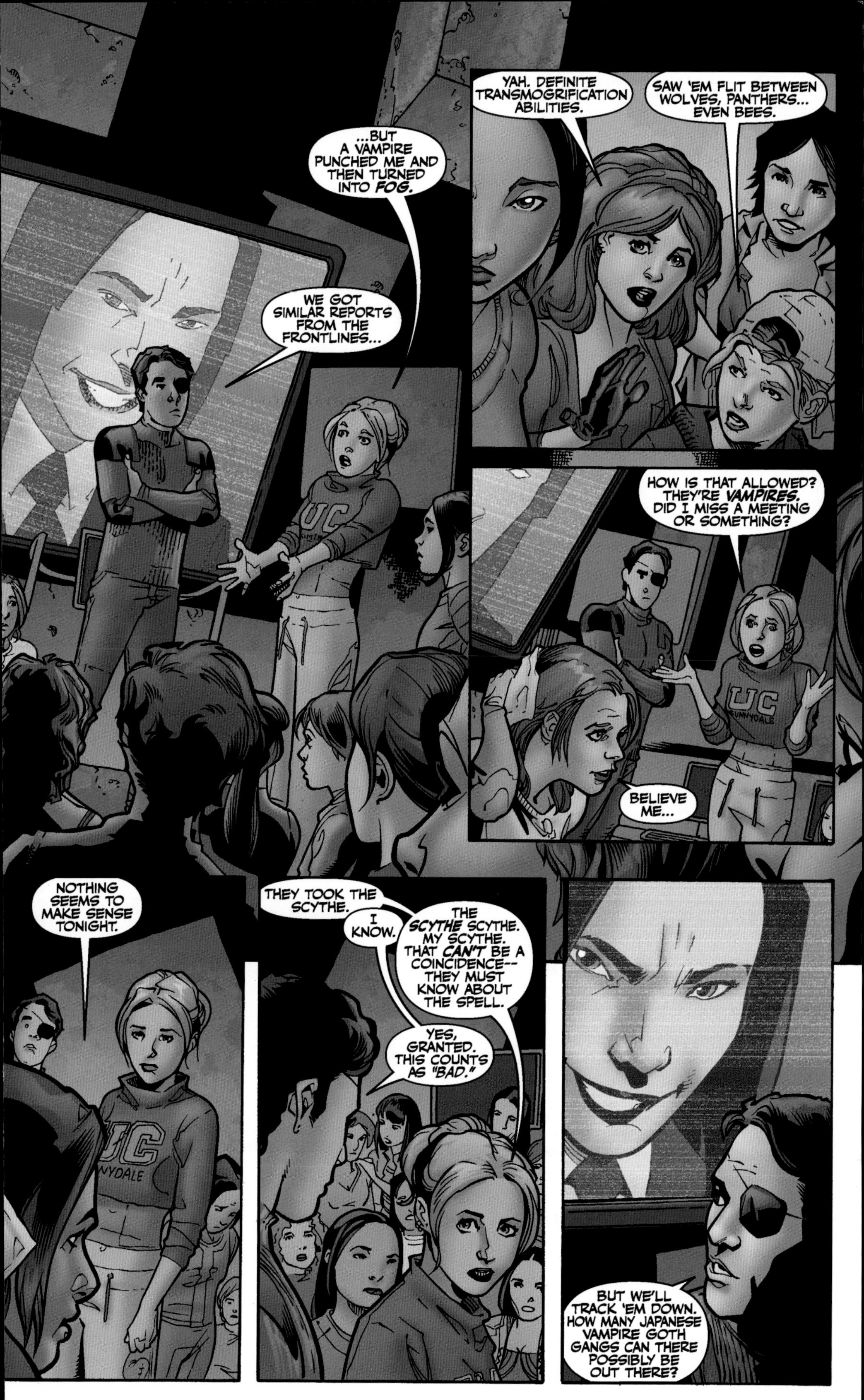
...BUT A VAMPIRE PUNCHED ME AND THEN TURNED INTO *FOG.*
WE GOT SIMILAR REPORTS FROM THE FRONTLINES...
YAH. DEFINITE TRANSMOGRIFICATION ABILITIES.
SAW 'EM FLIT BETWEEN WOLVES, PANTHERS... EVEN BEES.
HOW IS THAT ALLOWED? THEY'RE *VAMPIRES.* DID I MISS A MEETING OR SOMETHING?
BELIEVE ME...
NOTHING SEEMS TO MAKE SENSE TONIGHT.
THEY TOOK THE SCYTHE.
I KNOW.
THE *SCYTHE* SCYTHE. MY SCYTHE. THAT *CAN'T* BE A COINCIDENCE-- THEY MUST KNOW ABOUT THE SPELL.
YES, GRANTED. THIS COUNTS AS *"BAD."*
BUT WE'LL TRACK 'EM DOWN. HOW MANY JAPANESE VAMPIRE GOTH GANGS CAN THERE POSSIBLY BE OUT THERE?

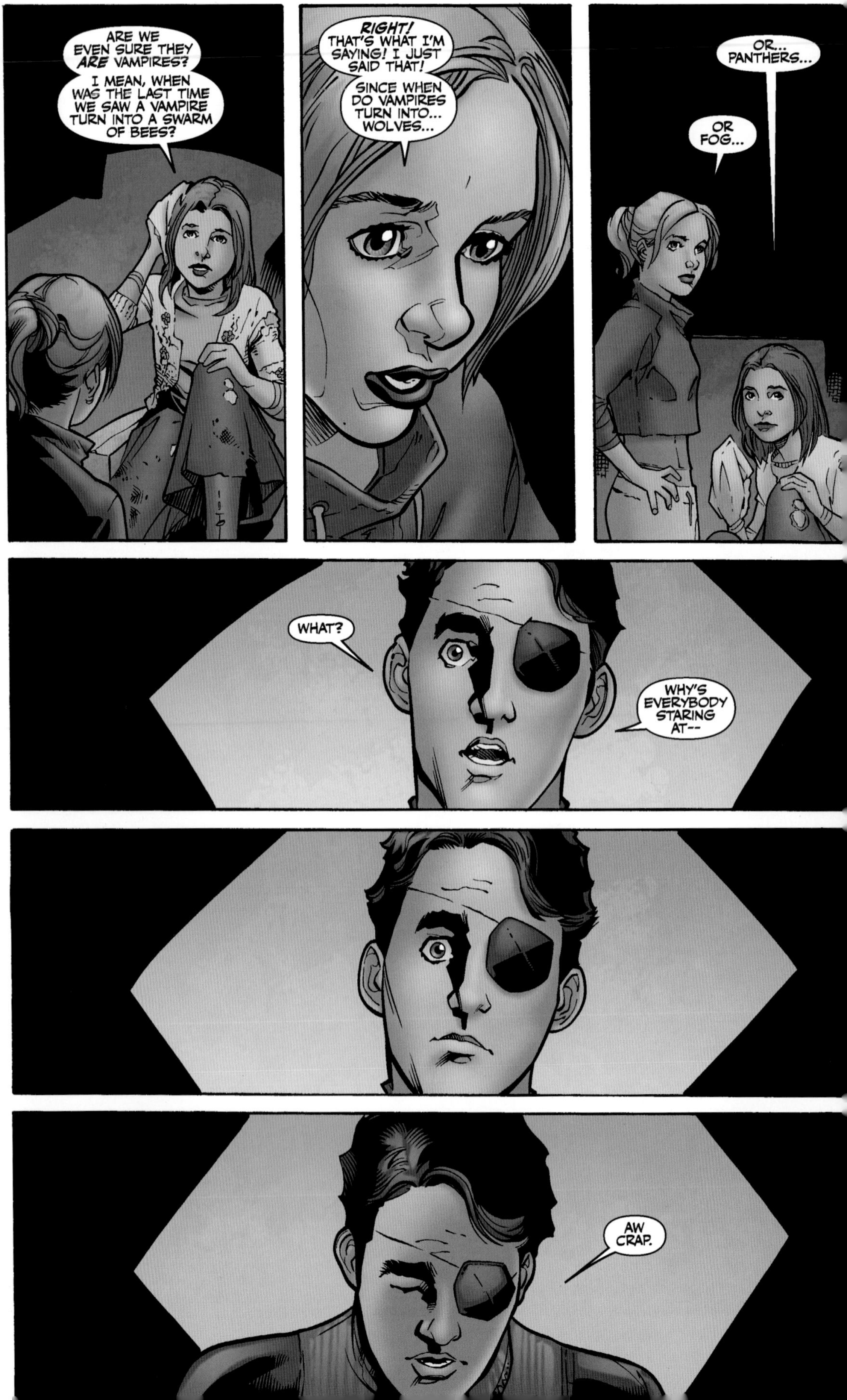
ARE WE EVEN SURE THEY *ARE* VAMPIRES?
I MEAN, WHEN WAS THE LAST TIME WE SAW A VAMPIRE TURN INTO A SWARM OF BEES?
RIGHT! THAT'S WHAT I'M SAYING! I JUST SAID THAT!
SINCE WHEN DO VAMPIRES TURN INTO... WOLVES...
OR FOG...
OR... PANTHERS...
WHAT?
WHY'S EVERYBODY STARING AT--
AW CRAP.

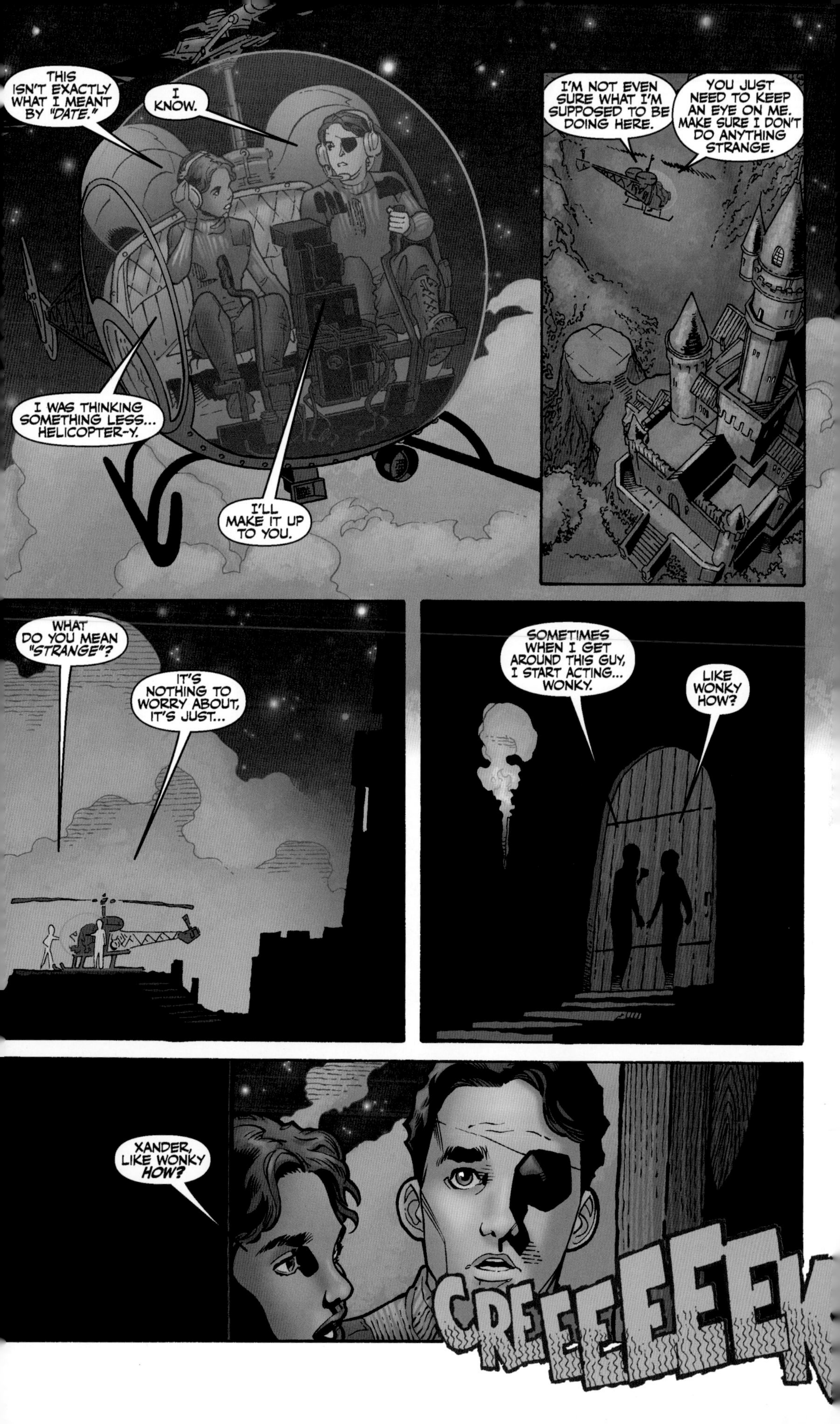
THIS ISN'T EXACTLY WHAT I MEANT BY *"DATE."*
I KNOW.
I WAS THINKING SOMETHING LESS... HELICOPTER-Y.
I'LL MAKE IT UP TO YOU.
I'M NOT EVEN SURE WHAT I'M SUPPOSED TO BE DOING HERE.
YOU JUST NEED TO KEEP AN EYE ON ME. MAKE SURE I DON'T DO ANYTHING STRANGE.
WHAT DO YOU MEAN *"STRANGE"*?
IT'S NOTHING TO WORRY ABOUT, IT'S JUST...
SOMETIMES WHEN I GET AROUND THIS GUY, I START ACTING... WONKY.
LIKE WONKY HOW?
XANDER, LIKE WONKY *HOW?*
CREEEEEK

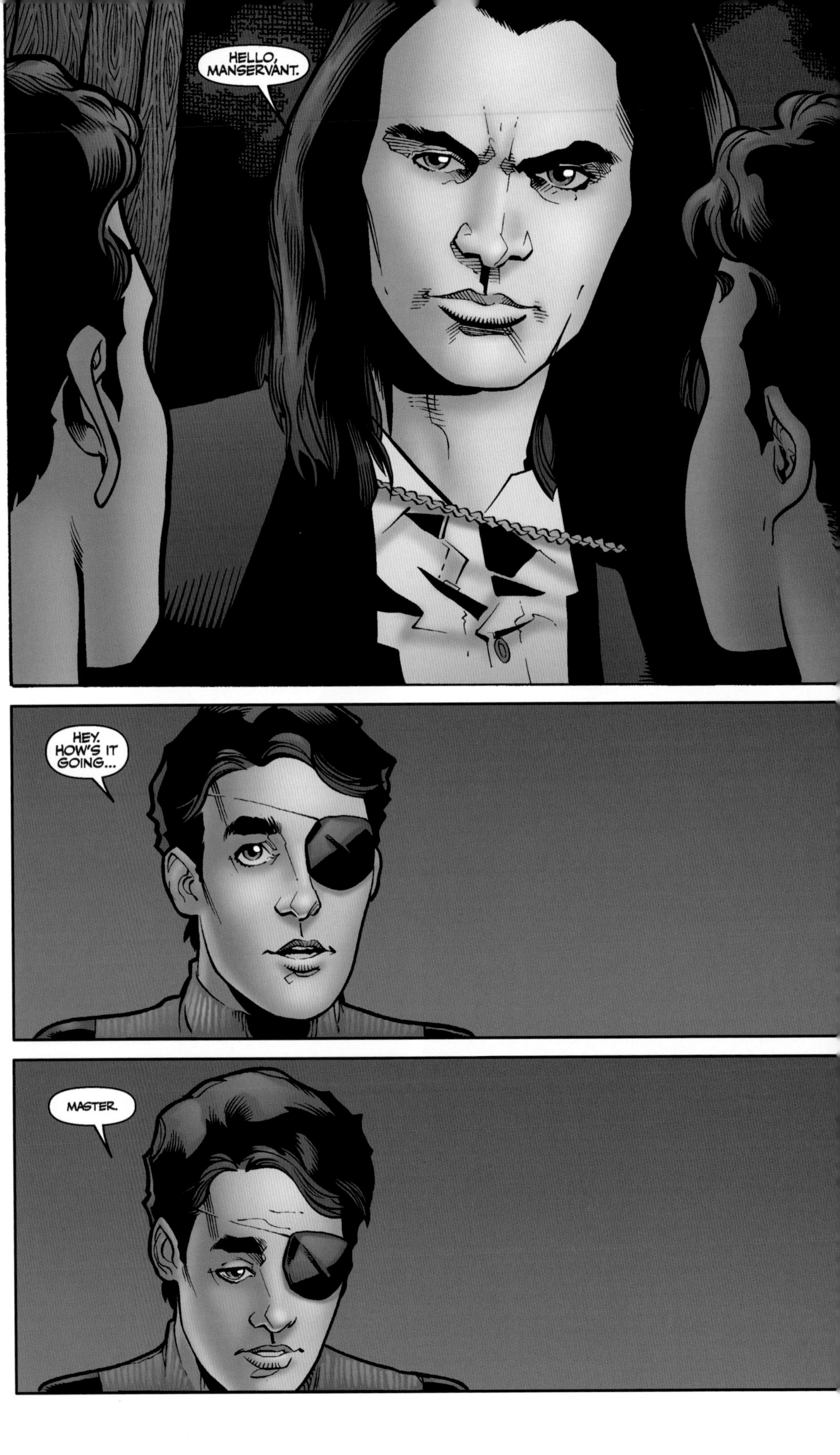
HELLO, MANSERVANT.
HEY. HOW'S IT GOING...
MASTER.

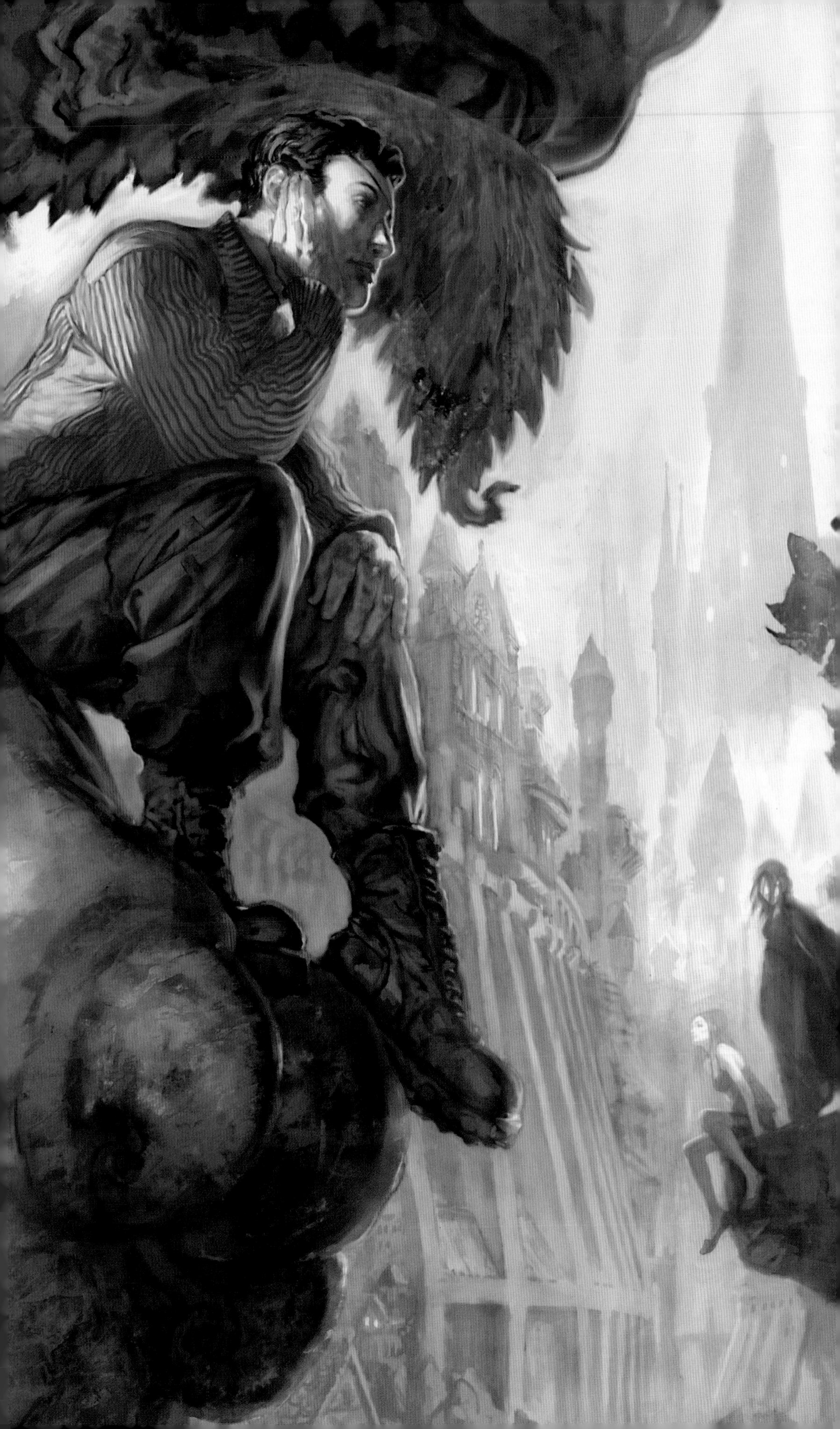

WOLVES AT THE GATE
PART TWO

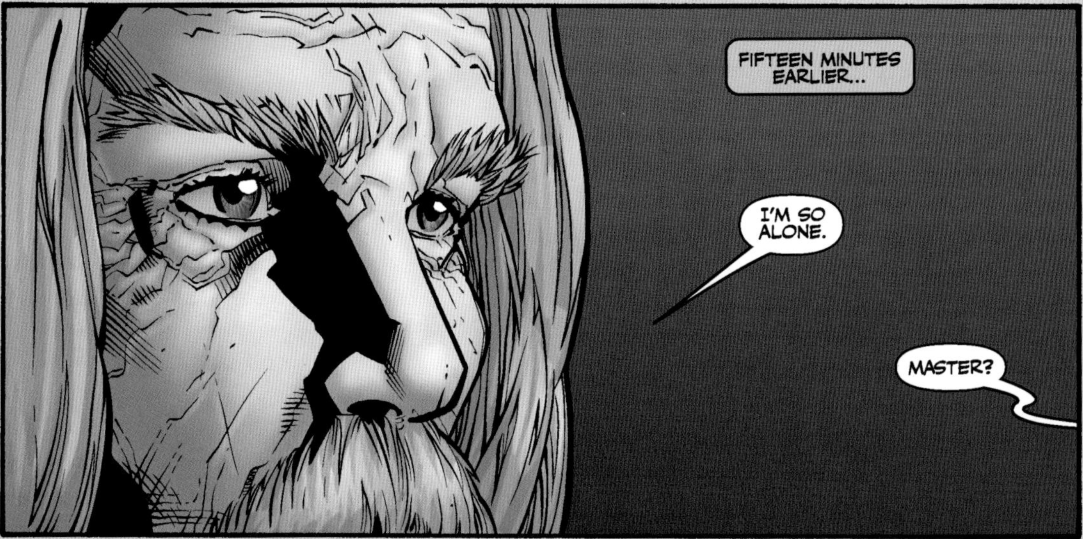
FIFTEEN MINUTES EARLIER...
I'M SO ALONE.
MASTER?

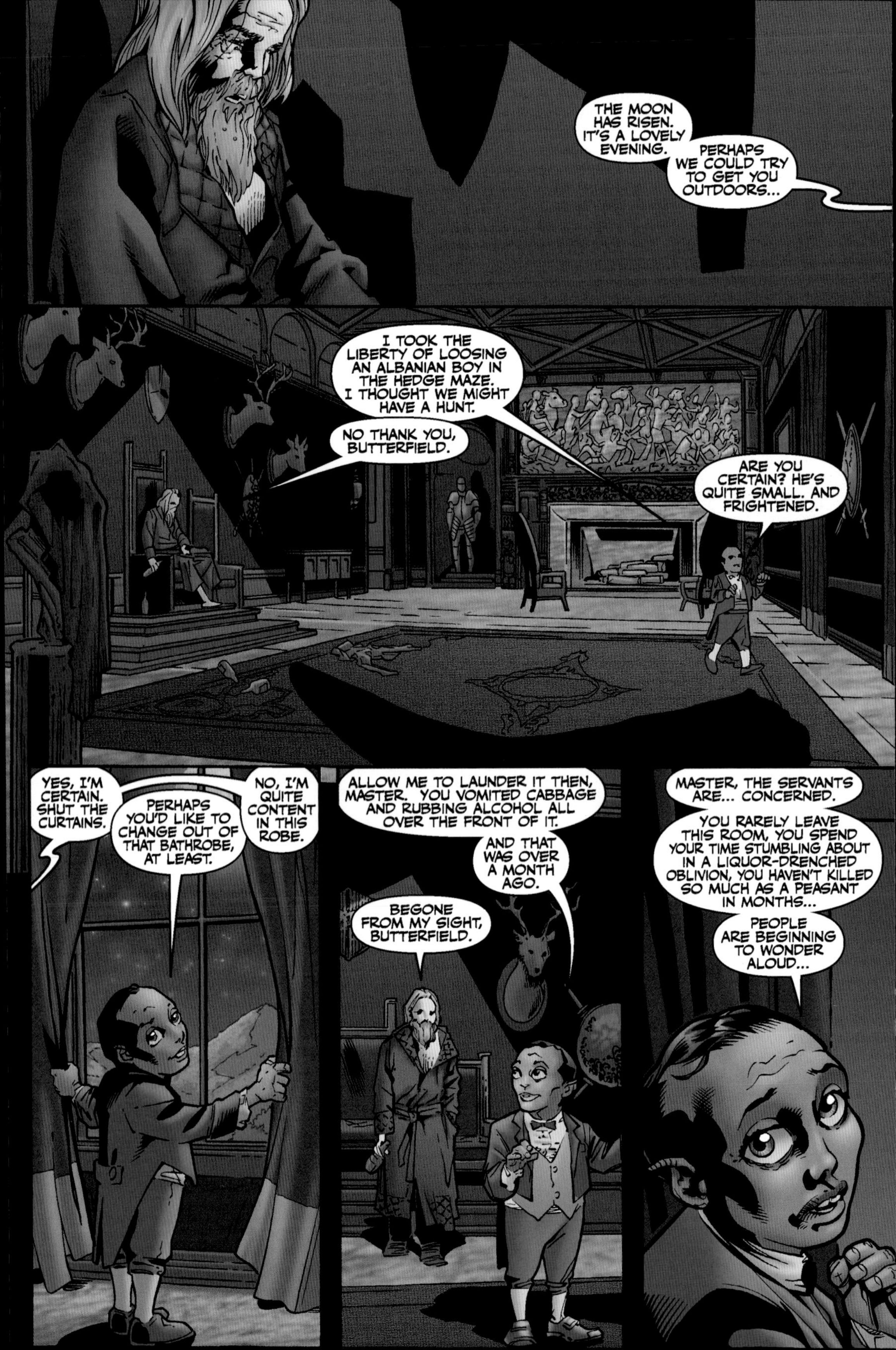
THE MOON HAS RISEN. IT'S A LOVELY EVENING.
PERHAPS WE COULD TRY TO GET YOU OUTDOORS...
I TOOK THE LIBERTY OF LOOSING AN ALBANIAN BOY IN THE HEDGE MAZE. I THOUGHT WE MIGHT HAVE A HUNT.
NO THANK YOU, BUTTERFIELD.
ARE YOU CERTAIN? HE'S QUITE SMALL. AND FRIGHTENED.
YES, I'M CERTAIN. SHUT THE CURTAINS.
PERHAPS YOU'D LIKE TO CHANGE OUT OF THAT BATHROBE, AT LEAST.
NO, I'M QUITE CONTENT IN THIS ROBE.
ALLOW ME TO LAUNDER IT THEN, MASTER. YOU VOMITED CABBAGE AND RUBBING ALCOHOL ALL OVER THE FRONT OF IT.
AND THAT WAS OVER A MONTH AGO.
BEGONE FROM MY SIGHT, BUTTERFIELD.
MASTER, THE SERVANTS ARE... CONCERNED.
YOU RARELY LEAVE THIS ROOM, YOU SPEND YOUR TIME STUMBLING ABOUT IN A LIQUOR-DRENCHED OBLIVION, YOU HAVEN'T KILLED SO MUCH AS A PEASANT IN MONTHS...
PEOPLE ARE BEGINNING TO WONDER ALOUD...

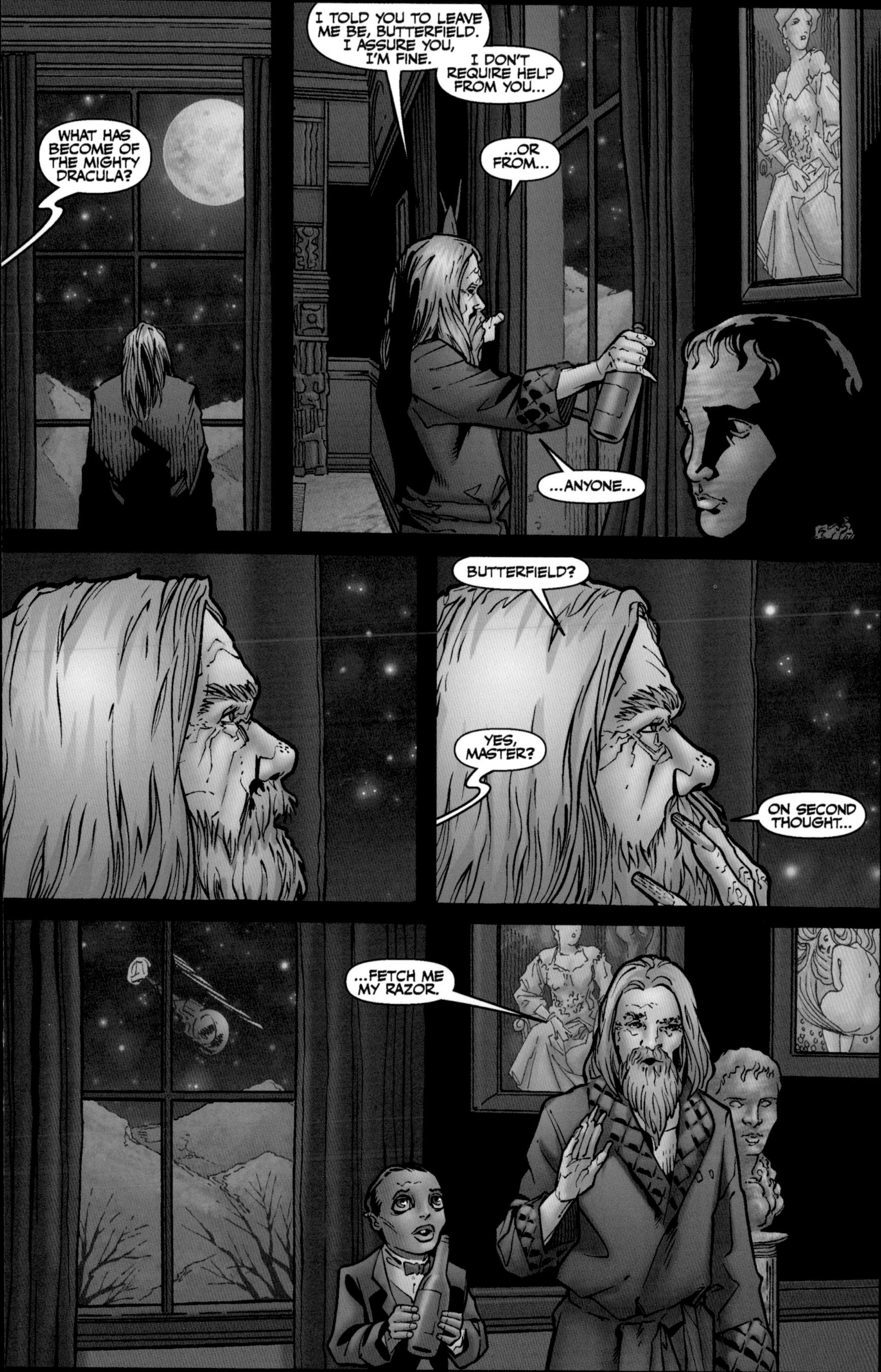
WHAT HAS BECOME OF THE MIGHTY DRACULA?
I TOLD YOU TO LEAVE ME BE, BUTTERFIELD. I ASSURE YOU, I'M FINE.
I DON'T REQUIRE HELP FROM YOU...
...OR FROM...
...ANYONE...
BUTTERFIELD?
YES, MASTER?
ON SECOND THOUGHT...
...FETCH ME MY RAZOR.

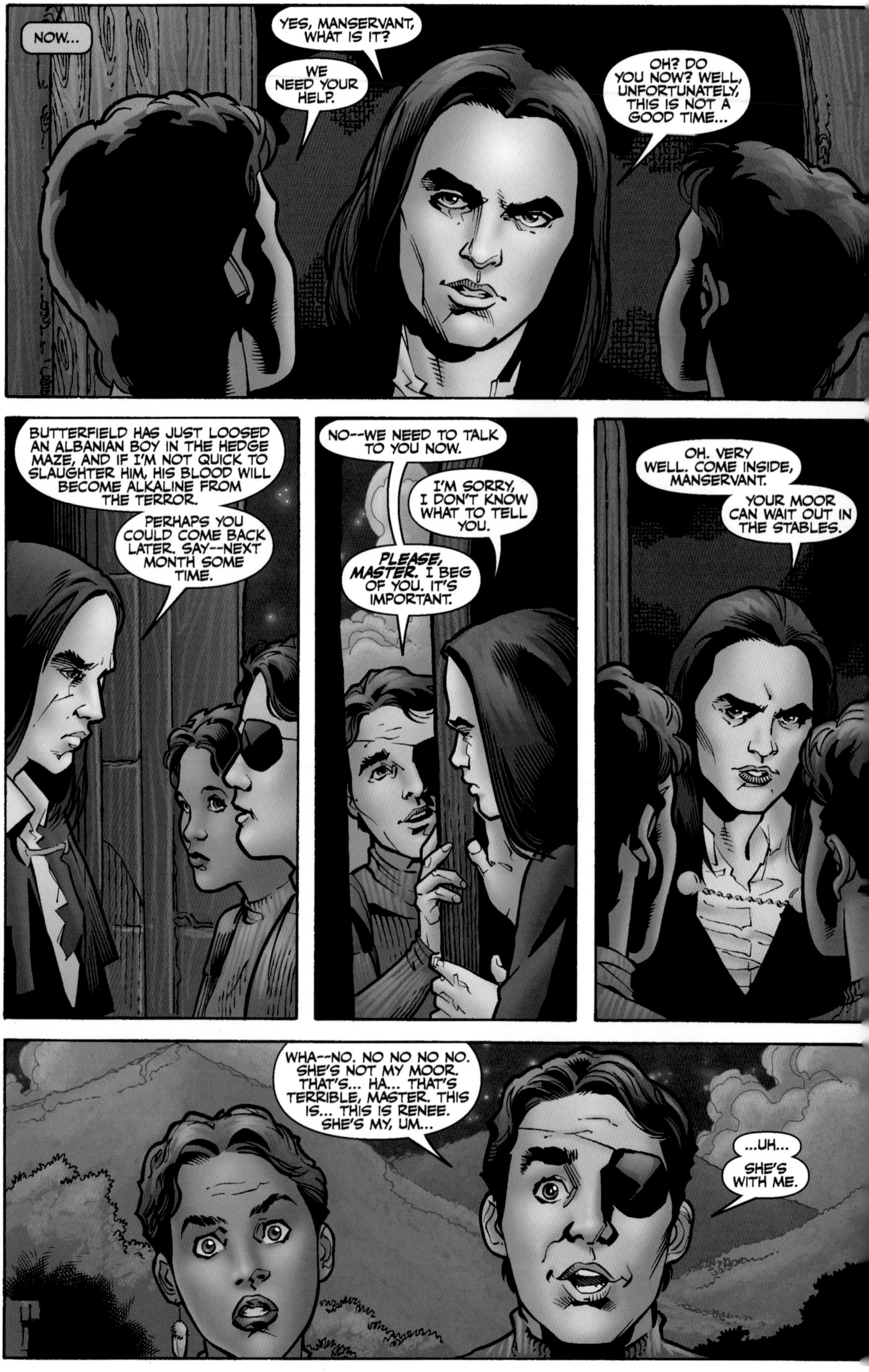
NOW...
YES, MANSERVANT, WHAT IS IT?
WE NEED YOUR HELP.
OH? DO YOU NOW? WELL, UNFORTUNATELY, THIS IS NOT A GOOD TIME...
BUTTERFIELD HAS JUST LOOSED AN ALBANIAN BOY IN THE HEDGE MAZE, AND IF I'M NOT QUICK TO SLAUGHTER HIM, HIS BLOOD WILL BECOME ALKALINE FROM THE TERROR.
PERHAPS YOU COULD COME BACK LATER. SAY--NEXT MONTH SOME TIME.
NO--WE NEED TO TALK TO YOU NOW.
I'M SORRY, I DON'T KNOW WHAT TO TELL YOU.
PLEASE, MASTER. I BEG OF YOU. IT'S IMPORTANT.
OH. VERY WELL. COME INSIDE, MANSERVANT.
YOUR MOOR CAN WAIT OUT IN THE STABLES.
WHA--NO. NO NO NO NO. SHE'S NOT MY MOOR. THAT'S... HA... THAT'S TERRIBLE, MASTER. THIS IS... THIS IS RENEE. SHE'S MY, UM...
...UH...
SHE'S WITH ME.

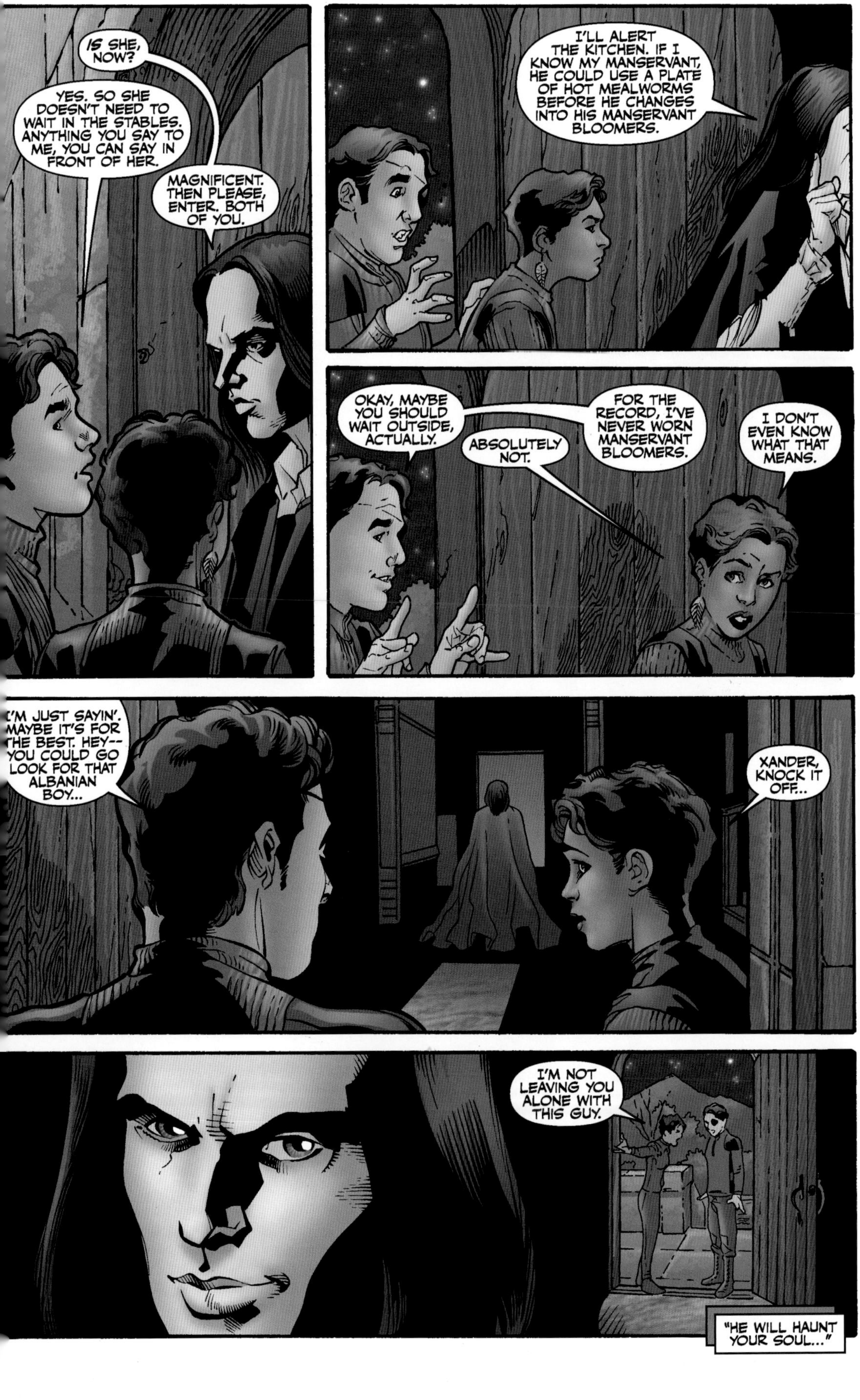
IS SHE, NOW?
YES. SO SHE DOESN'T NEED TO WAIT IN THE STABLES. ANYTHING YOU SAY TO ME, YOU CAN SAY IN FRONT OF HER.
MAGNIFICENT. THEN PLEASE, ENTER. BOTH OF YOU.
I'LL ALERT THE KITCHEN. IF I KNOW MY MANSERVANT, HE COULD USE A PLATE OF HOT MEALWORMS BEFORE HE CHANGES INTO HIS MANSERVANT BLOOMERS.
OKAY, MAYBE YOU SHOULD WAIT OUTSIDE, ACTUALLY.
ABSOLUTELY NOT.
FOR THE RECORD, I'VE NEVER WORN MANSERVANT BLOOMERS.
I DON'T EVEN KNOW WHAT THAT MEANS.
I'M JUST SAYIN'. MAYBE IT'S FOR THE BEST. HEY-- YOU COULD GO LOOK FOR THAT ALBANIAN BOY...
XANDER, KNOCK IT OFF...
I'M NOT LEAVING YOU ALONE WITH THIS GUY.
"HE WILL HAUNT YOUR SOUL..."

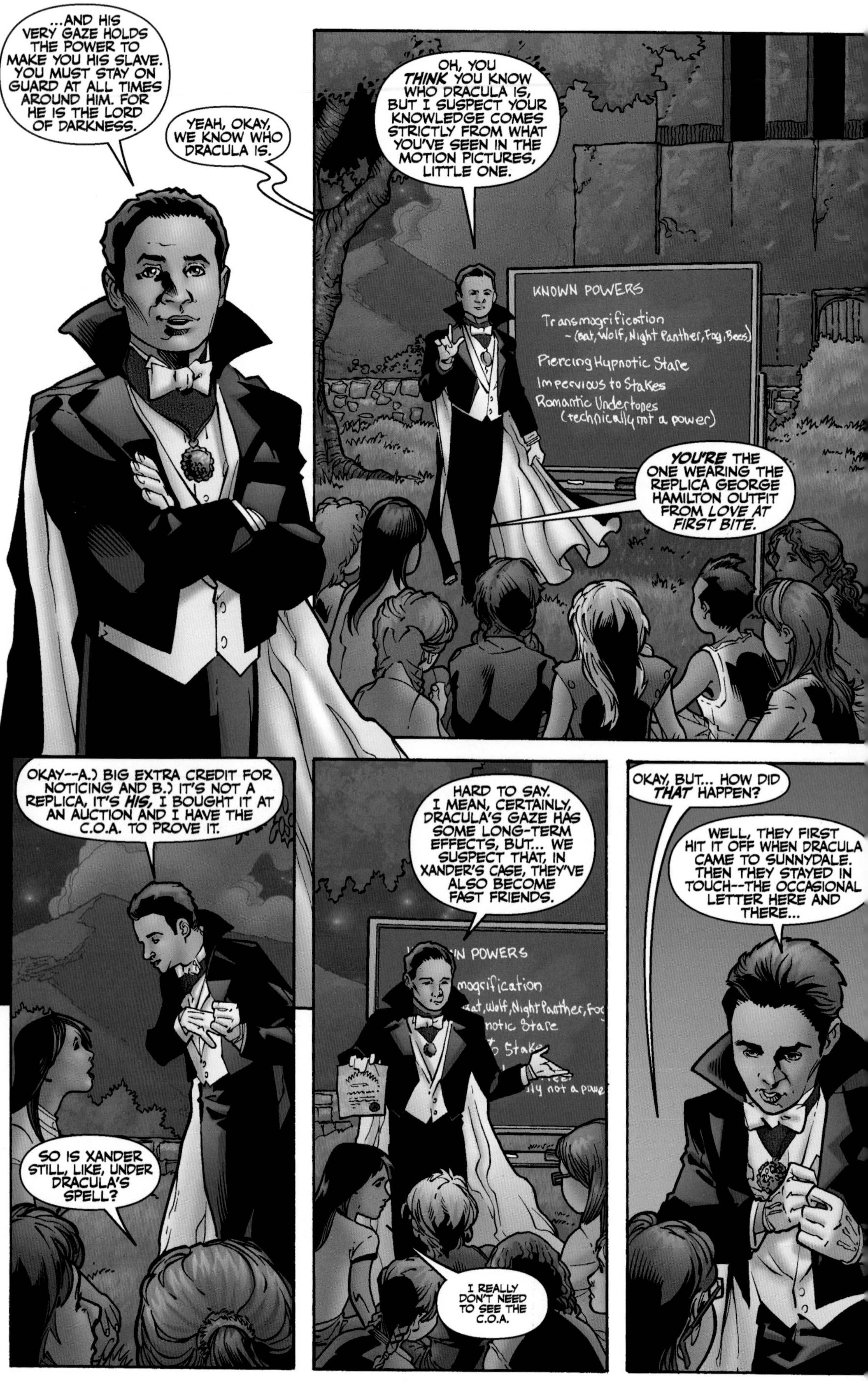
...AND HIS VERY GAZE HOLDS THE POWER TO MAKE YOU HIS SLAVE. YOU MUST STAY ON GUARD AT ALL TIMES AROUND HIM. FOR HE IS THE LORD OF DARKNESS.
YEAH, OKAY, WE KNOW WHO DRACULA IS.
OH, YOU THINK YOU KNOW WHO DRACULA IS, BUT I SUSPECT YOUR KNOWLEDGE COMES STRICTLY FROM WHAT YOU'VE SEEN IN THE MOTION PICTURES, LITTLE ONE.
KNOWN POWERS
Transmogrification
- (Bat, Wolf, Night Panther, Fog, Bees)
Piercing Hypnotic Stare
Impervious to Stakes
Romantic Undertones
(technically not a power)
YOU'RE THE ONE WEARING THE REPLICA GEORGE HAMILTON OUTFIT FROM LOVE AT FIRST BITE.
OKAY--A.) BIG EXTRA CREDIT FOR NOTICING AND B.) IT'S NOT A REPLICA, IT'S HIS, I BOUGHT IT AT AN AUCTION AND I HAVE THE C.O.A. TO PROVE IT.
SO IS XANDER STILL, LIKE, UNDER DRACULA'S SPELL?
HARD TO SAY. I MEAN, CERTAINLY, DRACULA'S GAZE HAS SOME LONG-TERM EFFECTS, BUT... WE SUSPECT THAT, IN XANDER'S CASE, THEY'VE ALSO BECOME FAST FRIENDS.
I REALLY DON'T NEED TO SEE THE C.O.A.
OKAY, BUT... HOW DID THAT HAPPEN?
WELL, THEY FIRST HIT IT OFF WHEN DRACULA CAME TO SUNNYDALE. THEN THEY STAYED IN TOUCH--THE OCCASIONAL LETTER HERE AND THERE...

AND THEN XANDER WENT AND LIVED WITH DRACULA FOR A FEW MONTHS.

WAIT-- *WHAT?*

YEAH--IT WAS SORT OF LIKE SEMESTER AT SEA, ONLY WITH HARPIES INSTEAD OF CO-EDS.

WHAT THE HELL ARE YOU TALKING ABOUT?

XANDER TOOK A LEAVE OF ABSENCE AND WENT TO TRANSYLVANIA. IT WAS RIGHT AFTER ANYA'S DEATH--HE NEEDED SOME GUY TIME.

AND--SO BUFFY JUST ALLOWED HIM TO GO *HANG OUT WITH DRACULA?*

IT WASN'T A BIG DEAL. DRACULA'S FOND OF XANDER. THEY HAVE A... UNIQUE RELATIONSHIP.

XANDER TAUGHT HIM TO RIDE A MOTORBIKE.

IN FACT, I SHOULD WRITE *"MOTORBIKING"* UP HERE UNDER POWERS...

KNOWN POWER

Transmogri
- (Bat, Panther, Bees)

Piercing

Imm
wer)

THIS IS SERIOUSLY HIS WORST LECTURE SINCE HIS ONE ON THAT WEAPON FROM *KRULL.*

HEY, I HEARD THAT! AND IT'S CALLED *THE GLAIVE,* THANK YOU VERY MUCH...

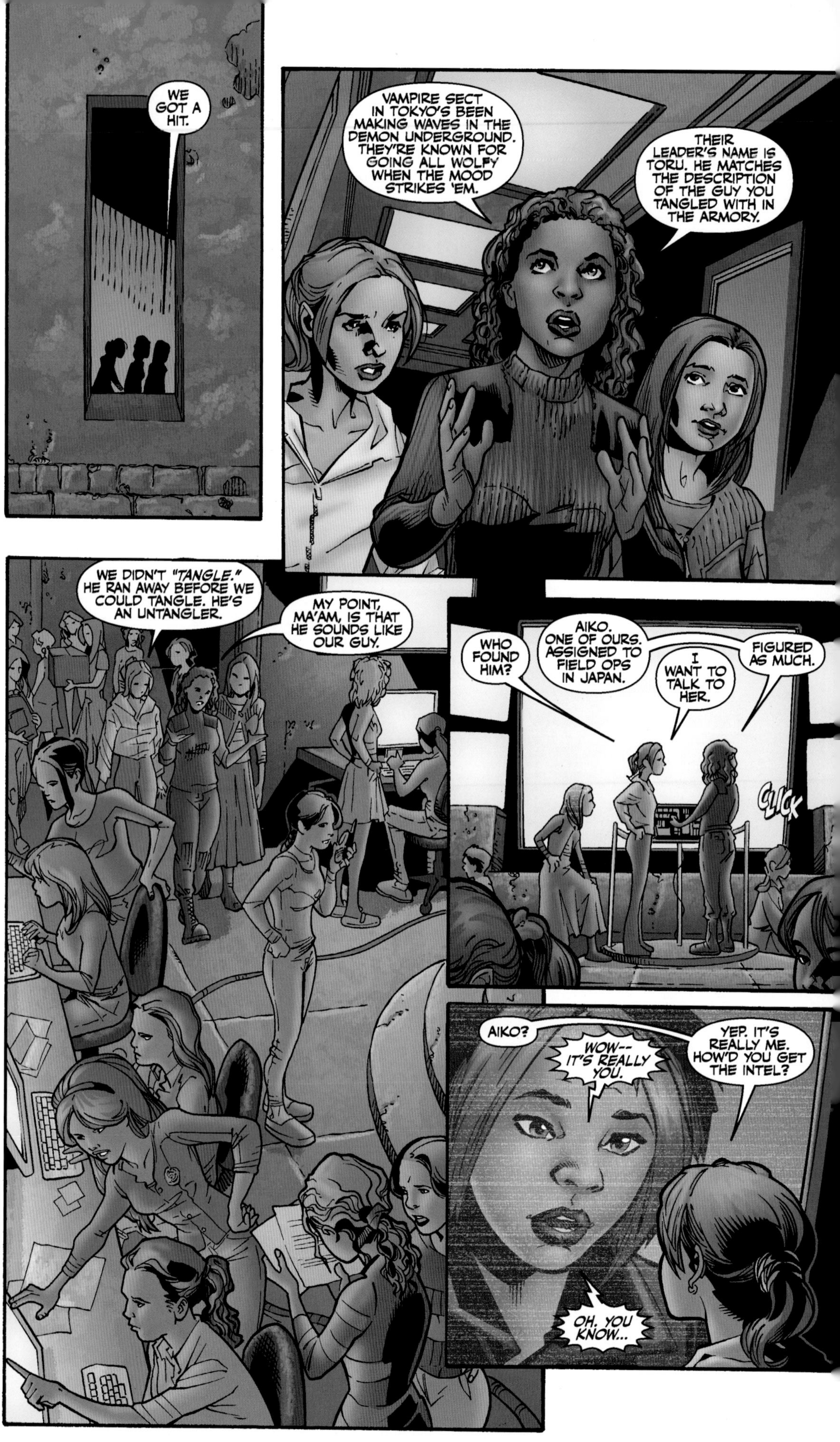
WE GOT A HIT.
VAMPIRE SECT IN TOKYO'S BEEN MAKING WAVES IN THE DEMON UNDERGROUND. THEY'RE KNOWN FOR GOING ALL WOLFY WHEN THE MOOD STRIKES 'EM.
THEIR LEADER'S NAME IS TORU. HE MATCHES THE DESCRIPTION OF THE GUY YOU TANGLED WITH IN THE ARMORY.
WE DIDN'T "TANGLE." HE RAN AWAY BEFORE WE COULD TANGLE. HE'S AN UNTANGLER.
MY POINT, MA'AM, IS THAT HE SOUNDS LIKE OUR GUY.
WHO FOUND HIM?
AIKO. ONE OF OURS. ASSIGNED TO FIELD OPS IN JAPAN.
FIGURED AS MUCH.
I WANT TO TALK TO HER.
CLICK
AIKO?
WOW-- IT'S REALLY YOU.
YEP. IT'S REALLY ME. HOW'D YOU GET THE INTEL?
OH. YOU KNOW...

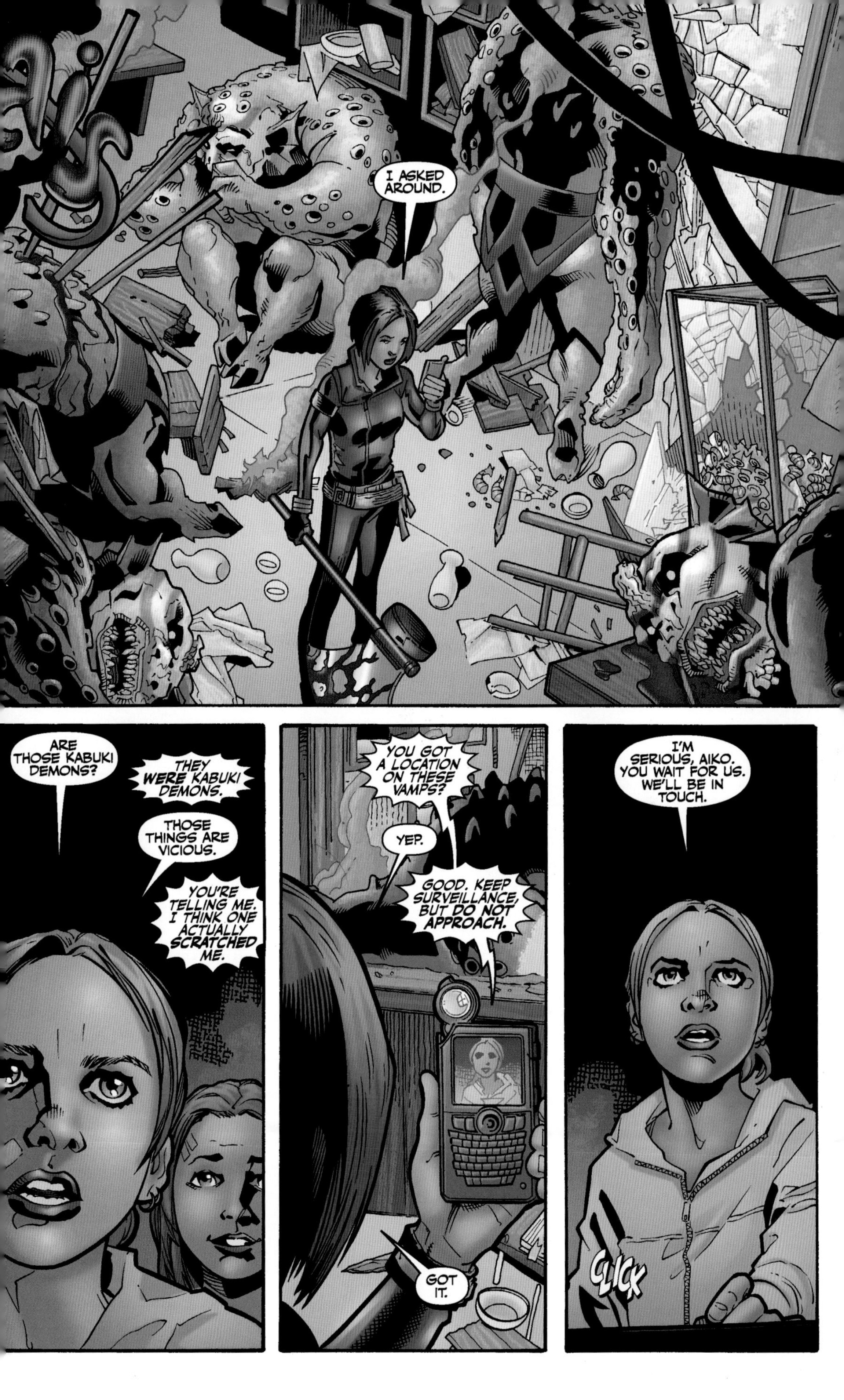
I ASKED AROUND.
ARE THOSE KABUKI DEMONS?
THEY WERE KABUKI DEMONS.
THOSE THINGS ARE VICIOUS.
YOU'RE TELLING ME. I THINK ONE ACTUALLY SCRATCHED ME.
YOU GOT A LOCATION ON THESE VAMPS?
YEP.
GOOD. KEEP SURVEILLANCE, BUT DO NOT APPROACH.
GOT IT.
I'M SERIOUS, AIKO. YOU WAIT FOR US. WE'LL BE IN TOUCH.
CLICK

SATSU?

YES?

PREP THE OTHERS. I WANT OUR TEAM SUITED UP AND READY FOR TRANSPO IN LESS THAN AN HOUR.

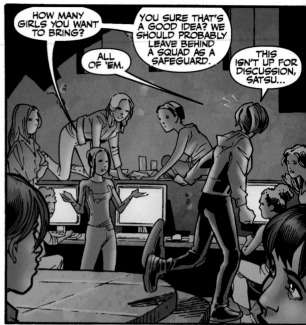

HOW MANY GIRLS YOU WANT TO BRING?

YOU SURE THAT'S A GOOD IDEA? WE SHOULD PROBABLY LEAVE BEHIND A SQUAD AS A SAFEGUARD.

ALL OF 'EM.

THIS ISN'T UP FOR DISCUSSION, SATSU...

I GAVE YOU AN ORDER. GET MOVING.

YES MA'AM.

HAVE WE HEARD FROM XANDER?

I'VE BEEN TRYING HIM. HE'S NOT RESPONDING.

YOU THINK HE'S IN TROUBLE?

WELL...

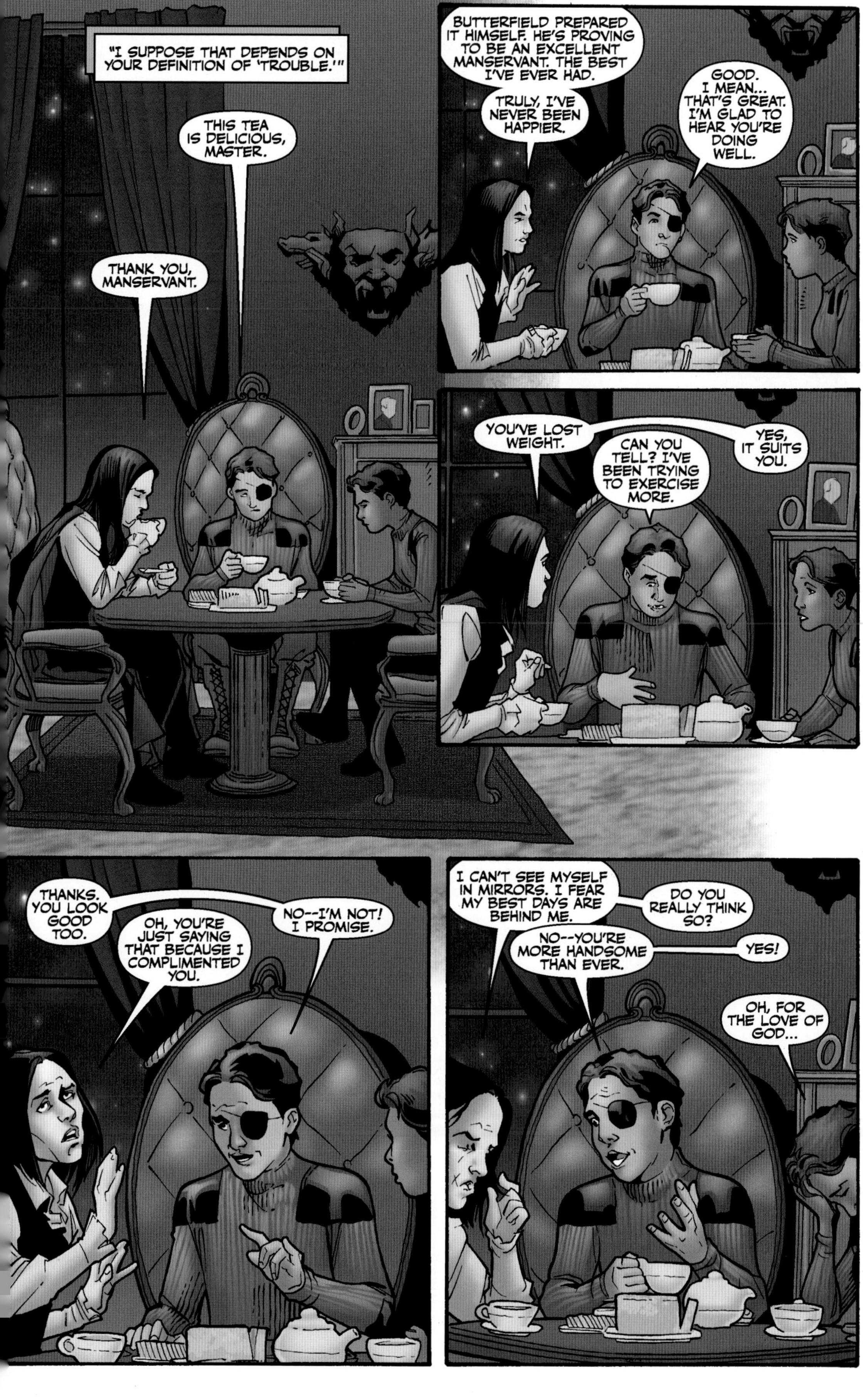
"I SUPPOSE THAT DEPENDS ON YOUR DEFINITION OF 'TROUBLE.'"
THIS TEA IS DELICIOUS, MASTER.
THANK YOU, MANSERVANT.
BUTTERFIELD PREPARED IT HIMSELF. HE'S PROVING TO BE AN EXCELLENT MANSERVANT. THE BEST I'VE EVER HAD.
TRULY, I'VE NEVER BEEN HAPPIER.
GOOD. I MEAN... THAT'S GREAT. I'M GLAD TO HEAR YOU'RE DOING WELL.
YOU'VE LOST WEIGHT.
CAN YOU TELL? I'VE BEEN TRYING TO EXERCISE MORE.
YES, IT SUITS YOU.
THANKS. YOU LOOK GOOD TOO.
OH, YOU'RE JUST SAYING THAT BECAUSE I COMPLIMENTED YOU.
NO--I'M NOT! I PROMISE.
I CAN'T SEE MYSELF IN MIRRORS. I FEAR MY BEST DAYS ARE BEHIND ME.
DO YOU REALLY THINK SO?
NO--YOU'RE MORE HANDSOME THAN EVER.
YES!
OH, FOR THE LOVE OF GOD...

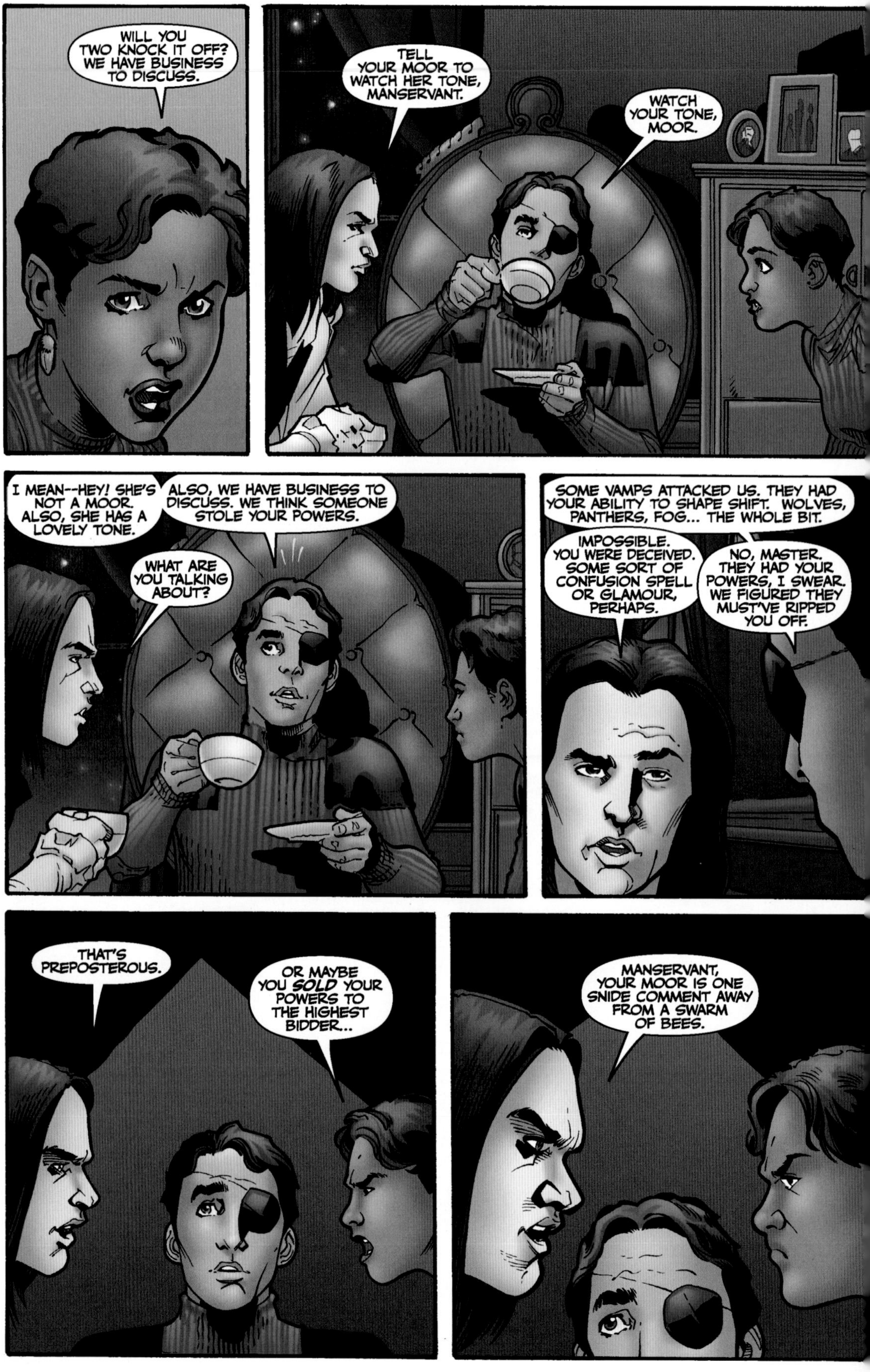
WILL YOU TWO KNOCK IT OFF? WE HAVE BUSINESS TO DISCUSS.
TELL YOUR MOOR TO WATCH HER TONE, MANSERVANT.
WATCH YOUR TONE, MOOR.
I MEAN--HEY! SHE'S NOT A MOOR. ALSO, SHE HAS A LOVELY TONE.
ALSO, WE HAVE BUSINESS TO DISCUSS. WE THINK SOMEONE STOLE YOUR POWERS.
WHAT ARE YOU TALKING ABOUT?
SOME VAMPS ATTACKED US. THEY HAD YOUR ABILITY TO SHAPE SHIFT. WOLVES, PANTHERS, FOG... THE WHOLE BIT.
IMPOSSIBLE. YOU WERE DECEIVED. SOME SORT OF CONFUSION SPELL OR GLAMOUR, PERHAPS.
NO, MASTER. THEY HAD YOUR POWERS, I SWEAR. WE FIGURED THEY MUST'VE RIPPED YOU OFF.
THAT'S PREPOSTEROUS.
OR MAYBE YOU *SOLD* YOUR POWERS TO THE HIGHEST BIDDER...
MANSERVANT, YOUR MOOR IS ONE SNIDE COMMENT AWAY FROM A SWARM OF BEES.

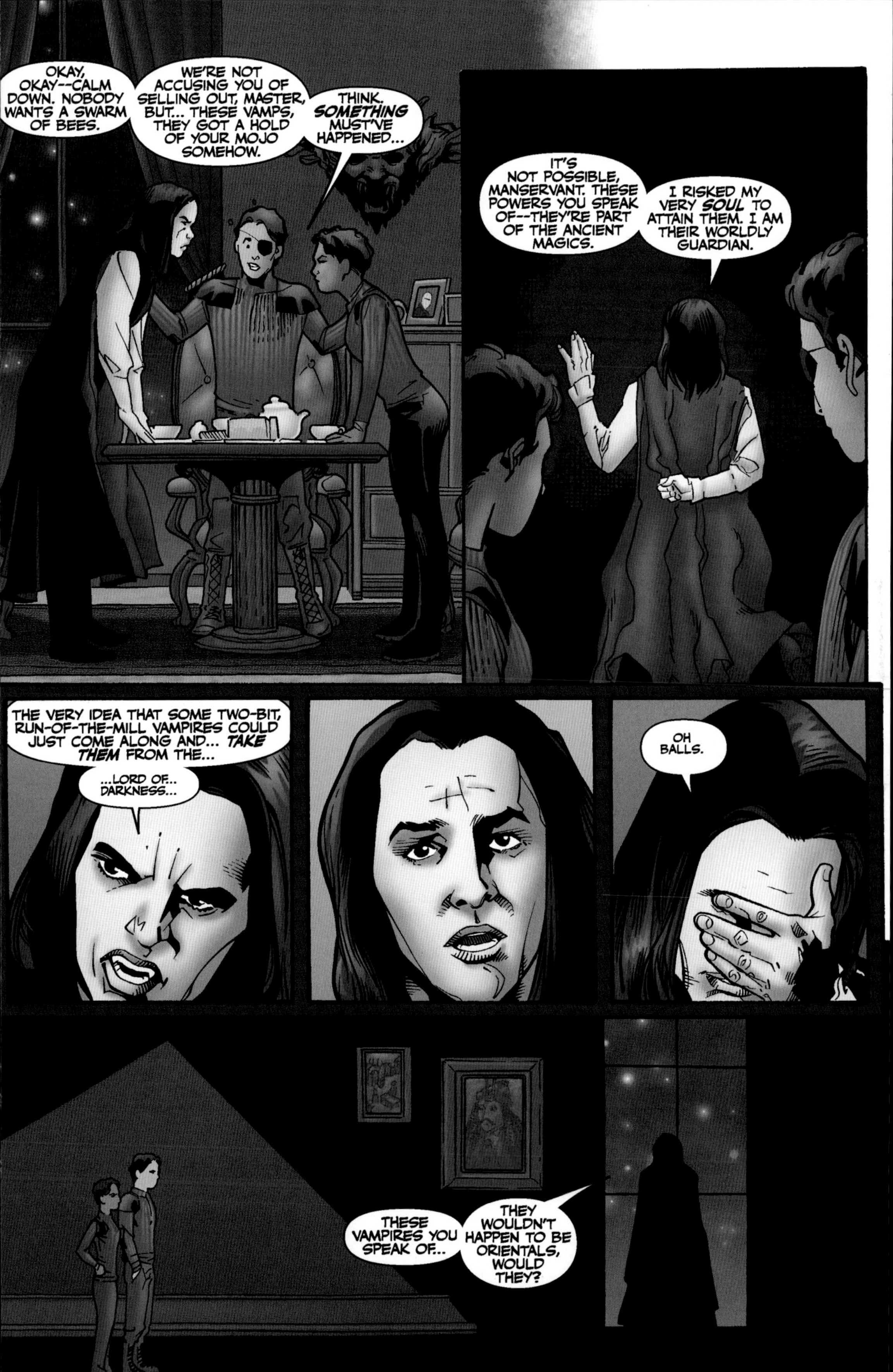
OKAY, OKAY--CALM DOWN. NOBODY WANTS A SWARM OF BEES.
WE'RE NOT ACCUSING YOU OF SELLING OUT, MASTER, BUT... THESE VAMPS, THEY GOT A HOLD OF YOUR MOJO SOMEHOW.
THINK. SOMETHING MUST'VE HAPPENED...
IT'S NOT POSSIBLE, MANSERVANT. THESE POWERS YOU SPEAK OF--THEY'RE PART OF THE ANCIENT MAGICS.
I RISKED MY VERY SOUL TO ATTAIN THEM. I AM THEIR WORLDLY GUARDIAN.
THE VERY IDEA THAT SOME TWO-BIT, RUN-OF-THE-MILL VAMPIRES COULD JUST COME ALONG AND... TAKE THEM FROM THE...
...LORD OF... DARKNESS...
OH BALLS.
THESE VAMPIRES YOU SPEAK OF...
THEY WOULDN'T HAPPEN TO BE ORIENTALS, WOULD THEY?

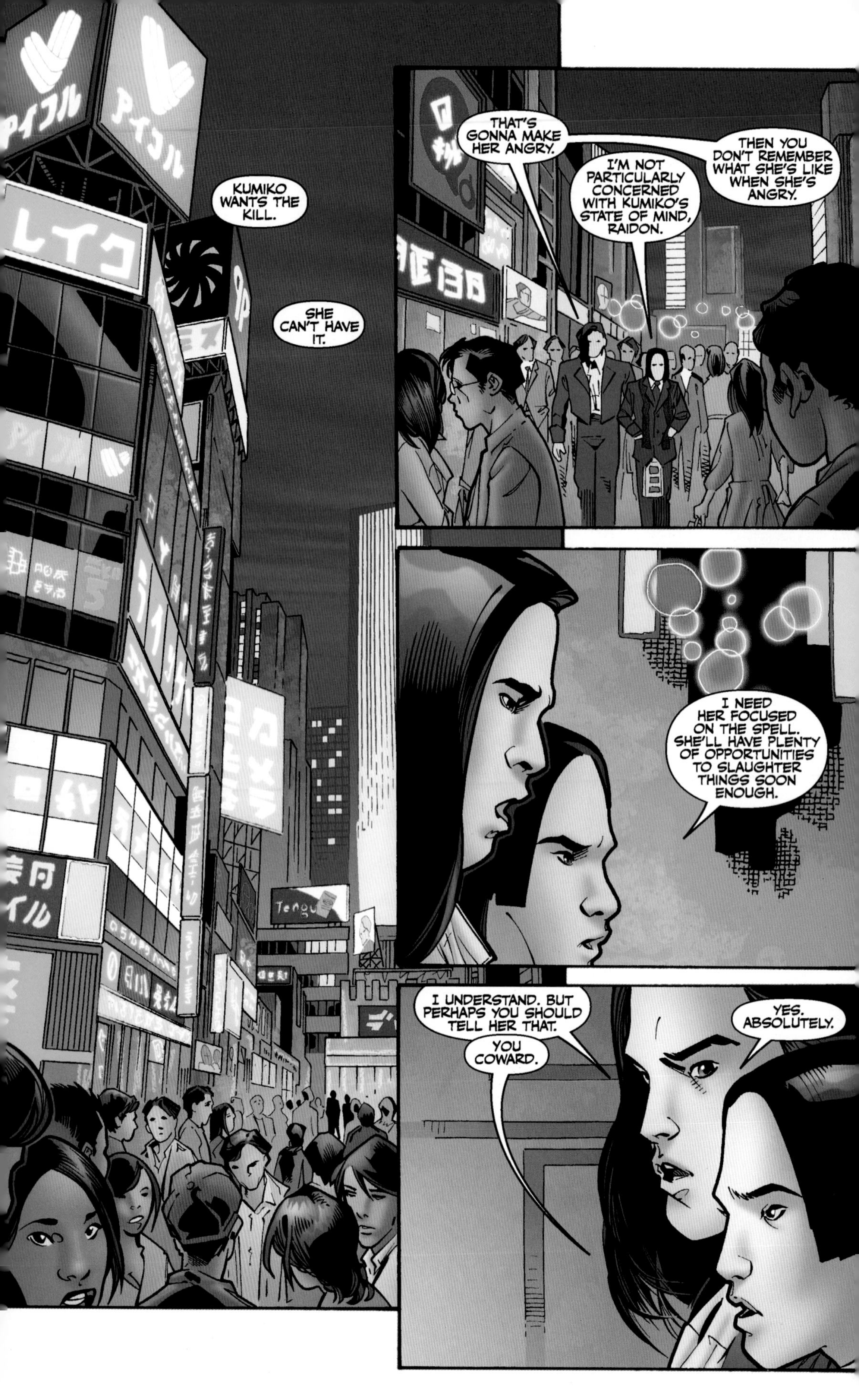
KUMIKO WANTS THE KILL.
SHE CAN'T HAVE IT.
THAT'S GONNA MAKE HER ANGRY.
I'M NOT PARTICULARLY CONCERNED WITH KUMIKO'S STATE OF MIND, RAIDON.
THEN YOU DON'T REMEMBER WHAT SHE'S LIKE WHEN SHE'S ANGRY.
I NEED HER FOCUSED ON THE SPELL. SHE'LL HAVE PLENTY OF OPPORTUNITIES TO SLAUGHTER THINGS SOON ENOUGH.
I UNDERSTAND. BUT PERHAPS YOU SHOULD TELL HER THAT.
YOU COWARD.
YES. ABSOLUTELY.

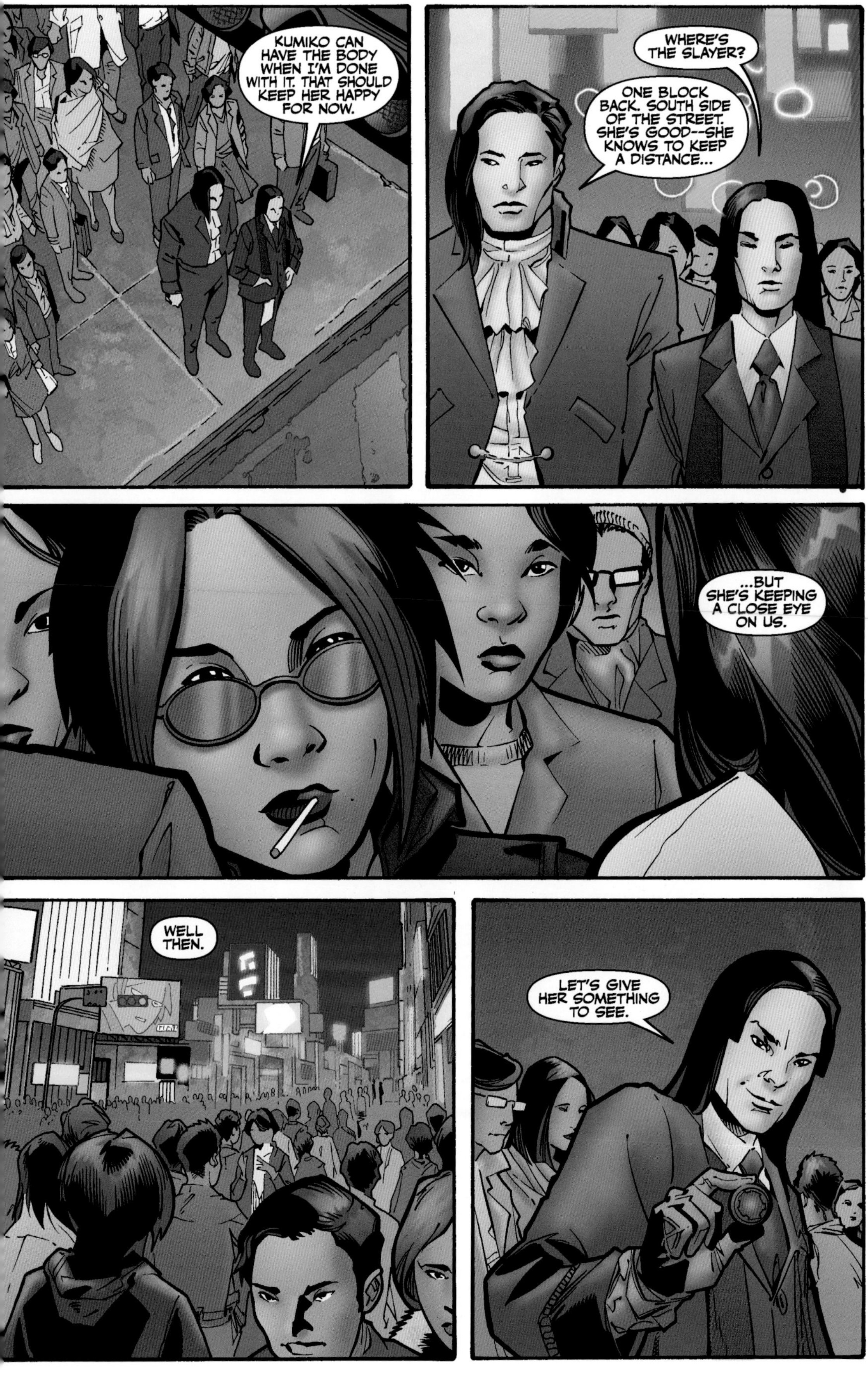

KUMIKO CAN HAVE THE BODY WHEN I'M DONE WITH IT. THAT SHOULD KEEP HER HAPPY FOR NOW.
WHERE'S THE SLAYER?
ONE BLOCK BACK. SOUTH SIDE OF THE STREET. SHE'S GOOD--SHE KNOWS TO KEEP A DISTANCE...
...BUT SHE'S KEEPING A CLOSE EYE ON US.
WELL THEN.
LET'S GIVE HER SOMETHING TO SEE.

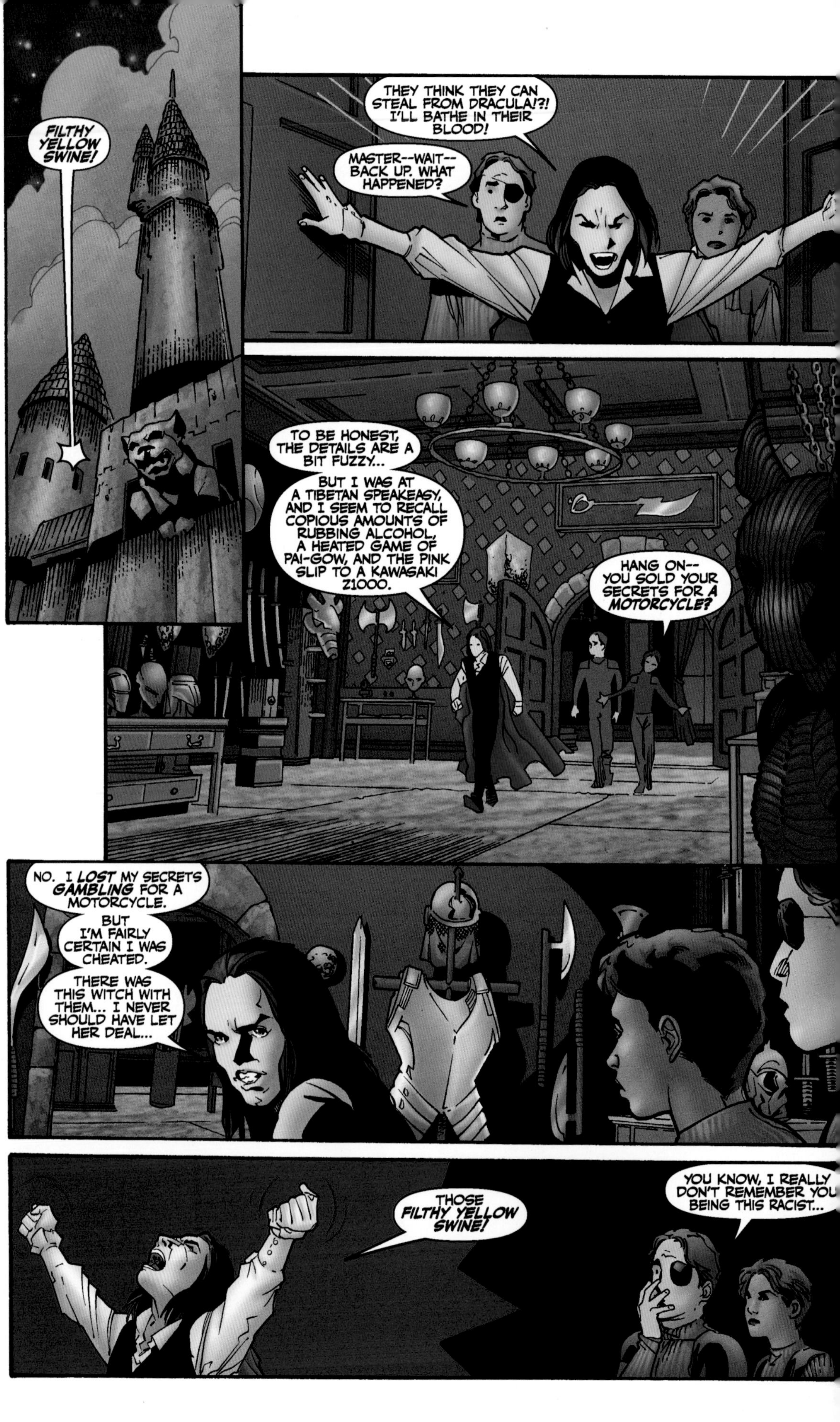
FILTHY YELLOW SWINE!
THEY THINK THEY CAN STEAL FROM DRACULA!?! I'LL BATHE IN THEIR BLOOD!
MASTER--WAIT-- BACK UP. WHAT HAPPENED?
TO BE HONEST, THE DETAILS ARE A BIT FUZZY...
BUT I WAS AT A TIBETAN SPEAKEASY, AND I SEEM TO RECALL COPIOUS AMOUNTS OF RUBBING ALCOHOL, A HEATED GAME OF PAI-GOW, AND THE PINK SLIP TO A KAWASAKI Z1000.
HANG ON-- YOU SOLD YOUR SECRETS FOR A MOTORCYCLE?
NO. I LOST MY SECRETS GAMBLING FOR A MOTORCYCLE.
BUT I'M FAIRLY CERTAIN I WAS CHEATED.
THERE WAS THIS WITCH WITH THEM... I NEVER SHOULD HAVE LET HER DEAL...
THOSE FILTHY YELLOW SWINE!
YOU KNOW, I REALLY DON'T REMEMBER YOU BEING THIS RACIST...

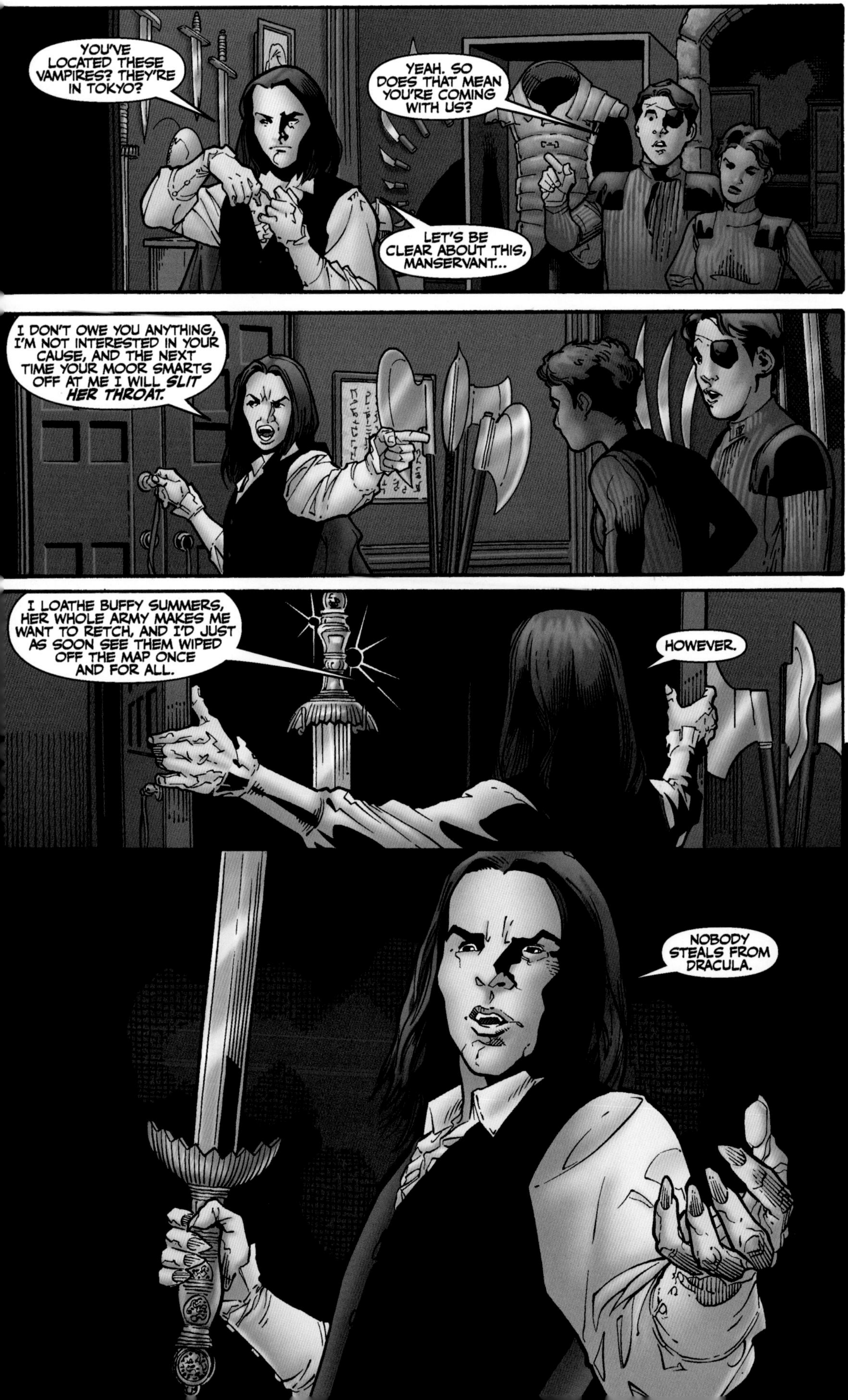
YOU'VE LOCATED THESE VAMPIRES? THEY'RE IN TOKYO?
YEAH. SO DOES THAT MEAN YOU'RE COMING WITH US?
LET'S BE CLEAR ABOUT THIS, MANSERVANT...
I DON'T OWE YOU ANYTHING, I'M NOT INTERESTED IN YOUR CAUSE, AND THE NEXT TIME YOUR MOOR SMARTS OFF AT ME I WILL SLIT HER THROAT.
I LOATHE BUFFY SUMMERS, HER WHOLE ARMY MAKES ME WANT TO RETCH, AND I'D JUST AS SOON SEE THEM WIPED OFF THE MAP ONCE AND FOR ALL.
HOWEVER.
NOBODY STEALS FROM DRACULA.

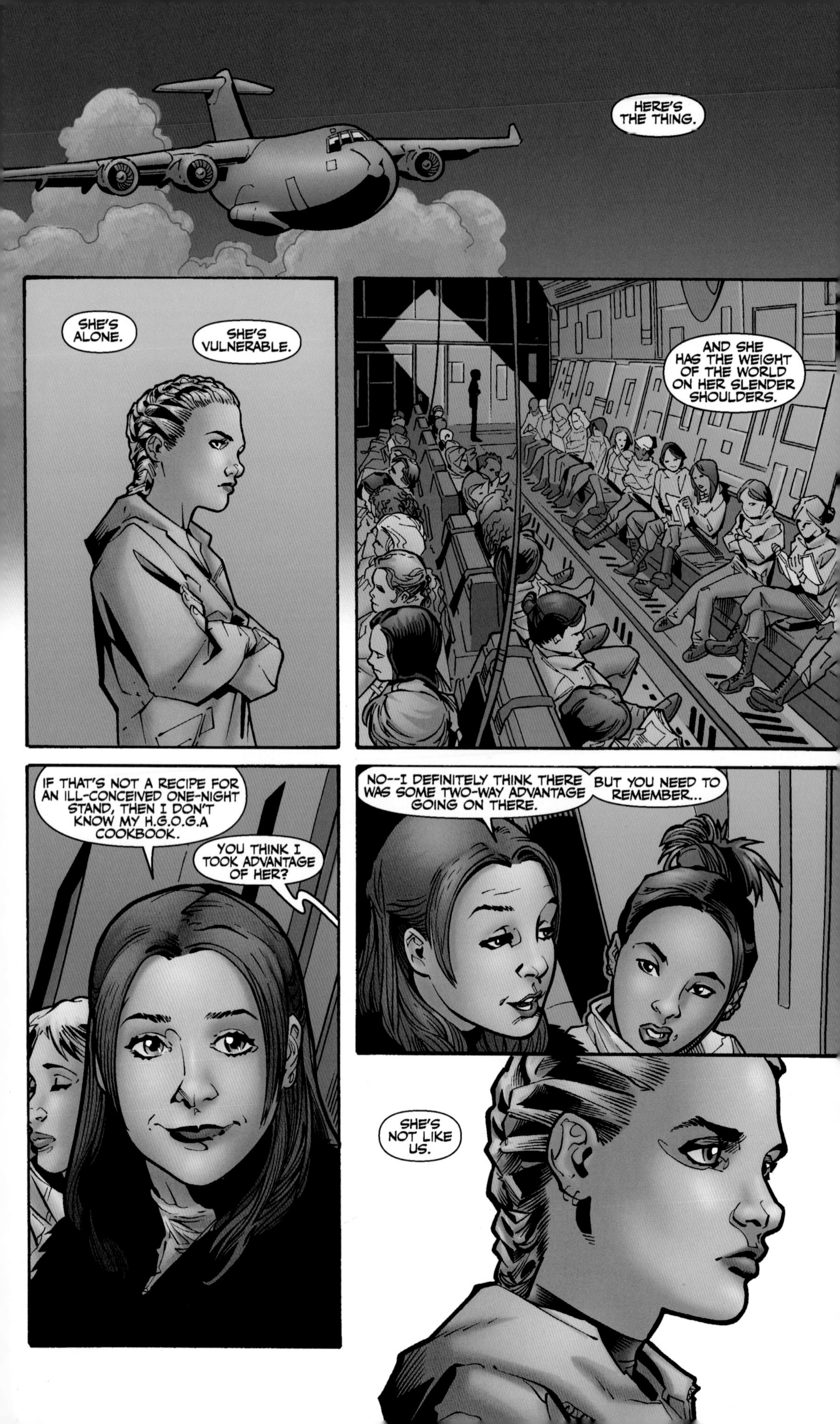
HERE'S THE THING.
SHE'S ALONE.
SHE'S VULNERABLE.
AND SHE HAS THE WEIGHT OF THE WORLD ON HER SLENDER SHOULDERS.
IF THAT'S NOT A RECIPE FOR AN ILL-CONCEIVED ONE-NIGHT STAND, THEN I DON'T KNOW MY H.G.O.G.A COOKBOOK.
YOU THINK I TOOK ADVANTAGE OF HER?
NO--I DEFINITELY THINK THERE WAS SOME TWO-WAY ADVANTAGE GOING ON THERE.
BUT YOU NEED TO REMEMBER...
SHE'S NOT LIKE US.

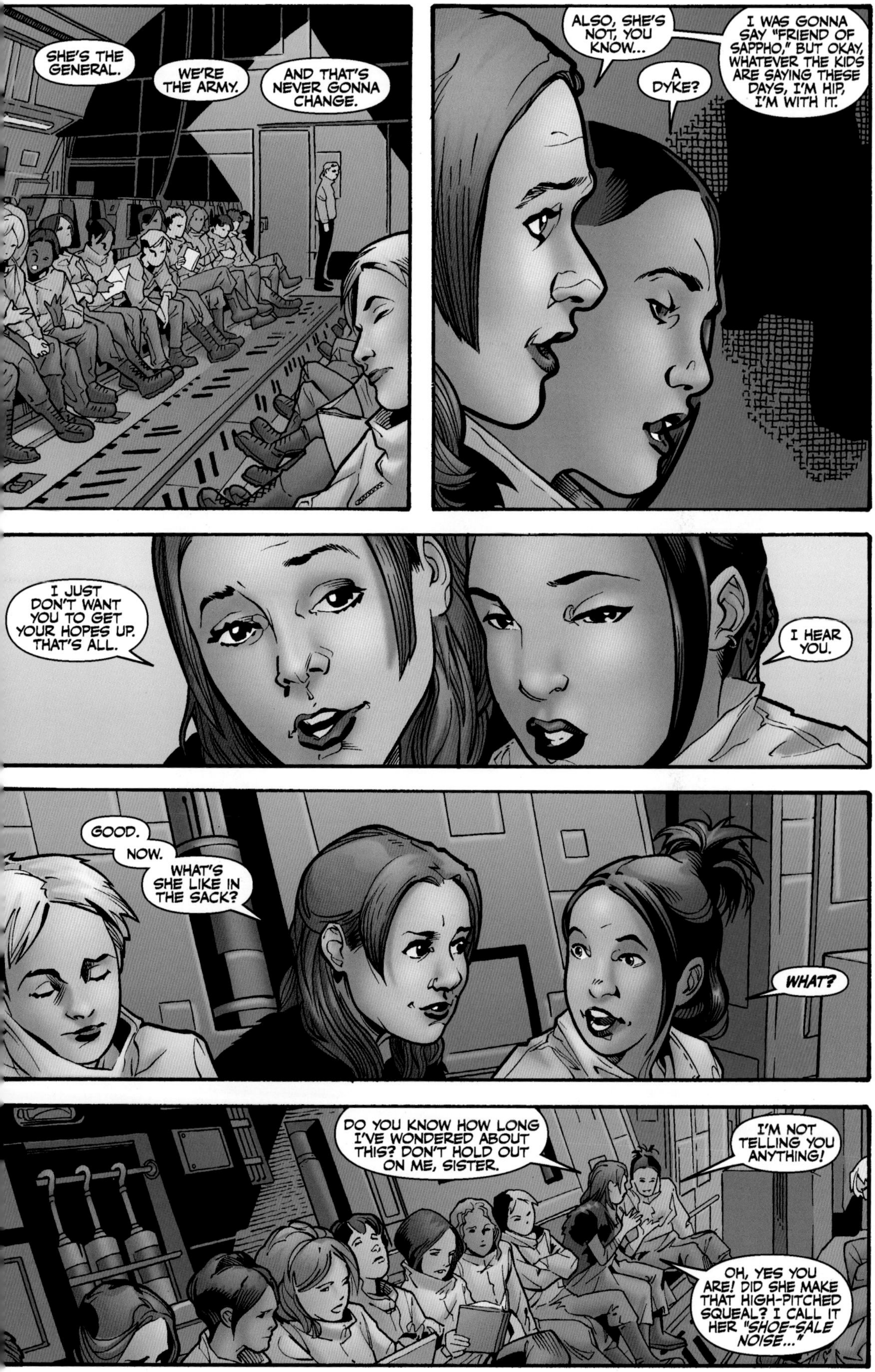
SHE'S THE GENERAL.
WE'RE THE ARMY.
AND THAT'S NEVER GONNA CHANGE.
ALSO, SHE'S NOT, YOU KNOW...
A DYKE?
I WAS GONNA SAY "FRIEND OF SAPPHO," BUT OKAY, WHATEVER THE KIDS ARE SAYING THESE DAYS, I'M HIP, I'M WITH IT.
I JUST DON'T WANT YOU TO GET YOUR HOPES UP. THAT'S ALL.
I HEAR YOU.
GOOD.
NOW.
WHAT'S SHE LIKE IN THE SACK?
WHAT?
DO YOU KNOW HOW LONG I'VE WONDERED ABOUT THIS? DON'T HOLD OUT ON ME, SISTER.
I'M NOT TELLING YOU ANYTHING!
OH, YES YOU ARE! DID SHE MAKE THAT HIGH-PITCHED SQUEAL? I CALL IT HER "SHOE-SALE NOISE..."

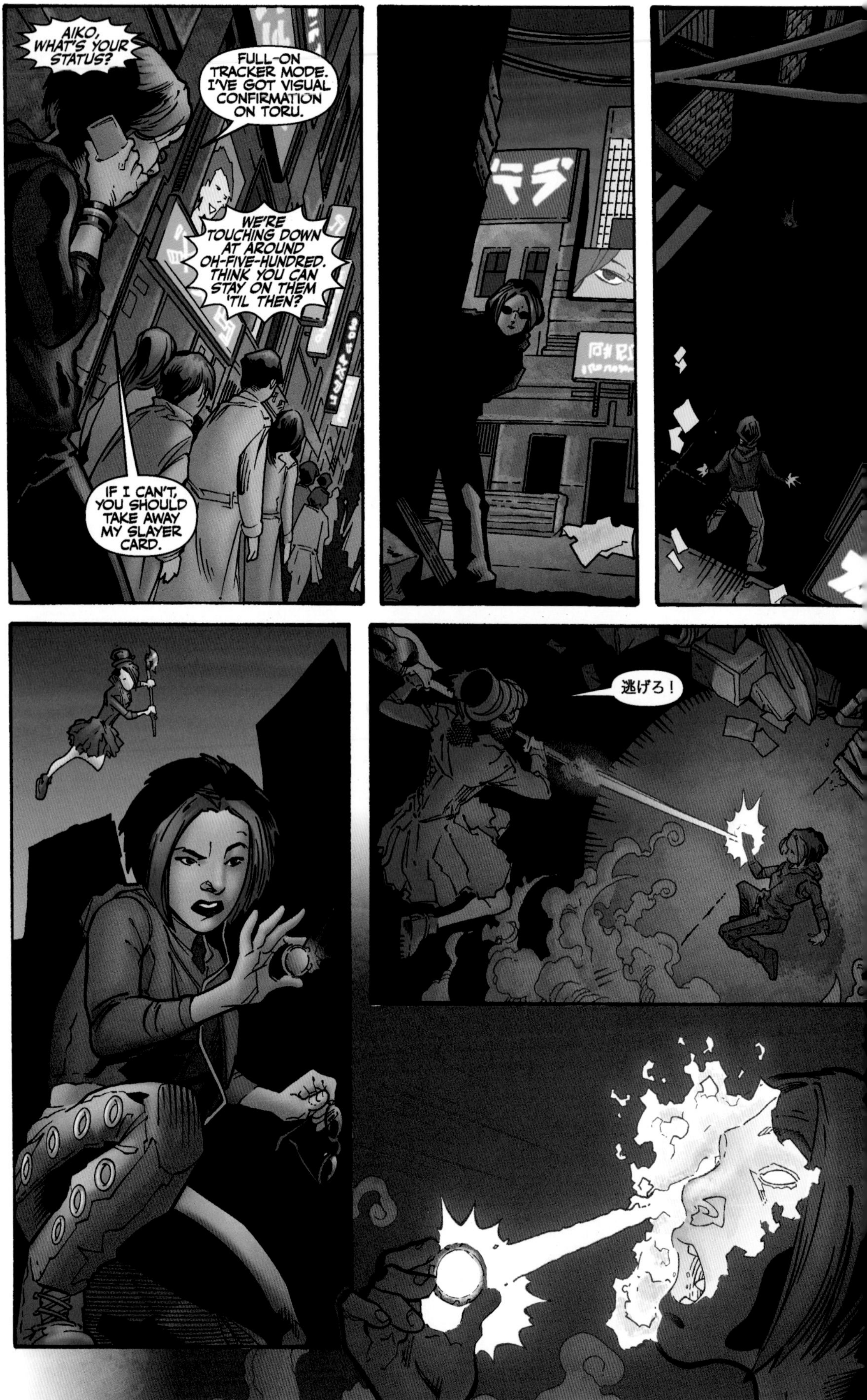
AIKO, WHAT'S YOUR STATUS?
FULL-ON TRACKER MODE. I'VE GOT VISUAL CONFIRMATION ON TORU.
WE'RE TOUCHING DOWN AT AROUND OH-FIVE-HUNDRED. THINK YOU CAN STAY ON THEM 'TIL THEN?
IF I CAN'T, YOU SHOULD TAKE AWAY MY SLAYER CARD.
逃げろ！

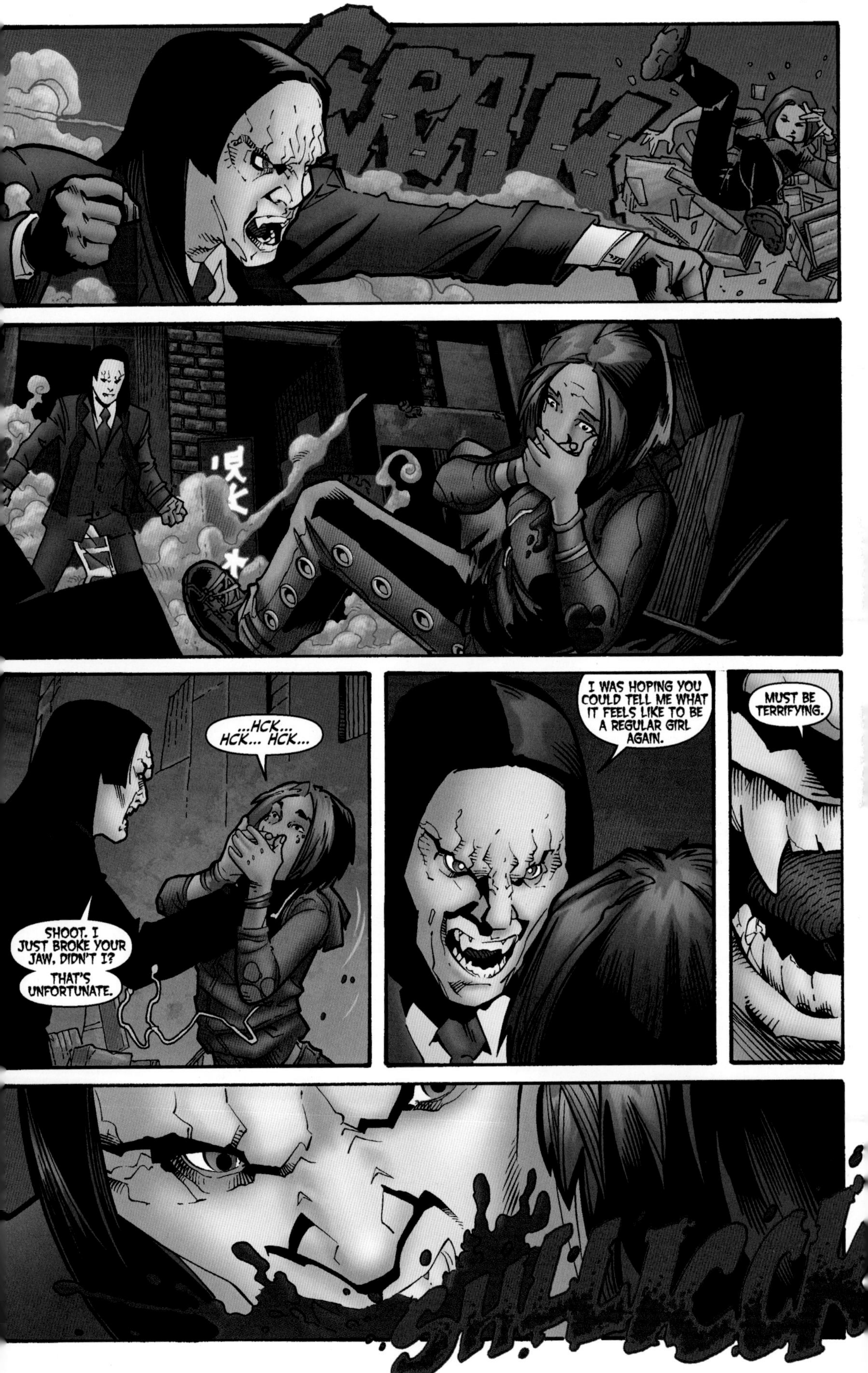
CRAK
...HCK... HCK... HCK...
SHOOT. I JUST BROKE YOUR JAW, DIDN'T I?
THAT'S UNFORTUNATE.
I WAS HOPING YOU COULD TELL ME WHAT IT FEELS LIKE TO BE A REGULAR GIRL AGAIN.
MUST BE TERRIFYING.
SHLLLUCCK

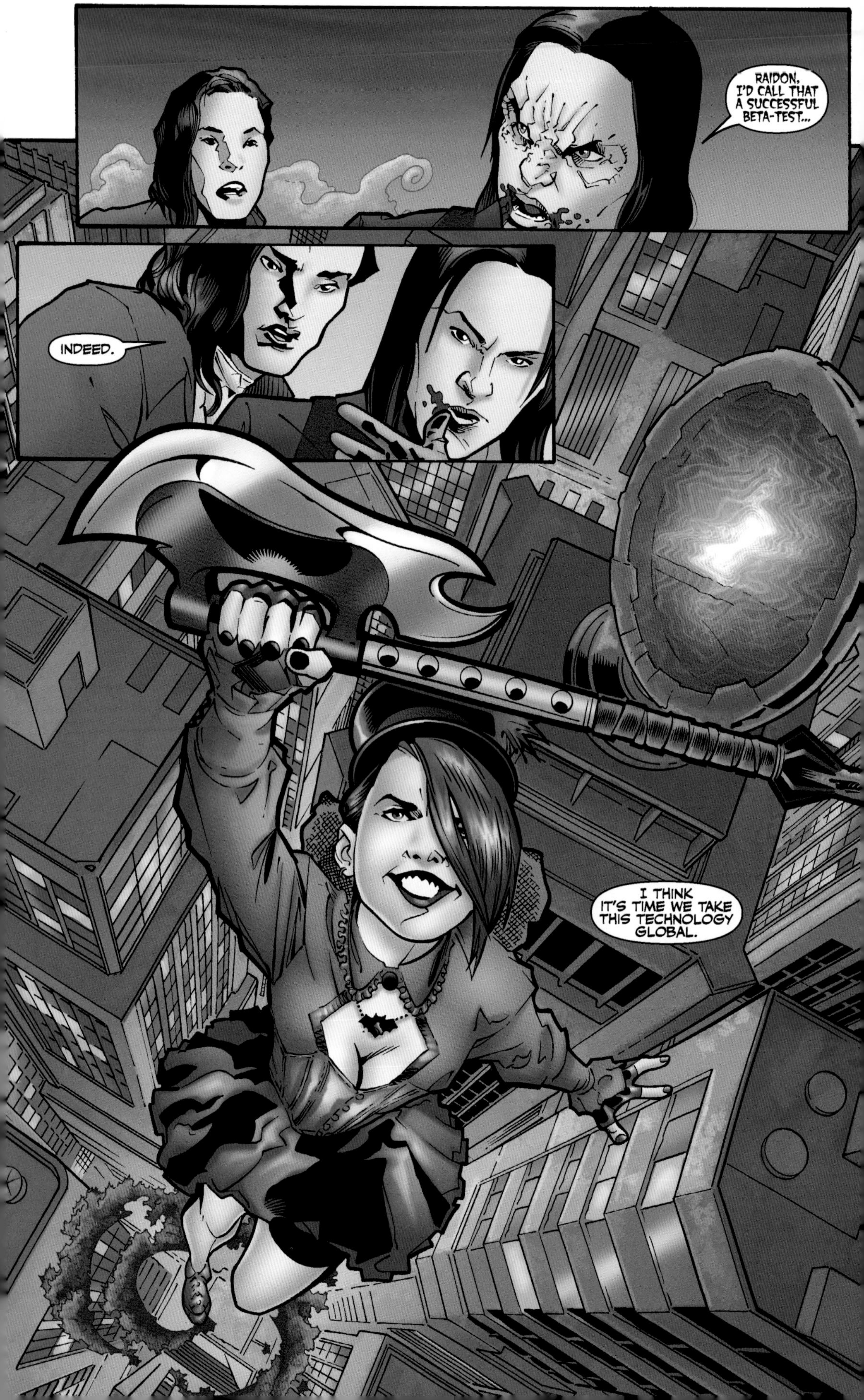
RAIDON, I'D CALL THAT A SUCCESSFUL BETA-TEST...
INDEED.
I THINK IT'S TIME WE TAKE THIS TECHNOLOGY GLOBAL.

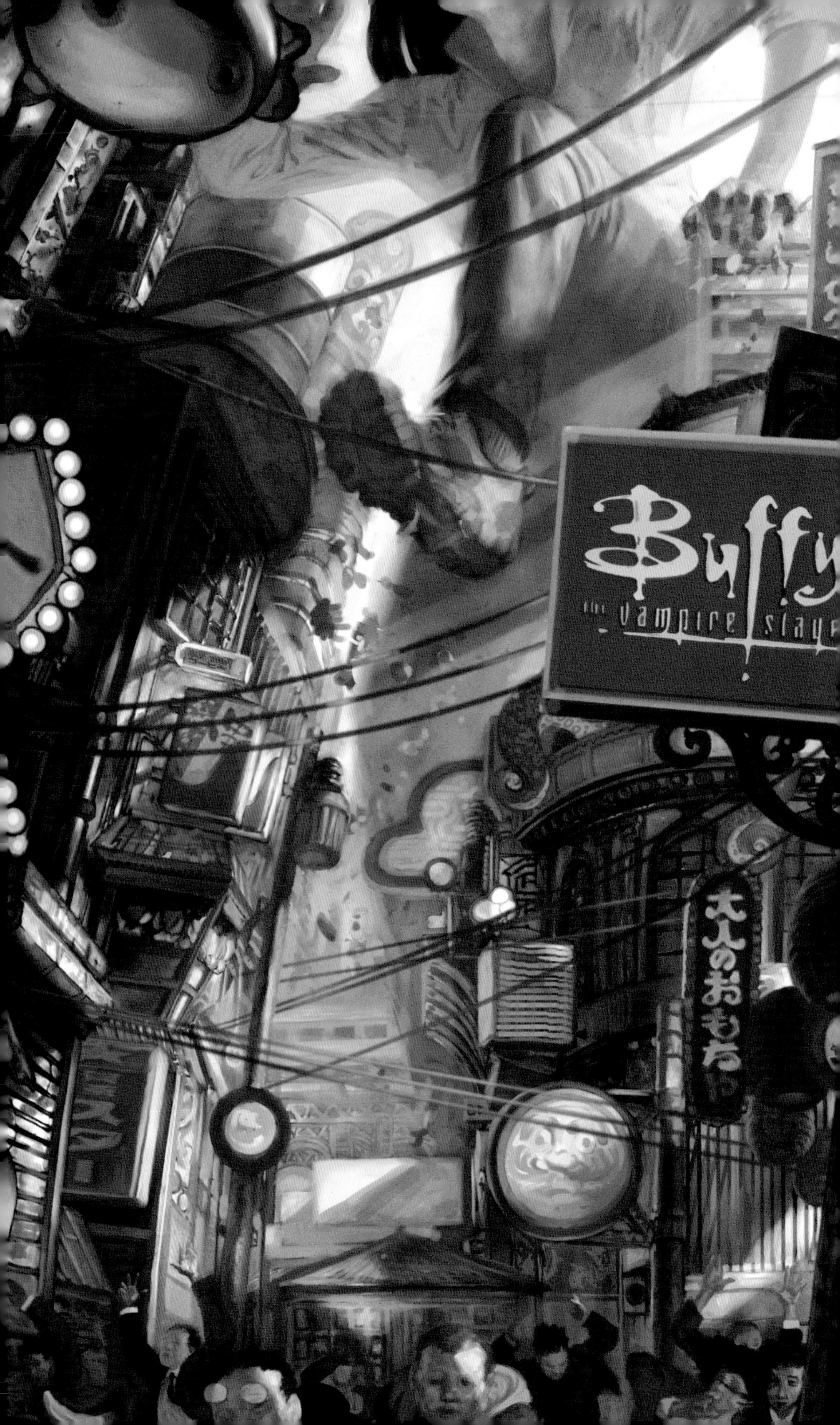
Buffy
vampire slaye

WOLVES AT THE GATE
PART THREE

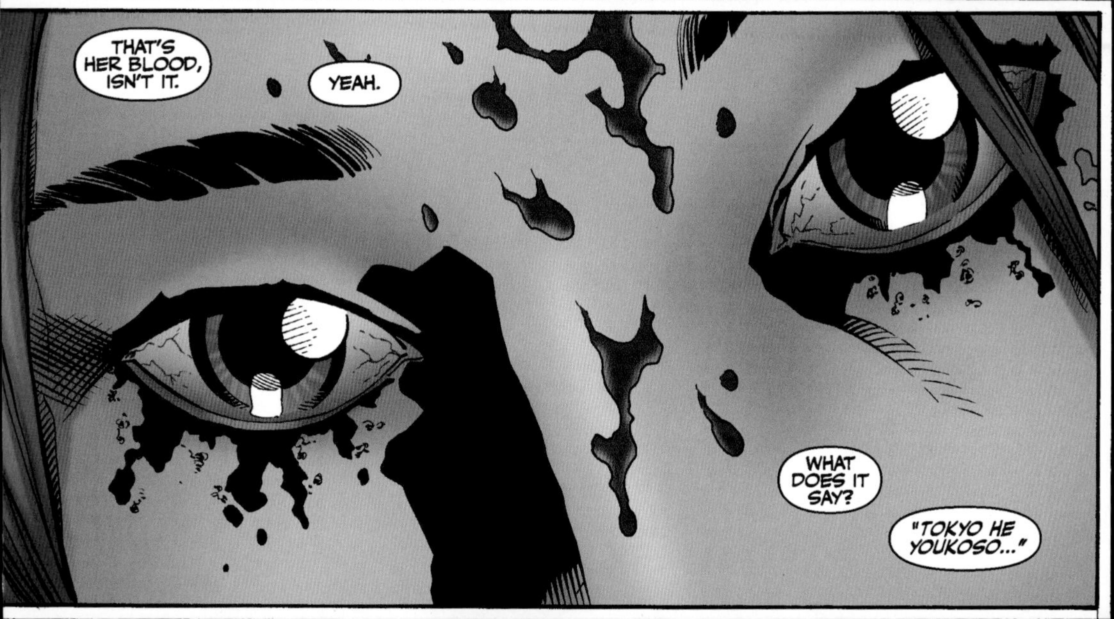

THAT'S HER BLOOD, ISN'T IT.
YEAH.
WHAT DOES IT SAY?
"TOKYO HE YOUKOSO..."

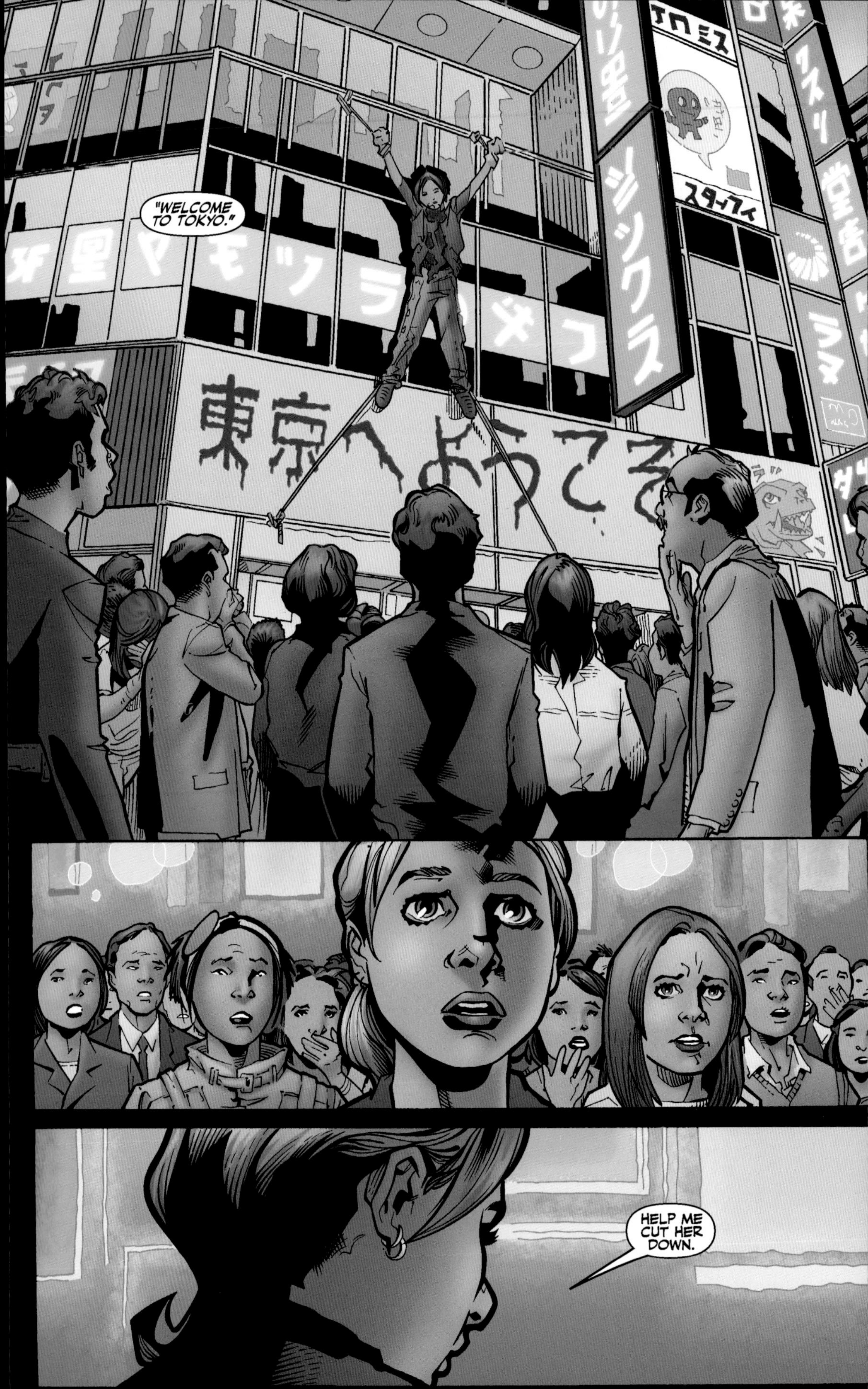
"WELCOME TO TOKYO."
東京へようこそ
HELP ME CUT HER DOWN.

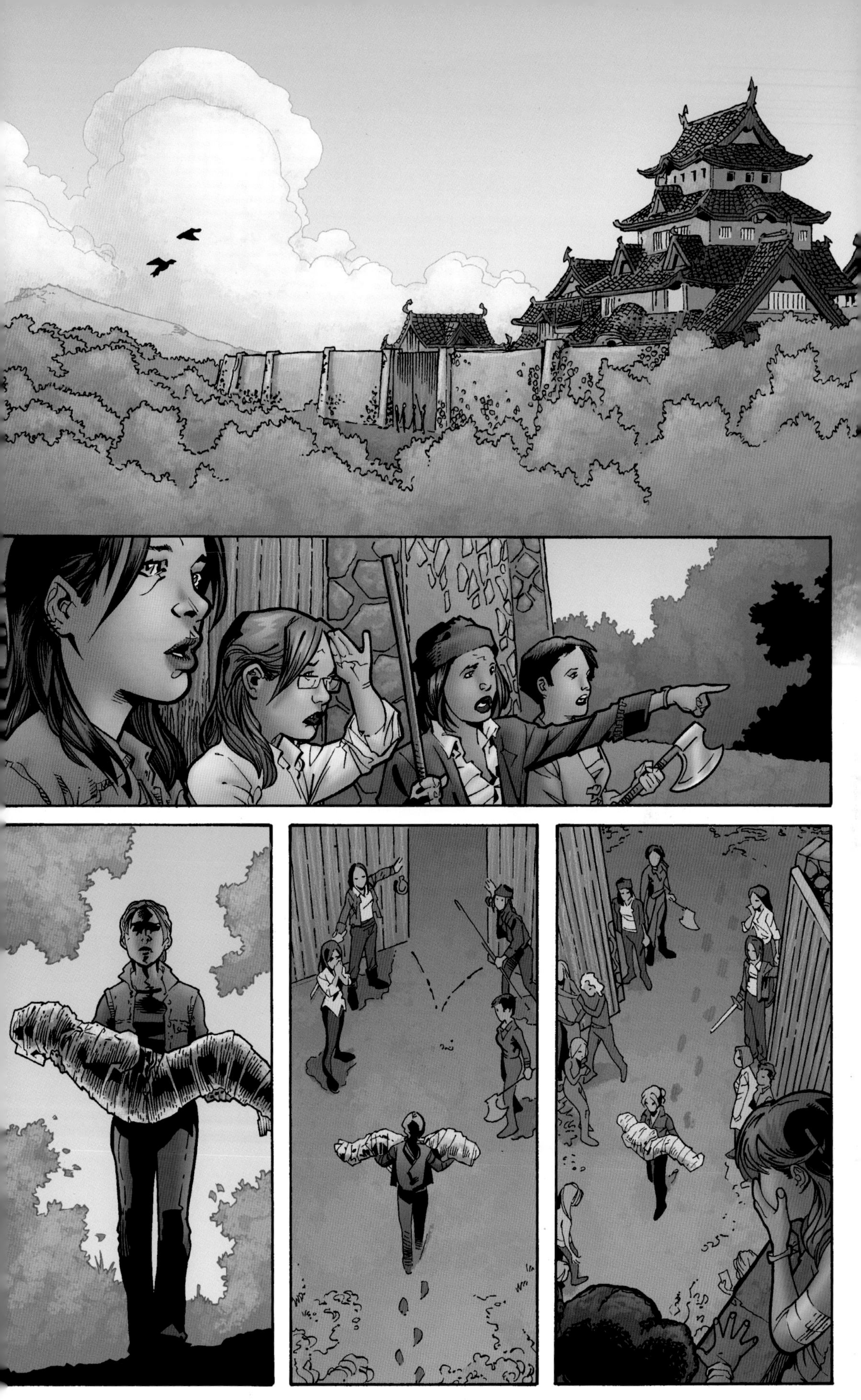

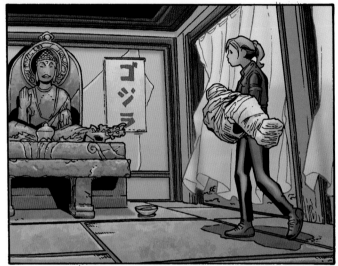

HOW LONG ARE YOU GONNA STAY UP HERE?

JUST 'TIL I FIGURE OUT WHAT TO DO NEXT.

NEED SOME HELP?

AT THE VERY LEAST, I COULD CONJURE UP SOME BLANKETS FOR YOU. WHO KNEW JAPAN WAS THIS COLD?

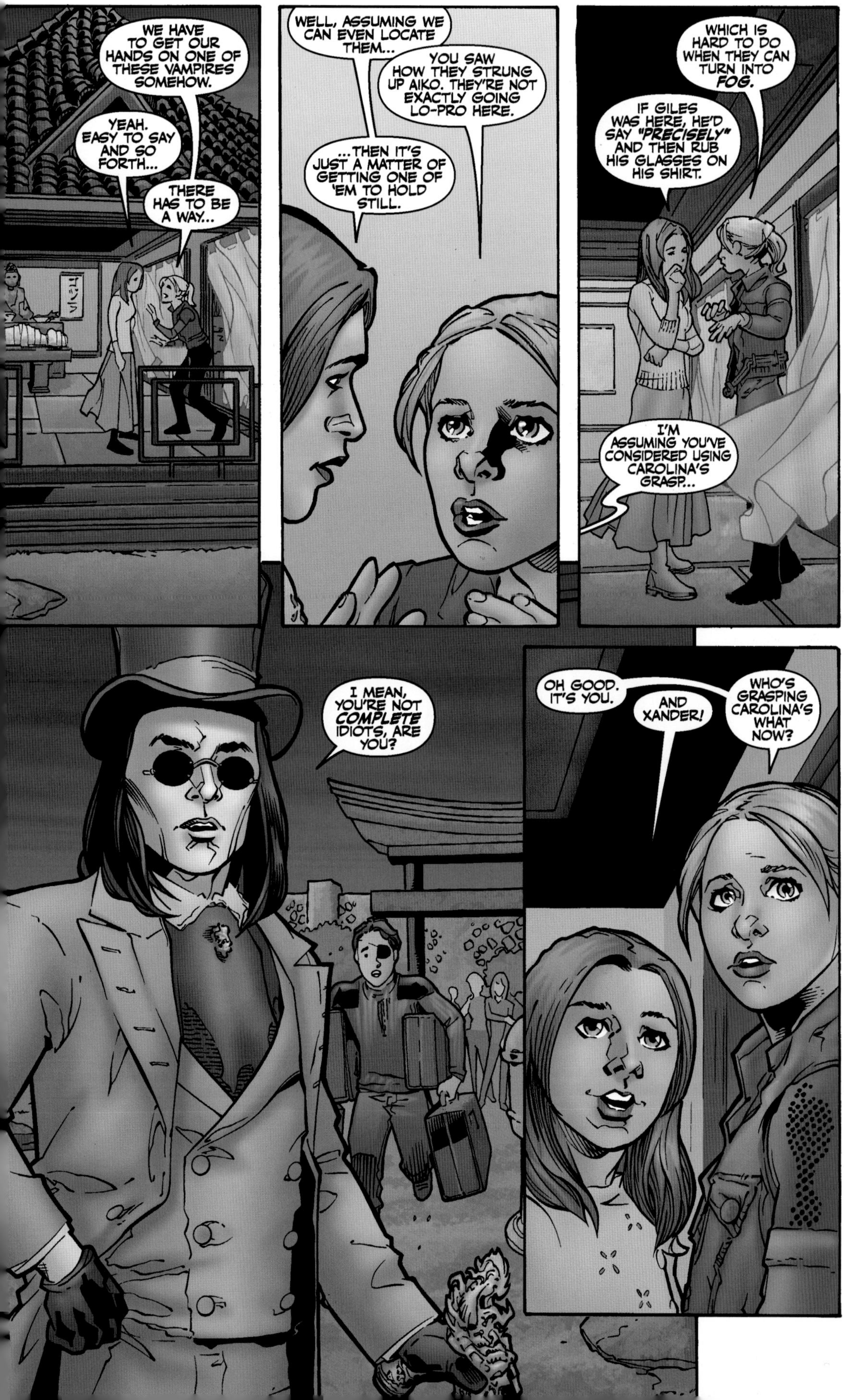
WE HAVE TO GET OUR HANDS ON ONE OF THESE VAMPIRES SOMEHOW.
YEAH. EASY TO SAY AND SO FORTH...
THERE HAS TO BE A WAY...
WELL, ASSUMING WE CAN EVEN LOCATE THEM...
YOU SAW HOW THEY STRUNG UP AIKO. THEY'RE NOT EXACTLY GOING LO-PRO HERE.
...THEN IT'S JUST A MATTER OF GETTING ONE OF 'EM TO HOLD STILL.
WHICH IS HARD TO DO WHEN THEY CAN TURN INTO FOG.
IF GILES WAS HERE, HE'D SAY "PRECISELY" AND THEN RUB HIS GLASSES ON HIS SHIRT.
I'M ASSUMING YOU'VE CONSIDERED USING CAROLINA'S GRASP...
I MEAN, YOU'RE NOT COMPLETE IDIOTS, ARE YOU?
OH GOOD. IT'S YOU.
AND XANDER!
WHO'S GRASPING CAROLINA'S WHAT NOW?

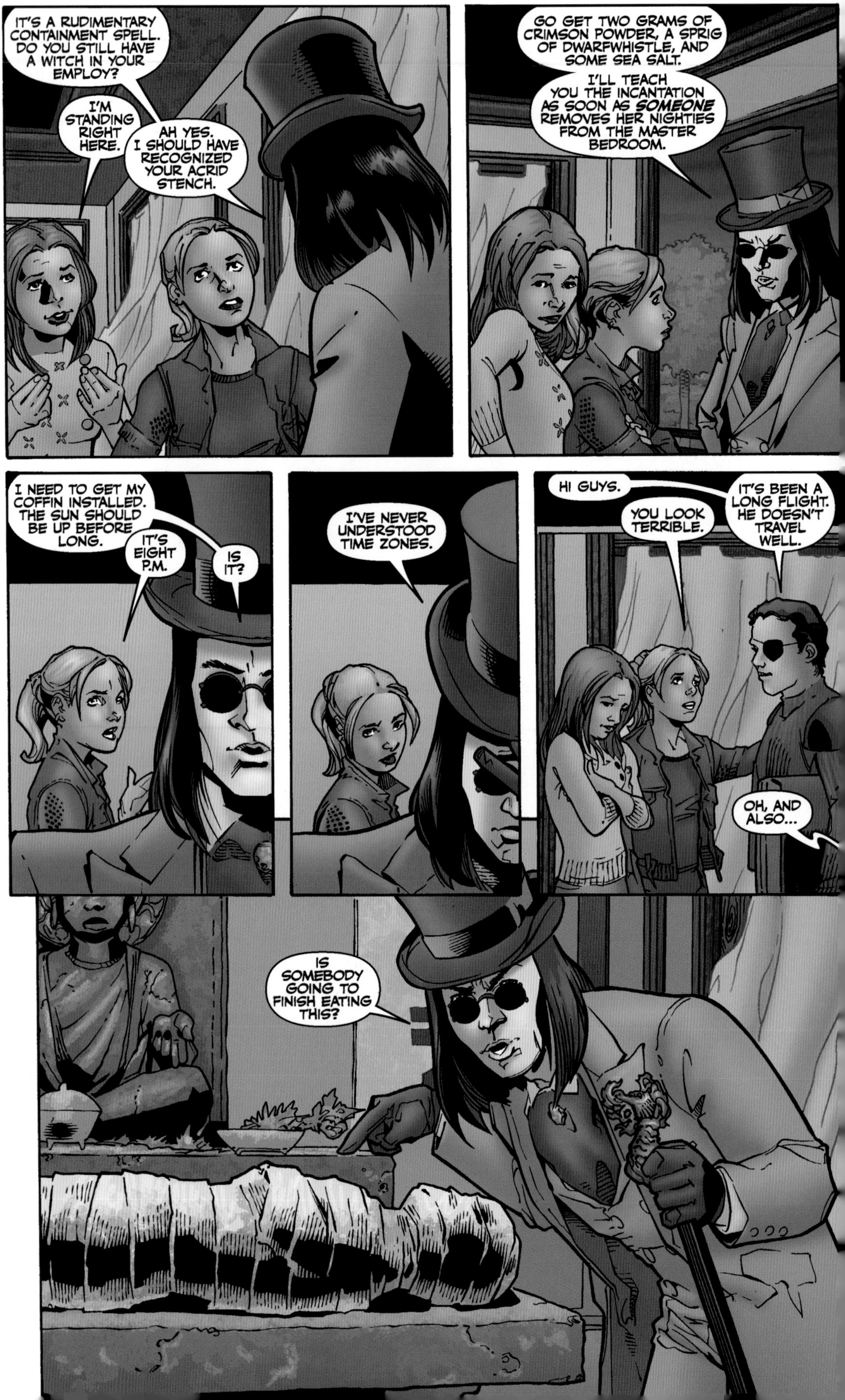
IT'S A RUDIMENTARY CONTAINMENT SPELL. DO YOU STILL HAVE A WITCH IN YOUR EMPLOY?
I'M STANDING RIGHT HERE.
AH YES. I SHOULD HAVE RECOGNIZED YOUR ACRID STENCH.
GO GET TWO GRAMS OF CRIMSON POWDER, A SPRIG OF DWARFWHISTLE, AND SOME SEA SALT.
I'LL TEACH YOU THE INCANTATION AS SOON AS SOMEONE REMOVES HER NIGHTIES FROM THE MASTER BEDROOM.
I NEED TO GET MY COFFIN INSTALLED. THE SUN SHOULD BE UP BEFORE LONG.
IT'S EIGHT P.M.
IS IT?
I'VE NEVER UNDERSTOOD TIME ZONES.
HI GUYS.
YOU LOOK TERRIBLE.
IT'S BEEN A LONG FLIGHT. HE DOESN'T TRAVEL WELL.
OH, AND ALSO...
IS SOMEBODY GOING TO FINISH EATING THIS?

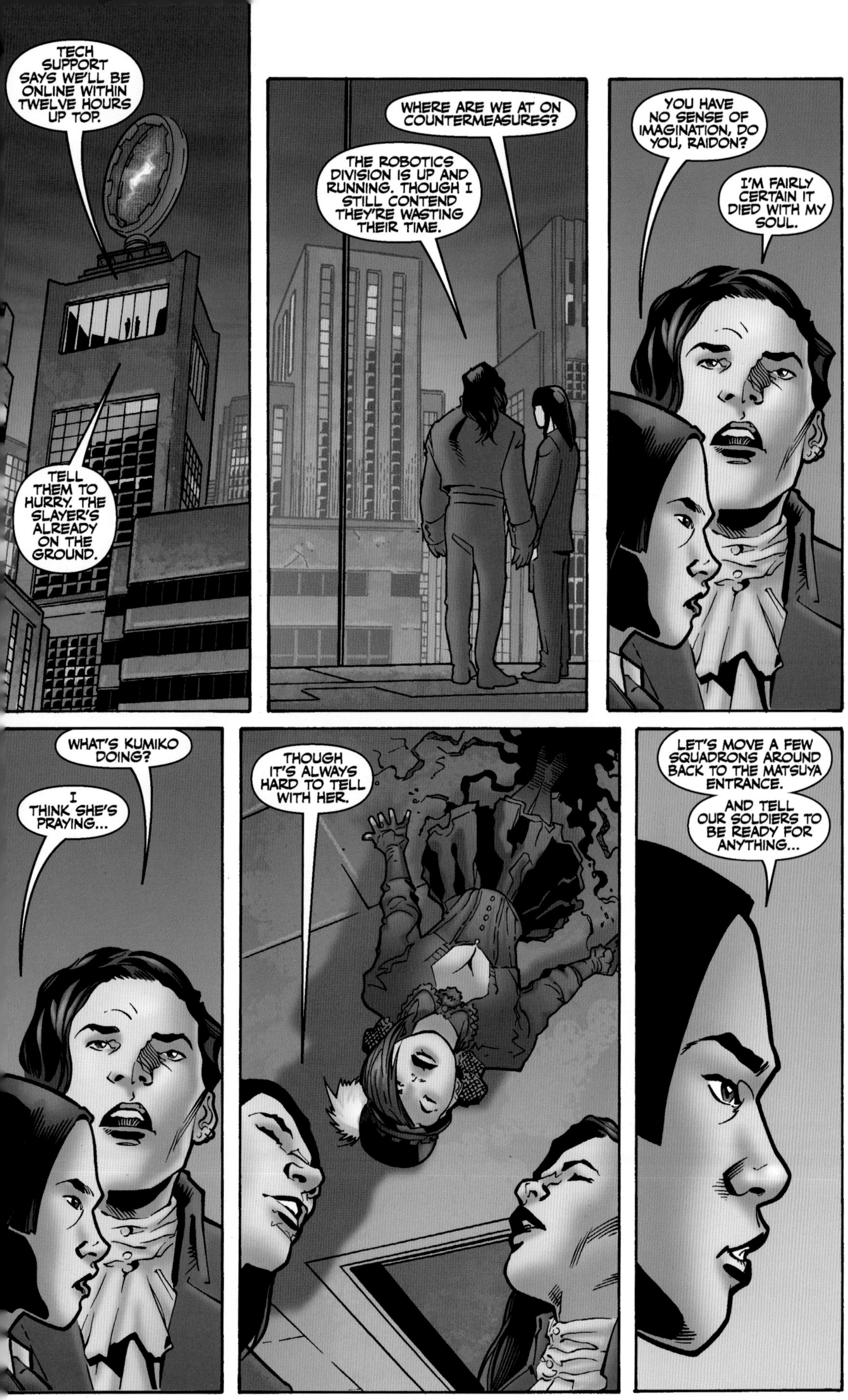
TECH SUPPORT SAYS WE'LL BE ONLINE WITHIN TWELVE HOURS UP TOP.
TELL THEM TO HURRY. THE SLAYER'S ALREADY ON THE GROUND.
WHERE ARE WE AT ON COUNTERMEASURES?
THE ROBOTICS DIVISION IS UP AND RUNNING. THOUGH I STILL CONTEND THEY'RE WASTING THEIR TIME.
YOU HAVE NO SENSE OF IMAGINATION, DO YOU, RAIDON?
I'M FAIRLY CERTAIN IT DIED WITH MY SOUL.
WHAT'S KUMIKO DOING?
I THINK SHE'S PRAYING...
THOUGH IT'S ALWAYS HARD TO TELL WITH HER.
LET'S MOVE A FEW SQUADRONS AROUND BACK TO THE MATSUYA ENTRANCE.
AND TELL OUR SOLDIERS TO BE READY FOR ANYTHING...

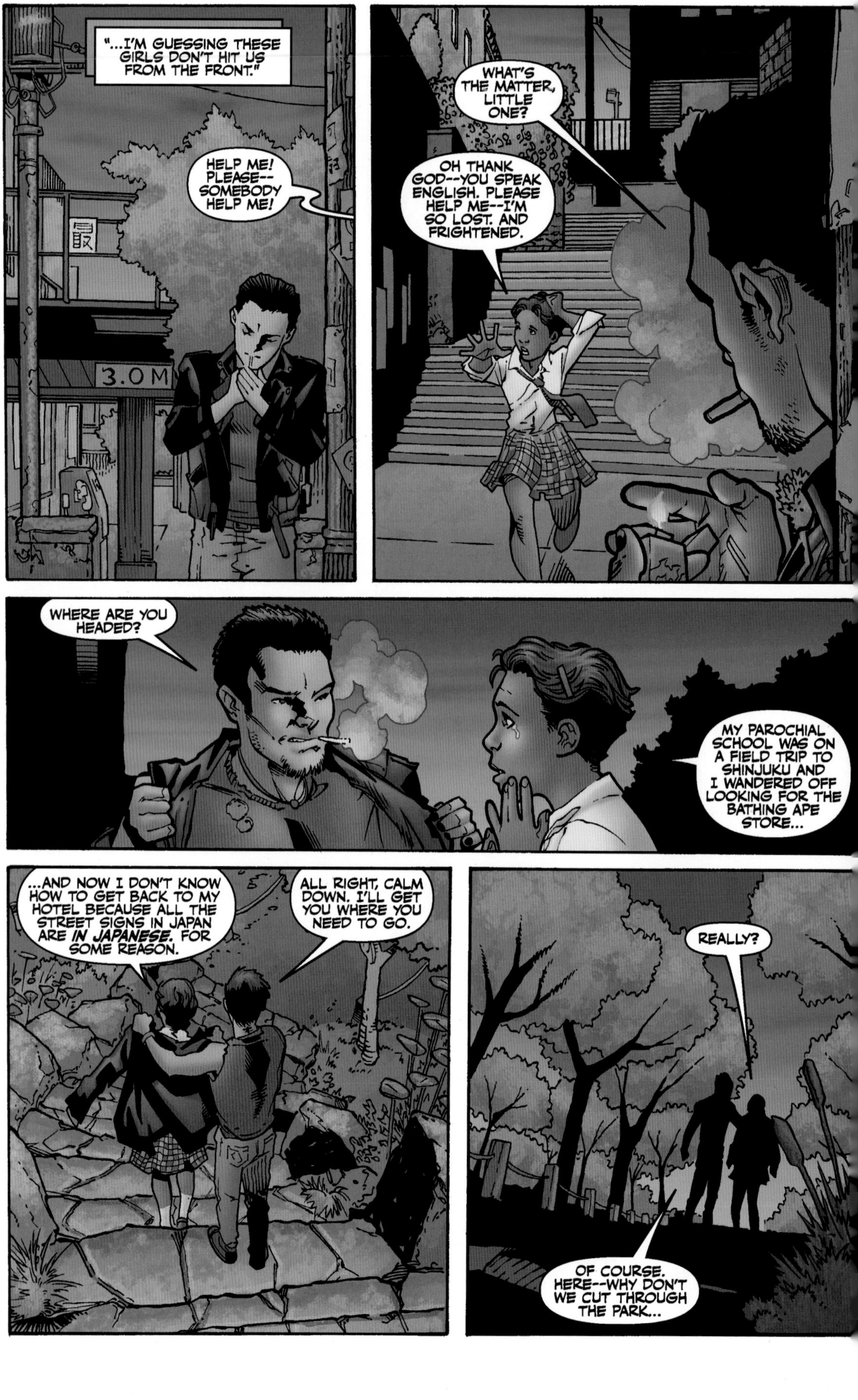

"...I'M GUESSING THESE GIRLS DON'T HIT US FROM THE FRONT."
HELP ME! PLEASE-- SOMEBODY HELP ME!
3.0M
WHAT'S THE MATTER, LITTLE ONE?
OH THANK GOD--YOU SPEAK ENGLISH. PLEASE HELP ME--I'M SO LOST. AND FRIGHTENED.
WHERE ARE YOU HEADED?
MY PAROCHIAL SCHOOL WAS ON A FIELD TRIP TO SHINJUKU AND I WANDERED OFF LOOKING FOR THE BATHING APE STORE...
...AND NOW I DON'T KNOW HOW TO GET BACK TO MY HOTEL BECAUSE ALL THE STREET SIGNS IN JAPAN ARE *IN JAPANESE.* FOR SOME REASON.
ALL RIGHT, CALM DOWN. I'LL GET YOU WHERE YOU NEED TO GO.
REALLY?
OF COURSE. HERE--WHY DON'T WE CUT THROUGH THE PARK...

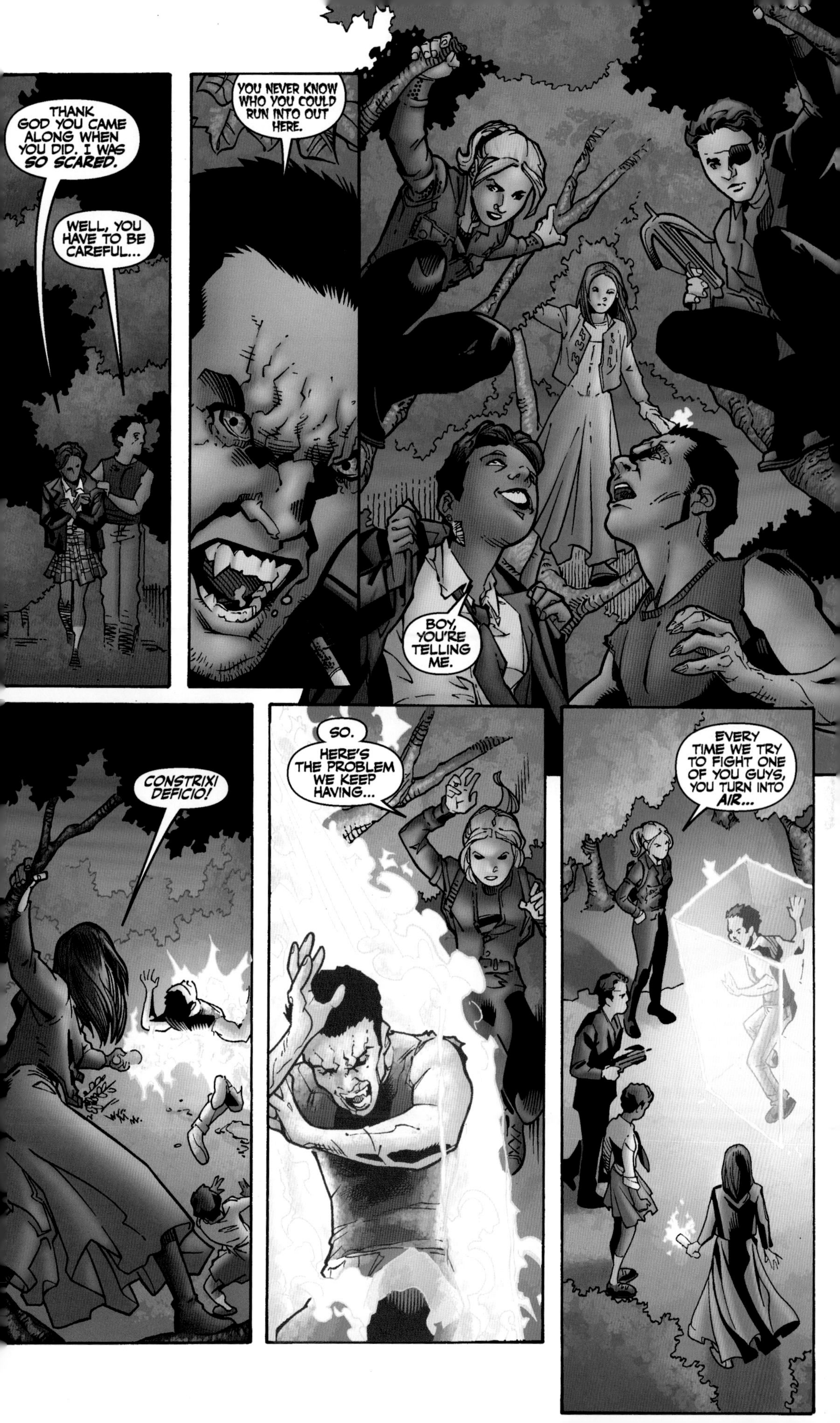
THANK GOD YOU CAME ALONG WHEN YOU DID. I WAS SO SCARED.
WELL, YOU HAVE TO BE CAREFUL...
YOU NEVER KNOW WHO YOU COULD RUN INTO OUT HERE.
BOY, YOU'RE TELLING ME.
CONSTRIXI DEFICIO!
SO.
HERE'S THE PROBLEM WE KEEP HAVING...
EVERY TIME WE TRY TO FIGHT ONE OF YOU GUYS, YOU TURN INTO AIR...

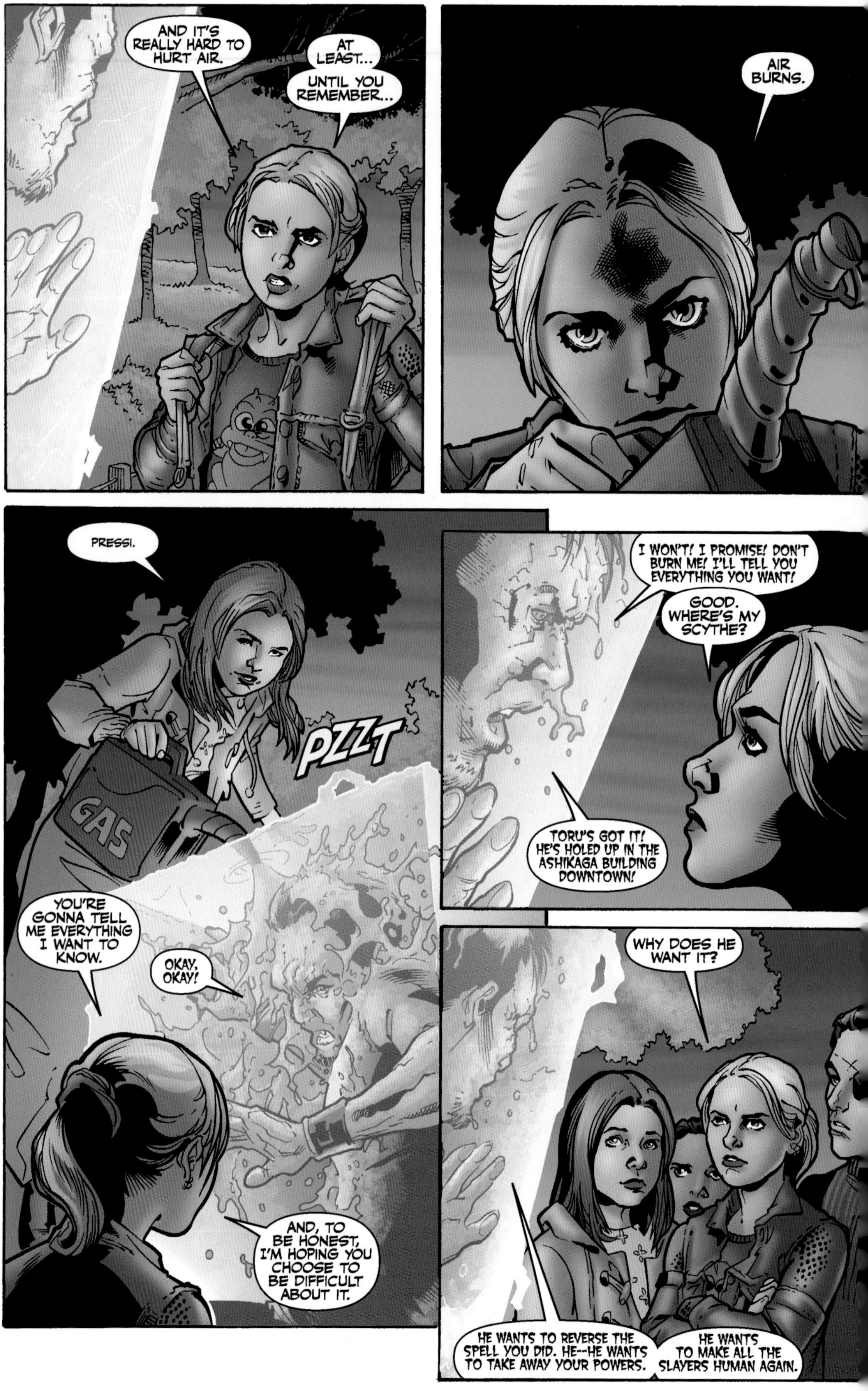
AND IT'S REALLY HARD TO HURT AIR.
AT LEAST...
UNTIL YOU REMEMBER...
AIR BURNS.
PRESSI.
PZZT
I WON'T! I PROMISE! DON'T BURN ME! I'LL TELL YOU EVERYTHING YOU WANT!
GOOD. WHERE'S MY SCYTHE?
TORU'S GOT IT! HE'S HOLED UP IN THE ASHIKAGA BUILDING DOWNTOWN!
YOU'RE GONNA TELL ME EVERYTHING I WANT TO KNOW.
OKAY, OKAY!
AND, TO BE HONEST, I'M HOPING YOU CHOOSE TO BE DIFFICULT ABOUT IT.
GAS
WHY DOES HE WANT IT?
HE WANTS TO REVERSE THE SPELL YOU DID. HE--HE WANTS TO TAKE AWAY YOUR POWERS.
HE WANTS TO MAKE ALL THE SLAYERS HUMAN AGAIN.

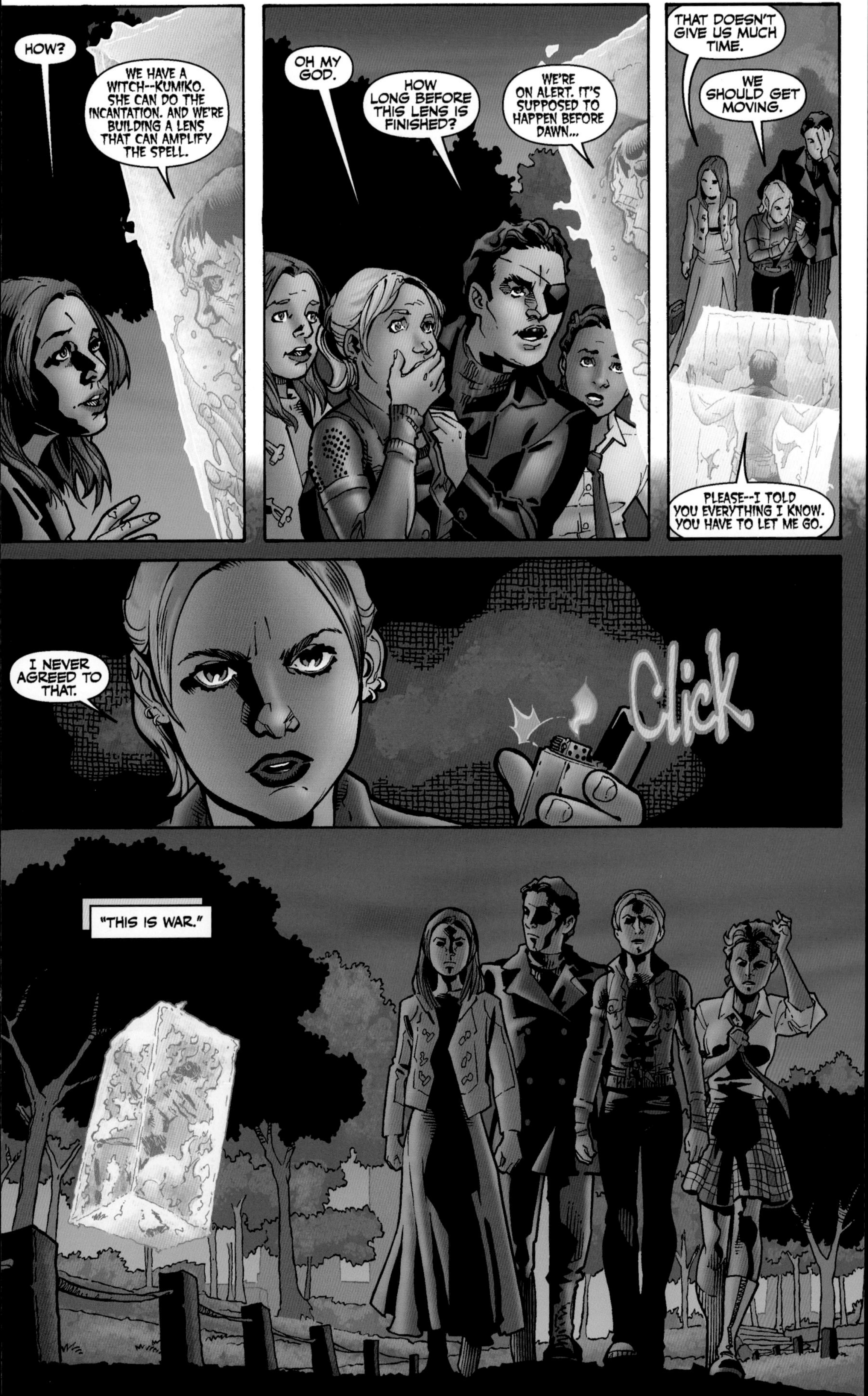
HOW?
WE HAVE A WITCH--KUMIKO. SHE CAN DO THE INCANTATION. AND WE'RE BUILDING A LENS THAT CAN AMPLIFY THE SPELL.
OH MY GOD.
HOW LONG BEFORE THIS LENS IS FINISHED?
WE'RE ON ALERT. IT'S SUPPOSED TO HAPPEN BEFORE DAWN...
THAT DOESN'T GIVE US MUCH TIME.
WE SHOULD GET MOVING.
PLEASE--I TOLD YOU EVERYTHING I KNOW. YOU HAVE TO LET ME GO.
I NEVER AGREED TO THAT.
Click
"THIS IS WAR."

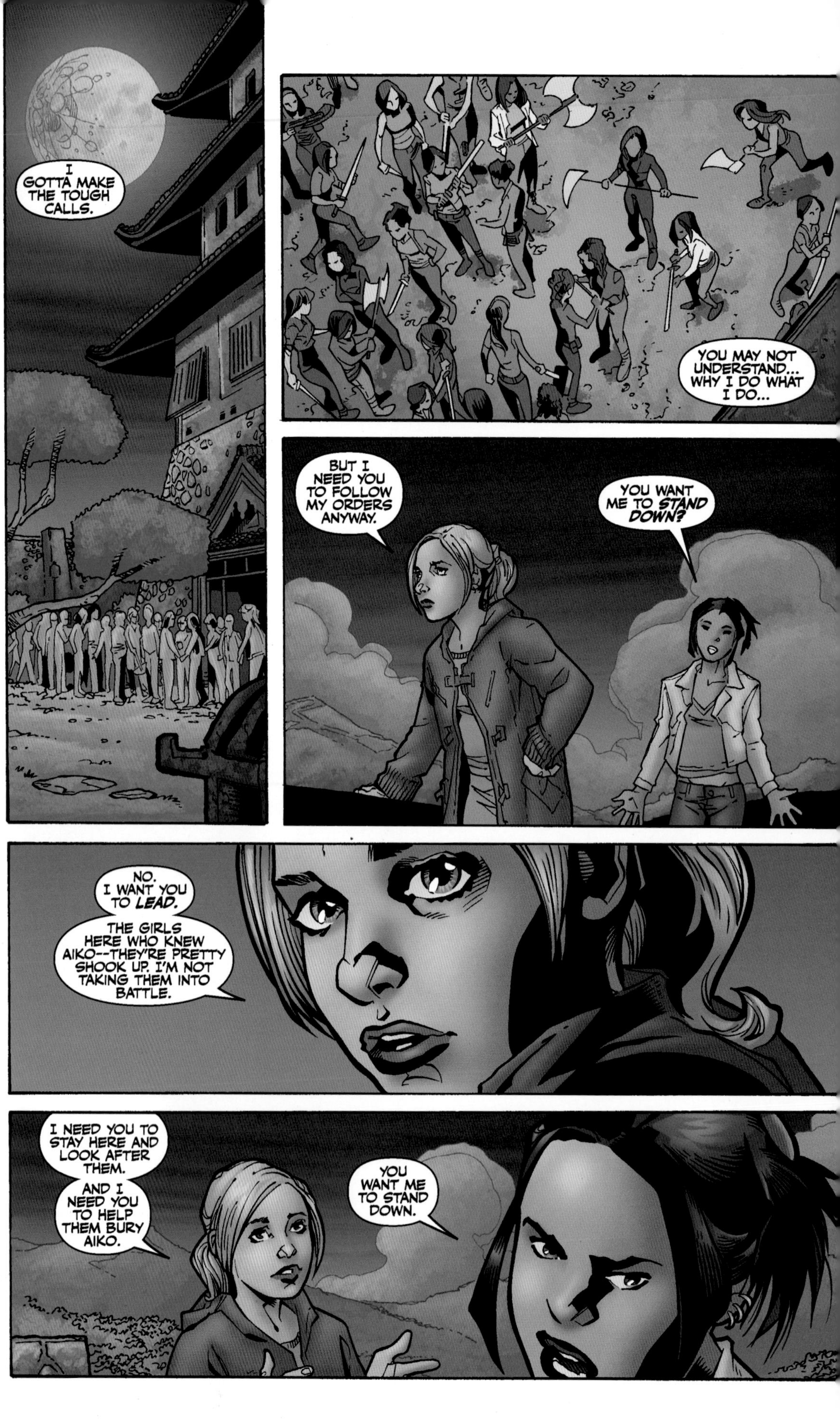
I GOTTA MAKE THE TOUGH CALLS.
YOU MAY NOT UNDERSTAND... WHY I DO WHAT I DO...
BUT I NEED YOU TO FOLLOW MY ORDERS ANYWAY.
YOU WANT ME TO STAND DOWN?
NO. I WANT YOU TO LEAD.
THE GIRLS HERE WHO KNEW AIKO--THEY'RE PRETTY SHOOK UP. I'M NOT TAKING THEM INTO BATTLE.
I NEED YOU TO STAY HERE AND LOOK AFTER THEM.
AND I NEED YOU TO HELP THEM BURY AIKO.
YOU WANT ME TO STAND DOWN.

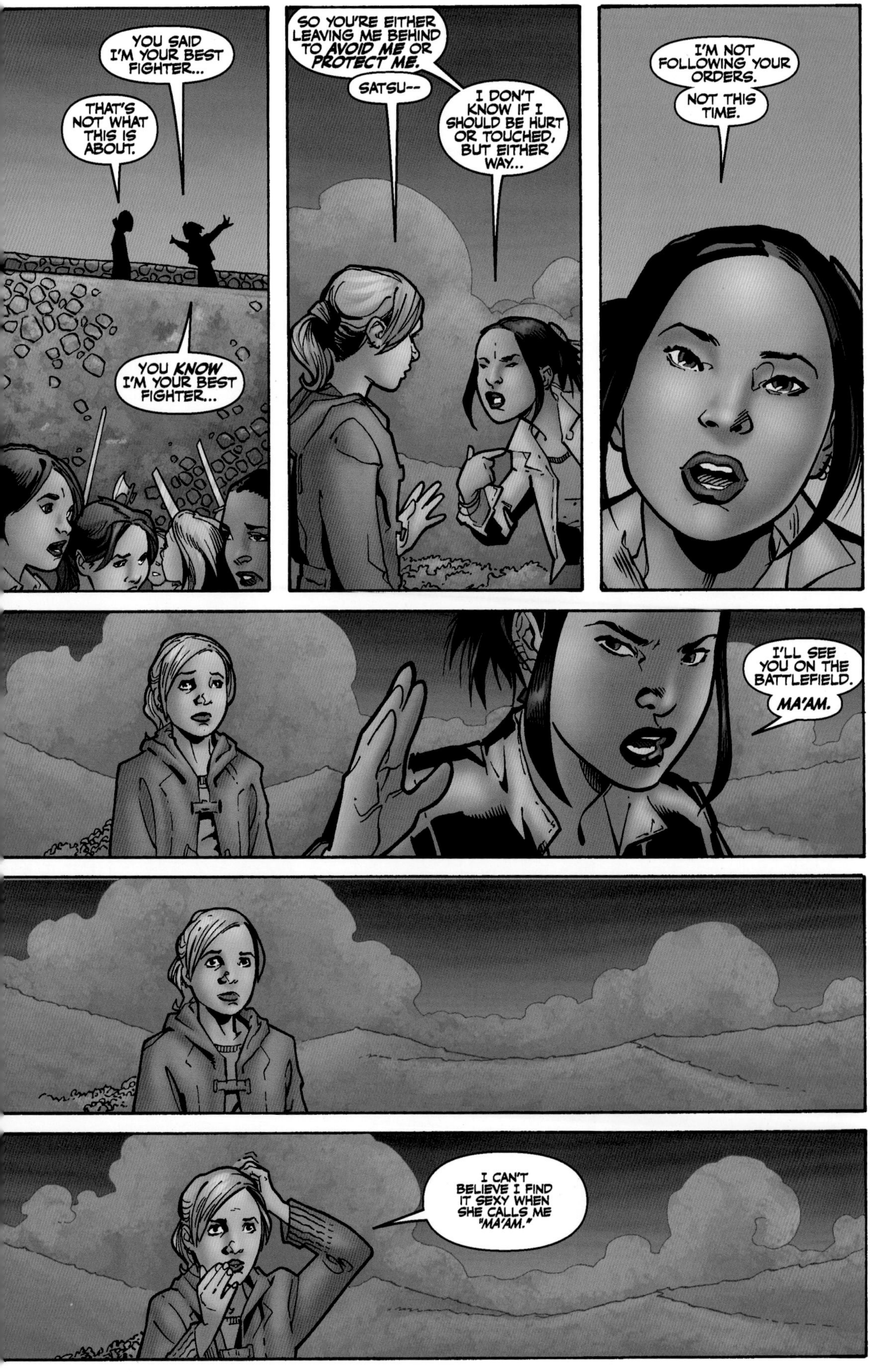
YOU SAID I'M YOUR BEST FIGHTER...
THAT'S NOT WHAT THIS IS ABOUT.
YOU KNOW I'M YOUR BEST FIGHTER...
SO YOU'RE EITHER LEAVING ME BEHIND TO AVOID ME OR PROTECT ME.
SATSU--
I DON'T KNOW IF I SHOULD BE HURT OR TOUCHED, BUT EITHER WAY...
I'M NOT FOLLOWING YOUR ORDERS.
NOT THIS TIME.
I'LL SEE YOU ON THE BATTLEFIELD.
MA'AM.
I CAN'T BELIEVE I FIND IT SEXY WHEN SHE CALLS ME "MA'AM."

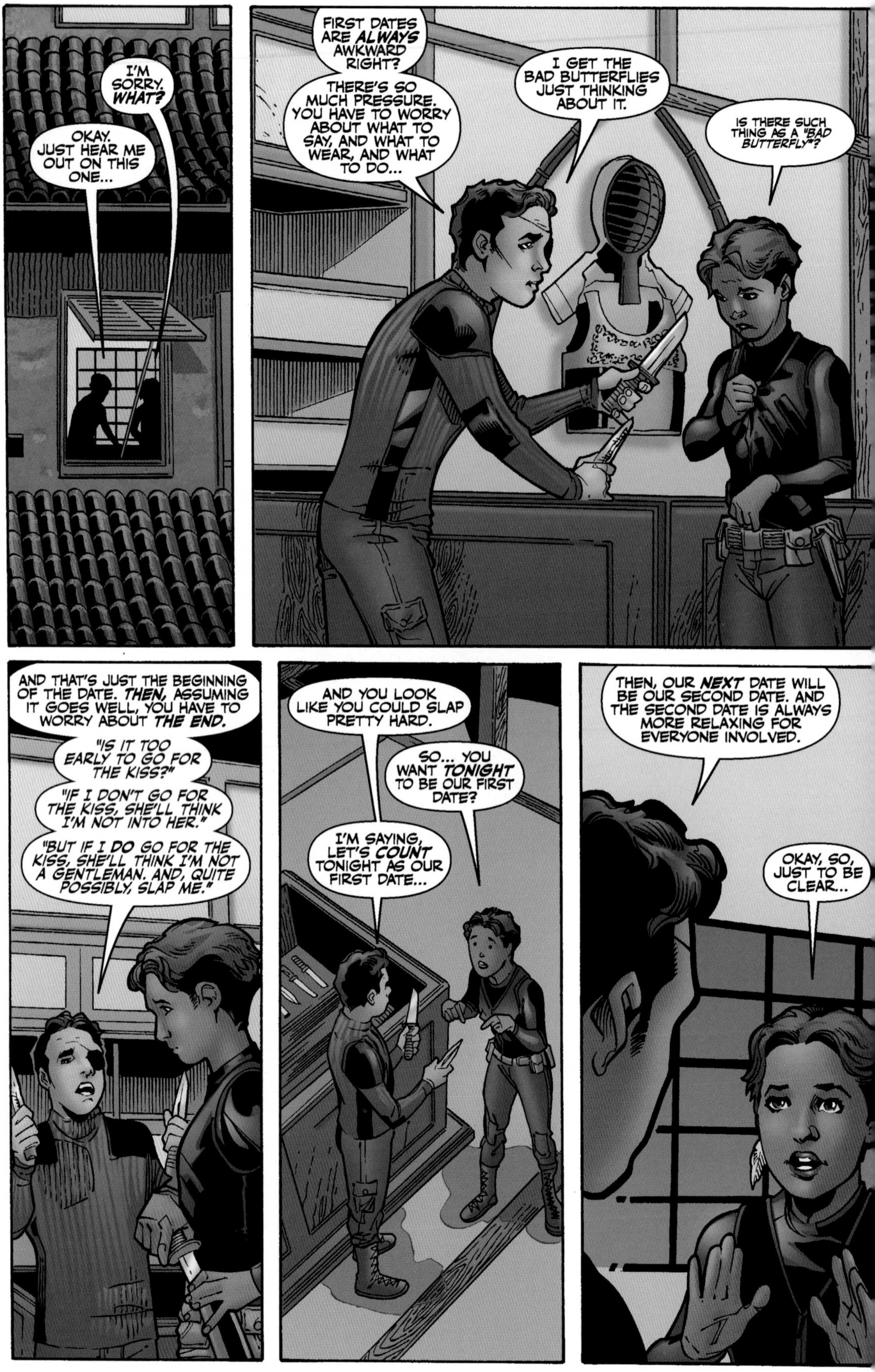

I'M SORRY. WHAT?
OKAY. JUST HEAR ME OUT ON THIS ONE...
FIRST DATES ARE ALWAYS AWKWARD RIGHT?
THERE'S SO MUCH PRESSURE. YOU HAVE TO WORRY ABOUT WHAT TO SAY, AND WHAT TO WEAR, AND WHAT TO DO...
I GET THE BAD BUTTERFLIES JUST THINKING ABOUT IT.
IS THERE SUCH THING AS A "BAD BUTTERFLY"?
AND THAT'S JUST THE BEGINNING OF THE DATE. THEN, ASSUMING IT GOES WELL, YOU HAVE TO WORRY ABOUT THE END.
"IS IT TOO EARLY TO GO FOR THE KISS?"
"IF I DON'T GO FOR THE KISS, SHE'LL THINK I'M NOT INTO HER."
"BUT IF I DO GO FOR THE KISS, SHE'LL THINK I'M NOT A GENTLEMAN. AND, QUITE POSSIBLY, SLAP ME."
AND YOU LOOK LIKE YOU COULD SLAP PRETTY HARD.
SO... YOU WANT TONIGHT TO BE OUR FIRST DATE?
I'M SAYING, LET'S COUNT TONIGHT AS OUR FIRST DATE...
THEN, OUR NEXT DATE WILL BE OUR SECOND DATE. AND THE SECOND DATE IS ALWAYS MORE RELAXING FOR EVERYONE INVOLVED.
OKAY, SO, JUST TO BE CLEAR...

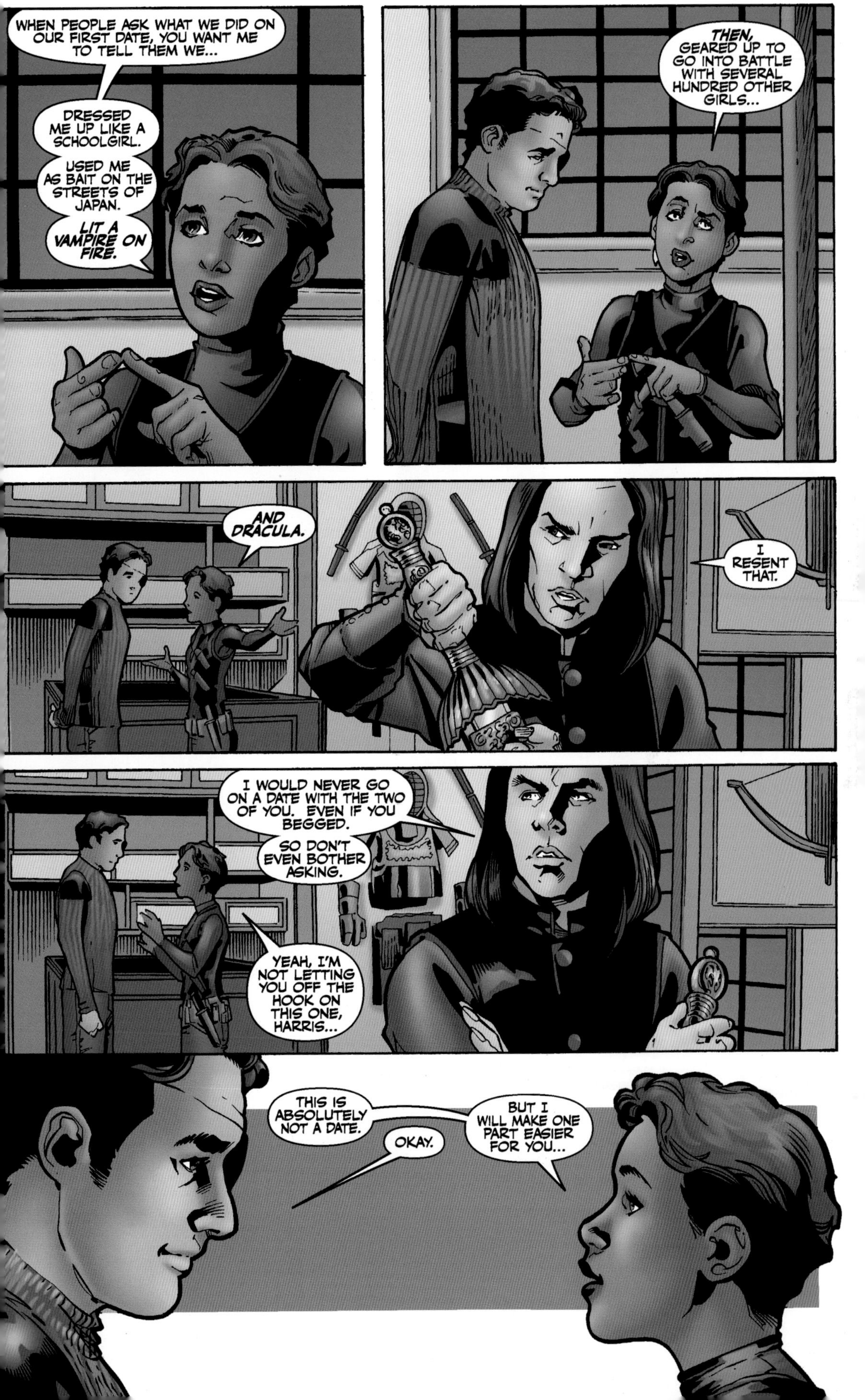
WHEN PEOPLE ASK WHAT WE DID ON OUR FIRST DATE, YOU WANT ME TO TELL THEM WE...
DRESSED ME UP LIKE A SCHOOLGIRL.
USED ME AS BAIT ON THE STREETS OF JAPAN.
LIT A VAMPIRE ON FIRE.
THEN, GEARED UP TO GO INTO BATTLE WITH SEVERAL HUNDRED OTHER GIRLS...
AND DRACULA.
I RESENT THAT.
I WOULD NEVER GO ON A DATE WITH THE TWO OF YOU. EVEN IF YOU BEGGED.
SO DON'T EVEN BOTHER ASKING.
YEAH, I'M NOT LETTING YOU OFF THE HOOK ON THIS ONE, HARRIS...
THIS IS ABSOLUTELY NOT A DATE.
OKAY.
BUT I WILL MAKE ONE PART EASIER FOR YOU...

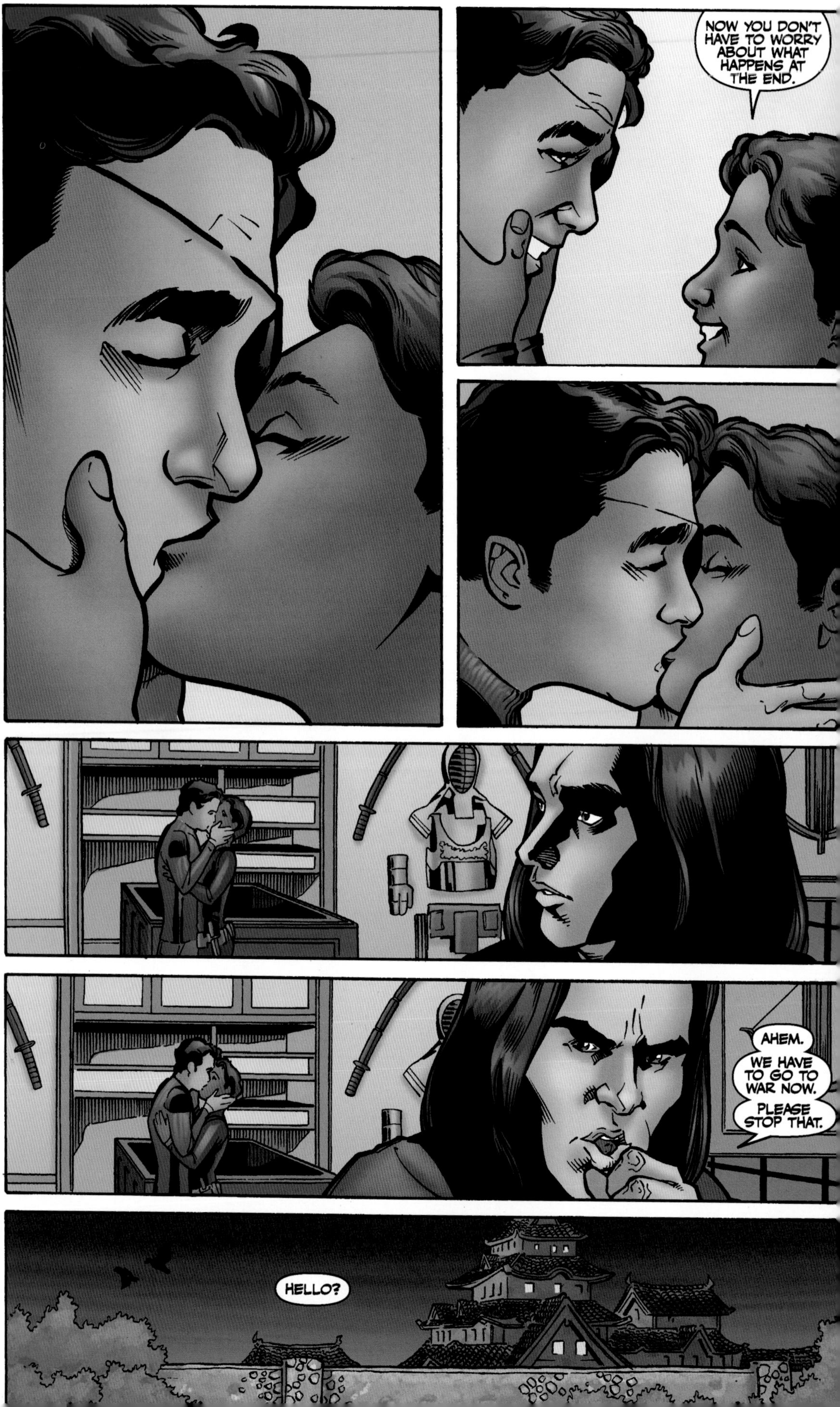
NOW YOU DON'T HAVE TO WORRY ABOUT WHAT HAPPENS AT THE END.
AHEM.
WE HAVE TO GO TO WAR NOW.
PLEASE STOP THAT.
HELLO?

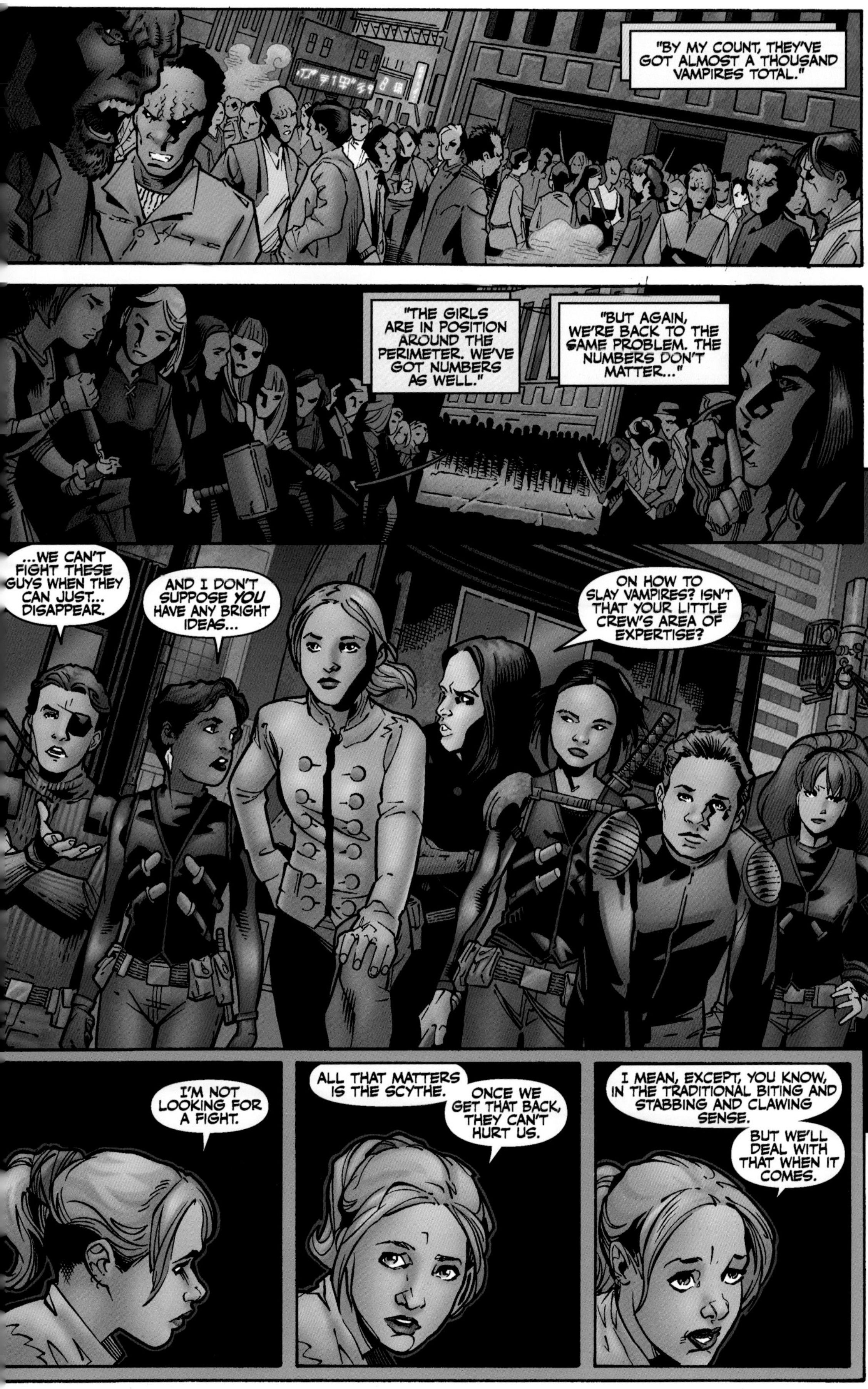
"BY MY COUNT, THEY'VE GOT ALMOST A THOUSAND VAMPIRES TOTAL."
"THE GIRLS ARE IN POSITION AROUND THE PERIMETER. WE'VE GOT NUMBERS AS WELL."
"BUT AGAIN, WE'RE BACK TO THE SAME PROBLEM. THE NUMBERS DON'T MATTER..."
...WE CAN'T FIGHT THESE GUYS WHEN THEY CAN JUST... DISAPPEAR.
AND I DON'T SUPPOSE YOU HAVE ANY BRIGHT IDEAS...
ON HOW TO SLAY VAMPIRES? ISN'T THAT YOUR LITTLE CREW'S AREA OF EXPERTISE?
I'M NOT LOOKING FOR A FIGHT.
ALL THAT MATTERS IS THE SCYTHE.
ONCE WE GET THAT BACK, THEY CAN'T HURT US.
I MEAN, EXCEPT, YOU KNOW, IN THE TRADITIONAL BITING AND STABBING AND CLAWING SENSE.
BUT WE'LL DEAL WITH THAT WHEN IT COMES.

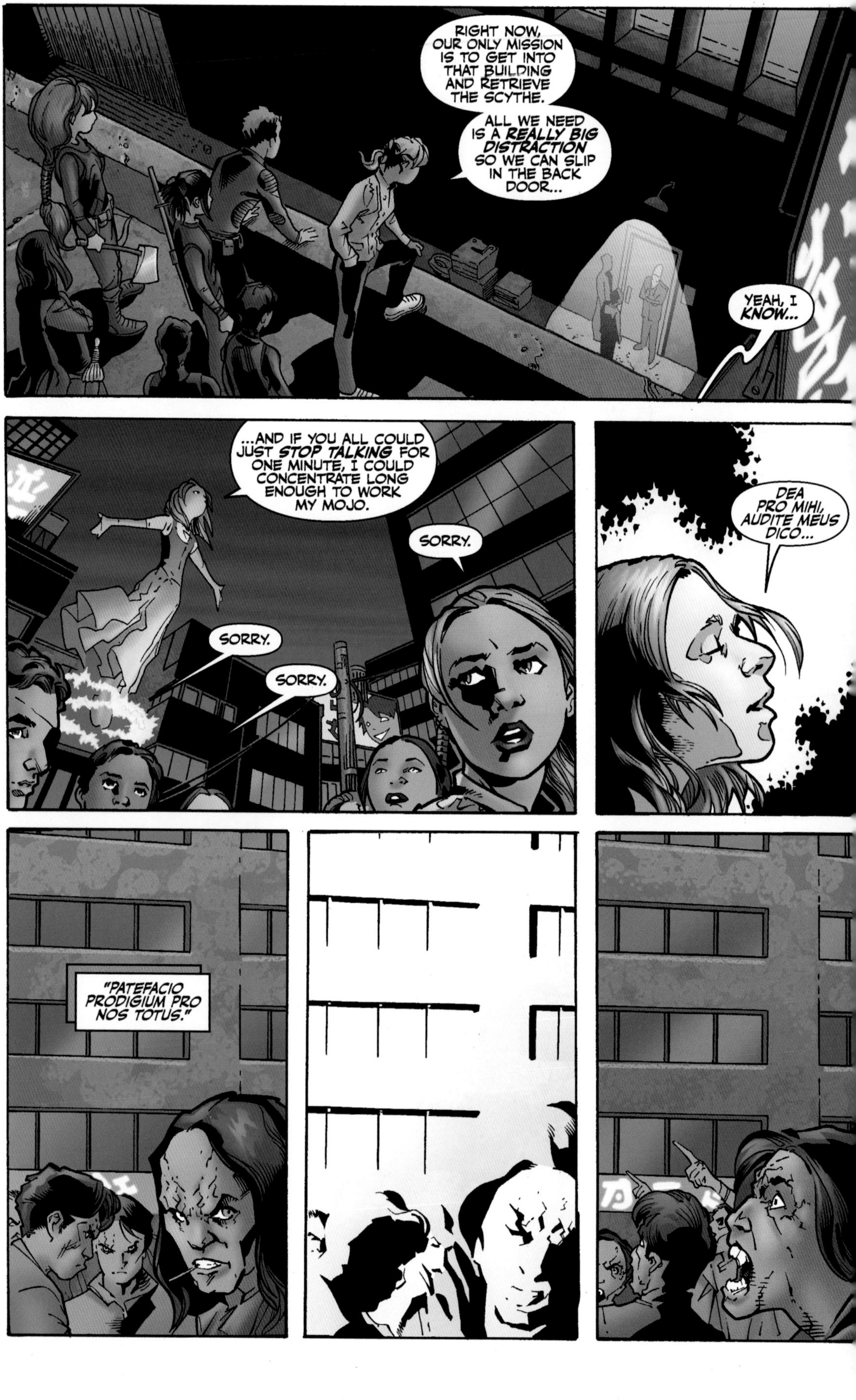
RIGHT NOW, OUR ONLY MISSION IS TO GET INTO THAT BUILDING AND RETRIEVE THE SCYTHE.
ALL WE NEED IS A REALLY BIG DISTRACTION SO WE CAN SLIP IN THE BACK DOOR...
YEAH, I KNOW...
...AND IF YOU ALL COULD JUST STOP TALKING FOR ONE MINUTE, I COULD CONCENTRATE LONG ENOUGH TO WORK MY MOJO.
SORRY.
SORRY.
SORRY.
DEA PRO MIHI, AUDITE MEUS DICO...
"PATEFACIO PRODIGIUM PRO NOS TOTUS."

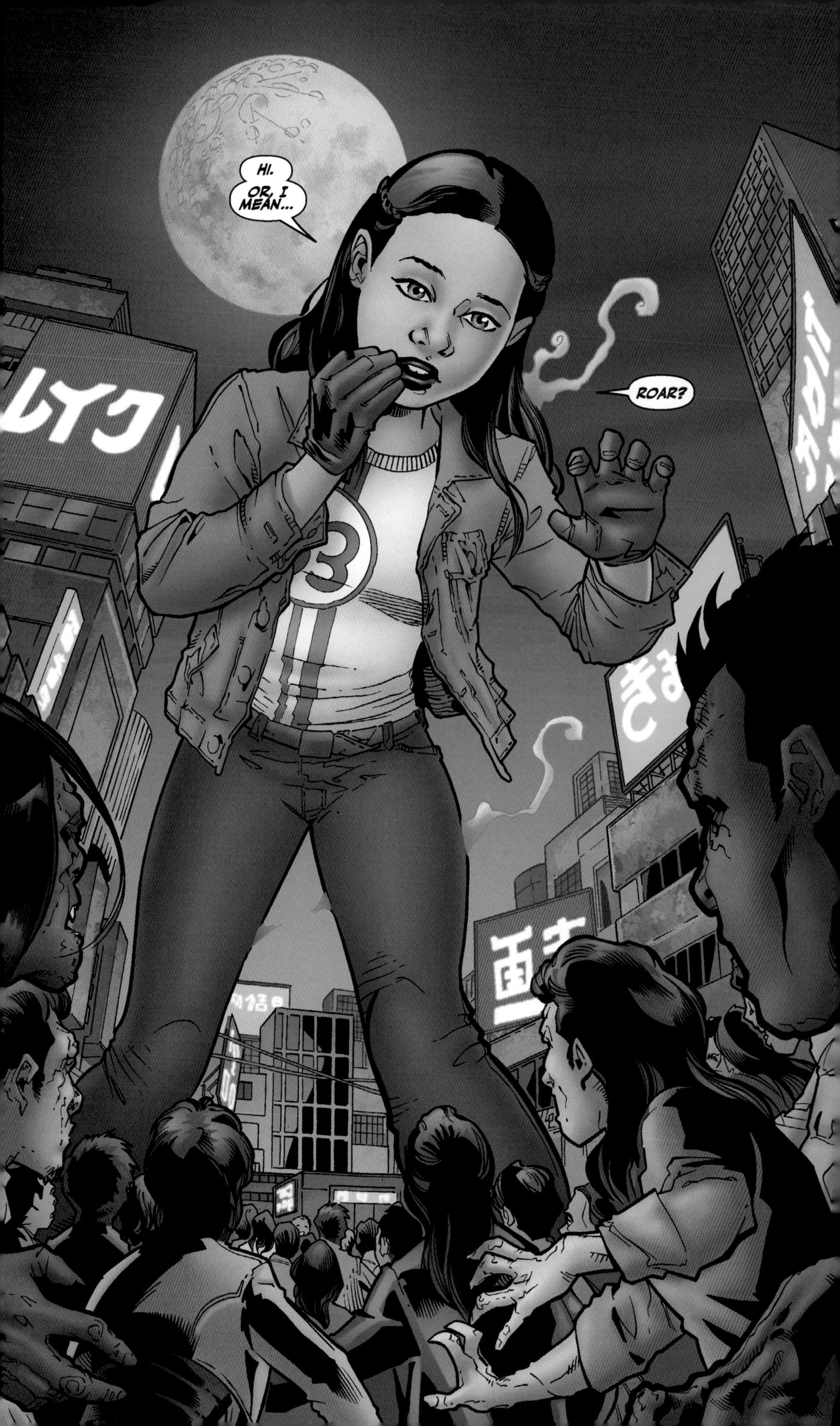
HI.
OR, I MEAN...
ROAR?

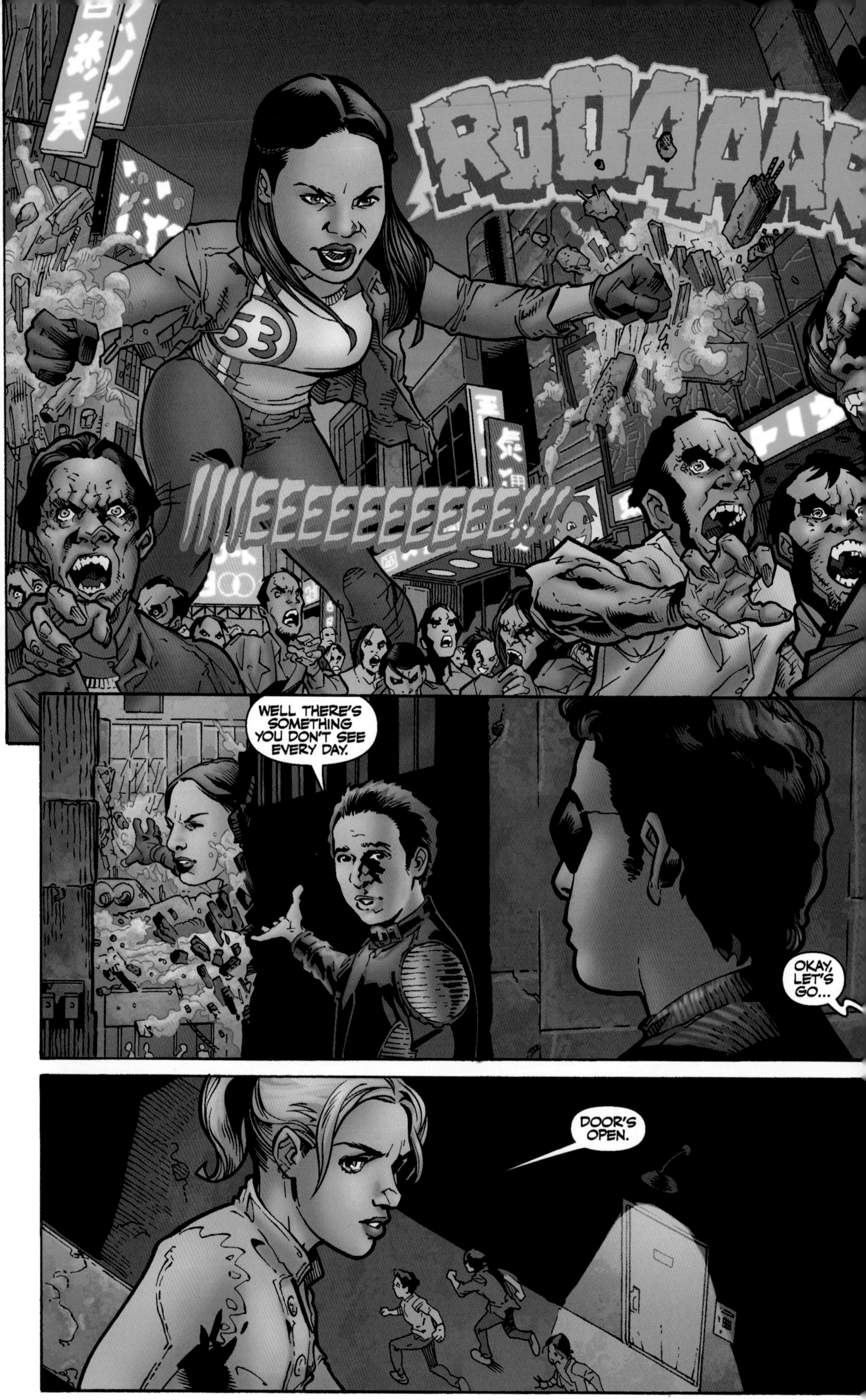
ROOAAAR
IIIIEEEEEEEEEEEE!!!
WELL THERE'S SOMETHING YOU DON'T SEE EVERY DAY.
OKAY, LET'S GO...
DOOR'S OPEN.

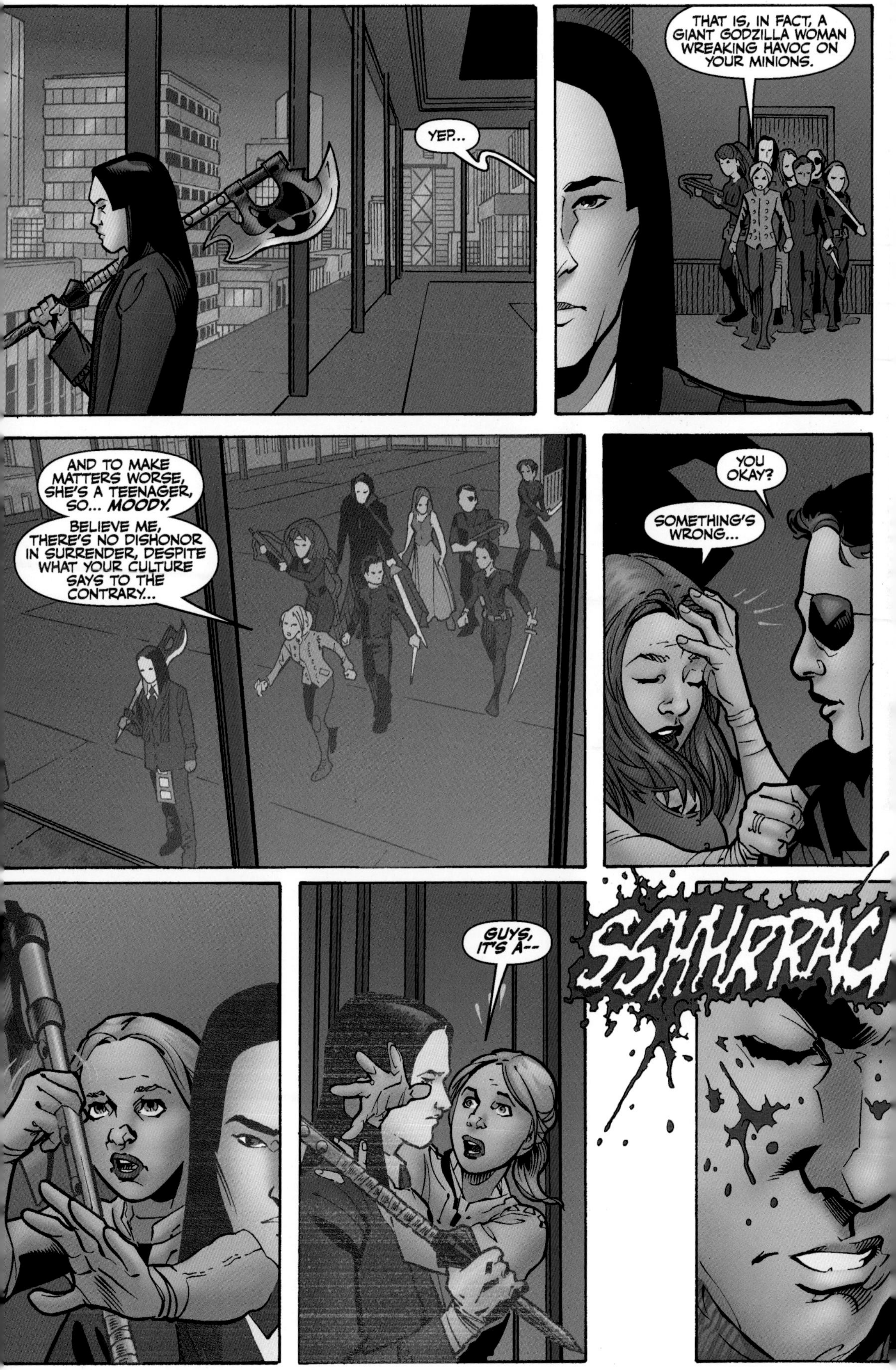
YEP...
THAT IS, IN FACT, A GIANT GODZILLA WOMAN WREAKING HAVOC ON YOUR MINIONS.
AND TO MAKE MATTERS WORSE, SHE'S A TEENAGER, SO... *MOODY.*
BELIEVE ME, THERE'S NO DISHONOR IN SURRENDER, DESPITE WHAT YOUR CULTURE SAYS TO THE CONTRARY...
YOU OKAY?
SOMETHING'S WRONG...
GUYS, IT'S A--
SSHHRRAC

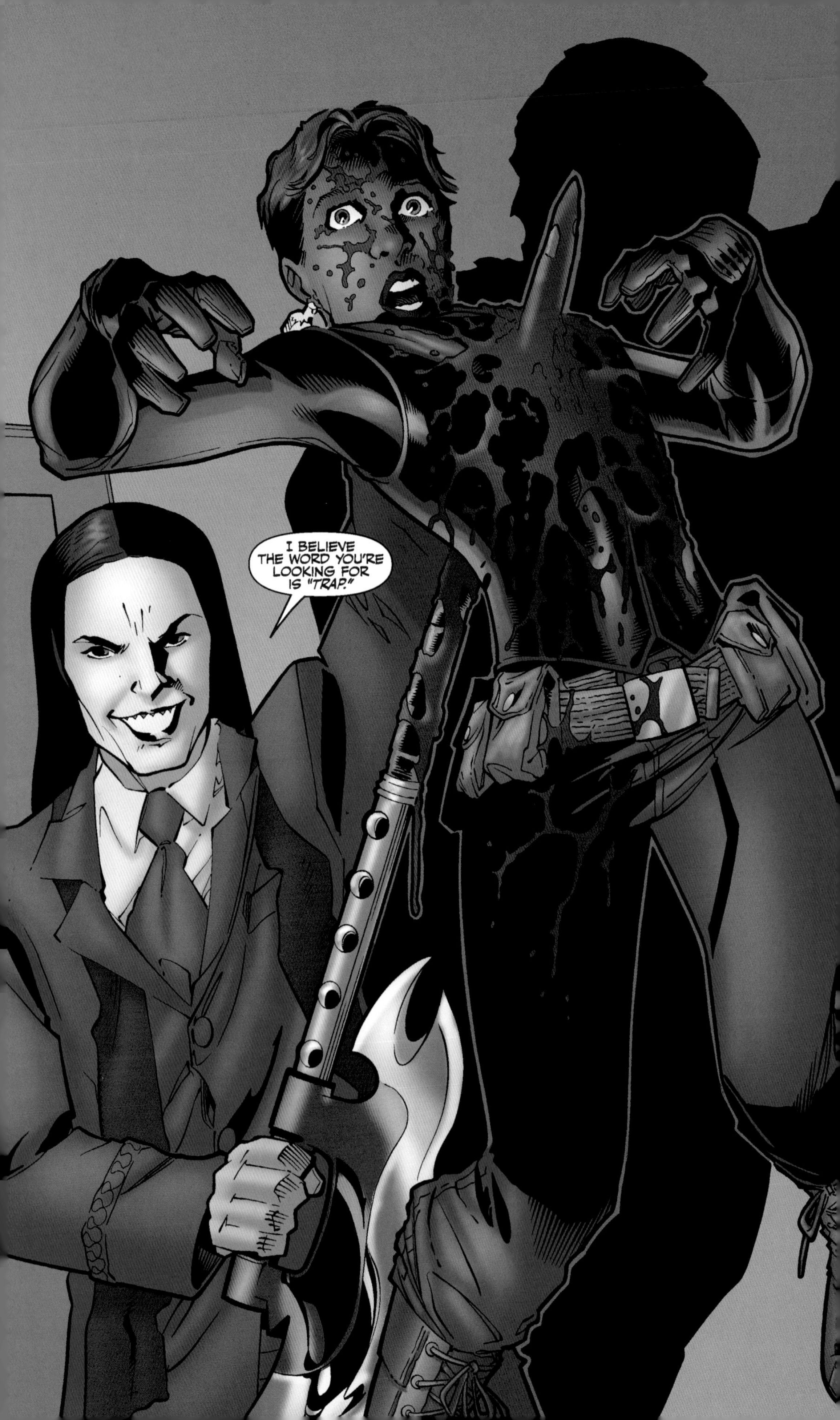
I BELIEVE THE WORD YOU'RE LOOKING FOR IS "TRAP."

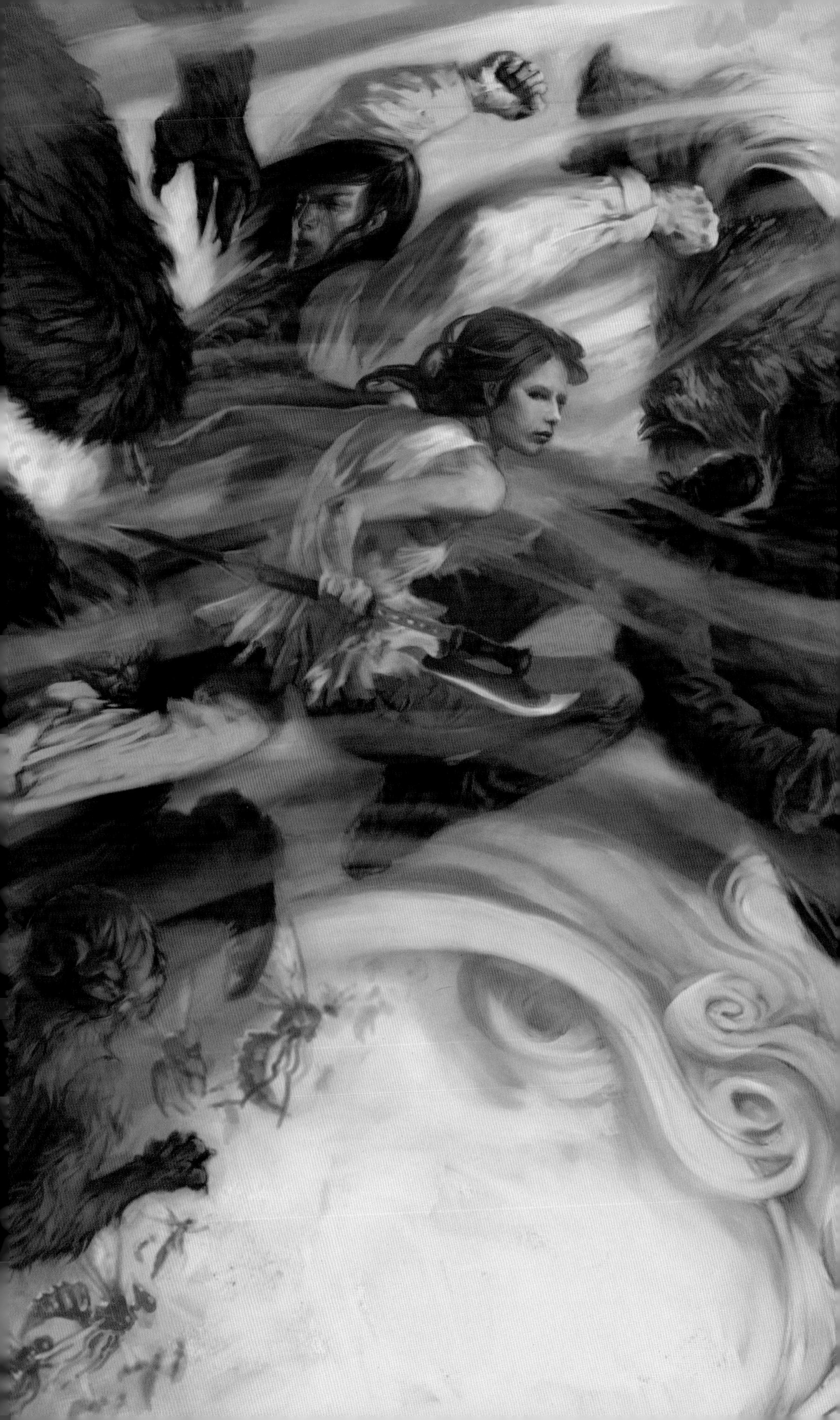

WOLVES AT THE GATE
CONCLUSION

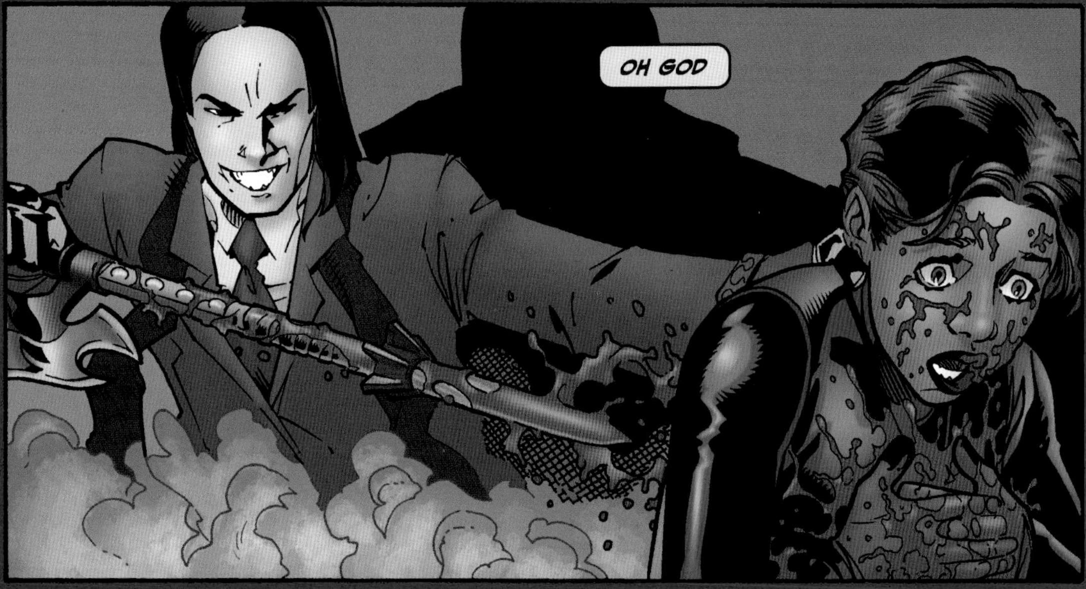
OH GOD

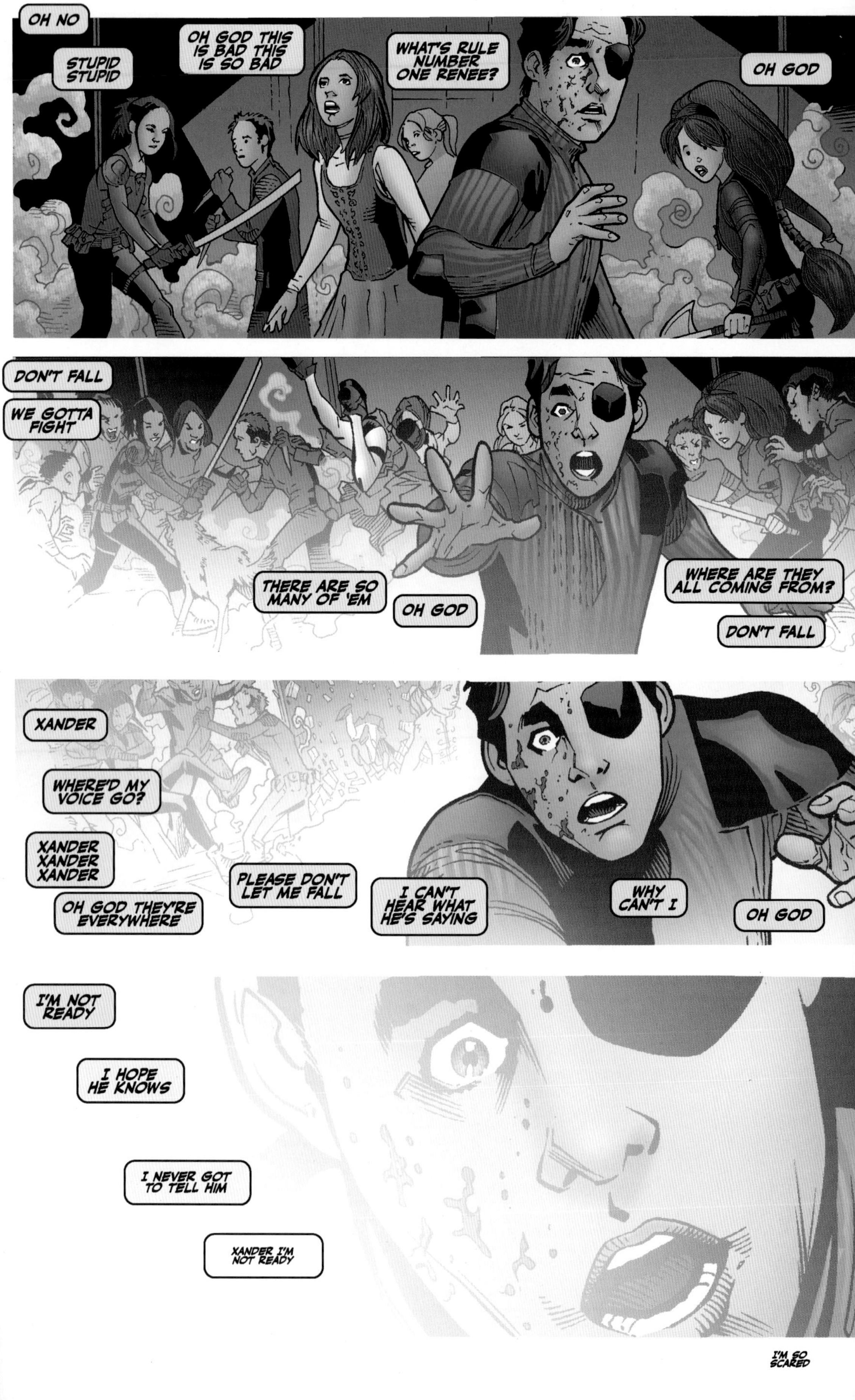
OH NO
STUPID STUPID
OH GOD THIS IS BAD THIS IS SO BAD
WHAT'S RULE NUMBER ONE RENEE?
OH GOD
DON'T FALL
WE GOTTA FIGHT
THERE ARE SO MANY OF 'EM
OH GOD
WHERE ARE THEY ALL COMING FROM?
DON'T FALL
XANDER
WHERE'D MY VOICE GO?
XANDER XANDER XANDER
OH GOD THEY'RE EVERYWHERE
PLEASE DON'T LET ME FALL
I CAN'T HEAR WHAT HE'S SAYING
WHY CAN'T I
OH GOD
I'M NOT READY
I HOPE HE KNOWS
I NEVER GOT TO TELL HIM
XANDER I'M NOT READY
I'M SO SCARED

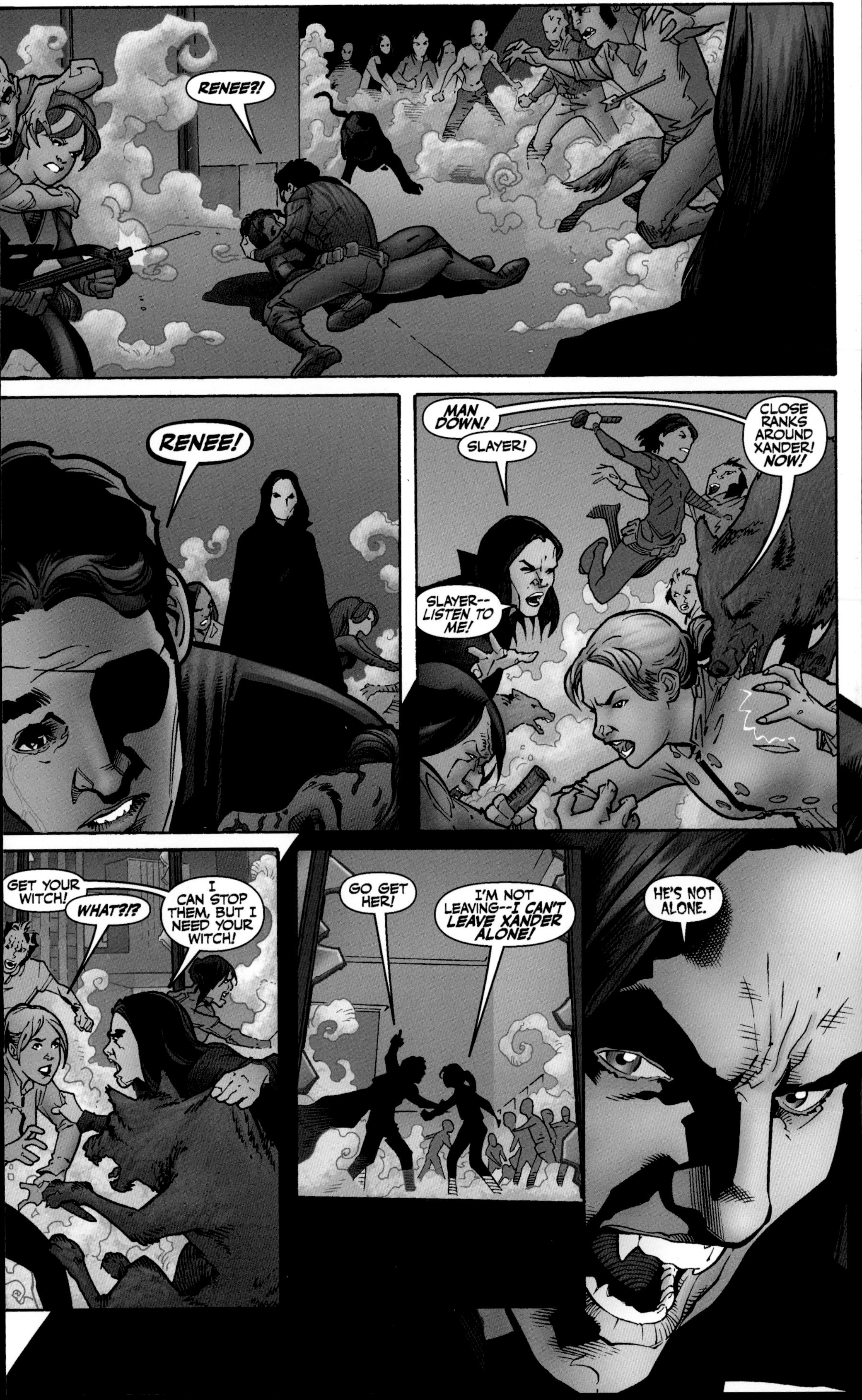
RENEE?!
RENEE!
MAN DOWN!
SLAYER!
CLOSE RANKS AROUND XANDER! NOW!
SLAYER-- LISTEN TO ME!
GET YOUR WITCH!
WHAT?!?
I CAN STOP THEM, BUT I NEED YOUR WITCH!
GO GET HER!
I'M NOT LEAVING--I CAN'T LEAVE XANDER ALONE!
HE'S NOT ALONE.

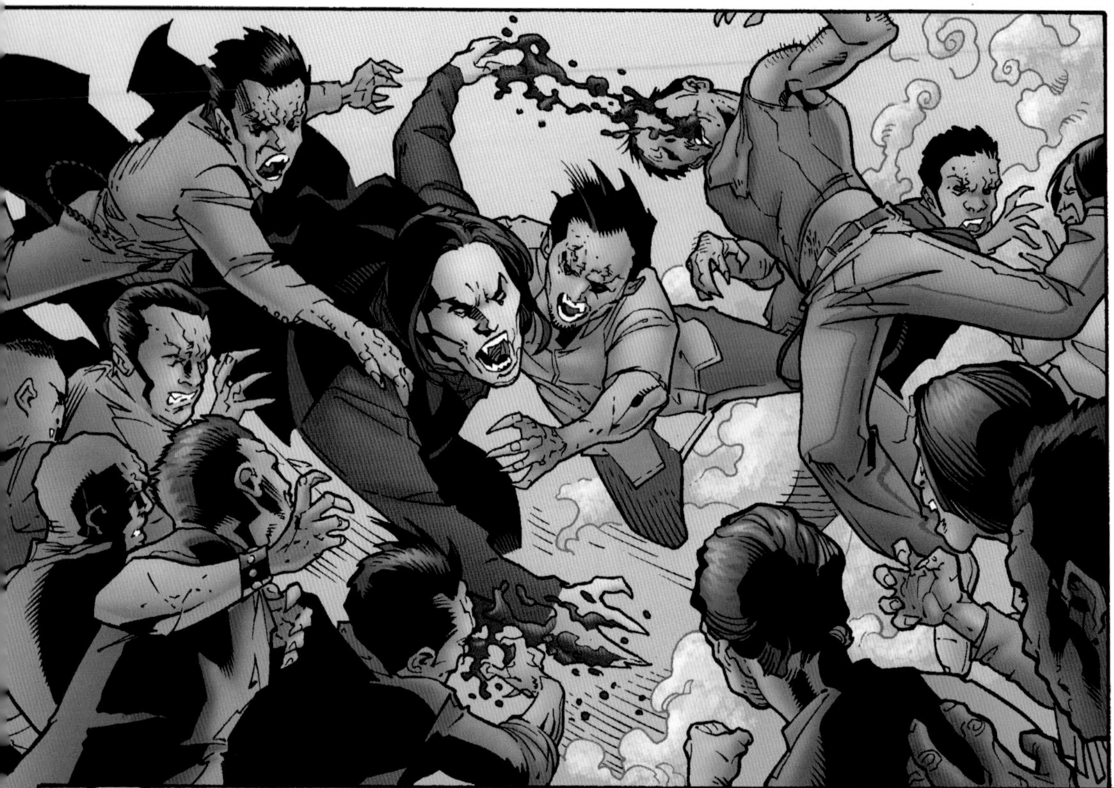

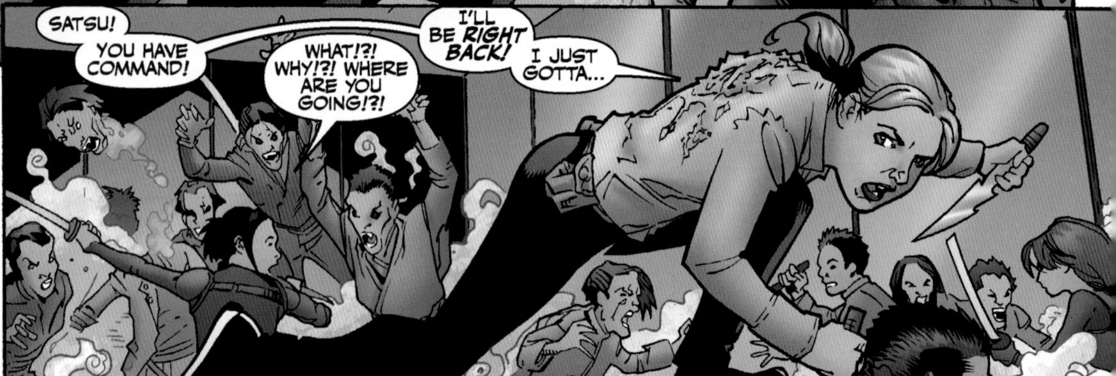
SATSU!
YOU HAVE COMMAND!
WHAT!?! WHY!?! WHERE ARE YOU GOING!?!
I'LL BE RIGHT BACK!
I JUST GOTTA...

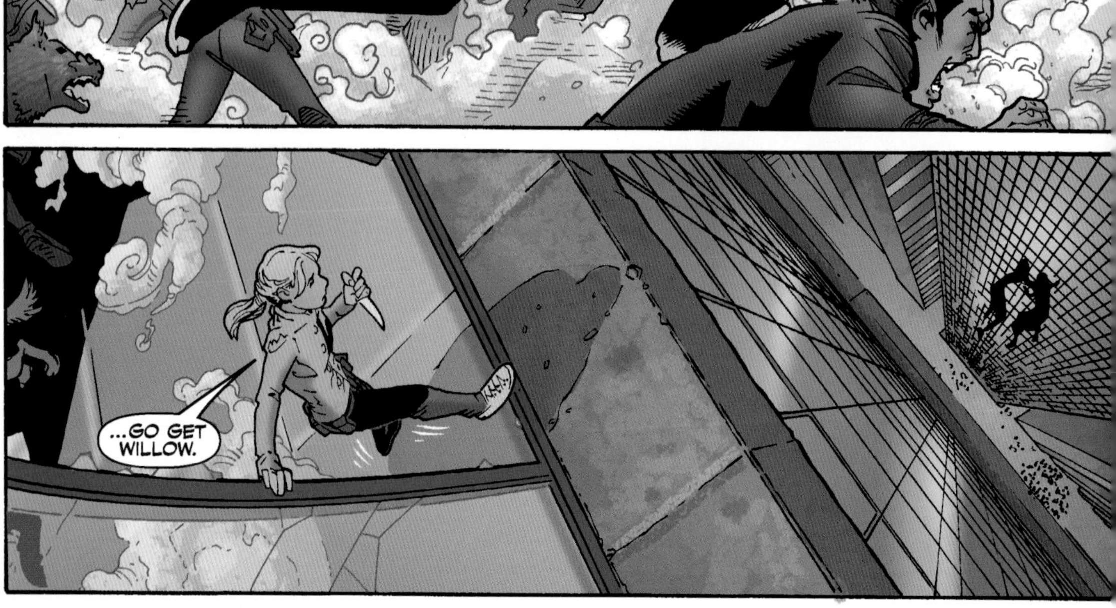
...GO GET WILLOW.

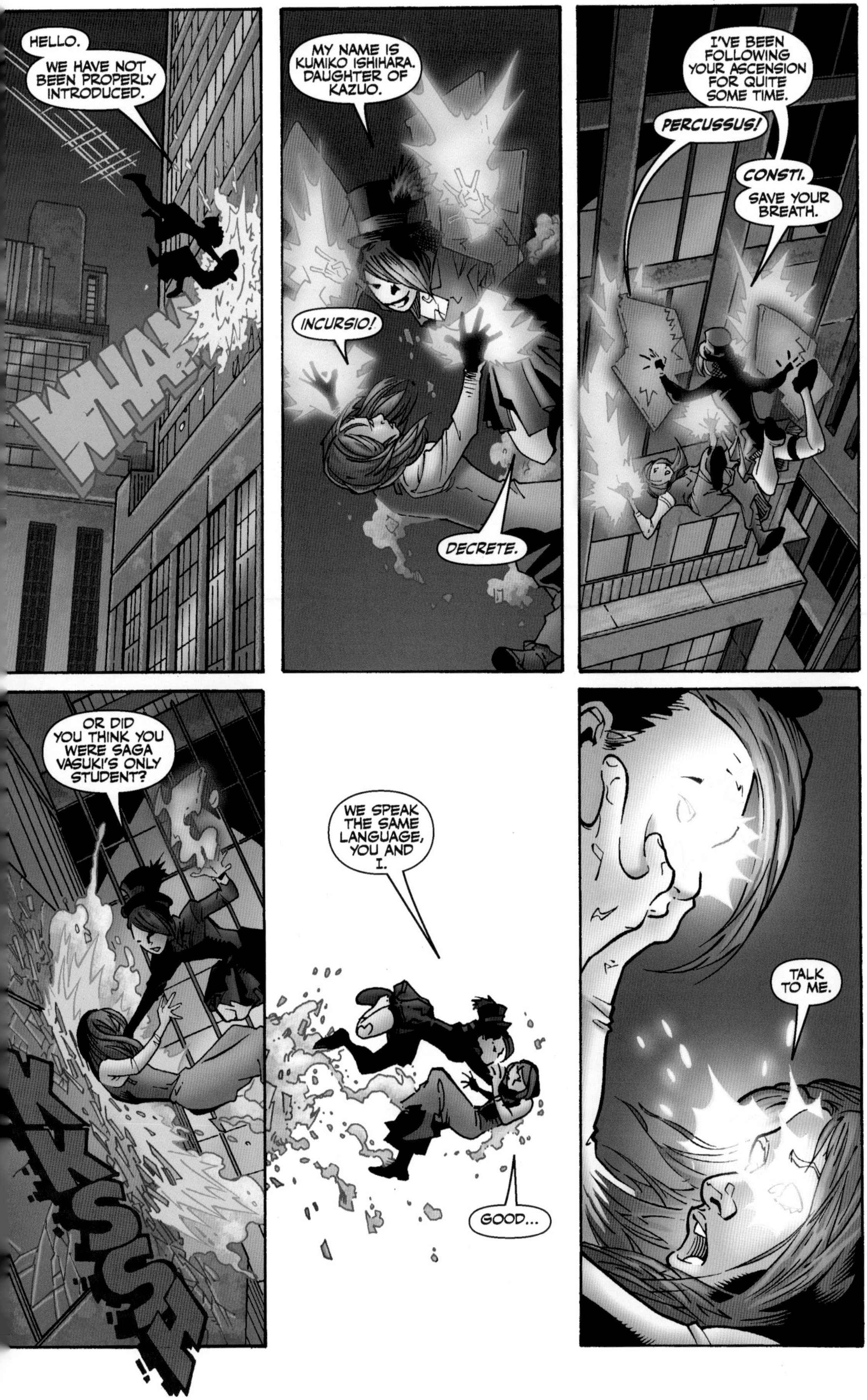
HELLO.
WE HAVE NOT BEEN PROPERLY INTRODUCED.
WHAM
MY NAME IS KUMIKO ISHIHARA. DAUGHTER OF KAZUO.
INCURSIO!
DECRETE.
I'VE BEEN FOLLOWING YOUR ASCENSION FOR QUITE SOME TIME.
PERCUSSUS!
CONSTI.
SAVE YOUR BREATH.
OR DID YOU THINK YOU WERE SAGA VASUKI'S ONLY STUDENT?
KSSSH
WE SPEAK THE SAME LANGUAGE, YOU AND I.
GOOD...
TALK TO ME.

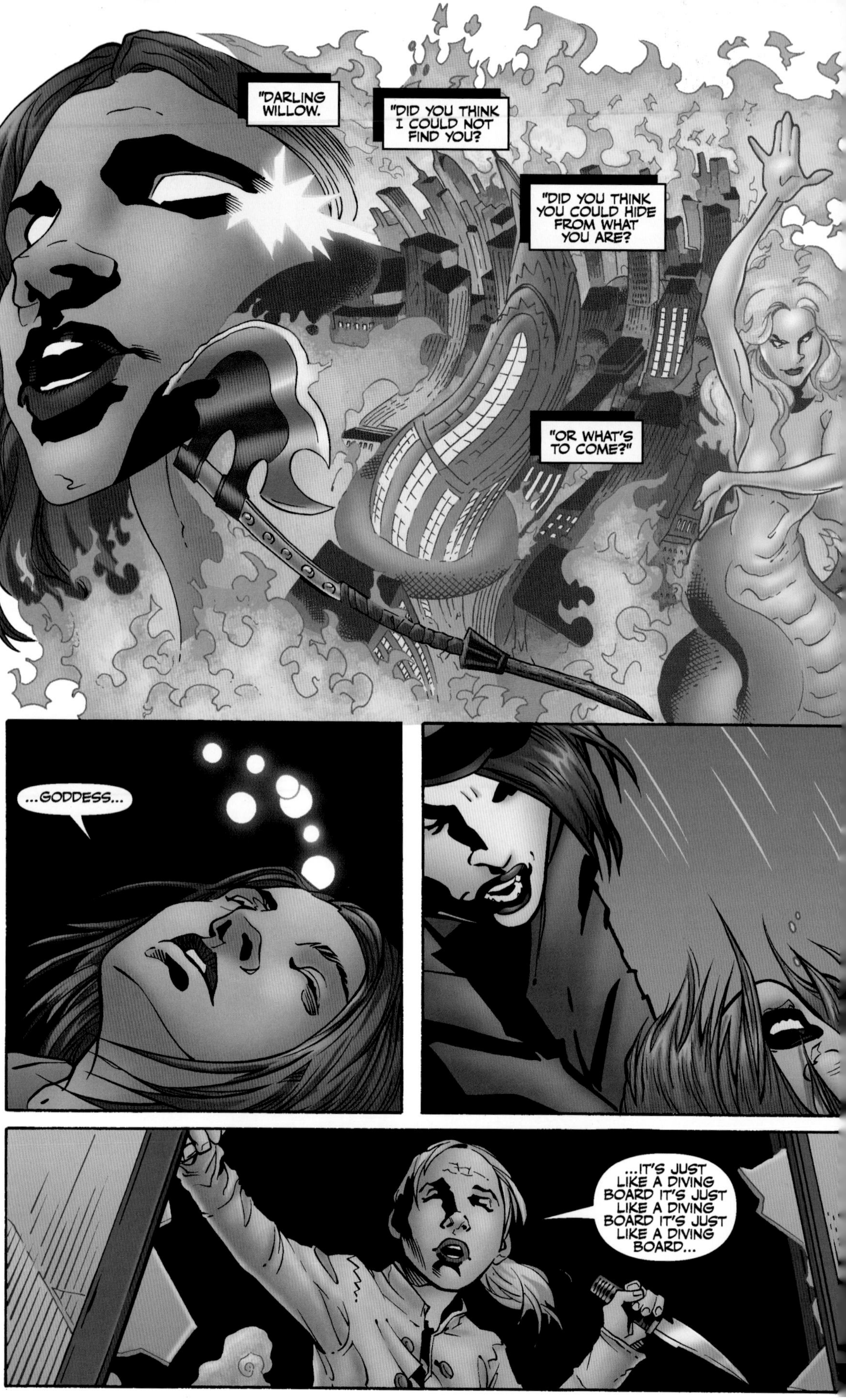
"DARLING WILLOW.
"DID YOU THINK I COULD NOT FIND YOU?
"DID YOU THINK YOU COULD HIDE FROM WHAT YOU ARE?
"OR WHAT'S TO COME?"
...GODDESS...
...IT'S JUST LIKE A DIVING BOARD IT'S JUST LIKE A DIVING BOARD IT'S JUST LIKE A DIVING BOARD...

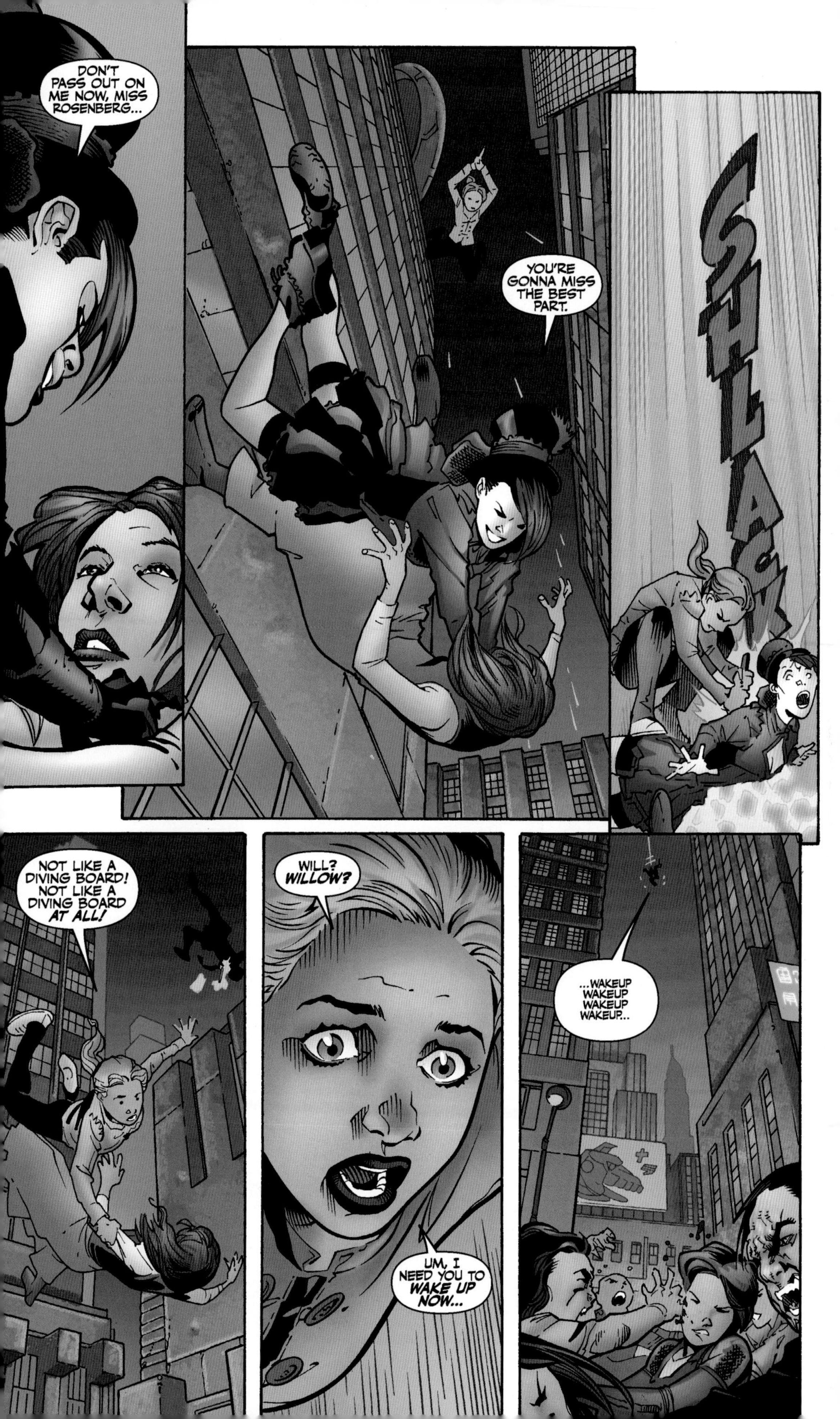
DON'T PASS OUT ON ME NOW, MISS ROSENBERG...
YOU'RE GONNA MISS THE BEST PART.
SHLACK
NOT LIKE A DIVING BOARD! NOT LIKE A DIVING BOARD AT ALL!
WILL? WILLOW?
UM, I NEED YOU TO WAKE UP NOW...
...WAKEUP WAKEUP WAKEUP WAKEUP...

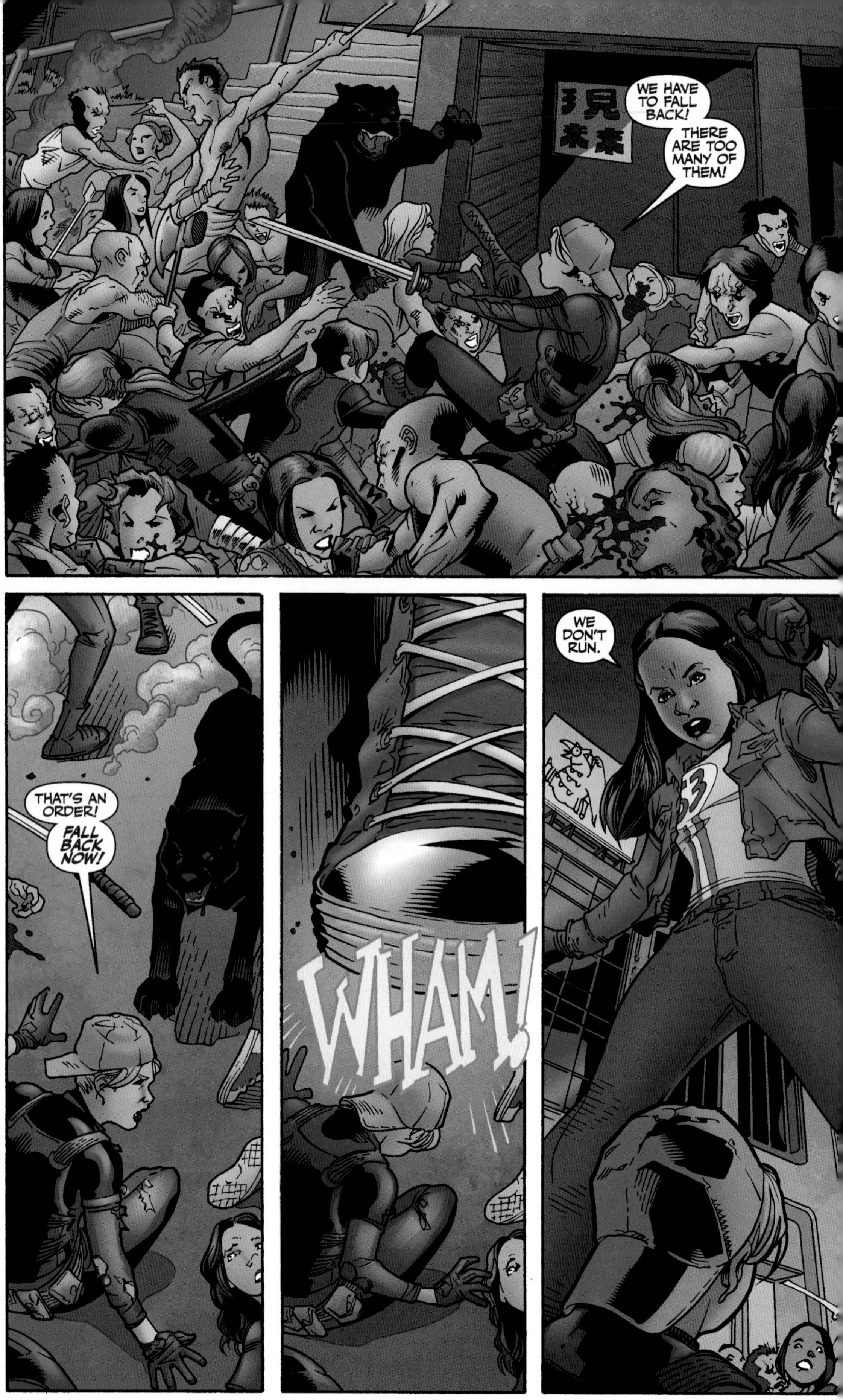
WE HAVE TO FALL BACK!
THERE ARE TOO MANY OF THEM!
THAT'S AN ORDER!
FALL BACK NOW!
WHAM!
WE DON'T RUN.

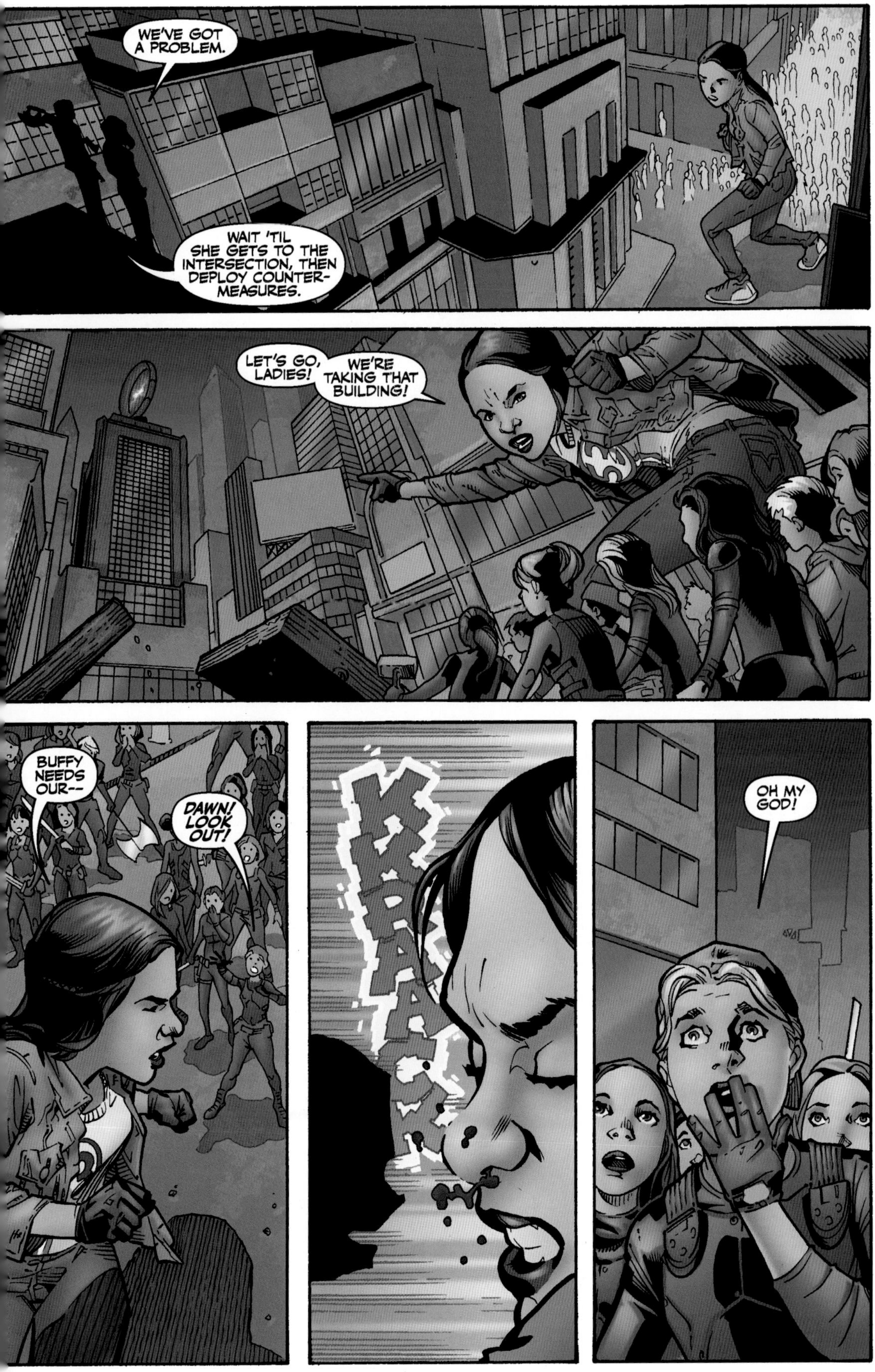
WE'VE GOT A PROBLEM.
WAIT 'TIL SHE GETS TO THE INTERSECTION, THEN DEPLOY COUNTER-MEASURES.
LET'S GO, LADIES!
WE'RE TAKING THAT BUILDING!
BUFFY NEEDS OUR--
DAWN! LOOK OUT!
OH MY GOD!

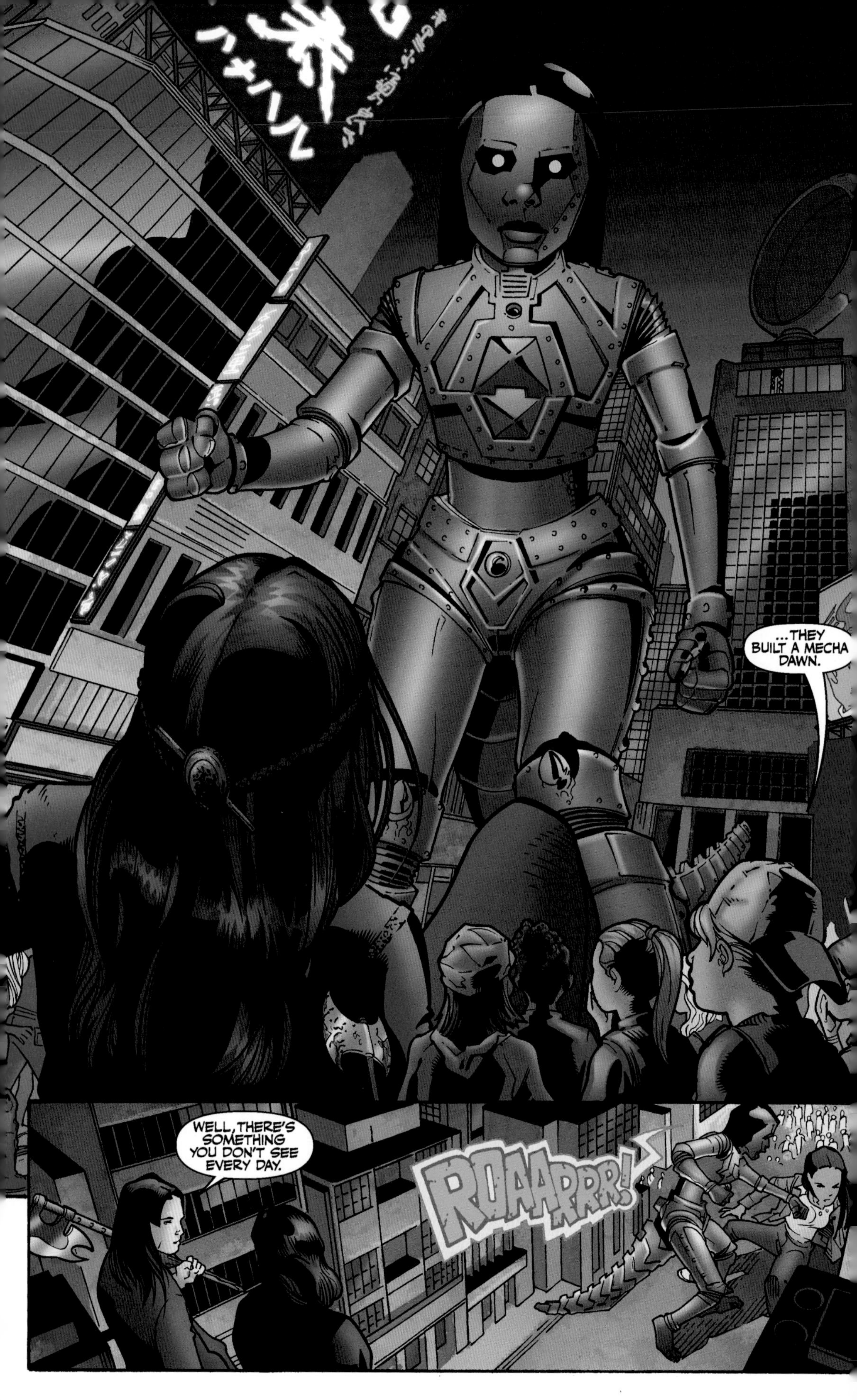
...THEY BUILT A MECHA DAWN.
WELL, THERE'S SOMETHING YOU DON'T SEE EVERY DAY.
ROAAARRR!

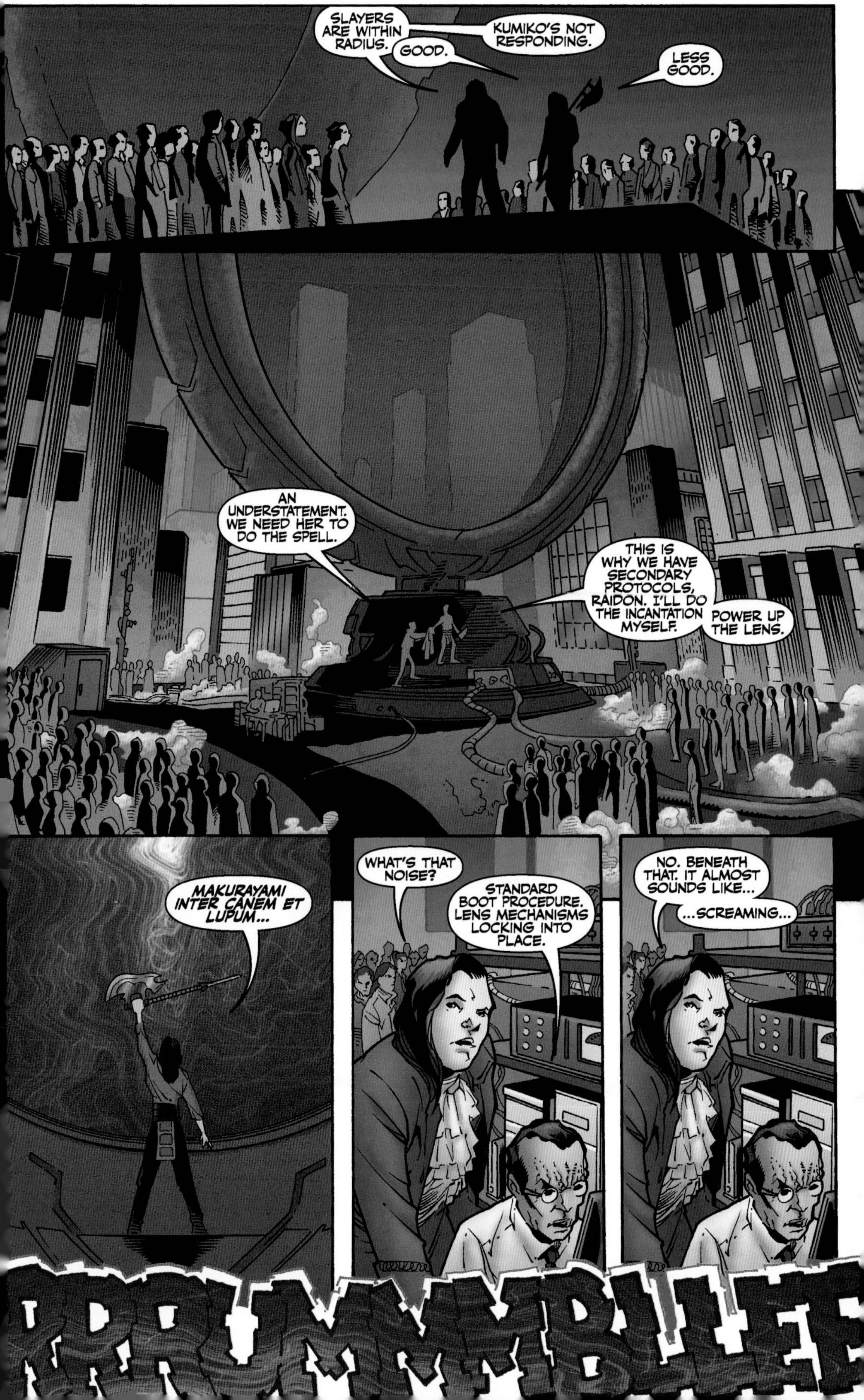
SLAYERS ARE WITHIN RADIUS.
GOOD.
KUMIKO'S NOT RESPONDING.
LESS GOOD.
AN UNDERSTATEMENT. WE NEED HER TO DO THE SPELL.
THIS IS WHY WE HAVE SECONDARY PROTOCOLS, RAIDON. I'LL DO THE INCANTATION MYSELF.
POWER UP THE LENS.
MAKURAYAMI INTER CANEM ET LUPUM...
WHAT'S THAT NOISE?
STANDARD BOOT PROCEDURE. LENS MECHANISMS LOCKING INTO PLACE.
NO. BENEATH THAT. IT ALMOST SOUNDS LIKE...
...SCREAMING...

GET THE SCYTHE!

ON IT!

OH HELL.

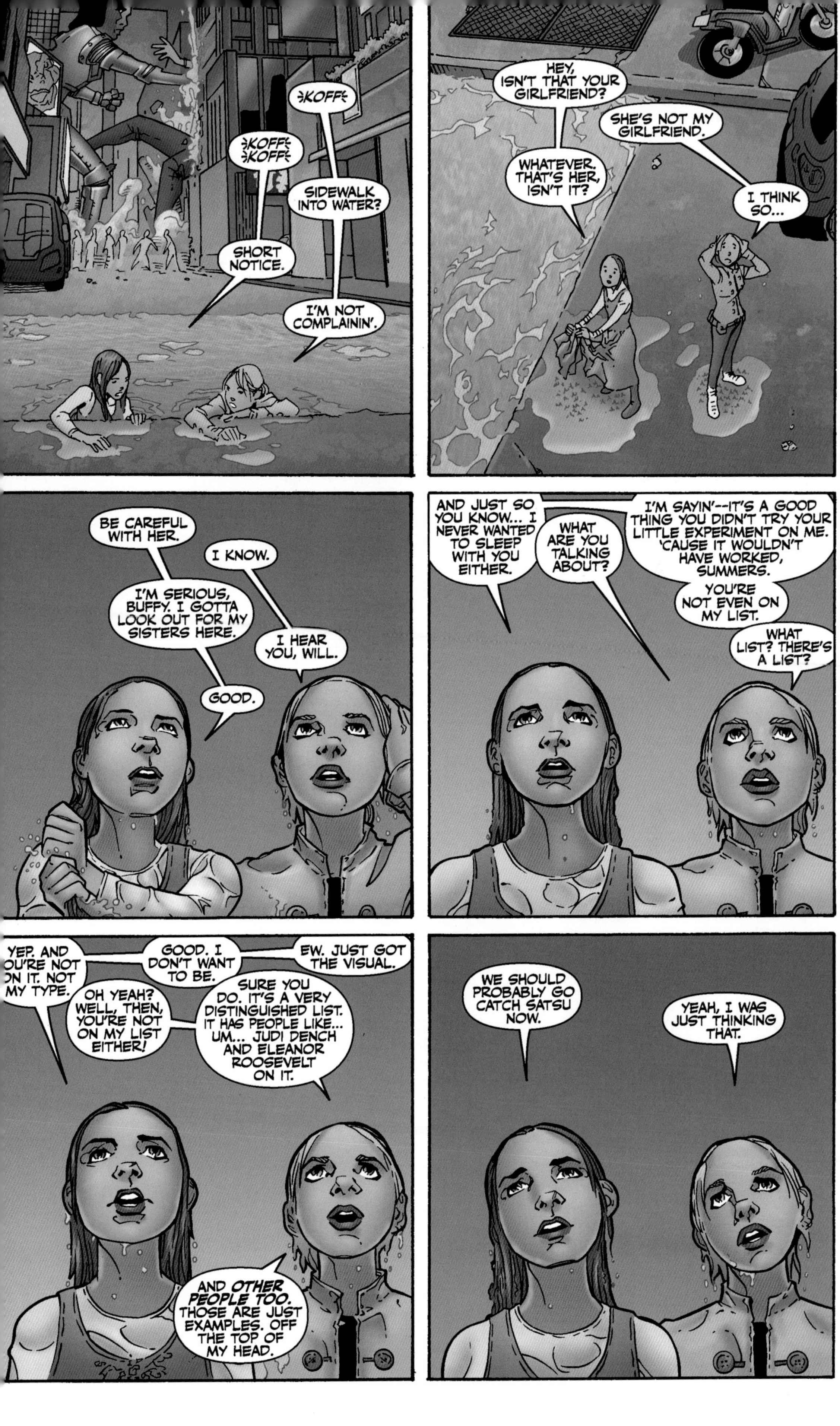

KOFF
KOFF *KOFF*
SIDEWALK INTO WATER?
SHORT NOTICE.
I'M NOT COMPLAININ'.
HEY, ISN'T THAT YOUR GIRLFRIEND?
WHATEVER. THAT'S HER, ISN'T IT?
SHE'S NOT MY GIRLFRIEND.
I THINK SO...
BE CAREFUL WITH HER.
I KNOW.
I'M SERIOUS, BUFFY. I GOTTA LOOK OUT FOR MY SISTERS HERE.
I HEAR YOU, WILL.
GOOD.
AND JUST SO YOU KNOW... I NEVER WANTED TO SLEEP WITH YOU EITHER.
WHAT ARE YOU TALKING ABOUT?
I'M SAYIN'--IT'S A GOOD THING YOU DIDN'T TRY YOUR LITTLE EXPERIMENT ON ME. 'CAUSE IT WOULDN'T HAVE WORKED, SUMMERS.
YOU'RE NOT EVEN ON MY LIST.
WHAT LIST? THERE'S A LIST?
YEP. AND OU'RE NOT N IT. NOT MY TYPE.
OH YEAH? WELL, THEN, YOU'RE NOT ON MY LIST EITHER!
GOOD. I DON'T WANT TO BE.
SURE YOU DO. IT'S A VERY DISTINGUISHED LIST. IT HAS PEOPLE LIKE... UM... JUDI DENCH AND ELEANOR ROOSEVELT ON IT.
EW. JUST GOT THE VISUAL.
AND *OTHER PEOPLE TOO.* THOSE ARE JUST EXAMPLES. OFF THE TOP OF MY HEAD.
WE SHOULD PROBABLY GO CATCH SATSU NOW.
YEAH, I WAS JUST THINKING THAT.

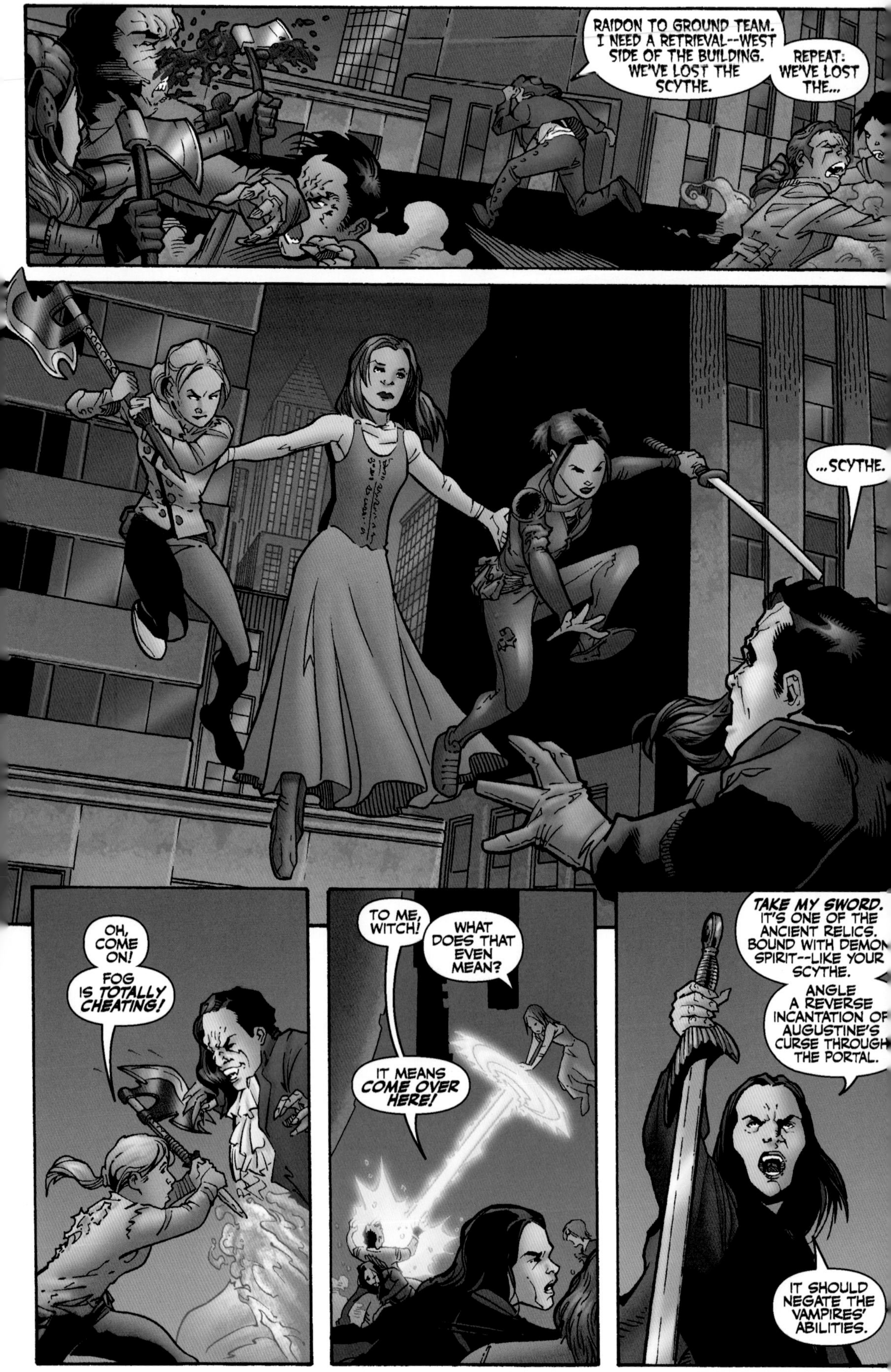
RAIDON TO GROUND TEAM. I NEED A RETRIEVAL--WEST SIDE OF THE BUILDING. WE'VE LOST THE SCYTHE.
REPEAT: WE'VE LOST THE...
...SCYTHE.
OH, COME ON! FOG IS *TOTALLY CHEATING!*
TO ME, WITCH!
WHAT DOES THAT EVEN MEAN?
IT MEANS *COME OVER HERE!*
TAKE MY SWORD. IT'S ONE OF THE ANCIENT RELICS. BOUND WITH DEMON SPIRIT--LIKE YOUR SCYTHE.
ANGLE A REVERSE INCANTATION OF AUGUSTINE'S CURSE THROUGH THE PORTAL.
IT SHOULD NEGATE THE VAMPIRES' ABILITIES.

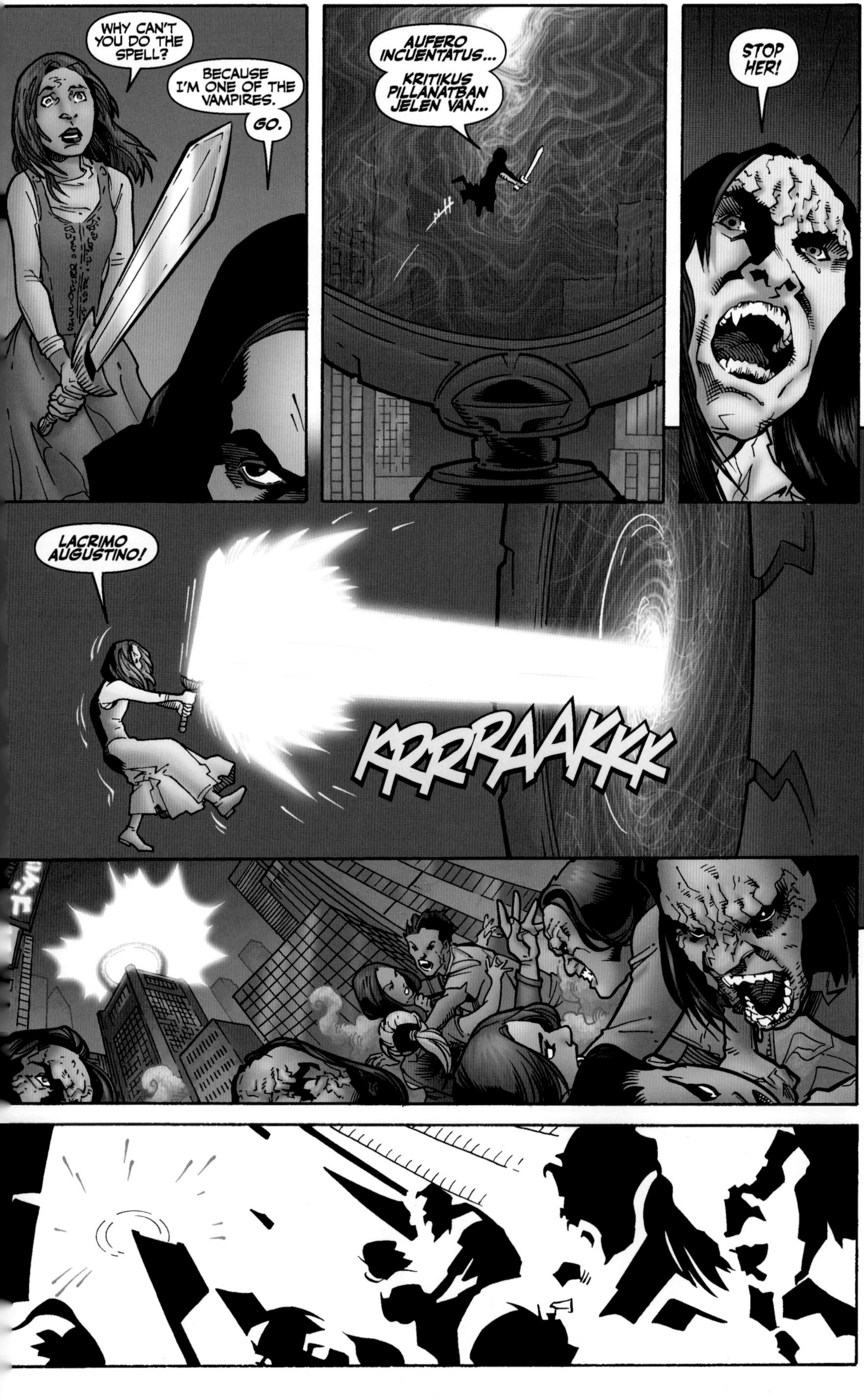
WHY CAN'T YOU DO THE SPELL?
BECAUSE I'M ONE OF THE VAMPIRES.
GO.
AUFERO INCUENTATUS... KRITIKUS PILLANATBAN JELEN VAN...
STOP HER!
LACRIMO AUGUSTINO!
KRRRAAKKK

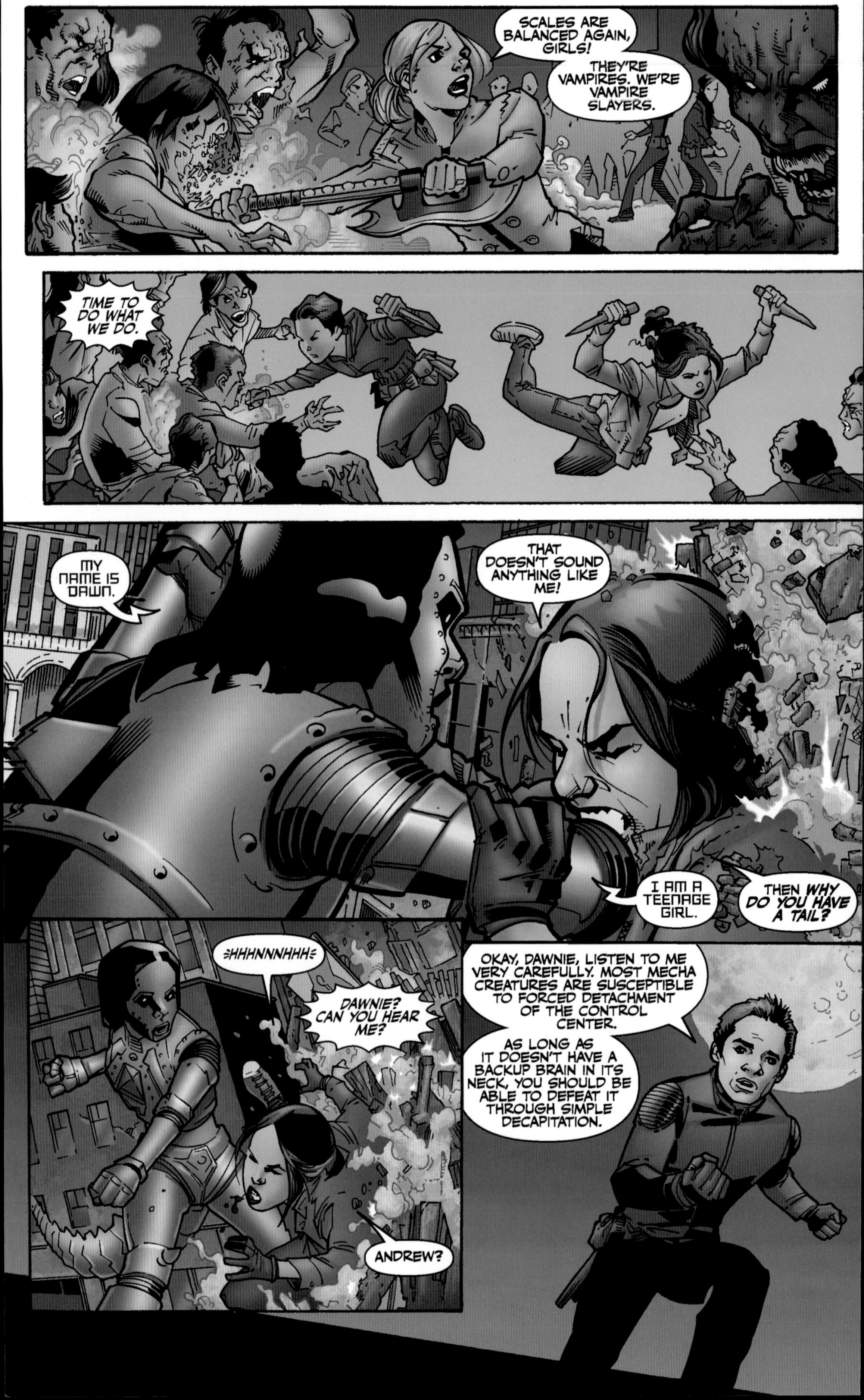
SCALES ARE BALANCED AGAIN, GIRLS!
THEY'RE VAMPIRES. WE'RE VAMPIRE SLAYERS.
TIME TO DO WHAT WE DO.
MY NAME IS DAWN.
THAT DOESN'T SOUND ANYTHING LIKE ME!
I AM A TEENAGE GIRL.
THEN WHY DO YOU HAVE A TAIL?
HHHHNNNHHH
DAWNIE? CAN YOU HEAR ME?
ANDREW?
OKAY, DAWNIE, LISTEN TO ME VERY CAREFULLY. MOST MECHA CREATURES ARE SUSCEPTIBLE TO FORCED DETACHMENT OF THE CONTROL CENTER.
AS LONG AS IT DOESN'T HAVE A BACKUP BRAIN IN ITS NECK, YOU SHOULD BE ABLE TO DEFEAT IT THROUGH SIMPLE DECAPITATION.

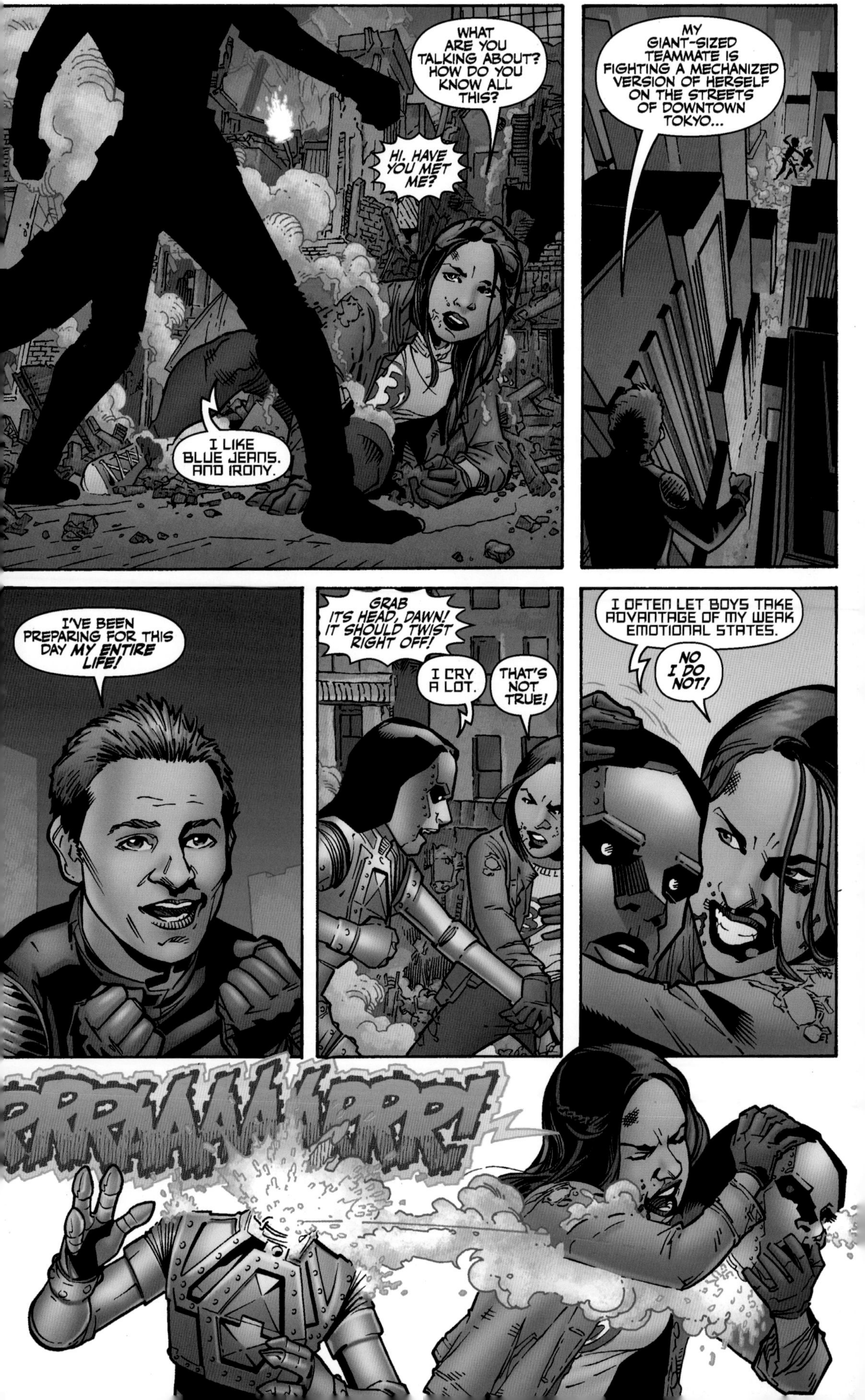
WHAT ARE YOU TALKING ABOUT? HOW DO YOU KNOW ALL THIS?
HI. HAVE YOU MET ME?
I LIKE BLUE JEANS. AND IRONY.
MY GIANT-SIZED TEAMMATE IS FIGHTING A MECHANIZED VERSION OF HERSELF ON THE STREETS OF DOWNTOWN TOKYO...
I'VE BEEN PREPARING FOR THIS DAY MY ENTIRE LIFE!
GRAB ITS HEAD, DAWN! IT SHOULD TWIST RIGHT OFF!
I CRY A LOT.
THAT'S NOT TRUE!
I OFTEN LET BOYS TAKE ADVANTAGE OF MY WEAK EMOTIONAL STATES.
NO I DO NOT!

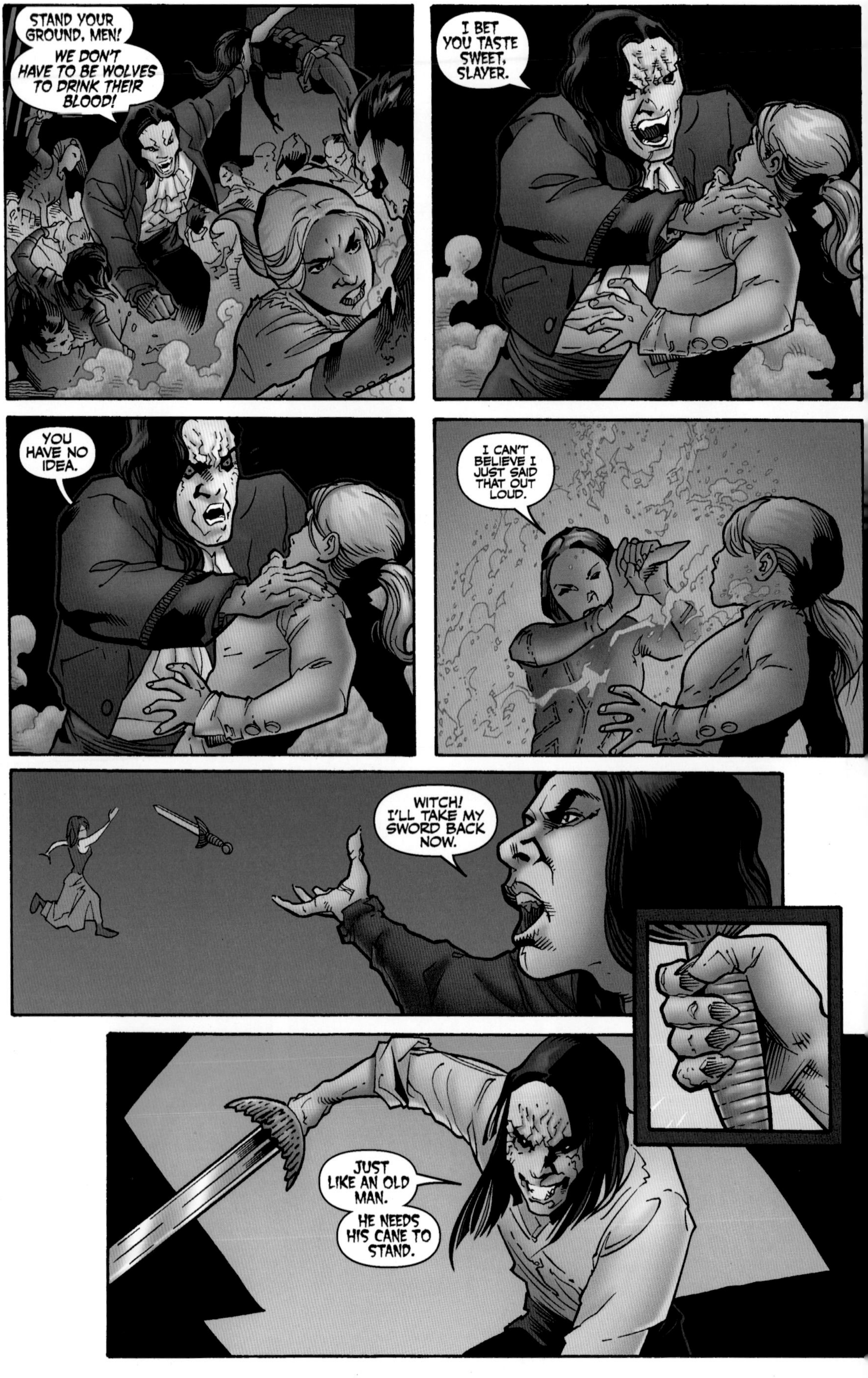
STAND YOUR GROUND, MEN!
WE DON'T HAVE TO BE WOLVES TO DRINK THEIR BLOOD!
I BET YOU TASTE SWEET, SLAYER.
YOU HAVE NO IDEA.
I CAN'T BELIEVE I JUST SAID THAT OUT LOUD.
WITCH! I'LL TAKE MY SWORD BACK NOW.
JUST LIKE AN OLD MAN.
HE NEEDS HIS CANE TO STAND.

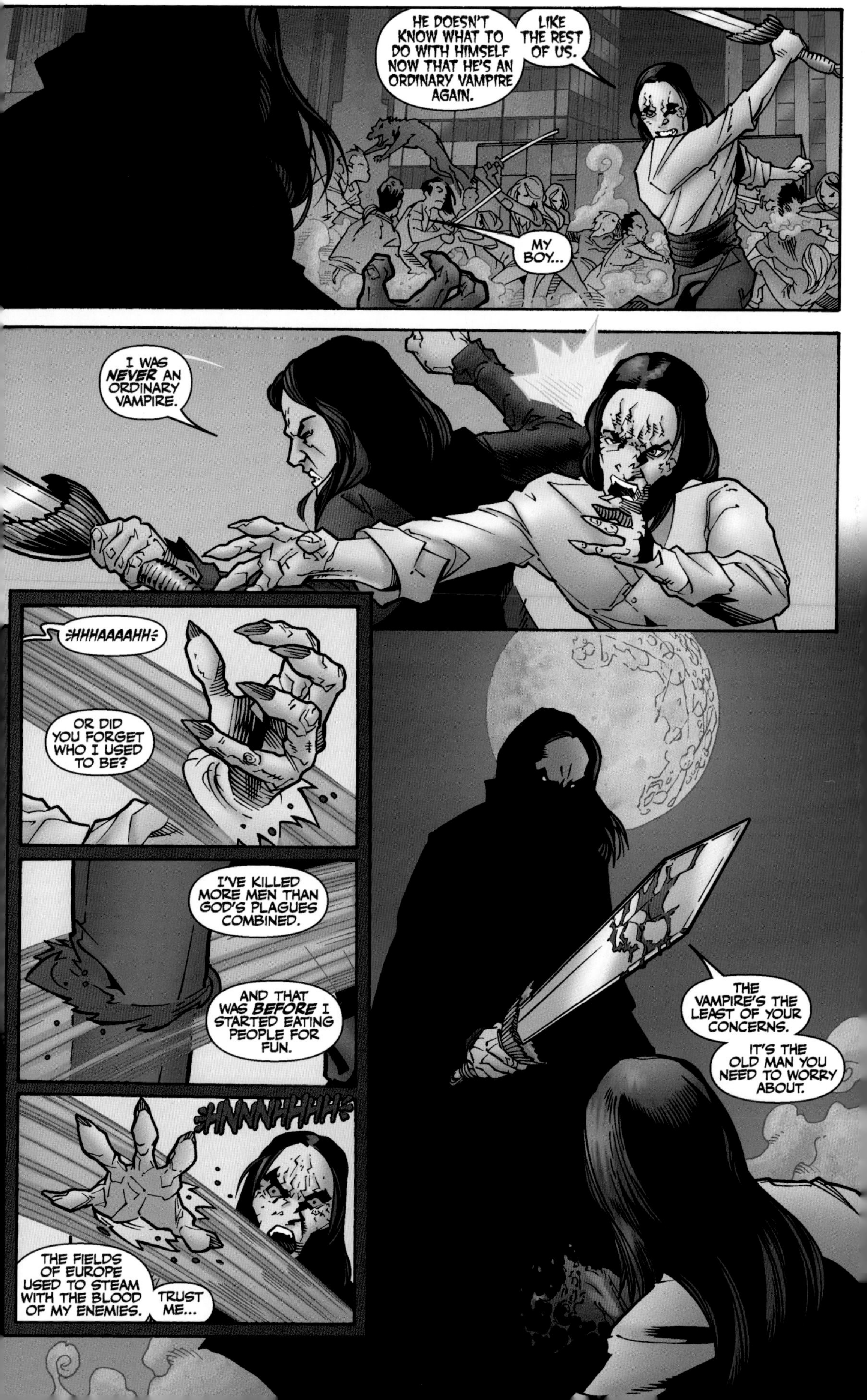
HE DOESN'T KNOW WHAT TO DO WITH HIMSELF NOW THAT HE'S AN ORDINARY VAMPIRE AGAIN.
LIKE THE REST OF US.
MY BOY...
I WAS NEVER AN ORDINARY VAMPIRE.
HHHAAAAAHH
OR DID YOU FORGET WHO I USED TO BE?
I'VE KILLED MORE MEN THAN GOD'S PLAGUES COMBINED.
AND THAT WAS BEFORE I STARTED EATING PEOPLE FOR FUN.
HNNNHHHH
THE FIELDS OF EUROPE USED TO STEAM WITH THE BLOOD OF MY ENEMIES.
TRUST ME...
THE VAMPIRE'S THE LEAST OF YOUR CONCERNS.
IT'S THE OLD MAN YOU NEED TO WORRY ABOUT.

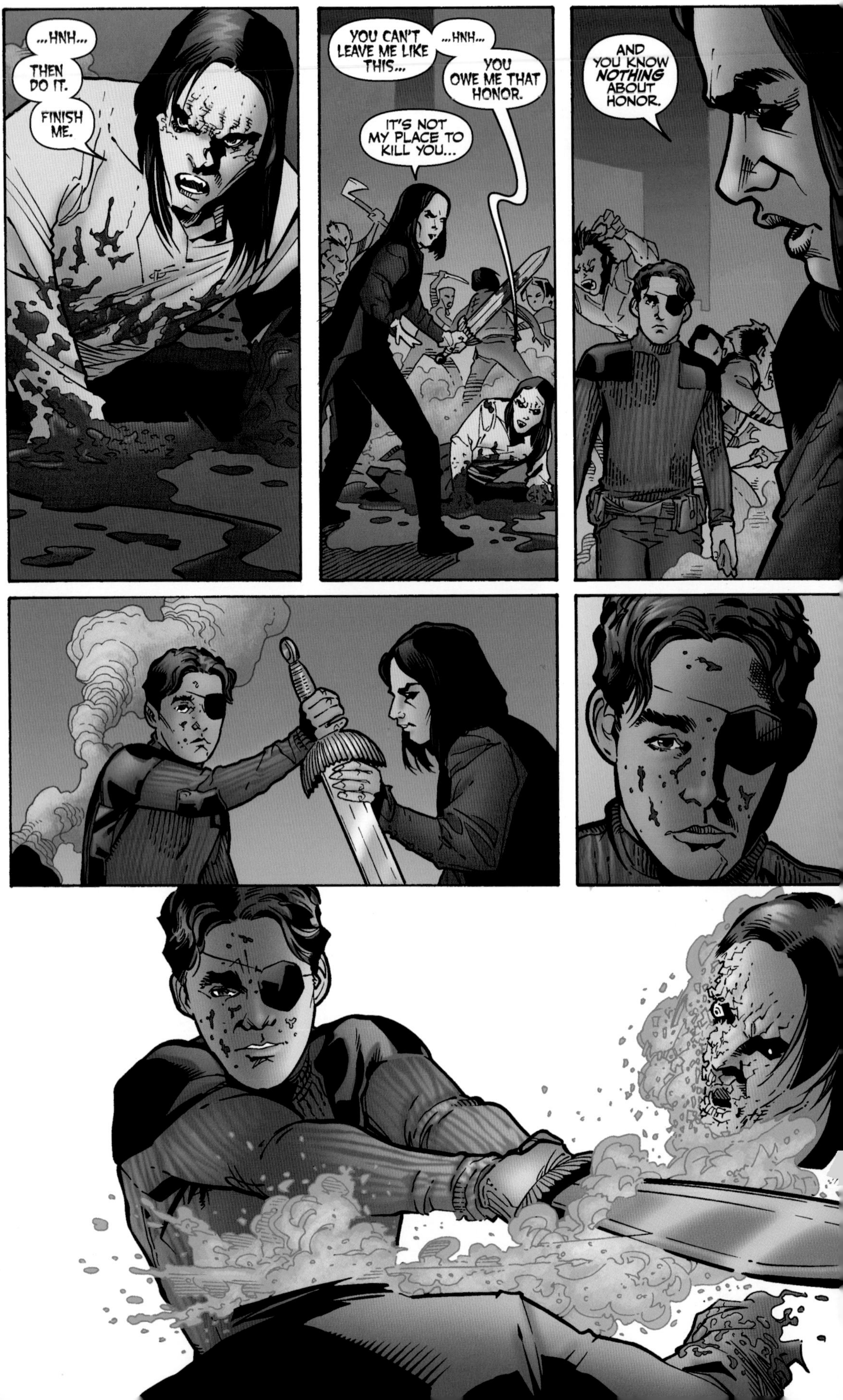
...HNH...
THEN DO IT.
FINISH ME.
YOU CAN'T LEAVE ME LIKE THIS...
...HNH...
YOU OWE ME THAT HONOR.
IT'S NOT MY PLACE TO KILL YOU...
AND YOU KNOW NOTHING ABOUT HONOR.

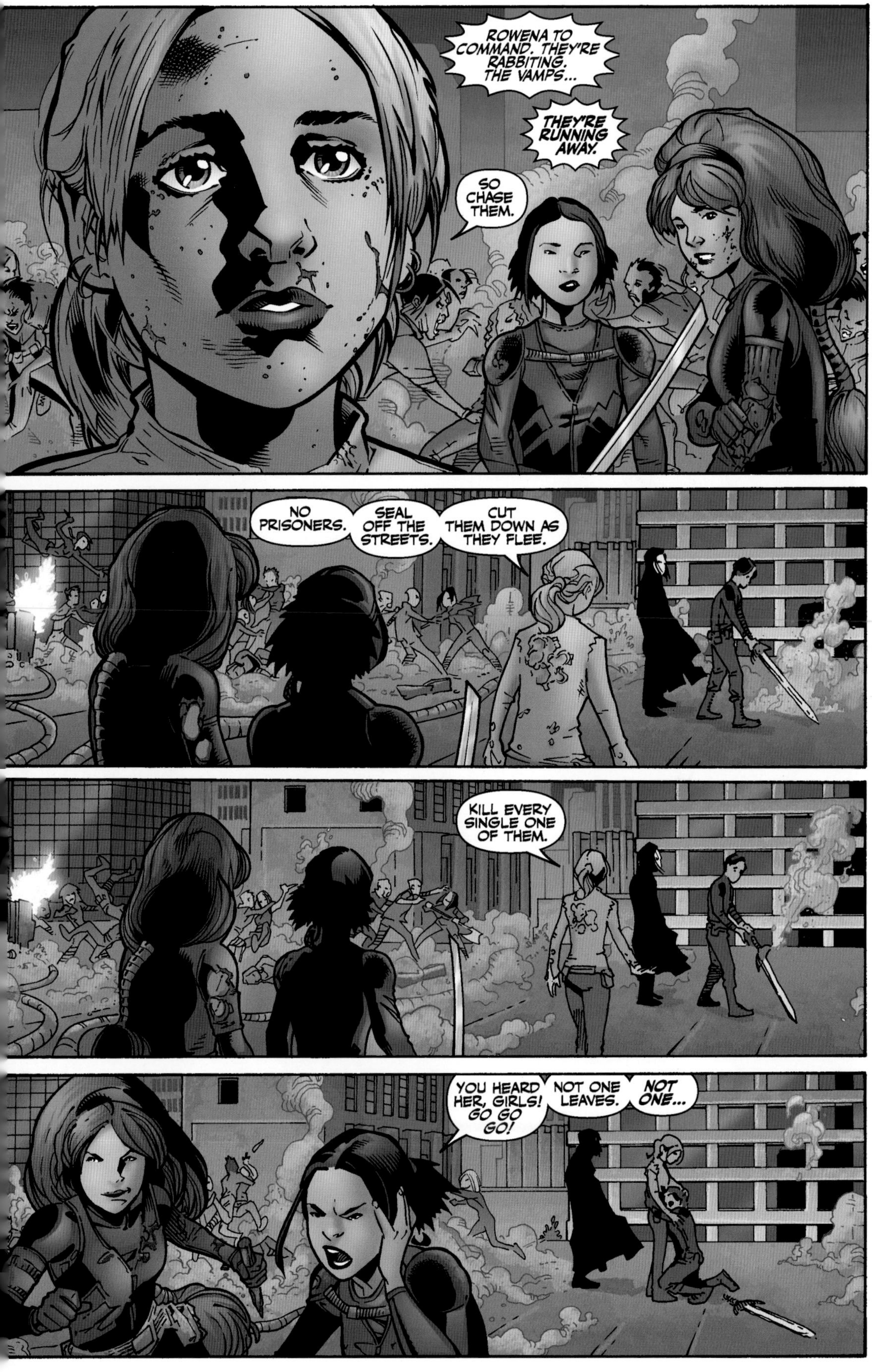
ROWENA TO COMMAND. THEY'RE RABBITING. THE VAMPS...
THEY'RE RUNNING AWAY.
SO CHASE THEM.
NO PRISONERS.
SEAL OFF THE STREETS.
CUT THEM DOWN AS THEY FLEE.
KILL EVERY SINGLE ONE OF THEM.
YOU HEARD HER, GIRLS! GO GO GO!
NOT ONE LEAVES.
NOT ONE...

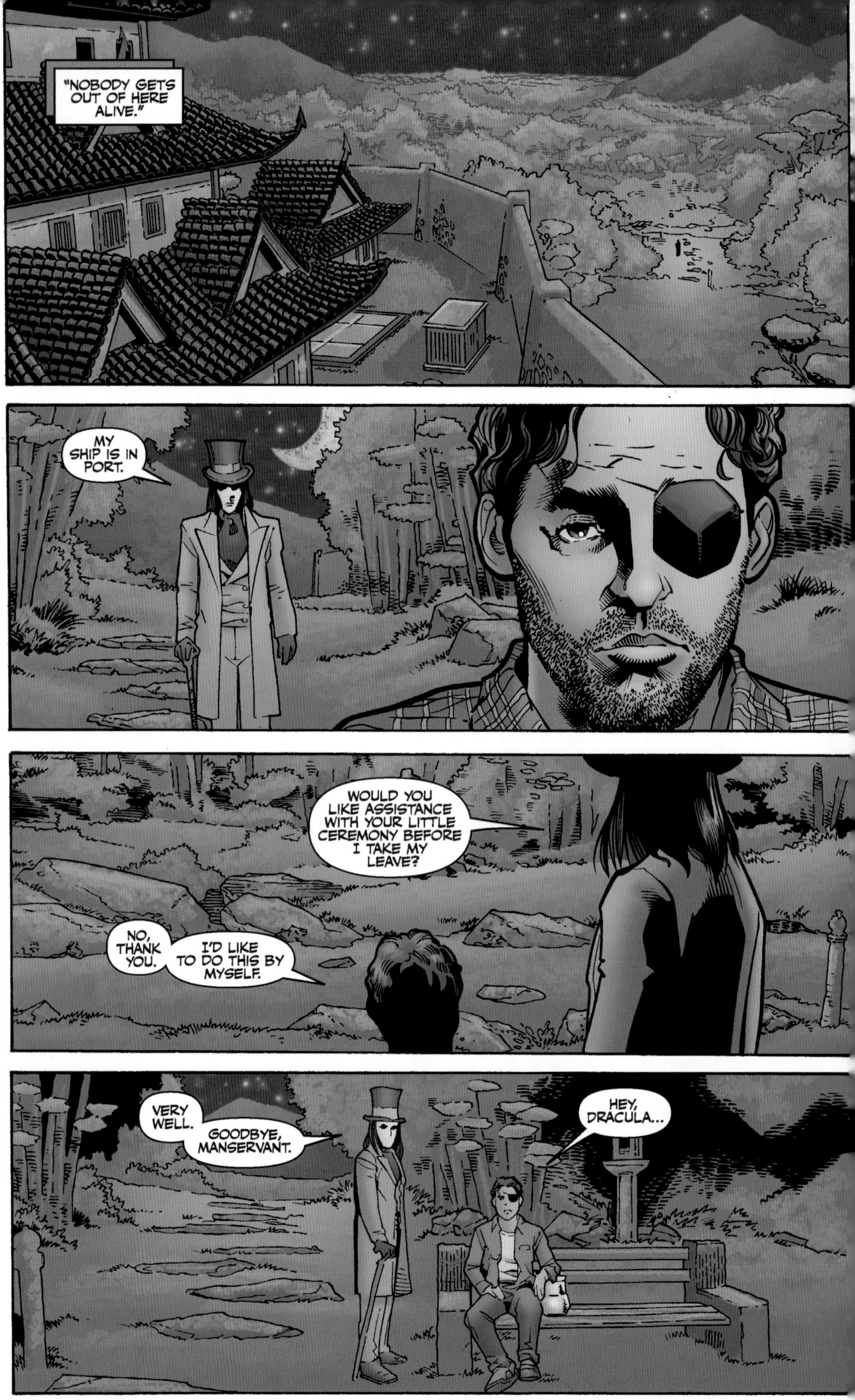
"NOBODY GETS OUT OF HERE ALIVE."
MY SHIP IS IN PORT.
WOULD YOU LIKE ASSISTANCE WITH YOUR LITTLE CEREMONY BEFORE I TAKE MY LEAVE?
NO, THANK YOU.
I'D LIKE TO DO THIS BY MYSELF.
VERY WELL.
GOODBYE, MANSERVANT.
HEY, DRACULA...

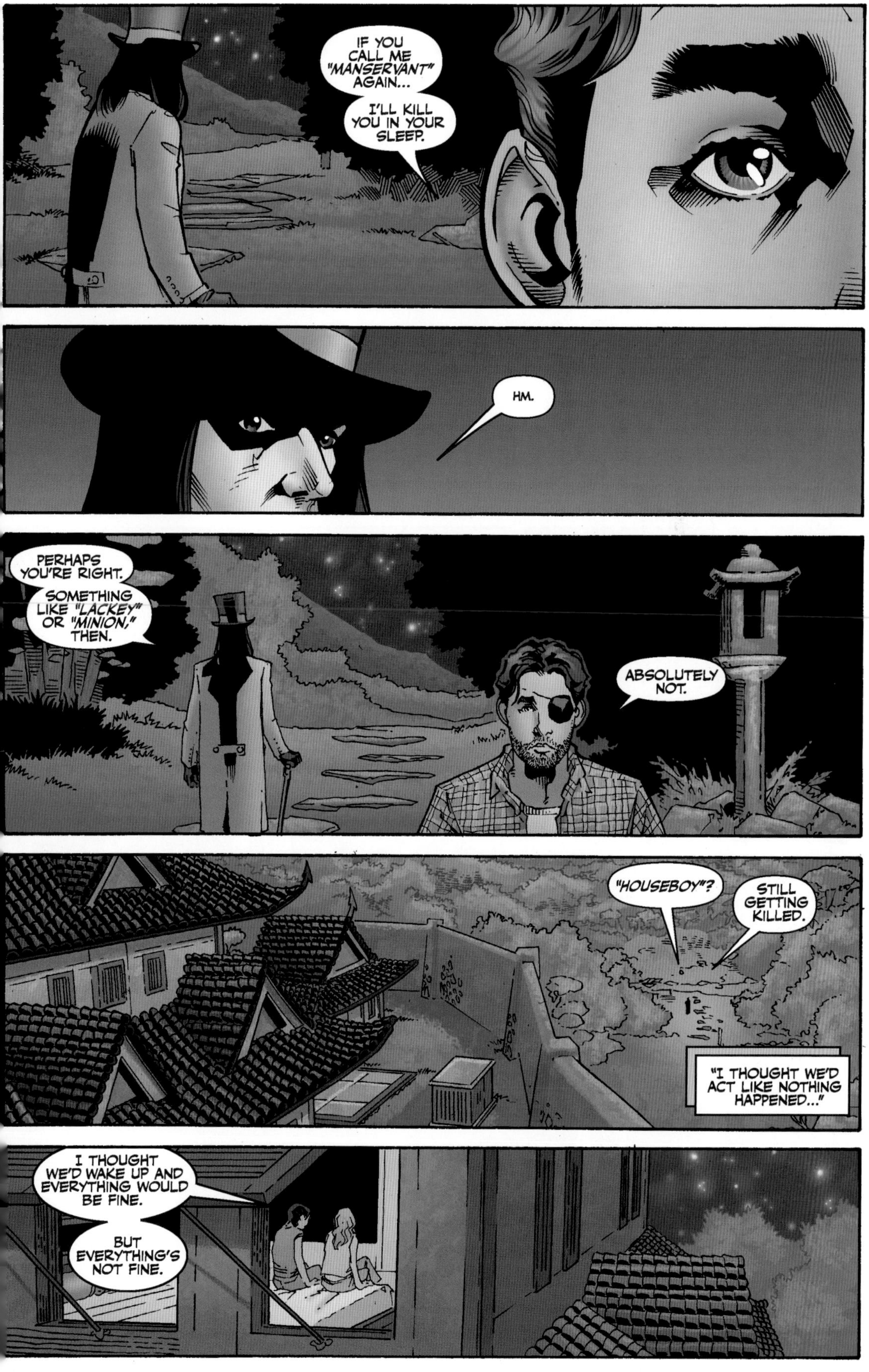
IF YOU CALL ME "MANSERVANT" AGAIN...
I'LL KILL YOU IN YOUR SLEEP.
HM.
PERHAPS YOU'RE RIGHT.
SOMETHING LIKE "LACKEY" OR "MINION," THEN.
ABSOLUTELY NOT.
"HOUSEBOY"?
STILL GETTING KILLED.
"I THOUGHT WE'D ACT LIKE NOTHING HAPPENED..."
I THOUGHT WE'D WAKE UP AND EVERYTHING WOULD BE FINE.
BUT EVERYTHING'S NOT FINE.

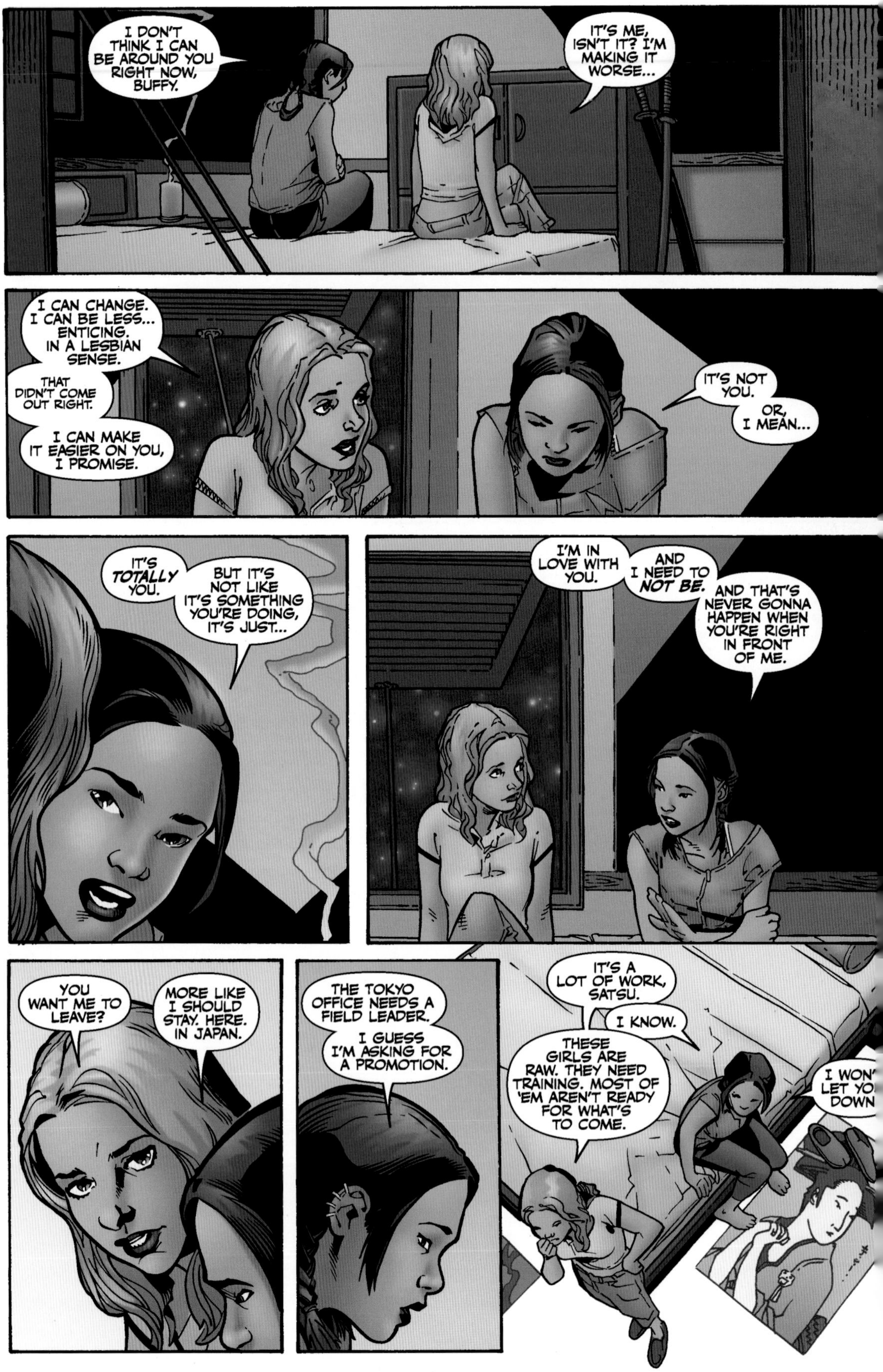
I DON'T THINK I CAN BE AROUND YOU RIGHT NOW, BUFFY.
IT'S ME, ISN'T IT? I'M MAKING IT WORSE...
I CAN CHANGE. I CAN BE LESS... ENTICING. IN A LESBIAN SENSE.
THAT DIDN'T COME OUT RIGHT.
I CAN MAKE IT EASIER ON YOU, I PROMISE.
IT'S NOT YOU.
OR, I MEAN...
IT'S TOTALLY YOU.
BUT IT'S NOT LIKE IT'S SOMETHING YOU'RE DOING, IT'S JUST...
I'M IN LOVE WITH YOU.
AND I NEED TO NOT BE.
AND THAT'S NEVER GONNA HAPPEN WHEN YOU'RE RIGHT IN FRONT OF ME.
YOU WANT ME TO LEAVE?
MORE LIKE I SHOULD STAY. HERE. IN JAPAN.
THE TOKYO OFFICE NEEDS A FIELD LEADER.
I GUESS I'M ASKING FOR A PROMOTION.
IT'S A LOT OF WORK, SATSU.
I KNOW.
THESE GIRLS ARE RAW. THEY NEED TRAINING. MOST OF 'EM AREN'T READY FOR WHAT'S TO COME.
I WON' LET YO DOWN

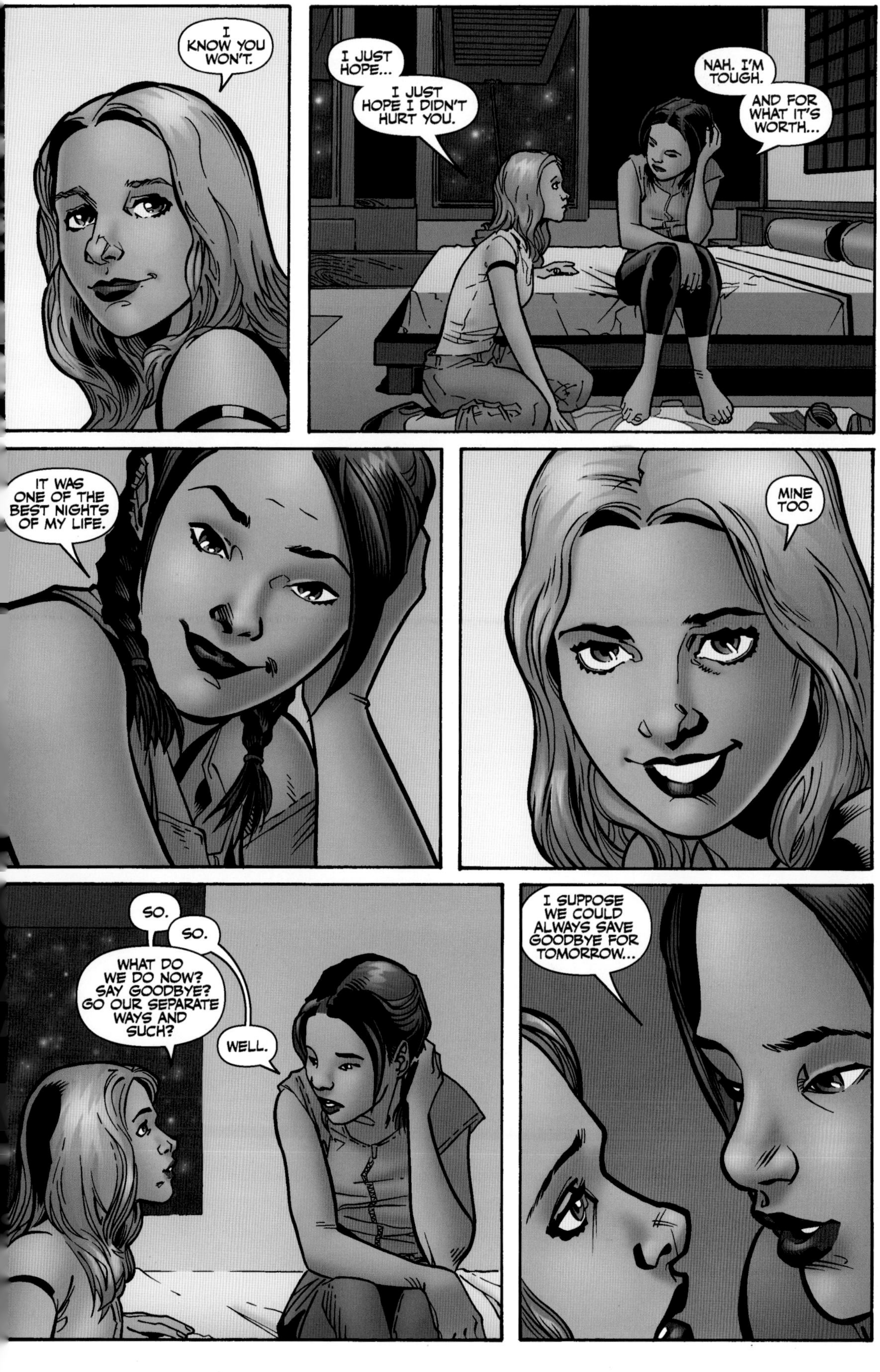
I KNOW YOU WON'T.
I JUST HOPE...
I JUST HOPE I DIDN'T HURT YOU.
NAH. I'M TOUGH.
AND FOR WHAT IT'S WORTH...
IT WAS ONE OF THE BEST NIGHTS OF MY LIFE.
MINE TOO.
SO.
SO.
WHAT DO WE DO NOW? SAY GOODBYE? GO OUR SEPARATE WAYS AND SUCH?
WELL.
I SUPPOSE WE COULD ALWAYS SAVE GOODBYE FOR TOMORROW...

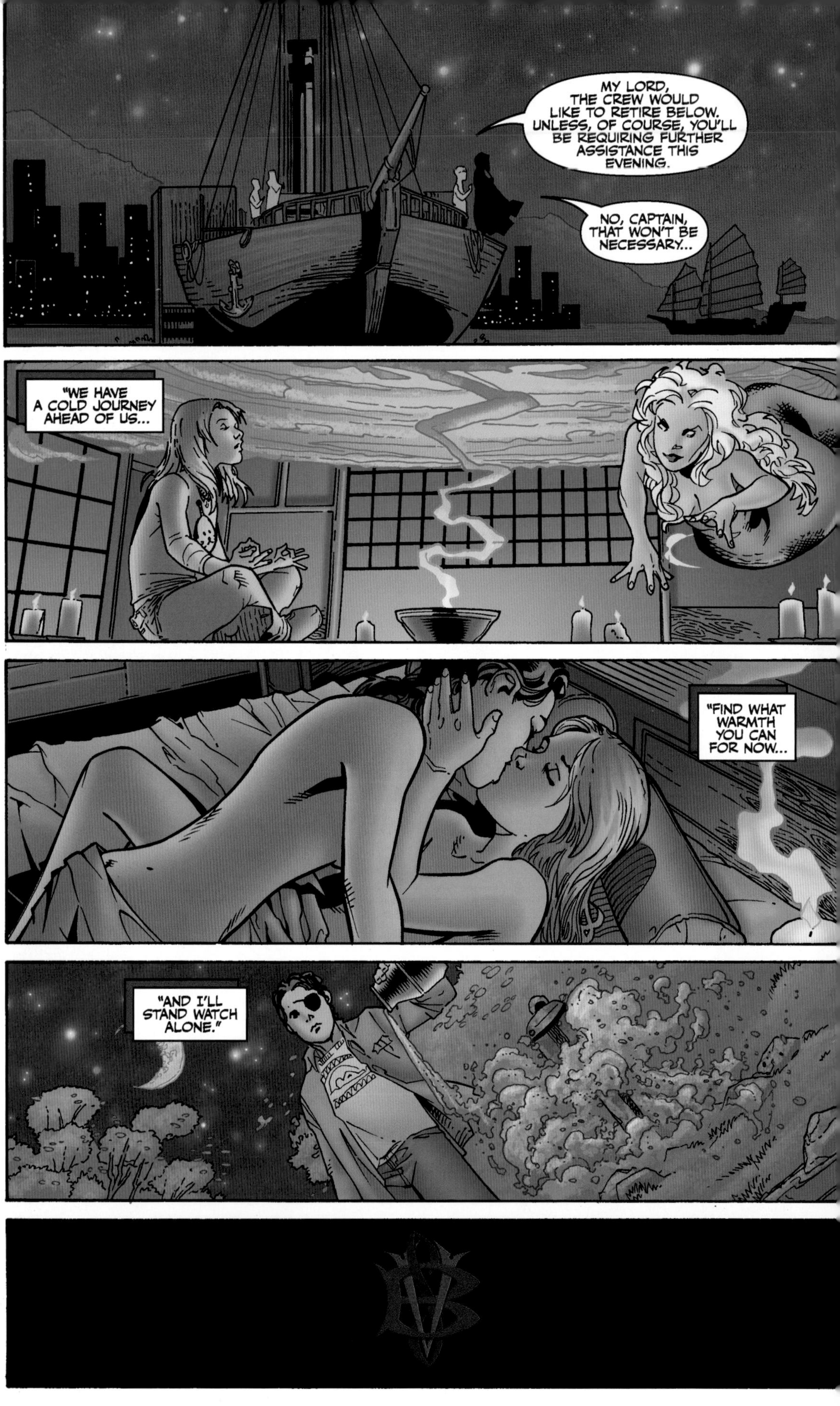
MY LORD, THE CREW WOULD LIKE TO RETIRE BELOW. UNLESS, OF COURSE, YOU'LL BE REQUIRING FURTHER ASSISTANCE THIS EVENING.
NO, CAPTAIN, THAT WON'T BE NECESSARY...
"WE HAVE A COLD JOURNEY AHEAD OF US...
"FIND WHAT WARMTH YOU CAN FOR NOW...
"AND I'LL STAND WATCH ALONE."

COVERS FROM

BUFFY THE VAMPIRE SLAYER

ISSUES #11–14

By

GEORGES JEANTY

with

DEXTER VINES
& MICHELLE MADSEN

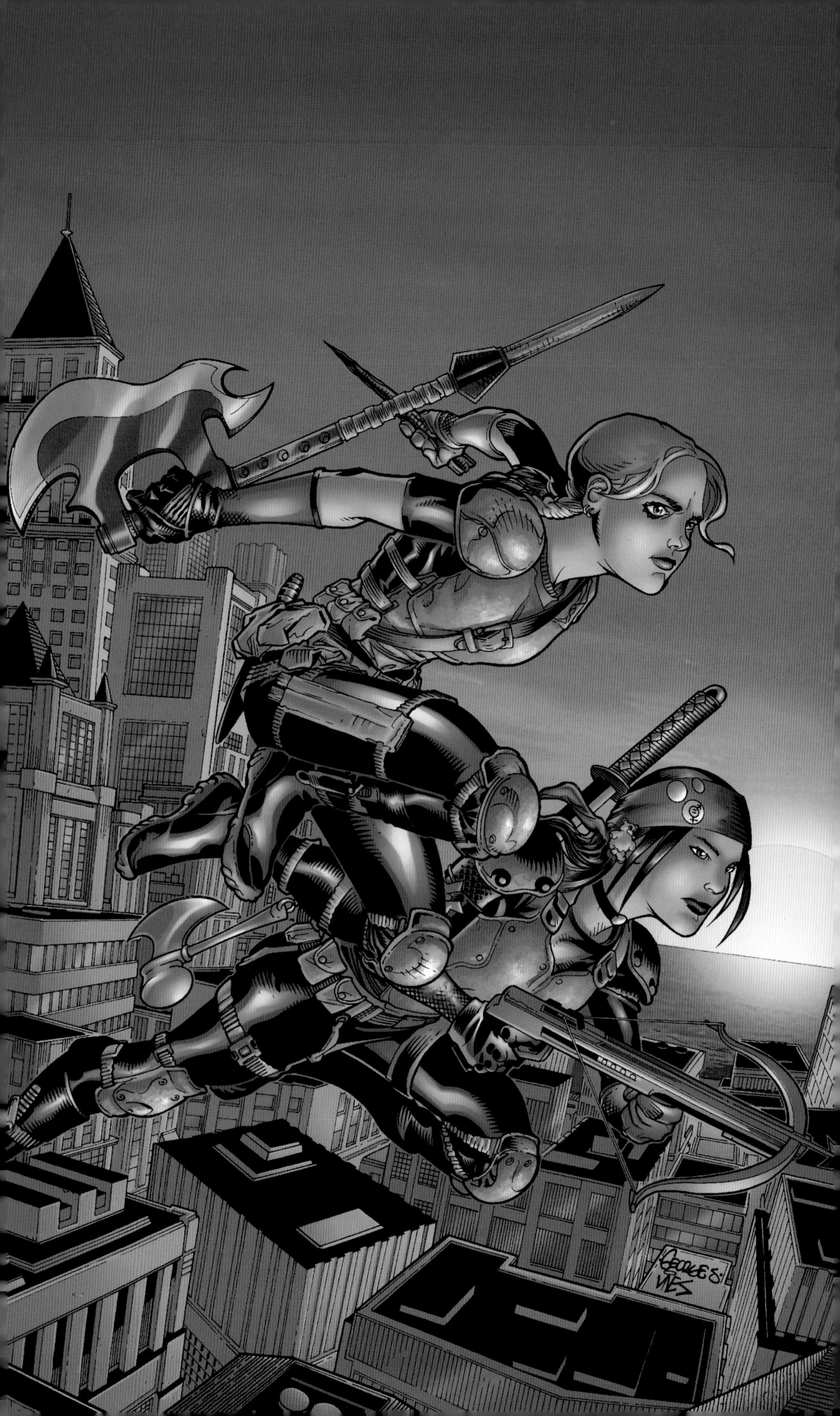

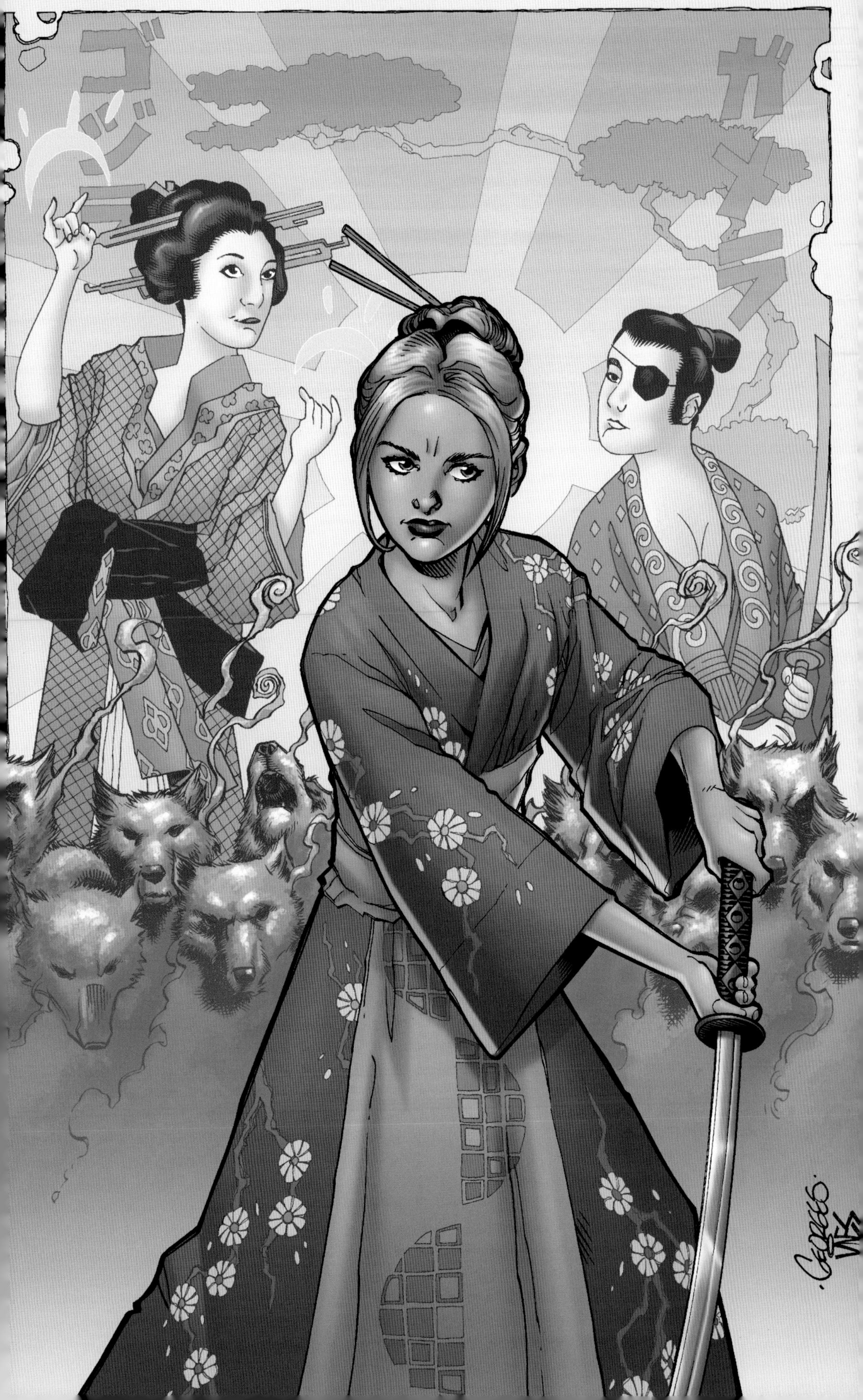

ゴジ
ガメラ

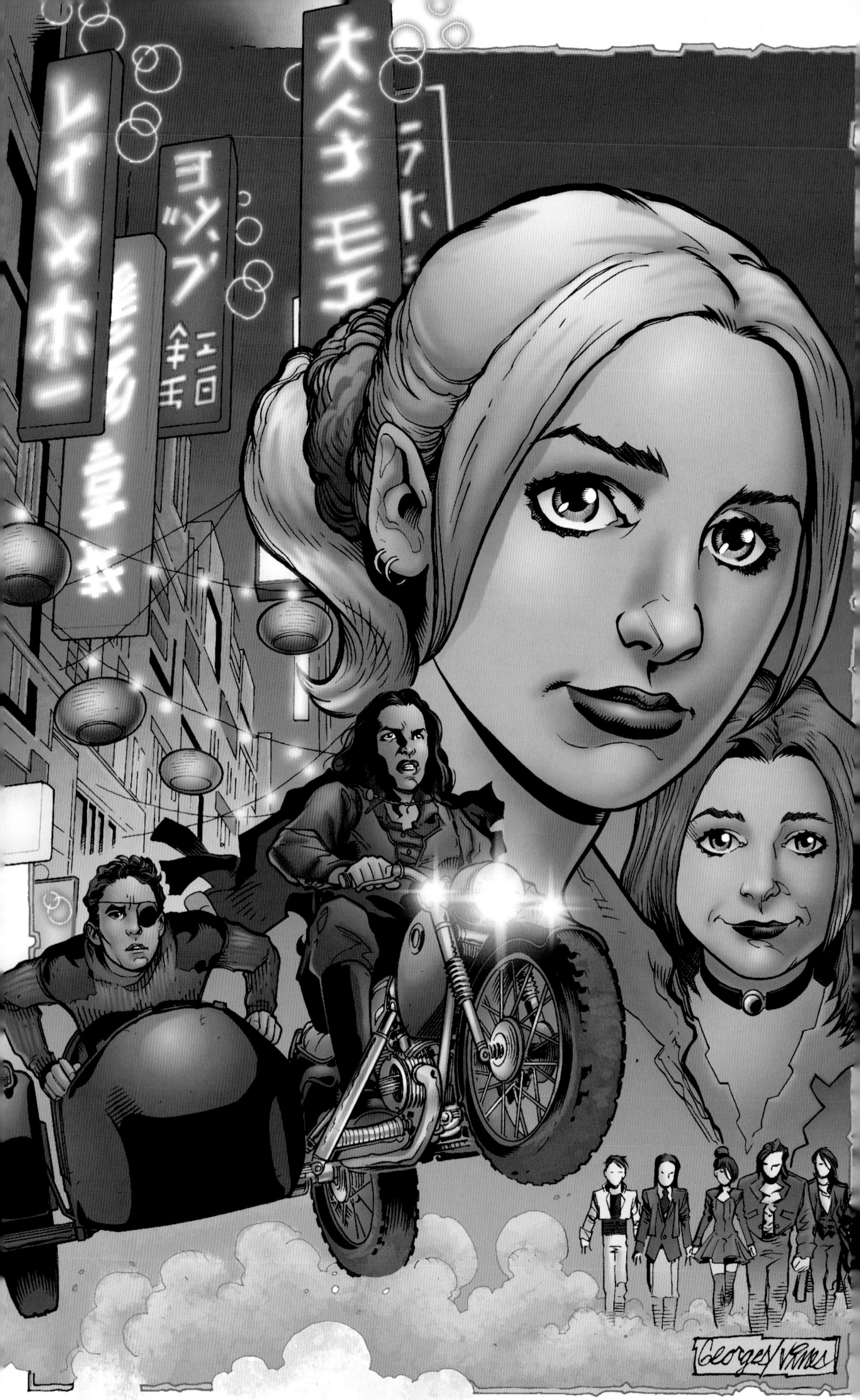
Georges/Vines

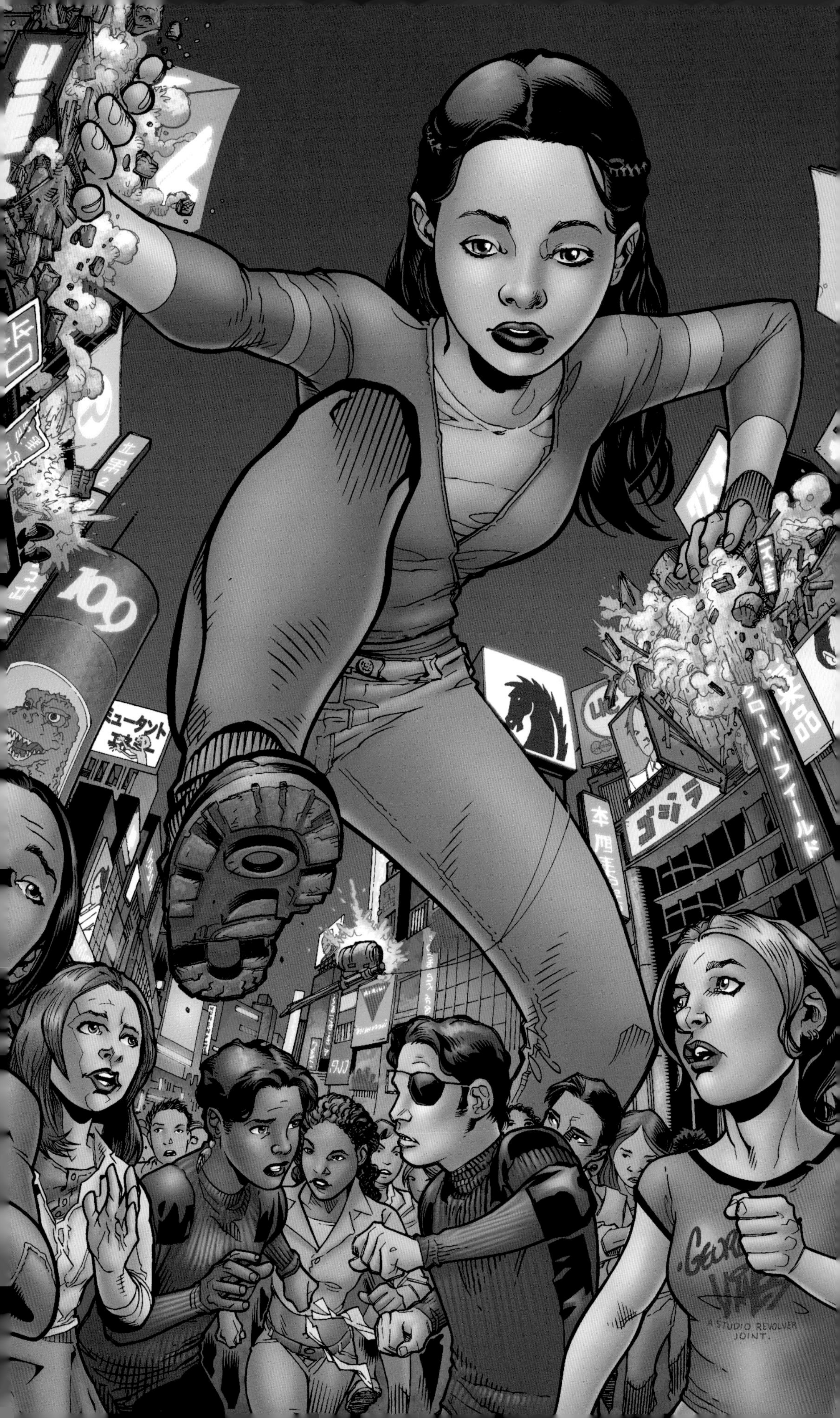
109
ミュータント
ゴジラ
クローバーフィールド
A STUDIO REVOLVER JOINT.

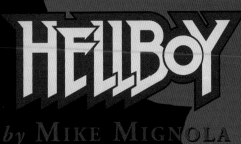

HELLBOY™

by MIKE MIGNOLA

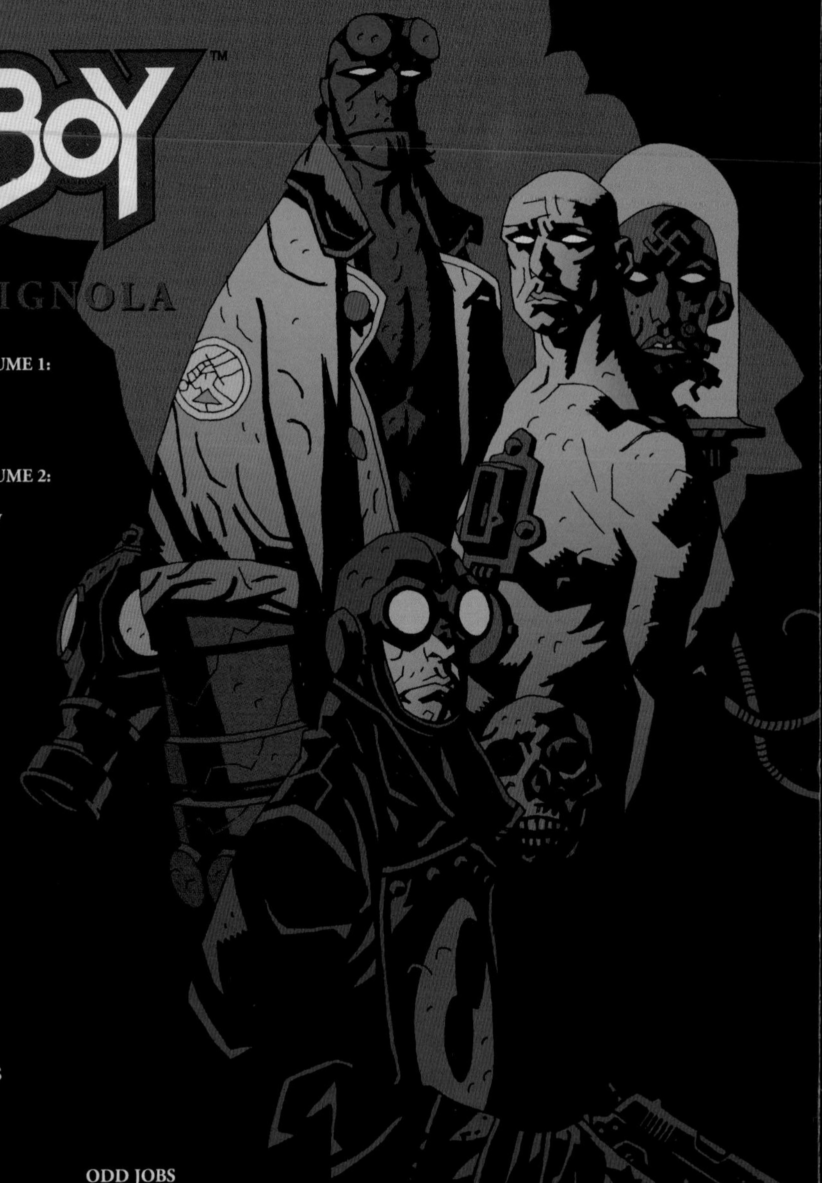

HELLBOY LIBRARY EDITION VOLUME 1:
SEED OF DESTRUCTION
AND WAKE THE DEVIL
ISBN 978-1-59307-910-9 | $49.95

HELLBOY LIBRARY EDITION VOLUME 2:
THE CHAINED COFFIN
AND THE RIGHT HAND OF DOOM
ISBN 978-1-59307-989-5 | $49.95

SEED OF DESTRUCTION
with John Byrne
ISBN 978-1-59307-094-6 | $17.95

WAKE THE DEVIL
ISBN 978-1-59307-095-3 | $17.95

THE CHAINED COFFIN
AND OTHERS
ISBN 978-1-59307-091-5 | $17.95

THE RIGHT HAND OF DOOM
ISBN 978-1-59307-093-9 | $17.95

CONQUEROR WORM
ISBN 978-1-59307-092-2 | $17.95

STRANGE PLACES
ISBN 978-1-59307-475-3 | $17.95

THE TROLL WITCH AND OTHERS
By Mignola, Corben, and Russell
ISBN 978-1-59307-860-7 | $17.95

DARKNESS CALLS
ISBN 978-1-59307-896-6 | $19.95

THE ART OF HELLBOY
ISBN 978-1-59307-089-2 | $29.95

HELLBOY: THE COMPANION
ISBN 978-1-59307-655-9 | $14.95

HELLBOY WEIRD TALES
Volume 1
ISBN 978-1-56971-622-9 | $17.95

Volume 2
ISBN 978-1-56971-953-4 | $17.95

To find a comics shop in your area,
call 1-888-266-4226
For more information or to order direct:
• On the web: darkhorse.com
• E-mail: mailorder@darkhorse.com
• Phone: 1-800-862-0052
Mon.–Fri. 9 AM to 5 PM Pacific Time

ODD JOBS
Short stories by Mignola,
Poppy Z. Brite, Chris Golden, and others
Illustrations by Mignola
ISBN 978-1-56971-440-9 | $14.95

ODDER JOBS
Short stories by Frank Darabont,
Guillermo del Toro, and others
Illustrations by Mignola
ISBN 978-1-59307-226-1 | $14.95

ODDEST JOBS
Short stories by China Miéville,
Ken Bruen, Mark Chadbourn, and others
Illustrations by Mignola
ISBN 978-1-59307-944-4 | $14.95

B.P.R.D.: HOLLOW EARTH
By Mignola, Chris Golden,
Ryan Sook, and others
ISBN 978-1-56971-862-9 | $17.95

B.P.R.D.: THE SOUL OF VENICE
By Mignola, Mike Oeming, Guy Davis,
Scott Kolins, Geoff Johns, and others
ISBN 978-1-59307-132-5 | $17.95

B.P.R.D.: PLAGUE OF FROGS
By Mignola and Guy Davis
ISBN 978-1-59307-288-9 | $17.95

B.P.R.D.: THE DEAD
By Mignola, John Arcudi, and Guy Davis
ISBN 978-1-59307-380-0 | $17.95

B.P.R.D.: THE BLACK FLAME
By Mignola, Arcudi, and Davis
ISBN 978-1-59307-550-7 | $17.95

B.P.R.D.: THE UNIVERSAL MACHINE
By Mignola, Arcudi, and Davis
ISBN 978-1-59307-710-5 | $17.95

B.P.R.D.: GARDEN OF SOULS
By Mignola, Arcudi, and Davis
ISBN 978-1-59307-882-9 | $17.95

B.P.R.D.: KILLING GROUND
By Mignola, Arcudi, and Davis
ISBN 978-1-59307-956-7 | $17.95

DARK HORSE COMICS™ *drawing on your nightmares*™
darkhorse.com

STAR WARS®

KNIGHTS OF THE OLD REPUBLIC

Volume 1: Commencement
ISBN: 978-1-59307-640-5

Volume 2: Flashpoint
ISBN: 978-1-59307-761-7

Volume 3: Days of Fear, Nights of Anger
ISBN: 978-1-59307-867-6

$18.95 each!

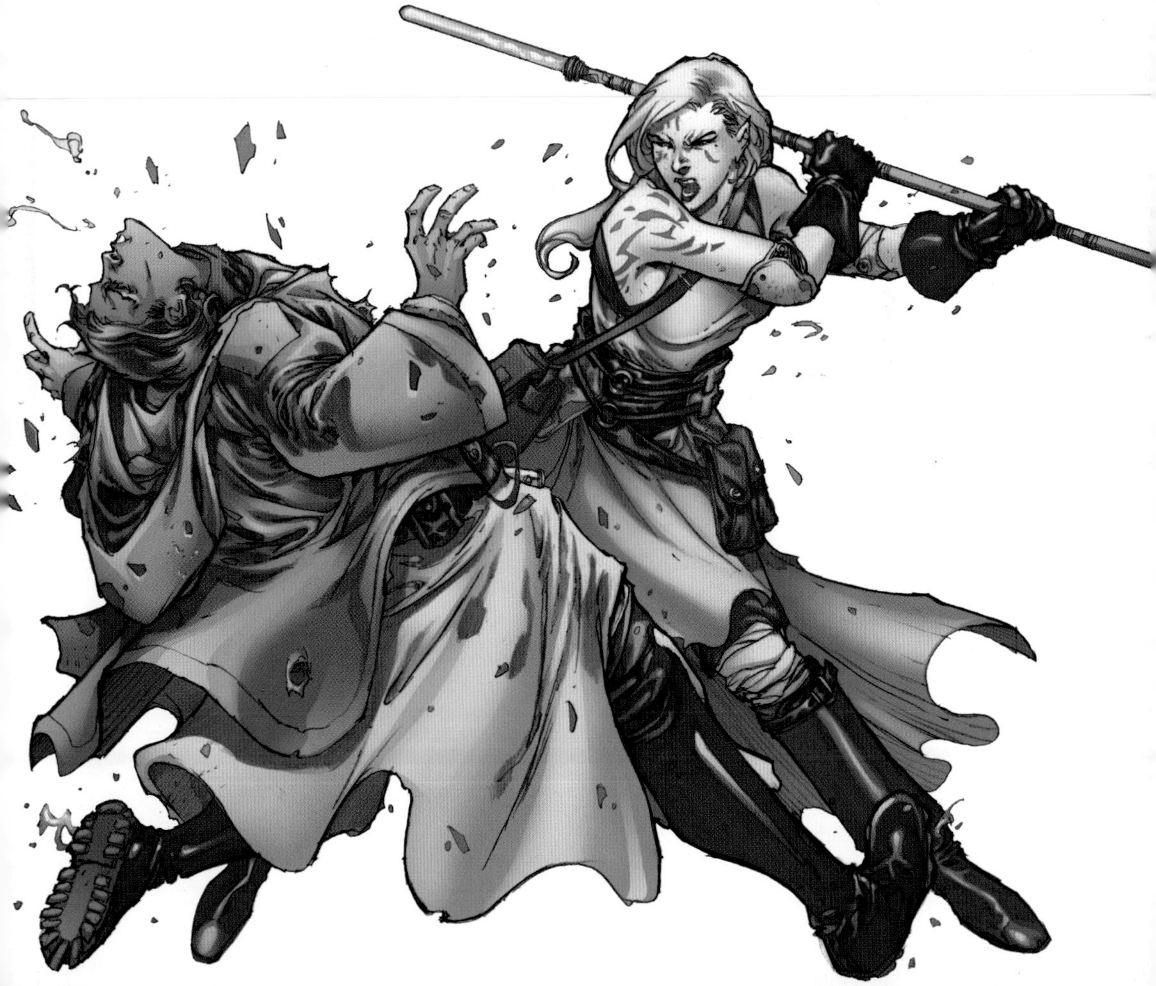

TO FIND A COMICS SHOP IN YOUR AREA, CALL 1-888-266-4226.
For more information or to order direct: *On the web: darkhorse.com *E-mail: mailorder@darkhorse.com
*Phone: 1-800-862-0052 Mon.-Fri. 9 A.M. to 5 P.M. Pacific Time.

DARK HORSE COMICS

FROM JOSS WHEDON

BUFFY THE VAMPIRE SLAYER SEASON 8:

VOLUME 1: THE LONG WAY HOME
Joss Whedon and Georges Jeanty
ISBN 978-1-59307-822-5 | $15.95

VOLUME 2: NO FUTURE FOR YOU
Brian K. Vaughan, Georges Jeanty, and Joss Whedon
ISBN 978-1-59307-963-5 | $15.95

VOLUME 3: WOLVES AT THE GATE
Drew Goddard, Georges Jeanty, and Joss Whedon
ISBN 978-1-59582-165-2 | $15.95

TALES OF THE SLAYERS
Joss Whedon, Amber Benson, Gene Colan, P. Craig Russell, Tim Sale, and others
ISBN 978-1-56971-605-2 | $14.95

TALES OF THE VAMPIRES
Joss Whedon, Brett Matthews, Cameron Stewart, and others
ISBN 978-1-56971-749-3 | $15.95

FRAY: FUTURE SLAYER
Joss Whedon and Karl Moline
ISBN 978-1-56971-751-6 | $19.95

SERENITY, VOLUME 1: THOSE LEFT BEHIND
Joss Whedon, Brett Matthews, and Will Conrad
ISBN 978-1-59307-449-4 | $9.95

ALSO FROM DARK HORSE . . .

BUFFY THE VAMPIRE SLAYER OMNIBUS

VOLUME 1
ISBN 978-1-59307-784-6 | $24.95

VOLUME 2
ISBN 978-1-59307-826-3 | $24.95

VOLUME 3
ISBN 978-1-59307-885-0 | $24.95

VOLUME 4
ISBN 978-1-59307-968-0 | $24.95

VOLUME 5
ISBN 978-1-59582-225-3 | $24.95

BUFFY THE VAMPIRE SLAYER:
PANEL TO PANEL
ISBN 978-1-59307-836-2 | $19.95

BUFFY THE VAMPIRE SLAYER:
CREATURES OF HABIT
ISBN 978-1-56971-563-5 | $17.95

MYSPACE DARK HORSE PRESENTS, VOLUME 1
Featuring "Sugarshock" by Joss Whedon and Fábio Moon
ISBN 978-1-59307-998-7 | $17.95

Buffy the Vampire Slayer

GEORGE
OWENS

DARK HORSE BOOKS®
darkhorse.com

AVAILABLE AT YOUR LOCAL COMICS SHOP OR BOOKSTORE!
To find a comics shop in your area, call 1-888-266-4226.
For more information or to order direct: • On the web: darkhorse.com • E-mail: mailorder@darkhorse.com • Phone: 1-800-862-0052
Mon.–Fri. 9 AM to 5 PM Pacific Time.

*Prices and availability subject to change without notice

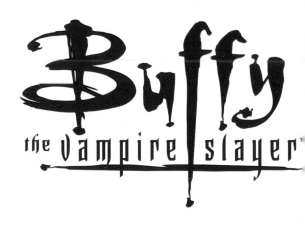

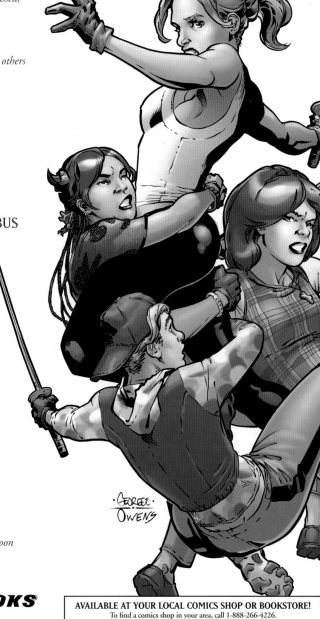